The Darkened Light of Joshua Clay

A Story of Grace and Redemption

Book One of The Scrollbearer Saga

Written by:
J. Scott

Published by J. Scott Publishing, an imprint of Sparky Bites Publishing.
ISBN (Hardcover): 978-1-968023-01-0
ISBN (Paperback): 978-1-968023-00-3
ISBN (eBook): 978-1-968023-02-7
ISBN (Audiobook): 978-1-968023-03-4

First Edition, August 2025
The Darkened Light of Joshua Clay: A Story of Grace and Redemption
Book One of The Scrollbearer Saga

Written by J. Scott
Cover Design by J. Scott
Characters Created by J. Scott
Edited by J. Scott
For more information, visit sparkybitespublishing.com

Based on the original poem *The Darkened Light of Joshua Clay* by J. Scott, originally written in 1988 and registered under copyright in 2021 by J. Scott.

While the poem serves as the foundation, this novel expands upon its themes, introducing new characters and deeper context to explore its world.

Printed in the United States of America

To my father—my hero, my guide, and the man I have spent my life striving to be like. Your wisdom carried me through dark times, your strength shaped my path, and your words inspired this story.

To my mother—gone, but never forgotten. Your love shaped me, and your memory continues to guide me. This book carries a piece of you within its pages.

To my wife—my steadfast partner, my source of love and encouragement. Without you, this journey would not have been the same. Thank you for standing beside me through it all.

To my sons—my greatest legacy. – "It's necessary to go through the fire to be tempered and refined."- I hope these words carry you through the hard times the way they carried me. May you always walk forward with strength, wisdom, and the knowledge that you are deeply loved.

And to Father Brian—gone now, but never forgotten. You showed me that faith is bigger than any one belief, that we are all God's children. The poem that started this journey exists because of you.

To all who have supported me along the way—thank you. This book would not exist without you.

*"Break the Word, and light shall fade;
blacken the sky, and silence the dove.
The burden once loosed will bind the soul,
yet the penitent may find the light above."*

(from the Scroll of the Covenant, Fragment I)

Table of Contents

Prologue: The Bells Toll

The bells never tolled when the world obeyed the law. Not the law of men, nor the law of war, but a law older than time—woven into faith, love, and the very foundation of all things meant to remain unshaken.

Yet, Joshua Clay broke it.

The moment his conviction faltered, his choice severing what was meant to remain whole, the world shifted—not through the clash of armies or the spilling of blood, but in something far deeper: judgment.

The bells did not warn or mourn; they declared. And as the first toll resonated across the land, the sky began to darken. Not with the sudden violence of a storm, but as if something ancient had recoiled, as if the heavens themselves had drawn back in silent witness to what had just begun.

The light thinned, dimming at the edges, fading not with shadow or tempest, but with an unnerving certainty—as though it knew the shape of the doom that was coming, even before the first terrified voice whispered its name.

Prologue: The Bells Toll

It was not an eclipse, nor a celestial omen; it was a sentence being etched upon the very fabric of existence. Because the bells did not merely ring; they weighed. Each toll pressed into the air, coiling in the lungs, prickling across the skin, sinking into the fragile space between thought and breath.

It was not the simple absence of air, not mere suffocation, but something far more insidious: the crushing weight of knowing, of understanding the irreversible shift.

For the bells did not simply announce judgment; they carried it forward, a creeping tendril stretching through the land, through the marrow of those yet to decide their allegiance, through the very hearts of those who had already made their choice. They were the harbingers of doom, their resonance a whispered promise of what was to come.

Across the land, the murmurs began—words spoken in hushed breath, in fearful tones, in voices uncertain whether to flee or to kneel before the inevitable force that had been set in motion.

Because the bells had never rung before, never needed to in a world that once held true. And now that they had begun, they would not stop. One toll for the moment Joshua Clay stepped beyond the boundaries of faith. A second for the first heart that wavered beneath his fractured lead. A third for the instant the encroaching darkness claimed its dominion over the land.

And yet—beneath the relentless toll, beneath the suffocating weight of knowing, beneath the pervasive whisper that insisted there was no turning back—there were some who did not recoil in fear at the sound. Some who stood beneath its resonating power felt it not as a finality, but as something else entirely, something far more perilous.

A choice.

The bells did not simply tally the fallen, nor merely weigh the souls that surrendered to the encroaching night. Instead, they waited—for those who still possessed the sliver of time to choose their path. And the toll itself was not just a marker of the irrevocable past; it called out to those who still drew breath, a final reckoning, the last gasp before surrender, the ultimate step before light—or shadow.

When the bells ring in this broken world, only two paths lie bare: surrender to the fading light, or consumption by the encroaching dark. Once their judgment has tolled, the consequences are absolute.

Yet, even amidst this stark dichotomy, whispers persisted of a third, more treacherous path – a descent into the fading echoes of another's forsaken soul, a desperate gamble to mend what had been shattered. The price of such a perilous salvation, however, was rumored to be a shared ascent into the light, or a shared fall into the deepening night.

And once the final bell rings, judgment is next.

The Weight We Bear

The Weight of Silver

"It's necessary to go through the fire to be tempered and refined."

That's what my father always said. It wasn't meant for me directly, at least not at first. He'd say it when recounting stories about Jonah—the man whose name lingered like an unbroken shadow over our family. Jonah, the betrayer, the one who shattered the ground we all walked on. A bitter taste still rises in my mouth whenever I think of him.

Now on this broken road, that same lingering bitterness coats my thoughts as I continue my solitary trek toward Joshua's purgatory, like the chains of my family's past are weighing me down. I have to wonder if my father was right. Would I repeat past mistakes, or finally break free?

Though the road ahead was uncertain, I knew I'd have to keep moving and try to find my own path, even though the shadows of my ancestors had always managed to find me before.

Maybe that's what my father meant. Maybe the fire he was talking about wasn't punishment—it was refinement. Maybe the suffering our family endured had a purpose, a way of burning away the worst parts of us and leaving something stronger behind. Or maybe it wasn't like that at all. Maybe the fire didn't care about strength or redemption, and all it left behind was ash.

The coin I carried served as a constant, albeit painful, reminder of my legacy. Its edges, digging into my skin whenever I touched it, felt more like a physical representation of a burden than an artifact. The story tied to the coin played out in my mind with unwavering clarity, as if I were a silent observer.

Grace's voice echoed in my mind, sharp and unforgiving. I heard the story so many times I could feel its weight, I could hear the silence after, I could feel the gravity of the conversation pressing against Jonah like the crushing weight of a burden willingly taken—a choice made that might never be unmade, not because it couldn't be, but because he wouldn't let it.

"You were named for peace," she'd said, deliberate, precise, each syllable measured, "but look at you now—you're not just trying to be something you're not, but forcing—no, *demanding* everyone else to play along. Like you're God. Like reality itself should bow to your will just because you command it."

A low voice, barely audible, replied, "We've changed."

At least, that's the version I grew up with.

Had he laughed? Had he scoffed? Had he flinched? I didn't know. Maybe he'd believed in his own illusion so fully that the words barely touched him—or maybe they'd cut so deeply he had to pretend they hadn't struck at all. But Grace hadn't raised her voice. She hadn't fought. She'd only looked at him, steady, unwavering, refusing to bend beneath whatever power he thought he wielded.

"Look at what you've done. Look at what you've become."

And then—her hand had closed around his, pressing something small, solid, undeniable into his palm.

A coin.

She hadn't explained it. She'd only placed it there, her touch light but final, as though the weight of it was enough to say everything left unsaid.

Then she spoke the two words that sealed our family's fate.

"Carry this."

They weren't a request. They weren't even a command. They were a curse. A burden that wouldn't end with him. It would pass through the years, through the blood, until it landed here—with me.

And now I carry it. Not because I want to. But because I have to. Carrying it doesn't make me feel refined or tempered or stronger. It just makes me feel—small.

The bells tolled in the distance, a constant reminder that time was running out—and that my destination might not exist at all.

I was so lost in thought, the weight of the past a tangible presence beside me, that the sudden appearance of someone else on the same desolate path that I'm on startled me.

A figure stood there, arms crossed, brow furrowed, as if my very existence was an unwelcome interruption. Her gaze was sharp, assessing, and I felt an immediate prickle of unease – a sense that this was someone forged in the same harsh crucible as this broken world. There was a significance about her stance, the set of her jaw, that resonated with a deep, unsettling familiarity, even though I couldn't place her.

She didn't move, didn't speak, her scrutiny making me feel like an insect pinned beneath her gaze. Finally, her voice cut through the silence, direct and wary. "Who are you?"

My own reply felt thin, inadequate against the unspoken tension. "Just someone passing through." Passing through to what? To more guilt? To a reckoning I wasn't sure I could face?

Her gaze swept over me, searching, probing. Then her eyes dropped to my hand, where the cold edges of the coin pressed against my palm. I instinctively tightened my grip, trying to conceal it within my fist.

"What's that?" Gillie's voice sharpened, her gaze locking onto my closed hand.

Hesitantly, I drew the coin into view, its cold surface mirroring the chill in the air. "It's just a keepsake." I lied, the word brittle against the weight of her stare.

Her eyes narrowed. "A keepsake?" The skepticism in her tone cut through me, and in that instant, I saw the flicker of understanding—followed by grim certainty. "A descendant of Jonah?" The accusation struck like a blade, hanging between us, demanding an answer.

My throat tightened. "I… I don't know what you're talking about," I muttered, but even I knew how weak the denial sounded.

"Don't lie." Her words lashed out, sharp enough to make me flinch. "That coin screams your history. It's one of the thirty pieces, isn't it? The silver that bought our ruin."

The truth landed like a stone in my gut. I met her gaze, quieter now. "You know the story."

"Of course I do." Her voice carried the weight of every lost soul who had heard it before. "Jonah betrayed Joshua. And Grace—Grace gave him that cursed piece of silver. Told him to carry it. And now it's yours. The grand inheritance of guilt."

I dropped my gaze to the dusty road, unable to meet her stare. What could I say? The truth was etched in the coin I held.

She exhaled, almost weary now. "My name's Gillie," she said, still wary, but there was something steadier in her tone. "and on this broken road, you carrying that…" Her gaze flicked back to the coin, scrutinizing it as if it carried all the weight of history. "…it tells me everything I need to know about you."

I swallowed hard, feeling stripped bare beneath her stare. "What are you really carrying?" she pressed. "Because that's no keepsake."

The lie was useless now. "It's a burden," I admitted, the words reluctant, raw. "A curse."

Gillie studied my face, her features masked—pity, disgust, or something heavier stirring beneath the surface. "A curse passed down from the betrayer."

I nodded slowly. The weight of it settled deeper, suffocating, undeniable. My name stuck in my throat, a stain I didn't want touching hers.

"So, you're just… carrying it?" she asked, the disbelief shifting into something sharper, something edged with accusation. "Walking around with the price of our damnation in your hand?"

The injustice of it flared within me, a brief spark against the overwhelming shame. "I don't have a choice," I said, my voice low but firm. "It's my inheritance."

Her eyes lingered on the coin. "Why don't you just throw it away?"

I stared at the silver in my hand, its chill biting into my skin. "I can't," I said. "I'm bound to it… or it's bound to me."

I'd tried once—standing at the edge of a river, the current rushing fast and dark beneath me. I threw the coin in with everything I had. But the instant it left my hand, pain lanced through my chest like a cracked rib. I dropped to my knees, gasping. It felt like a part of me had been ripped away. I never saw the coin fall. Only felt it return. Cold. Heavy. Mine.

She exhaled through her nose, the sound sharp and tired. "Well," she said, stepping back, "I don't have time to stand here trading family histories with someone carrying that thing."

Her gaze flicked again to the coin, and her lip curled. "It reeks of betrayal. I need to get going."

I felt the heat rise in my throat—a sting of protest I didn't let out. What was there to argue?

Instead, I asked, "Where are you going?"

"To Joshua's purgatory," she stated, her voice firm and resolute, leaving no room for argument. "Someone has to try and fix what your precious ancestor broke."

A flicker of disagreement sparked within me. Joshua broke the law. Jonah… he just helped him. But I swallowed the urge to argue. Now wasn't the time to start a war. A fragile hope, born of necessity, flickered within me. "Then we're heading the same way," I said, my voice barely above a whisper. "Maybe… maybe we can work together."

Her sharp look cut me off, extinguishing that fragile hope. "We are heading the same way," she acknowledged, her gaze still hard. "But don't mistake that for some kind of partnership. If I go along with this… arrangement… it's because having another pair of hands might be useful. Nothing more." A tense silence stretched between us, her gaze unwavering.

"No," I said simply, the weight of her conditional acceptance adding a layer of unease to my burden. "But walking the same broken road… maybe we could at least keep an eye out for each other." The words felt less like a plea born of a desperate loneliness and more like an attempt to find some common ground.

She hesitated, her gaze flicking between me and the desolate path ahead. Finally, a frustrated sigh escaped her lips. "Fine. But don't slow me down," she muttered, already turning to start down the path.

I followed, the coin's jagged edges pressed into my palm, a constant reminder of the chasm between us and the heavy weight of the journey ahead.

The road stretched before us, cracked and broken, its surface split into jagged fragments that clawed at the soles of my boots. Whatever had once held it together was long gone, eroded by time and neglect. Weeds had sprouted from the gaps—not vibrant or alive, but pale, sickly things that grew like the world had forgotten what green was supposed to look like. The air was thick with the smell of damp earth and decay, every breath dragging something heavy into my lungs.

The weight of her words settled heavily. The kin of a traitor. The phrase echoed in my mind, a stark reminder of the chasm between us, a chasm dug by a man I never knew but whose shadow defined me. Yet, we were heading to the same place, driven by the same broken world. A desperate thought took root.

No reprieve waited ahead. Only more weight to bear. And as we walked, I couldn't help but wonder: would this fire burn away the impurity I carried, leaving me tempered and refined? Or would it consume me entirely, leaving nothing but ash?

The Weight of Ruin

It wasn't always like this. Stories whispered of a time before—a world painted in hues we could now only imagine.

Clear skies, they said. Golden fields stretching to meet a gentle horizon. Bustling towns where laughter echoed through sunlit streets. Now, only the hollowed remnants of that world remained—ruins that clawed at the sky, a constant, jagged testament of what had been permanently lost.

Look anywhere, and you'd find it—a pervasive brokenness.

Abandonment clung to the air like a shroud. What once held purpose had been twisted into something grotesque, something unrecognizable.

Houses had collapsed inward, their empty frames sagging like the rib cages of forgotten corpses. Rivers, once lifeblood, now flowed dark and sluggish, their surfaces disturbed by shadows that writhed in defiance of any natural reflection.

"They say it started with him," Gillie's voice sliced through the oppressive silence. She didn't look my way—her gaze fixed on the unforgiving path beneath her boots. A steady voice, yes, but the weight of this broken world had etched a permanent sharpness into its tone. "With Joshua, I mean."

No immediate reply escaped me. Earlier, she laid the blame squarely at Jonah's feet. Now it's Joshua. It seems the weight of this world shifts the blame depending on who's carrying it.

What could I offer? She spoke a truth that clung to us both, a bitter knowledge we couldn't shed. The fall of Joshua Clay wasn't a mere tragedy; it was a creeping curse, a virulent sickness that had spread its tendrils into every corner of existence, leaving nothing untouched. We were the inheritors of that ruin, living in its perpetual twilight. Some simply lacked the courage to acknowledge the depth of the darkness.

"The darkness isn't the only legacy he left us," she continued, her voice now a low, almost bitter murmur. "The bells, the gnawing fear, the endless desolation—it never stops. It's a constant companion, always there, a shadow we can't outrun. People don't even raise a fist against it anymore. They just… exist. Or they fade away."

Her words hung in the stagnant air, a storm cloud too dense to break apart. An urge to argue, to push back against the sheer bleakness of her pronouncements, rose within me. But what defense could I offer against such a stark reality? She spoke the truth we both lived.

Before the darkness consumed us, a fragile hope had flickered. Before these skeletal ruins, life had pulsed with vibrant energy. Before the bells began their mournful toll, dreams had taken flight. The ancient law of Faith and Love had offered solace, a bedrock of peace. Then, that sacred law shattered, and with it, everything else.

Humanity hadn't simply stumbled; it had been pulverized, broken down piece by agonizing piece, like glass dropped repeatedly onto unforgiving stone until only dust remained.

The bells were a constant torment, their ceaseless chiming a dull ache in the back of our minds, a relentless reminder of what we carried—this inherited guilt—and the vibrant world we had lost.

Silence felt like a forgotten language. I couldn't recall a time when the bells weren't a part of the world's grim symphony. Yet, the stories of that silent peace, whispered like forbidden secrets, filled me with an unbearable longing.

Laughter echoing through bustling streets, the air thick with the intoxicating fragrance of blooming flowers—these memories, passed down like precious relics, felt like fragments of a beautiful, unreachable dream.

Despair had become our constant companion, a gnawing presence that never loosened its grip. And those who could no longer bear its crushing weight? They simply vanished. Into the shrouded unknown. Into the silent promise of purgatory. Into the oblivion that offered an escape from the endless toll. Perhaps they found a semblance of peace there. Perhaps they simply ceased to care.

Now, I walked this fractured path, driven by a fragile ember of hope. A perilous journey, shrouded in uncertainty, yet carrying the faintest whisper of possibility.

Each step was fueled by a stubborn belief: redemption, however improbable, remained within our reach. That one day, the bells would finally fall silent, and humanity might rise from the ashes of its own making.

This journey wasn't mine alone; it was a desperate plea for all of us, a flickering beacon against the vast, encroaching darkness.

"You blame him for everything," I said eventually, my voice quiet but holding a note of unwavering conviction.

Gillie stopped abruptly, pivoting to face me, her glare sharp enough to shatter stone.

"Don't you?"

The question struck with unexpected force, and for a fleeting moment, I found myself adrift, unsure of the answer that lay buried within me.

Did I blame Joshua? How could I not, when the very ground beneath our feet was fractured by his choices, by his catastrophic fall? Yet, to lay the entirety of the blame at his feet felt… incomplete. Wrong, even. An easy absolution I couldn't quite accept, not even in the silent chambers of my own mind.

"It's not that simple," I finally managed, meeting her unwavering gaze. "He wasn't the only one who fell. Everyone else—your family, my family, the entire world—they stood by, silent witnesses. No one tried to pull him back from the precipice. They simply let it happen."

Her eyes narrowed, sharp and unyielding, refusing to concede even a sliver of my point. "He made a choice. He betrayed Grace, betrayed his own soul. That's what shattered the world. Not my family. Not yours. Him."

An easy path lay before me, the seductive simplicity of blaming Joshua alone. But the truth was a tangled web, far more difficult to unravel.

Joshua hadn't walked his path to ruin in solitude. That was the haunting truth that clung to me—not just his descent, but the complicity of my own bloodline.

Jonah had been there, a shadow at his side, close enough to offer salvation. But instead of guiding him toward the radiant light of Grace, Jonah had been the undertow, exploiting every weakness, dragging him further into the suffocating darkness.

Greed. Lust. Envy. Pride. Cracks in Joshua's once-unbreakable armor, widened by subtle manipulation until the beacon of hope we had all clung to transformed into something broken, something dangerous.

A brief closing of my eyes offered no escape from the weight that settled on my chest. My great-grandfather hadn't just betrayed Joshua; he'd betrayed the very essence of Grace, betrayed his own soul in the process. And that betrayal hadn't ended with their fall. It had rippled outward, a destructive wave pulling everyone down into the abyss.

"It wasn't just Joshua," I murmured, the words an internal lament more than a direct address to Gillie. "It was Jonah too. He could've been the hand that pulled him back, but instead, he was the force that dragged him deeper."

Gillie's expression remained a rigid mask. Hard eyes, a tightly clenched jaw—she had heard me, but her resolve refused to yield.

"Whatever poison Jonah whispered," she retorted, her voice sharp as shattered glass, "Joshua still made his choice. He possessed the will to fight back, to stand firm in Grace's light. But he didn't. He surrendered. That's the moment the world broke—when he chose the darkness."

An argument hung on the tip of my tongue, a desperate urge to push back against the stark simplicity of her judgment. But the crushing weight of Jonah's betrayal held me captive.

Perhaps she was right. Perhaps Joshua's choices held the ultimate responsibility. But that truth didn't absolve Jonah, didn't erase his damning role. And there was no ground to be gained in this debate, no convincing her to see the shades of gray that haunted my own thoughts.

We walked on, the silence a heavy shroud, thick with unspoken confessions and buried truths.

In the distance, a solitary chime, hollow and mournful, rippled through the mist—a constant echo in this broken world. It wasn't the first time I'd heard it, and a grim certainty told me it wouldn't be the last.

The sound rippled through the stagnant air, a tangible echo of judgment settling deep within my bones, a constant reminder that some acts, once committed, could never be undone.

Ahead, the path twisted toward the empty shells of abandoned houses, stripped bare and weary, standing like desolate husks beneath a perpetually colorless sky.

Glass lay fractured underfoot. Roofs sagged under the relentless weight of years. This was the world Joshua had left behind—a place that stubbornly refused to die but had long forgotten how to truly live.

Gillie's voice, softer now yet laced with an icy coldness, cut through the quiet. "All of this," she said, her gaze sweeping across the desolate landscape. "And you still think he deserves saving?"

A hesitation snagged my steps as my gaze traced the hollowed-out ruins of what might have once been a home, a vibrant town, a life brimming with promise. Walls stripped bare of meaning. Trees twisted into skeletal forms. Ground that had long surrendered to the relentless decay.

The weight of it all pressed against me—heavy, unrelenting—a burden that didn't simply rest on my shoulders but settled deep within my soul, a constant reminder that some debts could never be repaid, some burdens never truly laid down.

Did Joshua deserve saving? The question twisted through the labyrinth of my mind as I glanced at Gillie's unforgiving profile.

How could anyone deserve salvation when this desolation was their legacy? When their choices had fractured the world beyond any apparent hope of repair?

Yet, even as anger, sharp and righteous, welled in my chest, something else stirred within me. Quieter, more elusive, harder to define.

"Everyone deserves saving," I said softly, the words escaping before my mind could fully process their implications.

No immediate reply. But the look she cast my way—hard, cold, conveying a profound disbelief in my naiveté—lingered long after she turned back to the path.

My gaze drifted back to the ruins, turning over the fragmented memories of the world before his fall, a world whispered in hushed tones.

Lush fields stretching to an impossible horizon. Rivers flowing clear and strong, teeming with life. Villages echoing with the warmth of community and the unrestrained joy of laughter.

All of it, swallowed by the ash and the silence.

And yet… even amidst the pervasive wreckage, stubborn threads of life persisted. Trees splitting the crumbling stone. Moss clinging to the weathered remnants of walls. Life, in its myriad forms, clinging on in defiant resilience.

Perhaps Gillie's judgment was correct. Perhaps Joshua Clay had forfeited any right to salvation.

But as I looked at the winding path ahead, leading us deeper into the remnants of his ruin, I couldn't shake the persistent thought of the fire that awaited us.

If there existed even the faintest chance to mend this broken world—to pull a single spark of light from the suffocating darkness—wasn't it a risk worth taking?

The world had burned once because of him. If the fire ahead held even the smallest promise of hope, then I had to believe it was a path worth walking, no matter the cost.

The Weight of Original Sin

When the world fell, it didn't shatter all at once. It fractured, piece by piece, every crack exposing the rot that had already been there, hidden beneath layers of pride and pretense. That's the thing no one likes to admit—the fall didn't create the darkness in people. It just gave them permission to stop hiding it.

Joshua's betrayal wasn't the first. That much was clear to anyone willing to look. The seeds of the fall had been planted long before he made his choice—buried deep in the hearts of men and women who thought they could make bargains with the eternal without paying the price. It was his fall, though, that gave the darkness its shape. His sins that let it spill into the cracks and devour what was left of the light.

I walked in silence, the weight of the thought pressing heavy on my chest as the deadened landscape stretched out before us. Gillie stayed a step ahead, her shoulders squared, her movements sharp and deliberate. She didn't turn back, but I could feel the tension radiating off her, the anger simmering just beneath her skin. We were both thinking about the same thing, though neither of us said it aloud.

The world hadn't just become dark. It had become cruel.

When the bells started tolling, they marked the boundaries of what remained—dividing those who tried to hold on to the light from those who let the darkness claim them.

Humanity, fractured by its own nature, had split into pieces. The greedy, the violent, the proud—they rose like weeds, choking the life out of anything that dared to grow toward hope. Communities fell apart, neighbors turned on each other, families dissolved into strangers, all driven by the same festering truth. Without the light, there was nothing left to keep the worst parts of people in check.

"*Do you think it was always in us?*" I asked suddenly, the words escaping before I could stop them.

Gillie glanced back over her shoulder, her expression unreadable. "What?"

"The darkness," I said, glancing at the ashen sky above us. "Do you think it was always there? Or did it take him falling to bring it out?"

She stopped walking, turning to face me fully. Her jaw was tight, her arms crossed over her chest. "Are you asking if this is all Joshua's fault?"

I hesitated, feeling the weight of her gaze. "I guess I'm asking if it would've happened anyway. If someone else would've fallen, even if he didn't."

Her eyes narrowed, sharp and unwavering. "It doesn't matter," she said flatly. "He did fall. He made his choice, and we're all paying for it now."

"But if it was always there," I pressed, "then maybe…"

"Maybe what?" she snapped, cutting me off. "Maybe it's not his fault? Maybe the world was already broken?" She let out a sharp, bitter laugh, the sound cutting through the air like glass. "You think that makes it better? That knowing the world was rotten before he betrayed Grace somehow makes what he did okay?"

"That's not what I'm saying," I said quickly, though the words felt weak in the face of her anger.

"Then what are you saying?" she demanded, her voice rising. "Because from where I'm standing, all of this…" she gestured sharply to the desolate landscape around us, to the hollow shells of buildings and the twisted branches of trees that bore no fruit— "all of this ruin comes back to him. He opened the door, and the rest of the world shoved its way through."

I didn't respond right away. What could I say to that? She wasn't wrong, not entirely. The fall had made monsters out of good men and beasts out of the rest. It had turned a world of promises into a wasteland of betrayals. But it wasn't just Joshua who had fallen. It wasn't just him who had turned his back on the light. He had been the first, yes. But the rest of us had followed.

I closed my eyes briefly, trying to gather my thoughts. "Maybe it's not about him," I said quietly. "Maybe it's about all of us. Maybe the fall wasn't just his. Maybe it was ours, too."

Gillie scoffed, shaking her head. "That's a nice thought," she said bitterly. "But it's not going to help us. We can't save the world. We're barely holding it together as it is."

She turned and started walking again, her movements stiff and deliberate. I followed, the weight of my words hanging in the air between us.

Purgatory's edge loomed closer now, the ground growing softer beneath our boots, and the trees ahead stretched higher, their twisted branches forming a canopy that blocked out the remnants of the dull, gray light. The bell tolled again, low and resonant, sending a shiver down my spine.

Joshua's fall hadn't just broken the world. It had broken us, and I couldn't help but wonder if there was anything left worth saving—or if the fall was still happening, piece by piece, with every step we took closer to Joshua's purgatory.

The Weight of the Swamp

The path narrowed with each step, winding deeper into a forest where trees seemed to writhe in place. Their trunks bent at unnatural angles, as though twisted by some unseen agony, and branches curled inward, hunched figures bracing against an invisible weight. Beneath our boots, the ground softened, sinking with each footfall, as if the very foundation was unraveling, struggling to maintain its form.

A colder, sharper air descended, carrying a faint, acrid smell that clung to the back of my throat—a metallic tang reminiscent of iron left too long in the rain, decayed but unbroken, awaiting the final touch of time.

Silence enveloped us, yet it was a silence that spoke volumes, a stillness that breathed. Unseen eyes seemed to press against my skin, a palpable weight. Each step grew heavier, the pull forward more insistent, as if the destination itself was already drawing us into its unseen grasp.

"It's not much farther," Gillie finally muttered, her voice tight, strained, a self-reassurance as much as a statement to me. A quick glance back revealed her hard but uneasy expression, the clench of her jaw betraying the tension her words tried to conceal.

For some time, the path had been constricting. Initially, it was subtle—shrubs encroaching on the edges, overgrown brush crowding our way, forcing careful footing between weathered roots and fallen limbs.

But then, the shift became undeniable. Jagged lines fractured the dirt beneath us, fissures splitting where the ground had once been firm. Trees pressed closer, their trunks leaning inward, relentlessly narrowing the space until walking side by side became impossible.

Gillie took the lead, her movements sharp and determined as she stepped over the thick trunk of a fallen tree. I followed, my hands gripping the rough bark as I hauled myself over the obstacle. More barriers littered our progress—broken limbs jutting into the path, undergrowth tangling around our ankles, snagging at our clothes.

Then, the trees ahead converged, an open space suddenly sealed shut. Towering pines on either side of the trail had woven together, their thick branches interlocking, a deliberate barrier.

Gillie slowed, her eyes scanning the dense cluster of limbs. "We can go through," she stated, a hard certainty in her voice. "The path's just beyond this patch, I can see it." Her conviction seemed fragile, a thin shield against the unknown.

I hesitated, glancing back at the way we had come. Distant but unbroken, the familiar road offered an alternative, a path of least resistance. Yet, that wasn't our purpose here.

"We go through," Gillie repeated, not waiting for my agreement. She pushed forward, forcing her way into the dense trees, their tightly packed trunks resisting her advance. Branches fought back, snagging at her sleeves, catching on her blade's hilt, brushing sharply against her face.

Instinctively, I raised my arms to shield my eyes as I followed. Limbs swiped at me, shifting as I moved, demanding I duck, twist, keep my head low in a constant struggle.

Then, the ground beneath us betrayed us. The steady dirt gave way to something yielding, something treacherous. Muck sucked at my boots, a subtle pull at first, testing its hold, threatening to drag me down into its unseen depths. Branches overhead obscured any attempt to see what I had stepped into.

Limbs bent inward, filling every available space, denying even a downward glance, forcing my focus relentlessly forward. There was only movement—the constant press and push against branches that seemed determined to hold us captive.

"We're almost there," Gillie gasped, her breath sharp and uneven. "The path's right ahead."

We pressed on, each step a battle against the lashing branches that slowed our progress, demanding a fight for every inch gained.

Then, abruptly, we broke through the suffocating embrace of the trees. I straightened, shaking off the broken twigs and clinging pine needles, my breath coming in sharp, uneven gasps.

I lifted my head. The world had undergone a stark transformation. The path had vanished. But it wasn't just the path; everything had changed. This was unlike any swamp I had ever witnessed.

Behind us, the dense, suffocating trees dissolved into a swirling mist, swallowed by the shifting air. Uneven layers of ground stretched out before us, wet and wrong, stagnant water pooling thickly between twisted roots that clawed at the sky like the skeletal remains of something long dead. A heavy, unnatural mist curled around it all, pressing in as if intent on drowning the entire landscape.

Then, a bell tolled. Loud, deep, immediate. The sound resonated in my ribs, reverberating through my chest, a physical presence as if I had stepped directly into its mournful call.

Next came the weight. Not just a sound, but a tangible force, pressing against my shoulders, constricting my breath, settling into my limbs like an unfamiliar burden. The very air felt heavier, thicker. The swamp clung to us, a wet, suffocating embrace, like guilt made manifest, like something unseen had coiled itself around us the moment we had trespassed into its domain.

Gillie exhaled sharply, shifting her stance, adjusting to the sudden pressure, but she remained silent.

We turned back. The road we had traveled was still visible, unchanged, untouched—a stark contrast to the alien landscape before us. But ahead lay only the oppressive swamp.

"*I swear I saw it,*" Gillie whispered, her voice thin and uncertain.

"We did," I confirmed, though a knot of doubt tightened within me.

And yet, it was gone, swallowed by the encroaching mist that swirled at the edges of our vision, closing in like a predator.

Somewhere in the distance, yet undeniably inescapable, another bell tolled its mournful note.

The threshold had been crossed. Joshua's purgatory was this oppressive swamp. And the weight of it had already begun to settle upon us.

Entering the Swamp

The Breath of Purgatory

The swamp was alive, but not like something meant to exist.

It didn't grow—it fed.

It didn't breathe—it smothered.

Every step pulled us deeper, its weight pressing in, thick and suffocating. The air carried something rotten, clinging to my skin like damp decay, heavy in my throat. Even the shallowest breath burned, as though the swamp itself refused to let us take it in.

The ground shifted beneath us, unstable, treacherous. Mud gripped our boots, dragging at each step, sucking, pulling. Water pooled in unseen pockets, waiting, lurking. The trees loomed overhead, limbs warped and curling inward—as if recoiling from something unseen.

The mist thickened, wrapping around us in slow, deliberate tendrils, threading through the trees, winding around my legs. It didn't whisper—but it pressed in, settling into the back of my mind like a presence I couldn't shake.

Gillie pushed forward, her steps slowing as the path vanished into decay.

"We're here," Gillie muttered ahead of me, her voice thin and strained, cutting through the oppressive silence. Her steps faltered as the path disappeared beneath layers of muck and rot. The confidence she carried before was gone, replaced by something more fragile—hesitation. "I can feel it."

I didn't respond. There wasn't anything I could say, not when the truth of it was so heavy, so all-encompassing. We were surrounded by it now, wrapped in the suffocating grip of something that seeped into every corner of existence. It was more than a landscape or a destination; it was an intrusion, a weight pressing against my thoughts, my breath, my very being.

The bell tolled again, a hollow chime rolling through the mist, deep and unrelenting. It didn't come from any single direction—it came from everywhere at once, settling into the air, pressing into my chest like a weight that didn't belong to me.

I stopped.

The trees loomed above, their branches bending unnaturally, twisting as if reaching for something unseen. The mist blurred their outlines, shifting them into something that no longer resembled trees at all. The air was still—too still—thick with something unseen, something watching.

Gillie inhaled sharply, her breath uneven. "*It's worse than I thought*," she murmured. Though her voice was quiet, it carried an edge—something frayed, something uncertain.

She glanced at me, fingers flexing near the blade at her side. "You feel it too, don't you?"

I nodded, unable to trust my voice.

Every movement forward felt less like progress and more like surrender, as though the path behind us had already disappeared and there was no turning back.

Every inch of me screamed to turn around, to run, to claw my way back to solid ground, to light, to something familiar. But I didn't move.

I closed my eyes for a moment, willing my legs to keep going.

And then—

A whisper.

Not a voice. Not something spoken. More like a pressure, creeping along the edges of thought, pressing into the space behind my eyes, dragging itself inside.

I inhaled sharply, my breath uneven. The swamp seemed darker when I opened my eyes again, the mist thicker, the branches closer. It was like the land had shifted while I wasn't looking—but that wasn't the worst part.

Something pressed against my skull, light at first, a breath of sound, a faint hum threading between my ribs.

But then—

Then it sharpened.

A knife against bone.

A weight against memory.

A presence digging its fingers into my thoughts, settling inside them, twisting.

"We're not alone," I said finally, my voice hollow and small.

Gillie stiffened, her hand tightening on the knife as her gaze darted to the shadows at the edges of the path. "I know," she said.

She felt it too. The swamp wasn't empty. It never had been.

I didn't see it—not yet—but its presence threaded through me all the same. The weight of something watching, something waiting, something pressing into the silence.

The whispers deepened. Not voices. Not words. Just pressure, threading into my chest, tightening around my throat, pulsing against my skull like something trying to get in.

The silence wasn't silence at all. It was noise so faint it couldn't be heard—only felt. A low vibration thrumming in my bones, pulsing beneath my skin, forcing its way through.

The water ahead rippled, though no wind moved the air. Gillie drew her knife, her movements sharp and deliberate, and the sound of steel scraping against leather cut through the stillness like a warning.

"Stay close," she said, her voice low.

"I'm not going anywhere," I replied, though the weight of my words felt heavier than before. My eyes scanned the shadows ahead, searching for something I couldn't name—something I wasn't even sure I wanted to see.

We moved forward again, slower now, our steps careful and deliberate. The ground grew wetter, the mud deeper, and the mist clung tighter, wrapping around us like it had a mind of its own. I felt its chill seep into my skin, its weight pressing against my chest, until breathing felt like pulling air through water.

"I didn't realize how dark it would be here," Gillie muttered, her voice quieter now, stripped of its usual edge. She stopped walking, her gaze fixed on the black water ahead, as if it held answers neither of us wanted to face.

I didn't answer right away. The stillness around us was suffocating, pressing in with a heaviness that made it hard to breathe.

Finally, I said, "What did you think it would be like?"

She hesitated, her shoulders tensing as though the question itself was too much. "I don't know," she admitted, her voice uneven. "I thought… I thought it would be like walking through a memory, maybe. Or a story. Something distant, something we could observe and keep apart from. But this…" Her breath hitched slightly, and she shook her head. "This isn't just a memory. It's alive."

I nodded slowly, my eyes scanning the dark, shifting mist that wrapped around us like a living thing. "I thought it would feel like walking into a shadow. But it's not. It's heavier than that. It's like it's sinking into us, twisting everything around us into something worse."

She glanced at me, fingers twitching near her blade. "Do you think it'll get darker?"

I didn't know how to answer. The truth was, I didn't think it could get darker… but I wasn't sure if that was hope or desperation talking. Instead, I looked at the twisted roots clawing through the muck, at the branches overhead, and felt the weight of the air pressing against my chest.

"It might," I said finally. "But we have to keep going."

Another bell tolled—deeper, lower, heavier—rolling through the thick air like something ancient stretching awake. The ground beneath us shuddered, the weight of the sound pressing into my chest, vibrating through my ribs. It wasn't just noise—it was felt. A slow, deliberate resonance that settled into everything, threading through the mist, winding through the tangled roots beneath our feet.

I froze. My breath caught. My pulse quickened.

Beside me, Gillie stood motionless, her blade catching the dim, shifting light, her gaze scanning the swamp like she expected something to step out from the shadows.

"*This isn't a swamp,*" I murmured, the words slipping out before I could stop them. "*It's a grave.*"

Gillie didn't answer. She didn't have to.

The mist curled tighter, blurring the edges of the world. The water thickened beneath our steps—dragging, resisting, turning each movement into something that felt less like forward motion and more like surrender.

Then… a whisper.

Thin. Threading through the silence between breaths.

"The twelve gather."

The words curled through the mist—not loud, not commanding, just there, just undeniable—settling into the air like a weight yet to fall.

Then, another whisper.

"The gathering storm approaches."

The sound wasn't sharp or sudden—it was woven into the atmosphere, a quiet declaration rather than a warning, a statement rather than a threat. The words sat between us like something spoken by the swamp itself, something that carried more truth than we were ready to understand.

Gillie stiffened beside me, her breath uneven. My own pulse sat heavy in my throat, the meaning of the words settling into me before I even fully understood them.

Another bell rang—deeper, heavier, weighted—and with it, the swamp trembled, the vibration spreading outward, threading through the trees, pulsing through the ground.

It wasn't loud.

It wasn't abrupt.

But it was everywhere.

Neither of us spoke.

Neither of us moved.

And yet, the swamp had already begun to pull us forward.

The mist tightened, the water growing heavier beneath our feet. The bell tolled again, its mournful echo curling through the shifting air, urging us onward.

Somewhere, in the depths of this haunted place, the judgment of one soul awaited.

And if we failed him, the punishment would not be his alone.

Reflections of Joshua

We shouldn't have come.

That thought weighed on me more with every step. The swamp pressed in around us, the air thick and suffocating, dragging us deeper with every breath. The realization hit slow, heavy, and inevitable. This wasn't just a place—it was alive, aware, and we had crossed its threshold without fully grasping the cost.

I turned, glancing back the way we'd come, my chest tightening as my eyes met only the swirling mist.

The path was gone. The trees behind us had shifted, their limbs closing in like a cage, and the pools of stagnant water all looked the same— indistinguishable, endless. My stomach churned, a sick knot forming as the truth settled over me like a weight I couldn't shake.

Gillie stopped beside me, her breath sharp. Her gaze darted over the mist, her lips pressing into a hard line. "The way out," she muttered, her voice tight with unease. "It's gone."

I swallowed hard, my hands tightening as though grasping something unseen. "No," I said, though I wasn't sure who I was trying to convince—her or myself. "It has to be there. It has to…"

"It's not," she cut in sharply. Her tone wasn't angry, just cold and brittle, like she didn't have the energy to soften it. Her hand hovered near her blade, her knuckles white. "The swamp… it's shifting. It's closing us in."

A whisper reached me then—soft and fleeting, brushing against my mind like the edge of a memory. At first, I thought I imagined it. But then it came again, curling through the mist like smoke. The sound wasn't loud; it didn't need to be. It slid under my skin and settled deep in my chest.

"*Not until it's done,*" it murmured. The words were faint, slipping through the air as though meant for each of us differently. But they carried an edge of finality that made my breath catch.

"Not until the purpose is fulfilled."

The mist pressed in tighter, shifting as though it, too, had acknowledged the words. There was no explanation, no further warning— just the statement.

Gillie stiffened, her head snapping toward me. "Did you hear that?" she hissed, her voice a mix of sharpness and dread.

I nodded, though I couldn't bring myself to speak. My fingers gripped the coin tighter as the whispers came again, carrying the same haunting message. They weren't voices—not in the way people spoke—but something else entirely. Something alive. Something that understood.

A sharp crack echoed through the mist, and I turned sharply, my heart pounding. Joshua stood ahead of us, his back rigid, his hands trembling at his sides as he stared into the black water pooling at his feet. When he spoke, his voice wasn't flat or distant—it was raw, trembling with anger.

"Who the hell are you?"

Gillie froze, her hand tightening around the hilt of her blade. "What are you talking about?"

Joshua whirled on us, his eyes wild, his expression flickering between fury and confusion.

"Who the hell are you?" he demanded again, his voice cracking. "Why are you here? Did Grace send you? Is this another one of her tricks?"

"Joshua…" I began, but he cut me off, taking a step closer, his gaze narrowing.

"No," he spat, his breath coming in ragged bursts. "You're not real. You can't be. She wouldn't send anyone. She wouldn't…"

His voice faltered, but the anger didn't fade.

"You're not real," he repeated, his fists clenched. "This place isn't real. It's not… it's not…"

His gaze flicked to the water again, and something in his posture broke, his shoulders slumping as his voice dropped to a whisper.

"It's me," he said, almost to himself. "It's all me."

The water rippled again, slower this time, and I found myself staring despite every instinct screaming at me to look away. The surface twisted, darkened, then began to shift. At first, I couldn't make sense of the shapes forming beneath the water—they flickered, blurred, like reflections seen through shattered glass. But then they sharpened, and I realized they weren't reflections at all. They were fragments.

Faces. Places. Sins.

Gillie stepped closer, her hand instinctively reaching for the blade strapped to her side.

"Don't look," she said sharply, her gaze cutting to me. "It's just another trick."

Joshua didn't move. His eyes were locked on the pool as the images beneath its surface shifted—first a woman's face, then his own, younger, pleading, desperate.

"*It's not a trick*," he whispered, his voice trembling. "*It's real. It's me.*"

Entering the Swamp

"It's showing him," Gillie muttered through clenched teeth, her expression hardening. "It's showing him everything."

The swamp rippled again, and the images deepened. Grace's face appeared, her eyes piercing, unrelenting, her mouth moving as though she were speaking words that didn't reach us. Joshua's breath hitched, and he stumbled back, his hands trembling.

"*I didn't know,*" he whispered, his voice breaking. "*I didn't mean to.*"

The swamp didn't care. It wasn't letting go.

"This is what it does," Gillie said, stepping between Joshua and the water, her knife flashing in the dim light. "It keeps us here. It drags us under."

I shook my head, taking a slow, shaky step forward. The whispers curled through the mist again, wrapping around my chest, my thoughts.

"Not until it's done," they murmured. "Not until he chooses."

Joshua turned to me, his gaze hollow, his voice trembling.

"How do we leave this place?" he asked, though there was no hope in his tone. Only desperation. Only fear.

The truth was—we might not. Not unless he did. Not unless he chose right. And if he didn't . . . we'd fall with him.

I wanted to lie—to tell him there was still a way back. That we could just turn around and the swamp would let us go. But the truth had already settled deep in my chest like a stone.

"We can't," I said softly, the words falling from my lips like a truth I hadn't wanted to admit. "Not until it's over."

And if you fall, I thought, we fall too.

Gillie's gaze darkened, her anger barely held in check.

I lowered my gaze as Joshua turned away from the pool. The weight of his past clung to all of us now.

Gillie met my eyes—not long, just a flicker. But in that moment, I saw something beneath her steel: not pity, not forgiveness… just the barest hint of understanding. A shared weight.

And then she looked away, back to the path. Back to the mission

"Then we keep moving," she said firmly, her voice cutting through the oppressive stillness. "We don't stop. Not for this. Not for anything."

Joshua hesitated, his chest heaving as his eyes lingered on the water. But then he nodded, his steps slow, hesitant, as he turned away from the pool.

The whispers faded slightly, the mist shifting just enough to reveal the narrow path ahead.

Another bell tolled, louder this time, and the weight of the swamp deepened as we pressed forward.

The path was winding, unrelenting, and every step felt like dragging ourselves through the weight of Joshua's sins.

But we kept moving.

There was no other choice.

The Tolling Bells

The next toll didn't just ring—it vibrated.

The sound hummed through the mist, deep and constant, threading through the air like something buried beneath the surface had stirred awake. It didn't crash or echo—it settled, stretching through the ground, traveling through the roots and waterlogged earth beneath our feet.

The swamp shuddered.

I felt it beneath my boots, a subtle, pulsing tremor—not violent, not sudden, but steady, pressing inward, sinking into the bones of the place itself. The air sharpened, shifting as though the swamp had taken a breath and was holding it.

Gillie stiffened beside me, her breath catching. Her gaze flicked toward the mist-draped trees, scanning the shifting shadows between the tangled limbs.

"What was that?" she asked, voice low, deliberate—like she didn't want to admit the unease tightening her jaw.

I opened my mouth to respond, but before I could, the next toll came—clearer this time, heavier, rolling through the swamp like thunder breaking the silence. It wasn't a sound so much as a pull, a vibration that reverberated in my chest and tightened around my ribs.

The air felt colder, the dampness sharp against my skin. I could see it in Gillie's face—she was bracing, too.

Joshua froze ahead of us, his shoulders tensing, his steps faltering for the first time since we entered.

"*The bell,*" he whispered, his voice trembling as if he was afraid of the words themselves. "*It's started.*"

Gillie frowned, glancing at me before fixing her glare on him. "Started what?" she asked, her tone sharp as she stepped closer. "What does it mean?"

Joshua hesitated, the shadows of the swamp pressing against him like they were holding him upright and threatening to drag him down all at once. The next toll echoed—low, weighted, vibrating through the ground like it had taken on physical form, threading into the earth beneath our feet.

He exhaled, slow and deliberate.

"The last twelve months have gathered," he said. His voice wasn't sharp, wasn't uncertain—it was resigned, like the words had been settled long before he spoke them.

Gillie's breath hitched. She turned toward him, brows drawn tight. "What does that mean?" she asked, the unease slipping into her voice despite her best effort to steady it.

Joshua didn't look at her. He didn't look at me.

He only stared into the mist, eyes locked on something neither of us could see.

"The last twelve months have gathered."

He said it again—not changing the words, not explaining them, only repeating them like a truth too large to fit into anything more.

The silence thickened, pressing against us, settling into the swamp.

Gillie swallowed. "Joshua."

"*The final year,*" he murmured, voice hollow, distant.

He inhaled like it hurt, like he was bracing for something heavier than the air around us.

"The 100th."

Gillie's mouth tightened, her fingers tightening briefly against the hilt of her knife. Her movements were sharp but unsteady as her gaze flicked toward the mist curling thicker around us.

She exhaled, slow and sharp.

Joshua didn't respond. He stared forward, his hollow gaze fixed on the mist as though he could see something waiting just beyond it. His hands twitched at his sides, clenched and trembling, and for a moment, I wondered if he was going to step back, to turn around and run. But the next toll rang through the swamp, cutting the thought short, and instead, he stepped forward.

Gillie swore under her breath, glancing at me before moving after him. "This isn't right," she muttered, her voice tight. "These bells—they're not just sounds. They're pulling him."

Entering the Swamp

"*They're pulling all of us*," I murmured, my hands tightening as if bracing against the weight of the swamp. I followed them, the bell's chime vibrating through the air again, deeper and darker with each toll.

The tolls weren't just calling Joshua. They knew us, too. Every step we took was watched, counted, weighed.

It wasn't just the bells that remembered. The swamp itself was listening.

And somewhere beneath that sound, a truth I hadn't let myself say aloud:

If Joshua is damned when the final bell rings . . . we are too.

Gillie grabbed Joshua's arm suddenly, her movements quick and forceful, stopping him mid-step.

"Listen to me," she said sharply, her voice cutting through the oppressive stillness. "You don't get to wander off every time this swamp whispers something at you. This is your last year, fine. But that doesn't mean you run toward the first thing that calls your name. Understand?"

Joshua's jaw tightened, his gaze fixed on hers. "You don't understand," he said softly, though his voice carried an edge. "I don't have time to wait."

Gillie scoffed, letting go of his arm and stepping back as she glared at him. "You think rushing toward the swamp's tricks is going to help you? You think this place has time for your impatience?" Her voice rose slightly, the bite in her tone sharp enough to cut through the mist.

I stepped between them before Joshua could respond, holding up a hand to stop him from pushing past her again.

"Stop," I said firmly, my voice steady despite the unease twisting in my chest. "We don't know what's waiting for us out there. We stick together. We move carefully."

Joshua shook his head, his hollow eyes flicking to me.

"The bells aren't just sounds," he said quietly. "They're marks. They're counting down."

"Counting down to what?" I asked, though part of me already knew the answer.

He didn't hesitate. "Judgment," he said, his voice trembling. "The God Forsaken Bell. The end."

The words hung between us, heavy and cold, as the fifth toll rang through the swamp, shuddering through the mist like a pulse. My chest tightened, the weight of the sound settling in my bones, and I realized then that he was right.

This wasn't just about the journey.
This was about time—time running out, time slipping away.
And the bells weren't going to let us forget it.

Gillie exhaled sharply, her hand hovering near her knife again as she glanced at me.
"Then we keep moving," she said, her voice steeling into something harder, colder. "Those bells aren't going to wait for us, and neither is his redemption."

I nodded, my hands tightening as the mist pressed closer, the swamp's weight settling heavier on my shoulders. Joshua didn't move for a moment, his gaze lingering on the path ahead, but finally, he nodded too. His steps were slow, hesitant, as though the swamp was pulling him forward and holding him back all at once. But he walked.

The next toll came, deep and resonant, and the shadows among the trees seemed to shift, observing us as we moved forward. The air grew colder, sharper, and I couldn't shake the feeling that the swamp was waiting for us to falter. I glanced at Gillie, her jaw tight as she kept her pace steady, her gaze fixed ahead, and Joshua moved just ahead of her, his breathing shallow but determined.

The sound carved through the mist, deep, resonant, pressing into the fabric of the swamp, but it wasn't alone.

The whispers came with it.

Soft at first. Insidious. Flickering at the edges of thought, barely distinguishable from the hum of silence. But they were there—they had always been there.

Joshua exhaled sharply, pressing a hand to his temple, fingers tightening against his skull.

"*Don't listen to them,*" he murmured, his voice strained, distant.

Gillie turned toward him, uneasy. "What?"

Joshua barely lifted his gaze. "The whispers," he said, his tone heavy, dull with exhaustion. "They come when you stop. They sink in. They pull at your mind, twist what's yours until it's not anymore."

The weight of his words pressed into the silence between them.

"They don't just speak," Joshua continued, his voice unsteady. "They dig inside, find the cracks, press into your fears, your failures, your regrets, and then…" He hesitated, jaw tightening. "Then they make you doubt what was ever real. They change things."

Gillie swallowed, the unease creeping further into her expression. "Change how?"

Joshua clenched his teeth. "They rewrite memories," he said, his voice hollow, weighted. "They take what you know and strip it bare, replacing it with something else, something wrong—but you don't realize it's happening until it's too late. The longer you linger, the more they sink in. And eventually…"

His fingers twitched at his sides.

"…eventually, they take you."

The bells tolled again, deeper this time.

Joshua's breath shuddered. "You have to keep moving," he whispered, his voice thin, urgent. "It's one of the rules of the swamp. If you stop… if you wait too long… the whispers will take you."

The words settled between us, heavy, undeniable.

The bells tolled once more.

And beneath their weight, the whispers grew louder.

Then the next toll rang—louder now, rolling through the swamp with a weight that made my knees tremble. The mist twisted tighter, shadows stretching longer, swallowing the spaces between us, but we kept moving. We had to.

The next toll followed—sooner than expected, sharp and commanding, threading through the air like it was pulling at something unseen. The bells were coming faster now—or maybe I was simply bracing for them, anticipating their arrival, feeling the inevitable weight of each one settle before it even rang.

The sound changed.

It wasn't just marking distance or warning of what lay ahead—it was marking something, some shift, something already waiting.

The swamp's breath grew icy, a tangible weight pressing down on us, as if the very mire sought to claim us. This heaviness permeated everything—the hushed air, the yielding earth, and within me, a cold dread coiled around my ribs, stealing the ease of my breath.

Time had already slipped.

The journey was underway.

There was no turning back.

Only the swamp.

Only the weight.

And now, all twelve had gathered. The year had begun.

The Shadow of Grace

It wasn't just the swamp pressing in—it was time.

Something had shifted, something had settled, and though none of us had spoken the words aloud, we could feel it. The last year had started. Joshua's final twelve months. And we were inside them now—walking through time itself, through its weight, through its undeniable presence pressing against our chests.

The realization didn't come as an abrupt thought. It came as a feeling—the thickening mist, the tightening air, the slow, deliberate resistance of the ground beneath our feet. There was no turning back, no stopping, because we had already been claimed by it, already stepped into something that had been waiting for us long before we arrived.

Joshua stiffened, his breath ragged, but he didn't speak.

Gillie, ahead of us, gripped her knife tighter, her breath shallow, her movements sharp—but uncertain. Even she felt it.

Another toll echoed through the swamp—not loud, not sudden, but deep, settling into the ground, threading through the tangled roots beneath our feet.

No one spoke

The swamp didn't need words.

The weight of it was already enough.

Gillie's step faltered, the fading bell seeming to draw a line of tension across her shoulders. Her breath hitched, and her fingers dug more firmly into the hilt of her knife, as if seeking anchor.

"Keep moving," she muttered, her voice low, deliberate. It wasn't a command—it was a warning.

Her gaze fixed on the path ahead, as though she could will it into clearing. "Don't let it get to you."

Joshua followed close behind, his steps slower, dragging. His gaze flicked between the mist and the shadows pressing closer, his breaths shallow, uneven. He didn't say anything, but I could feel his hesitance like the weight of the swamp itself. Each step seemed harder than the last, and I couldn't tell if it was the mud pulling him down or the pull of whatever lay ahead.

Another toll echoed through the swamp, its low chime vibrating through the mist, and I froze mid-step. It wasn't just a sound. It was a ripple, a pull that hummed through my chest, vibrating against my ribcage like it was trying to shake something loose.

I glanced at Gillie, but she didn't stop. Her shoulders were stiff, her eyes sharp, but her fingers were trembling against her knife.

"You feel that, don't you?" Joshua's voice was quiet, trembling, as though he didn't want to admit it. He stopped walking, his hollow eyes fixed on something just ahead, and I could see the way his chest heaved with shallow breaths.

"It's her. She's here."

Gillie stiffened, her gaze snapping to him like a whip.

"Her who?"

The words came sharp, clipped—more suspicion than curiosity.

Joshua didn't answer, didn't even blink.

Gillie exhaled sharply, shaking her head. "It's probably just the swamp playing tricks on you," she said, her voice dropping into something colder. "Don't let this place fool you. You know what it's doing."

Joshua shook his head, his jaw tightening.

"*You don't know,*" he murmured, almost to himself. His hand twitched at his side, as though he meant to reach out for something just out of sight. "*She's close. I can feel her. I have to—*"

"No," Gillie snapped, cutting him off. "You're not going anywhere."

But he didn't listen.

His steps quickened, his movements sharper as he pushed forward, and the mist seemed to part slightly in front of him, drawing him in like a hand pulling him toward its palm.

"Joshua, stop!" I shouted, moving after him, but my boots sank deeper into the mud, the resistance stronger now, holding me back. The shadows curled closer, wrapping around the trees and the edges of the mist like claws. I could feel the pull, sharp and heavy, dragging at every part of me.

And then the mist shifted.

It was slow at first—subtle, like the flicker of movement in the corner of your eye. But then it took shape, a figure emerging from the haze, soft and shimmering, almost unreal.

Joshua froze, his chest heaving, his eyes wide, and I knew before he spoke who it was.

The figure moved closer, her outline sharpening, her pale dress catching the faint light filtering through the trees. The air shifted as she approached—a sudden drop in warmth, like winter exhaled through her skin. A sweet, decaying scent followed, like lilacs left too long in water.

"*Grace,*" Joshua whispered, his voice breaking. His hand reached out toward her, trembling, and the figure tilted her head slightly, her face still blurred by the mist.

"It's… it's really her."

Gillie swore under her breath, grabbing his arm and yanking him back sharply.

"It's not her," she said, her voice cutting through the silence like a blade. "Joshua, look at her. Really look."

Joshua hesitated, his hand hovering mid-reach, his breaths quick and shallow.

"I can't," he whispered. "I don't…"

"Look at her," Gillie demanded, her grip tightening on his arm. "She's wrong. You know she's wrong."

I stepped closer, my gaze flicking to the figure. She was clearer now, her features sharpening, but something was off. Her movements were smooth but hollow, like a marionette pulled by invisible strings. Her lips parted as if she meant to speak, but no sound came.

She wasn't alive—not really.

She wasn't Grace.

Joshua's breaths quickened, his hand trembling as he pulled it back slowly. His gaze dropped to the ground, his jaw clenching as his shoulders sagged.

"She's gone," he said softly, his voice barely audible. "She's not here."

Gillie nodded, releasing his arm as the mist shifted again, the figure dissolving back into the haze. The clearing darkened, the shadows pressing closer, and I could see the way Joshua's hands shook at his sides. He didn't speak again, but his silence was heavy—filled with doubt, regret, and something darker.

The swamp didn't stop

The mist curled tighter.

And then the whispers pressed in.

Not like before.

Not subtle.

Not waiting.

They came all at once.

A sudden weight settled heavily in my chest, a foreign presence winding around my ribs like grasping claws. No words were spoken, no voices echoed, only this unwelcome intrusion, something clamping down, yanking, digging into my very being.

Entering the Swamp

Joshua inhaled sharply, his breath hitching—too fast, too unsteady. His eyes darted across the clearing, searching the mist, his fingers twitching at his sides.

Gillie clenched her teeth. Her posture shifted—tense, defensive, ready to run.

Another toll echoed through the swamp, louder now, and Joshua's head snapped up.

He felt it.

We all felt it.

The whispers didn't let go.

They tightened.

They pressed inside.

"We keep going," Gillie said firmly, her voice cutting through the silence like steel. "We don't stop. Not for this. Not for her. Not for anything."

I nodded, my steps firm as I followed her.

Joshua hesitated a moment longer, his gaze lingering on the shadows where Grace had stood, but then he moved, his steps slow and heavy.

The mist didn't lift—it wrapped tighter, more deliberate now. Heavy. Intentional.

And its whispers grew louder, filling the spaces between the tolling bells with words I couldn't understand but could feel—deep, and cold, and close.

The First Encounter

Raven's Arrival

The whispers clung to the air—breath against the skin, threading through thought. They had never truly left, not entirely, and even as we pressed forward, as the swamp thickened around us, their weight remained, settling deeper into the silence that followed.

Joshua's steps faltered, his breath uneven, his fingers twitching at his sides as he scanned the shifting mist. He wasn't looking for answers—he already knew none would come. Gillie moved beside him, her grip steady on the knife at her hip, her movements sharp, deliberate, her posture rigid as if she could brace herself against the unseen presence pressing in from all sides.

The air was different now, heavier, the silence pressing down like a held breath, unnatural in the way it settled between the trees. It wasn't relief—it was absence, calculated and waiting, something measured, something watching.

The First Encounter

Then, without sound, without warning, the mist parted, unraveling like frayed cloth, thinning just enough to reveal the figure standing at the center of the clearing. He had always been there; we just hadn't seen him.

At first glance, he looked human. Tall. Lean. His sharp features blurred in the haze.

But the longer I stared, the more the details refused to settle. His shape flickered with the mist, shifting between rigid edges and fluid motion. His clothing twisted—first tattered fabric, then something sleek and refined, then wild again, rough like raw hide stripped from something long dead.

He was more shadow than man. More suggestion than substance. Yet, somehow, more present than anything else we had encountered in the swamp.

His eyes caught the faint light filtering through the trees, their glow subtle but undeniable, tracking our movements as if he already knew how we would react before we even did. The corner of his mouth lifted, slow and deliberate, amusement curling at the edges of his expression like something meant to be seen, meant to be unsettling.

"Walking through our whispers so easily," he mused, his voice smooth, rich, layered with something too practiced to be anything but intentional. "Not many do."

His gaze flickered to Joshua, settling there, watching, assessing.

Gillie shifted beside me, her fingers brushing the hilt of her knife in a movement so slight it was nearly imperceptible, but he saw it. His smirk deepened, his posture unwavering, effortless in the way he owned the space around him.

"They linger, don't they?" he continued, tilting his head just slightly, as if waiting for confirmation, as if enjoying the weight of his own words. "Digging at the edges of your thoughts, winding their way inside. You'll learn to listen soon enough."

The mist curled in around us again, thickening at the edges, and in that moment, whether he was lying or not, whether he had created the whispers or merely claimed them, it no longer mattered.

Gillie's posture stiffened beside me, her hand brushing the hilt of her knife, ready but cautious. "Who are you?" she demanded, her voice steady, biting.

He tilted his head, his sharp gaze shifting to her, as if evaluating her worth. "*Ah, such simple minds,*" he murmured, his tone steeped in mockery. His lips pulled into a cruel smile, revealing teeth that gleamed like glass. "Who are we? That's your question? A dull one, but we shall humor you."

His form flickered violently, his silhouette rippling between masculine sharpness and something regal, feminine—more unsettling than I wanted to admit. "Are we Raven?" he said, his voice lilting with playfulness. "The guide? The shadow? The trickster? Or are we more? Are we chaos, hunger, inevitability?" His glowing eyes burned brighter, and the cruel edge in his smile deepened. "We know what you're here for. And we laugh."

Gillie narrowed her gaze, her hand tightening on the hilt of her knife. "You're just another puppet," she shot back, her voice biting through the mist. "Whatever game you're playing, we're not interested."

The air shifted violently, and Raven's smile faltered, his glowing eyes narrowing. "A puppet?" he said, his tone sharp, cutting through the air like a blade. The mist twisted tighter around his feet, as though responding to his anger. "You reduce us to something small, something powerless? How insulting. How limited."

His form rippled, growing taller, sharper, his glowing eyes burning like embers. "We're Raven," he said, his voice thunderous, reverberating through the clearing. "Not a puppet. Not a pawn. We're chaos itself."

Joshua flinched slightly at his outburst, but before he could speak, Raven's attention snapped back to him. His tone dropped, soft yet deliberate, drifting closer like smoke. "We have seen you before, Joshua Clay. Long before the swamp claimed you. You carried your soul to the edge, and we knew it would not be long before it shattered."

Joshua's breath hitched, his gaze faltering as the weight of Raven's words pressed against him. "*Stop,*" he said softly, though his voice trembled. "*You don't know me.*"

"Oh, but we do," Raven replied smoothly, his smile sharpening as his glowing eyes gleamed with cruel amusement. "You bargained once before, didn't you? With someone who made you believe the pain could be taken away. We remember it well. And we see how it still weighs on you—how it has shaped you."

Joshua froze, his hands trembling at his sides. "*I didn't know,*" he whispered, his voice breaking.

Raven's laughter was low, jagged, cutting through the stillness like shattering glass. "Of course you didn't. That's the beauty of desperation—it blinds you. But worry not; we're here for you now. We're ready to make it all go away."

Gillie stepped closer, her posture sharp and defensive. "Whatever bargain you think you're offering," she said coldly, "we're not buying."

Raven tilted his head, his glowing eyes narrowing as he studied her, amused but wary. "Ah, the defiant one," he said softly. "So eager to fight a battle you don't understand. Your labels amuse us, as does your confidence. But don't mistake it for control."

The bell tolled suddenly, deep and resonant, shuddering through the clearing like a pulse. Raven's form flickered again, his glowing eyes narrowing as he stepped back into the mist. "Your trials have begun," he said, his voice echoing faintly, layered with distant whispers. "The swamp delights in its guests, after all. Your resolve will be tested. Broken. Consumed."

Joshua's gaze dropped, his shoulders slumping slightly as though the weight of Raven's words had settled on him more heavily than the rest of us. Raven's glowing eyes lingered on him, his expression unreadable. "*We're here for you, Joshua Clay,*" he said softly, his voice resonant. "*Only you.*"

And just as suddenly as he had appeared, Raven dissolved into the mist, his form unraveling like smoke caught in a storm. The clearing fell silent again, but the weight of his presence lingered, suffocating and heavy.

None of us spoke for a long moment, frozen as the mist curled tighter around us. The air felt colder now, sharper, as though the swamp had absorbed Raven's fury and transformed it into something tangible.

Joshua moved first, his steps slow and deliberate as he turned back to the path. His shoulders sagged, his gaze fixed on the ground, and he didn't speak. Gillie followed close behind, her knife still drawn, her movements sharp and defensive.

I lingered a moment longer, the weight of the moment pressing against my chest like an anchor. Raven's laughter echoed faintly in my mind—mocking, haunting, unrelenting. His final words hung heavy in the air: "Only you."

The Weight of Names

Raven's presence lingered long after he had vanished.

It wasn't just the encounter—it was the weight of it, the way he had appeared without warning, without effort, and how the swamp hadn't seemed to touch him at all. His absence should have given us relief, but it didn't. If anything, it pressed against us even harder, settling over our shoulders like something unseen.

Then... I looked up.

The First Encounter

The sky loomed, low, unrelenting, ready to collapse at any moment. Dark clouds stretched thick overhead, folding inward, pressing down with a weight that had nothing to do with the air itself. It had been there the whole time, but now we felt it.

Was that the point?

Had Raven disappeared just long enough for us to notice it? Had he stepped back—not to leave, but to let the swamp itself close in, to show us how small we really were beneath it?

Every movement felt heavier. The silence stretched, broken only by the crunch of damp earth beneath our boots and the quiet pull of whispers threading through the air—too faint to catch, too persistent to ignore.

I tightened my grip on the coin in my pocket, its sharp edges pressing against my skin like a warning. Joshua walked ahead, his steps uneven, dragged down by something he wouldn't name. Gillie moved beside me, her knife close, her gaze sharp—darting to the shifting shadows, waiting for something to emerge.

Then—the air shifted. Not in any way I could see, not visibly, but in the way it felt. Like something waiting, like something drawing us forward, like something had already decided that we would arrive whether we wanted to or not.

Joshua froze. His breath hitched—short, shallow.

Gillie's fingers curled tighter around the hilt of her knife.

And then… he returned.

Raven stepped into view, unfolding with an unsettling calm. He didn't arrive. He didn't enter. He had never truly left. The weight of the sky pressed heavy against everything—but not him. It was as if the storm had parted just enough to let him through, untouched, unmoved.

Gillie stiffened. "You're back," she muttered, suspicion laced through the words.

Raven smiled, slow, easy. His dark eyes flicked toward her, amusement sharp at the edges.

"Did we ever leave?" he asked. "Or have you only just noticed?"

He let the question hang for a moment, his gaze flicking upward—toward the sky, toward the weight pressing down.

"We told you," he murmured, his voice smooth, deliberate. "You'd listen to the whispers eventually. Just like you did when you looked up."

Joshua shifted, his breath shallow. Gillie's hand tightened around the hilt of her knife, but she didn't speak.

Raven's smile widened, his tone softening into something almost playful.

"It's fascinating, really," he continued. "How easily you follow. A glance here, a step there. We didn't even have to try."

He took a step closer, his movements soundless, his presence filling the space between us.

"You looked up because we wanted you to. And you'll do other things, too. You'll listen. You'll follow. You'll succumb."

His gaze lingered on each of us in turn, his smile never faltering.

"It always happens," he said, almost casually. "The swamp doesn't break you all at once. It doesn't have to. It just… nudges."

He paused, his eyes narrowing slightly, his voice dropping lower.

"And we enjoy watching it happen."

His words twisted something in my chest, but I forced myself not to show it. "Where were you?" I asked cautiously, keeping my voice steady despite the tension coiling around us.

Raven didn't answer immediately. His gaze drifted past us, settling on the swirling mist ahead. "Where we needed to be," he said eventually. "Where the swamp wanted us."

Gillie narrowed her eyes, stepping forward with sharp deliberation, her knife gleaming faintly in the dim light. "If you're playing games, Raven, stop it now," she snapped. "We don't have time for this."

Raven tilted his head slightly, his faint smile sharpening. "You think this is a game, Gillie?" he asked, his voice calm but carrying an edge that made the air feel colder. "Everything here has purpose. Even you."

The weight of his words hung heavily in the air, the mist swirling tighter around him as though it were drawn to him. It felt like we weren't just facing Raven; we were confronting something larger—something that blurred the lines between him and the place we stood.

"What does that mean?" I pressed, my voice trembling despite my attempt to sound steady. "What purpose are you talking about?"

Raven's gaze slid to me, his expression unreadable. "Purpose," he repeated softly. "A question you've carried since you stepped into this place. Do you even know why you're here? Or why he sent you?"

Gillie stiffened at his words, her grip tightening further. "Who sent us?" she demanded sharply. "If you know something, then say it. Enough with the riddles."

Raven's faint smile deepened, but it held no warmth. "Answers?" he echoed. "Answers are heavy things. You think you want them, but the truth is, you may not be ready for the weight they carry."

Joshua flinched visibly, his trembling hands clenching at his sides as though bracing against something only he could feel. "*What weight?*" he murmured, his voice faint and uneven. "*What are you trying to say?*"

The mist stirred sharply, cold and pressing, and the swamp seemed to ripple with silent laughter. Raven's voice cut through it, low and resonant.

"You carry names like armor," he said, his tone steeped in mockery. "Legacies like shields. But do you understand what they mean? Or the choices they bind you to?"

Gillie's glare hardened, her jaw tightening. "Who are we bound to?" she demanded, her voice sharp and cutting. "If you know, then say it."

Raven tilted his head again, his gaze flicking between us. "You already know," he said quietly, his voice smooth but layered with something darker. "The blood in your veins speaks louder than any words we could offer."

The cryptic answer sent a chill through me, sharp and lingering. I clenched my fists, the pressure biting deeper into my skin as I tried to ground myself against the oppressive weight of his presence. "What do you mean?" I asked, my voice trembling.

Raven's faint smile returned, his expression laced with quiet amusement. "*You think knowing will save you,*" he said softly. "*But some truths are better left buried.*"

The mist shifted once more, swirling deliberately, and on the ground ahead of us, a shape began to take form—an outline, faint but unmistakable. A circle surrounded by jagged lines radiating outward like flames or thorns. It pulsed faintly with the same rhythm as the swamp's weight.

"What is that?" Gillie asked sharply, her voice cutting through the stillness. "What does it mean?"

Raven didn't respond immediately. Instead, his tone softened into something almost wistful. "A mark," he said. "A reminder. A name carved too deeply to be erased."

I froze, the breath catching in my throat as the symbol burned into my thoughts. It was familiar—hauntingly so—but its meaning remained maddeningly out of reach. "Whose name?" I asked quietly.

Raven tilted his head slightly, his dark gaze flicking to the symbol. "*Names,*" he murmured, "*are just shadows of what we leave behind.*"

His figure blurred at the edges then, dissolving slowly into the mist as though the swamp was pulling him away. "*Some truths,*" he said softly, "*are better left buried.*"

"Don't you dare disappear!" Gillie snapped, her frustration boiling over as she lunged forward. "We're not done here!"

But it was too late. The mist swallowed him whole, his figure dissolving into the haze until he was gone. The symbol flickered once, twice, and then it, too, vanished, leaving only the suffocating silence in its wake.

We stood there, frozen, the weight of his words pressing harder with every passing second. Gillie's grip on her knife was white-knuckled, her gaze burning into the empty space where Raven had been. Joshua didn't move, his hollow eyes fixed on the swirling mist, his breaths shallow and uneven.

"*What was he trying to tell us?*" I murmured, my voice barely audible. But no one answered—not Joshua, not Gillie, and certainly not the swamp. The only sound was the faint crunch of damp earth beneath our boots as we turned back to the path and began walking again, the weight of Raven's absence and the questions he'd left behind dragging heavily behind us.

Division Among Them

The weight of Raven's presence hung in the air like a storm cloud, thick and suffocating. His words hadn't just left questions; they'd left fractures. Each of us carried our own interpretation of what he said, and each of us wore it like armor—or maybe like chains.

Gillie marched ahead with sharp, purposeful strides, her knife still clutched tightly in her hand. She didn't glance back at me, but I felt her tension like a blade pressed against my spine. The silence wasn't empty; it crackled, alive with unspoken accusations and doubts.

Finally, Gillie stopped short and spun around, her glare cutting through the mist. "So," she snapped, her voice like flint striking steel. "Are you going to tell us what you're hiding, or do I have to spell it out for you?"

I stiffened, her words hitting harder than I'd expected. "What are you talking about?" I asked, though I could feel the answer already coiling in her gaze.

"You've been quiet," she said, her tone sharp and biting. "Too quiet. Ever since Raven showed up, you've been off. What is it? You know something about him—don't you? About what he said?"

Her accusation sent heat rising into my chest. "I'm trying to process," I said evenly, though my voice trembled beneath the weight of her stare. "You heard him just like I did. He wasn't exactly straightforward."

Gillie scoffed, crossing her arms. "Don't give me that. You've been holding onto something since before we even got here. The way he talked about legacies—bloodlines—you knew what he meant."

The words cut deeper than I wanted to admit. My thoughts churned, circling back to the symbol Raven had shown us. That crest—it was Jonah's. I knew it as surely as I knew my own name. But what did it mean? What did Raven mean when he spoke of names and shadows? My head ached with questions I didn't know how to answer.

"I don't know what you're talking about," I said finally, though the conviction in my voice wavered. "You think I understand this any better than you do?"

"Don't you?" Gillie shot back, stepping closer. "Because it sure seems like you've got a lot more context than the rest of us. You don't think it's suspicious that Raven kept looking at you—that he said things that felt like they were meant for you?"

"Stop it," Joshua said, his voice low but strained. He turned to face us, his hollow eyes dark with something unspoken. "This is what he wants. He wants us to fall apart."

Gillie wheeled on him, her frustration spilling over like water through a crack. "And what about you?" she demanded. "You haven't said a damn thing since he showed up. What is it you're afraid of, Joshua? That he was right about you?"

Joshua flinched, his shoulders stiffening under the weight of her words. "*Afraid?*" he murmured, his voice trembling. "*I don't have the luxury of being afraid. Not anymore.*"

Gillie's glare hardened, her hand tightening around the knife. "No, you don't," she snapped. "Because every mistake you made led us here. Every choice you made broke the world. And now we're the ones cleaning up after you."

"Enough!" I said sharply, stepping between them before the tension could ignite into something worse. "What's wrong with you? You think Raven's words were only about me? Or about him?" I pointed to Joshua, my chest tight with frustration. "He was talking about all of us."

Gillie's jaw tightened, her gaze locking with mine. "Don't turn this around on me," she said coldly. "If he wasn't just talking about you, then what was that symbol about? That wasn't my family's crest, was it?"

The accusation lodged itself firmly in my chest. "I don't know!" I admitted, my voice rising despite my effort to stay calm. "But maybe this isn't just about me. Maybe it's about your family, too. Don't think I didn't notice the way you reacted to what he said."

Her glare faltered, just for a second, before returning with renewed intensity. "What the hell is that supposed to mean?"

"It means you're projecting," I snapped, the words spilling out before I could stop them. "You're so desperate to pin this on me because it's easier than facing your own doubts."

Gillie's mouth opened like she was ready to throw the words back at me, but Joshua spoke first.

"And what about you?" he said softly, his voice quiet but sharp enough to cut through the tension. "You're both so quick to throw blame at each other. But what about me? What do you think I'm hiding?"

The question silenced us, the weight of his words pressing down like the swamp itself. His gaze dropped to the ground, his hollow eyes shadowed by guilt. "I've made my choices," he said, his voice trembling. "I've made my mistakes. And maybe the swamp will never let me forget them. But don't think for a second that I don't see how it's breaking all of us."

The stillness that followed was suffocating. Gillie turned sharply, stalking back toward the path. "Believe whatever you want," she muttered, her voice low and bitter. "But don't think I'll let this swamp take me down with you."

Joshua lingered for a moment, his gaze flicking to mine. There was something raw in his expression—a fragility I hadn't seen before. Then he turned and followed Gillie, his steps slow and unsteady.

I lingered, the reminder of my past gnawing at my flesh. Gillie's words echoed in my mind, twisting like a splinter I couldn't remove. Maybe she was right. Maybe I was carrying more than just a name, more than just a legacy. But if that was true, what did it mean for the path ahead? And could we hold together long enough to see it through?

Threads of Trust

The mist curled thick around us, shifting in slow, deliberate waves. It looked normal enough—dense, heavy, the kind of fog that pressed into the air like a living thing—but the longer I stared, the more the thought crept in.

Had I looked at it on my own?

Or had Raven made me?

The First Encounter

The question sat uneasily in my mind, twisting at the edges of my thoughts. He was gone—his shadow dissolved into the haze—but his presence hadn't left, not really. His words lingered, cutting deep and unrelenting, and now, standing in the shifting fog, I couldn't tell if I was seeing the swamp or if he had made me look at it just to prove that he could.

I swallowed hard, forcing the thought down.

None of us spoke as we trudged forward, but the silence between us was anything but empty. It was sharp, filled with questions we were too afraid… or too angry… to ask.

Joshua walked ahead, his steps uneven, his shoulders hunched under the weight of something unspoken. Gillie followed close behind him, her knife clutched tightly in her hand, her gaze cutting through the mist like she was looking for a fight.

I stayed in the middle, my thoughts circling around Raven's warnings and the jagged symbol scorched into the swamp floor.

There was something about it… something familiar… but I couldn't grasp it.

Gillie's voice sliced through the quiet, brittle and biting. "You think Raven was only talking about you, don't you?" she said sharply, glancing back at me. "About your family. About Jonah."

I tensed, her accusation setting me on edge. "I never said that," I replied, my voice carefully even. "But you heard him. This isn't just about me—it's about all of us."

Gillie scoffed, her laugh bitter. "Yeah, right," she muttered. "He knows exactly how to get in our heads. And don't act like he didn't get in yours. The way he talked about bloodlines, legacies… That wasn't just some coincidence."

Her words twisted like a knife, but I forced myself to push back. "What about you?" I said, my voice rising slightly. "You think his words didn't mean anything to you? You've been tense ever since he showed up. What did you think he was getting at?"

Gillie turned on me, her glare sharp and unwavering. "You don't know what my family's been through," she snapped. "You don't know the weight we've carried."

Joshua's pace faltered ahead of us, his steps slowing, though he didn't turn. The silence stretched thin, the weight of Gillie's words pressing down on all of us.

"What's your family's connection to all this?" I asked cautiously, my voice steady but edged with curiosity. "What are you saying?"

Gillie hesitated, her grip tightening on the knife. She glanced briefly at Joshua before finally speaking, her voice faltering. "Olivia," she said quietly, her tone heavy. "She was my grandmother."

The name hit me hard, the realization twisting in my gut. I froze mid-step, my thoughts spinning. But it was Joshua who stopped completely. Slowly, he turned, his hollow eyes fixed on Gillie. "*Olivia?*" he murmured, his voice trembling. "*But… she was so young.*"

"How do you know her?" I asked, my voice cutting into the tension as I stepped closer to him. "Who was she to you?"

Joshua's gaze dropped to the ground, his shoulders trembling. "*She was my daughter,*" he said softly, his voice breaking. "*Olivia was my daughter.*"

"Yeah," Gillie broke in, her voice sharp and unrelenting. "His daughter. My grandmother. And she deserved better than what you gave her."

Joshua flinched at her words, his hands clenching at his sides. "*I didn't know,*" he whispered, his voice cracking under the weight of her accusation. "*I didn't know she… She was just a child when I…*"

"She grew up," Gillie interrupted, her tone cold. "And she grew up without you."

Joshua's shoulders sagged further, his breath coming in shallow, uneven waves. "*She deserved better,*" he murmured, his voice trembling. "*She deserved everything I couldn't give her.*"

"She deserved a future," Gillie snapped. "But the swamp doesn't care about what we deserve. It devours everything—hope, light, people. You know that better than anyone."

Joshua stiffened, his hollow eyes darkening as he turned to face her fully. "*She was strong,*" he said softly, his voice shaking but resolute. "*Stronger than I deserved. Stronger than… anyone.*"

I stepped forward, forcing myself between them before the tension could spiral further. "Stop," I said firmly, my voice cutting through the haze. "This isn't getting us anywhere. Raven and the swamp—they want this. They want us divided. And if we keep fighting, we're giving them exactly what they want."

Gillie turned away abruptly, her steps sharp as she stalked back down the path. "Fine," she muttered, though her anger still lingered in the air. "But don't think this swamp cares about redemption."

Joshua lingered for a moment, his gaze dropping to the ground. His voice came softly, trembling. "*She used to laugh,*" he murmured. "*Even when everything was falling apart. She always found a way to make things brighter.*"

Gillie stiffened at his words, her grip tightening on the knife. Her attention stayed fixed on the path ahead. "*She was the only one who believed we could fix any of this,*" she said softly, her voice faltering for the first time. "*She never stopped trying. Even when it felt hopeless, she held onto the idea that we could rise again. She was—light. Our light. And she carried it alone,*" she said softly. "*Because no one else would.*"

I felt my chest tighten, my thoughts circling back to Raven's words: Only you. "That light… it's still here," I said quietly. "If Olivia believed in it, maybe we can, too."

Gillie scoffed again but didn't argue. She turned back to the path, her steps brisk and purposeful. Joshua followed, his movements slow and unsteady, as though the weight of her words had left him struggling to hold himself together.

I trailed behind them, the tension lingering in the air like a shadow. The mist coiled tighter, suffocating, as though the swamp itself was pulling us closer to the truth we feared. And still, Raven's voice echoed faintly in my mind, mocking and relentless: Only you.

Allies and Enemies

Marcus's Bargain

The silence stretched razor-thin, hanging between us like a thread ready to snap. Joshua moved ahead, shoulders hunched, his steps careful. Gillie followed close behind, knife in hand, her movements sharp with unease.

I lagged slightly behind, every breath heavy, weighted. Raven's words hadn't left us—they were crawling under our skin, threading into our thoughts, tightening their hold. The swamp felt different now. Not just heavy. Not just oppressive.

Like it had chosen.

Then—the veil of darkness lifted.

Not like mist shifting. Not like fog clearing.

Like something unseen had decided it was time. Like the shadows had been holding him, hiding him, waiting for this exact moment to step aside.

And there he stood.

A man in the middle of the path, like he had just appeared out of nothing.

Tall. Gaunt. Rigid, yet at ease, as though he had been waiting for this moment all along. His face was long, angular, his features sharp beneath the unnatural light. Shadows twisted over his pale skin, shifting, moving—almost alive.

His eyes gleamed—dark, calculating, patient.

He wasn't like Raven.

He wasn't like anyone.

Gillie froze beside me, her breath catching as her knife came up, the blade glinting faintly. "Another one of his tricks," she muttered, voice cold, knuckles white around the hilt. "I'm not falling for this."

The figure took a slow, deliberate step forward, his dark eyes scanning each of us in turn. He clasped his hands behind his back—unhurried, yet precise, like a man long accustomed to control. "Trick?" he repeated, his voice low and smooth, like silk dragging across stone. "No, not a trick. I'm as real as you, as this place." His gaze lingered on Joshua, then flicked to Gillie. "Put the blade away. It won't do you any good here."

Gillie didn't move. Her glare hardened. "Who are you?" she demanded. "What do you want?"

The man tilted his head slightly, a faint smile curling at the corners of his lips—too composed, too rehearsed. "*Ah, introductions,*" he murmured, amused. "My name is Marcus. And what I want?" His gaze swept toward the swirling mist. "That's not the question you should be asking. What you should ask is why I'm here."

I shifted uneasily, hands tightening at my sides. "Fine," I said, keeping my voice low. "Why are you here?"

Marcus turned to me, eyes sharp, clinical—like a scientist observing a subject. "I'm here," he said slowly, "because this swamp isn't done with you. And neither am I."

Joshua flinched. His shoulders tensed. Gillie's blade remained raised, but her knuckles twitched—uncertainty creeping in.

"You expect us to trust you?" she asked, voice like a blade itself.

Marcus's mouth curved again, more performance than expression. "Trust?" he echoed, as though tasting the word. "No, Gillie. I don't expect your trust. I expect you to listen. Because whether you believe me or not… I'm your guide."

A chill slid down my spine. The mist curled tighter around Marcus, the swamp seeming to fold toward him.

"Guide us where?" I asked, forcing the words out. They felt too loud in the silence.

Marcus extended a pale hand toward the path ahead. "To the end," he said simply. "To what you came here to find."

Gillie didn't blink. "We don't need anything from you," she said.

He chuckled softly—low and bitter, like the sound of something cracking. "You don't have the luxury of pride here. Not in this place. Not with what's ahead."

He paused, letting the silence breathe before turning slightly toward Joshua, his smile tightening.

"Trust me," he said, tone tilting toward something sardonic. "There's plenty of pride to go around here."

Joshua stiffened. Marcus didn't look away.

"Isn't that right, Joshua Clay?" he said, voice dipping to something almost tender. "Pride—it was your first, most cherished sin. And perhaps, your most ruinous."

Joshua's hollow eyes flickered, but he said nothing. The weight of that single sentence seemed to settle on his shoulders like a cloak soaked in lead.

The silence that followed wasn't just quiet—it was *watching*.

Marcus let it stretch, then stepped closer, eyes still on Joshua. "The swamp has taken a particular interest in you," he said. "You hear its whispers. You feel its pull."

Joshua's steps faltered. His gaze dropped, but he didn't speak.

"You need me," Marcus continued, his voice soft, curling like smoke. "You can't move forward without guidance. But nothing here comes without cost."

I felt the coin press cold against my leg, the edge sharp enough to remind me I was still present.

And Marcus waited. Smiling.

I hesitated, pulse quickening as the weight of Marcus's words settled over us. Gillie stepped forward, her blade still drawn, catching the faint shimmer of swamplight. "What are you offering?" she asked, her voice sharp, suspicious.

Marcus's lips parted just slightly—less a smile, more a show of teeth. "A way forward," he said. "Through the trials. Past the thresholds. To the truth you seek."

"And what do you want in return?" Gillie snapped, her posture rigid.

His eyes glinted. "A bargain," he said, the word slow, indulgent. "A piece of you. A fragment of soul. A memory, perhaps. Something small. Something . . . seemingly inconsequential. But enough."

Joshua's breath hitched as Marcus's gaze returned to him, unblinking.

"This offer is for all of you," Marcus continued, smoothly. "But it starts with you, Joshua Clay. The pain you've carried—the weight of your first bargain—it could be gone. All of it."

Joshua's eyes widened slightly, his posture faltering. *"Gone?"* he whispered, uncertain.

Marcus nodded slowly. This time, his expression softened—not in kindness, but in mimicry of it. "Yes. But the price isn't yours alone. If the others join you—if they also give a part of themselves—you'll finally be free."

The silence that followed was brutal.

Gillie's grip tightened on her knife. Her breathing turned shallow, hard. "So that's it?" she said, voice sharp. "You want us to cut ourselves open so he can walk away clean? No."

Joshua's voice cracked. "I didn't ask for this."

Marcus's gaze didn't shift. "No one asks for redemption," he said, calm as falling ash. "They only take it when it's offered."

Gillie's eyes burned. "You think we're that gullible? We're not giving you anything."

He laughed, sharp and sudden—a sound like bones snapping beneath weight. "Oh, you will," he said, certainty laced through every word.

"You won't even know what I've taken," Marcus said softly, "until it's gone."

He let the silence breathe.

"I'll let the swamp decide what's fair."

His voice dipped lower, almost reverent.

"It's so very good at understanding your worth."

"Because you have no choice."

Joshua's voice was small when it finally came. "What happens if we don't?"

Marcus tilted his head. His smile faded—not gone, just buried beneath something colder. "Then you remain here. Wandering. Lost. Until the swamp decides it's had enough of you."

The words landed like stones dropped into a still lake. No splash. Just weight.

Gillie shook her head, defiance unshaken. "There's always another way. We don't need you."

Marcus's gaze turned toward her, darker now, less amused. "*Ah*," he murmured, with a quiet mockery. "That fire. How bright it burns in the beginning—only to flicker when the wind turns."

He stepped forward, and the very air seemed to bend around him. "But you'll learn. This place does not forgive. It does not relent. It *demands*. And you'll pay."

"You carry so much weight," Marcus said, glancing between us. "What I offer isn't loss. It's relief. A memory taken is a burden lifted. A scar erased. Doesn't that sound… lighter?"

Joshua looked at me, then at Gillie, pain tightening every line in his face. "We don't have a choice," he said quietly. "We need him. We need to move forward."

Gillie wheeled on him, fury just beneath the surface. "You don't speak for all of us."

Marcus's voice slid between them, smooth as oil. "This isn't punishment," he said, almost tender. "It's mercy. Even Eden had a gate. I just happen to offer the way through."

I swallowed hard. The weight in my palm shifted—the coin pressing against my skin like it could feel the choice ahead. I curled my fingers around it, anchoring myself to that pressure.

A whisper—not a voice, not even words, just a pull—brushed the edge of my thoughts. It wasn't desperation. It was certainty.

I didn't want to say it. My mouth resisted, my chest tightening like the truth might cost me more than the coin ever could.

"We'll pay together," I said, stepping forward before the argument could crack further. My voice came out steadier than I felt. "It's the only way."

Marcus's gaze dropped to my hand. His face shifted—not surprised, but recognizing. He studied the coin with unsettling reverence.

"Wise," he said softly. "You'll find that wisdom often comes at great cost."

"Raven was right, you know. Names are just shadows of what you leave behind."

He extended his hand. Long, pale fingers moved like they weren't bound by flesh, gliding rather than reaching—*untethered*.

"Shall we begin?"

Gillie didn't move, but the tension in her limbs radiated like heat. Joshua stepped forward slowly, his breath hitching as he extended his hand toward Marcus's.

I hesitated.

A wave of reluctance rose in me, but so did the weight of the swamp pressing from all sides. The pressure of the path ahead. The truth we still didn't have.

I reached out.

Something moved in the mist behind him—barely a figure, barely a sound. Just enough to wonder if someone had done this before… and never walked back.

And in that moment—before our hands met—I knew: whatever we gave, we wouldn't get it back.

The Woman in the Mist

The moment Marcus's fingers brushed ours, the mist surged around us, a roaring tide of whispers drowning out everything else. The world dissolved into gray, the ground beneath our feet seeming to vanish as a pull—both physical and impossible—dragged us forward. It was like falling, but slower, stranger, as though the swamp had reached inside us and twisted something loose.

Something had shifted when Marcus let go. The swamp felt heavier now—not pressing down on us, but seeping in, like it was trying to fill the spaces left behind. I felt—less. As if something vital had been taken, something I wouldn't realize was missing until it was too late.

When the mist finally settled, the swamp was different. The air was sharper, colder, and every sound felt muffled, as though the swamp was holding its breath. The trees loomed taller now, their twisted branches clawing at the sky, and the ground beneath us was firmer, but unnervingly smooth—no roots, no muck, just cold, damp earth. The silence was unbearable, laced with an unease that scraped at the edges of thought.

I glanced at Gillie and Joshua, the gravity of what we'd just done pressed heavily on all of us. Gillie's hand hovered near the hilt of her knife, her jaw tight, her eyes darting through the mist. Joshua stood rigid, his breath shallow, his shoulders trembling. None of us spoke, but I could feel the question lingering between us:

What have we lost?

The answer wasn't clear—not yet. But something was missing. I felt it in the heaviness of my chest, in the aching emptiness where certainty used to be. The coin in my pocket seemed lighter now, its edges dulled, its grounding presence muted.

Gillie's face had hardened, her movements sharper, more deliberate, as though some part of her resolve had been stripped away.

Joshua hadn't even looked back, his steps slower, his posture hunched as if the swamp weighed heavier on him than it did on the rest of us.

The path ahead twisted sharply, disappearing into the haze that pressed closer with every step. It felt unfamiliar, unwelcome, even though we hadn't stopped moving. It wasn't just the swamp—it was us. Whatever bargain Marcus had made with us, it had taken something intangible, something vital, and left a void that the swamp was eager to fill.

The air shifted, subtle at first—like a breath held too long—before it rippled through the swamp in a way that made the mist seem alive.

The ground beneath us felt less solid, like it might give way with the slightest misstep, and the oppressive silence deepened into something heavier, something that pushed down on my chest with every step. The haze thickened, swirling with an almost deliberate movement, as though the swamp itself was reacting to what we had just done.

And then Gillie was the first to notice.

She froze mid-step, her head snapping toward the edge of the path. "We're being watched," she said, her voice low but sharp. Her hand tightened on the hilt of her knife, her knuckles white against the tension in her fingers.

Joshua stopped a few paces ahead, his shoulders stiffening. He glanced over his shoulder, his hollow eyes narrowing. "By who?" he asked, though his voice carried no real curiosity—just the weight of something he already feared.

I scanned the mist, my chest tightening as the shadows at the edges of my vision flickered and moved. At first, I thought it was just the swamp playing tricks again, twisting the light, warping the air to make us see things that weren't there.

But then I saw it—a faint outline, just beyond the trees.

It was a figure, barely visible through the swirling haze. They were cloaked, their movements slow but deliberate, their silhouette shrouded in an unearthly stillness. The mist coiled around them, giving the impression that they were a part of it—woven into its fabric.

Gillie's knife was halfway out of its sheath before I put a hand on her arm. "Wait," I said quickly, my voice barely above a whisper.

"Wait for what?" she snapped, her glare fixed on the figure. "If that's another one of this swamp's tricks, we can't just stand here and let it get the drop on us."

"They're not coming toward us," I said, though my voice wavered. "Look—they're just… standing there. Watching."

The figure didn't move closer. They stood at the edge of the trees, half-swallowed by mist, blurred but unmoving—like the swamp had carved them there. There was something about the way they stood—calm, deliberate, unthreatening—that made me hesitate. Whoever they were, they weren't like the swamp's other denizens. They didn't feel like Marcus, or Raven. They didn't feel wrong.

Joshua took a step forward, his breath shallow as he stared at the figure. "Do you feel that?" he asked quietly, his voice trembling.

"Feel what?" Gillie shot back, her glare snapping to him.

"It's…" He hesitated, his hollow eyes flicking back to the figure. "It's like they know us. Like they've been waiting."

Gillie rolled her eyes, her frustration evident. "Or it's the swamp, playing tricks on your mind again. Don't get sucked in."

But I couldn't shake the feeling that Joshua was right. There was something familiar about the figure, something I couldn't quite place. It wasn't just the way they watched us—it was the way their presence seemed to pull at the edges of my thoughts, gentle but insistent, like a memory trying to surface.

The figure's head tilted slightly, and from beneath the folds of their cloak came a voice—soft, but laced with knowing:

"You're not whole anymore, are you? I can feel it. A wound without blood."

The words sent a chill down my spine, sharp and surgical. Gillie stiffened beside me, her hand tightening on her knife. The figure didn't move any closer, but their gaze grew heavier, more insistent—like they could see straight through us.

Joshua stepped forward, his breath uneven. "Who are you?" he asked, voice barely more than a whisper.

The figure didn't respond. Instead, they raised one hand—slow, deliberate—and pointed further down the path, their gesture as precise as it was unreadable.

"What the hell does that mean?" Gillie muttered, her grip locked like a vice on the knife's hilt.

"It means we're supposed to follow," Joshua said quietly.

Gillie turned to him, incredulous. "Are you serious? We don't even know who—or what—that is."

He didn't look at her. His eyes stayed fixed on the figure, wide and glassy with something unspoken. "We have to," he said finally. "I can feel it. They're... helping us."

Gillie scoffed, frustration rising like steam. "Helping us? You think the swamp is helping us now? That this thing—" she gestured toward the cloaked figure "—is some kind of guide?"

"Gillie, stop," I said, stepping between them. "Look at them. They haven't moved. They haven't attacked. Maybe Joshua's right. Maybe this one's… different."

Her glare turned on me. "And if you're wrong? What then? We follow that thing into the fog and it tears us apart?"

"I don't know," I admitted. "But if they meant us harm, they could have done it already."

Gillie's jaw clenched, but after a long pause, she lowered her blade—barely. "Fine," she muttered. "But if this goes wrong, that's on you—not me."

Joshua was already moving, his steps slow and deliberate as he walked toward the direction the figure had pointed. The mist seemed to draw back for him, just slightly—like the path itself was adjusting to let him pass.

The figure lingered a moment longer, their cloaked form blending into the fog as they turned and disappeared into it.

But I didn't think they'd really gone. Not entirely.

We walked in silence. Each footstep landed heavy; each breath scraped against the stillness. I kept glancing back, half-expecting to see that cloaked silhouette still watching from the trees.

Instead, what I saw was something else.

The faint flicker of that strange light we'd glimpsed earlier—the same one that had vanished when Marcus appeared—reemerged, flickering just ahead in the fog. It pulsed faintly, like it was waiting for us to catch up.

The mist coiled around our legs like it didn't want us to leave this part of the swamp—but still, the path opened. Not cleared by wind or chance, but like something had chosen this moment. Just like before.

Just like Marcus.

Something was guiding us

Not trust—but something close enough to follow.

Behind us, the fog swallowed the space where the figure had stood, leaving only silence and the weight of what we'd left behind.

We didn't speak, not even when the light ahead began to pulse faster, brighter, as though reacting to our presence. It didn't feel like a warning.

It felt like a summons.

And ahead, past the flickering glow, the shadows began to move.

Not the shapeless kind—but the kind that could reach for you.

The Army of the Dark

The whispers tightened, coiling through the air like serpents—tempting, taunting, pressing into our ears. The path ahead twisted sharply, swallowed by a wall of shadows that didn't just move—they pulsed, alive with a rhythm that felt too deliberate.

We followed, slower now. Each step felt heavier. Each breath dragged through the thickening air. The swamp wasn't just watching anymore—it was guiding us. Nudging us forward toward something we hadn't agreed to.

The path split open into a clearing, and the shift was instant.

The ground was wrong—dry, cracked, leached of all life. The trees stood skeletal, their branches twisted toward the sky like contorted hands reaching in silent agony.

At the center, a faint light pulsed—eerie and cold.

One steady glow.

Beating in time with the whispers.

Marcus appeared again.

He stood at the far edge of the clearing—tall, still, the same shadowed smile curving his lips. His dark eyes gleamed with something too satisfied to be anything but cruel.

But he wasn't alone.

Figures stood beside him—distorted, flickering, not quite whole. They shifted like smoke caught between shapes, not fully human, not fully swamp. Something in between. Something worse.

Joshua froze.

His breath caught. His eyes locked onto the shapes behind Marcus.

"What is this?" he whispered, barely louder than the wind.

Gillie's knife was out in an instant, her stance rigid, gaze scanning the figures. "It's a trap," she hissed. "We never should've followed him."

Marcus stepped forward just slightly, his smile widening. "Ah," he said, voice smooth as silk curling around a blade. "How lovely of you to join us. I was beginning to think you'd gotten lost."

"Marcus," I said, stepping forward despite the churn in my chest, "who are they? What do you want with them?"

He tilted his head, the expression on his face hovering between amusement and warning. "You're looking at my… recruits," he said softly. "The beginnings of something greater than you can comprehend."

"Recruits for what?" Gillie's voice was low, hard.

"For the future," Marcus replied. His gaze drifted over us. We felt like footnotes beneath it. "The swamp is shifting. The balance is breaking. Something is coming, and when it arrives… those who stand with me will know power beyond imagination. And those who don't?"

His smile grew sharper.

"Well. The swamp doesn't take kindly to defiance."

Joshua's hands clenched at his sides. His breath was shaky. "What do you want from us?"

"Ah, Joshua," Marcus said, almost fondly. "You're already part of this, whether you accept it or not. But if you're asking for specifics. . . ."

He turned, gesturing toward one of the shadowed figures.

It moved.

Not walked—moved, like a puppet remembering how to be human. The mist parted around her, and my stomach twisted.

She stepped forward slowly—graceful, fluid—but wrong.

Her face was young. Familiar. Empty.

There was something hollow in her expression—but not blank. It was focused, like someone staring through glass at a world they no longer belonged to. Her eyes held no confusion, only vacancy shaped into obedience.

Her steps were too precise. Her silence too complete.

Whatever she was now . . . she wasn't entirely herself.

"Who is that?" Gillie asked sharply, her knife angling upward. Her grip was tight, knuckles white.

Marcus didn't take his eyes off the figure. "She was no one," he said, almost wistfully. "Adrift. Forgotten. The swamp devours those who drift. But sometimes—if someone intervenes—it can reshape them. Give them form. Purpose."

His gaze flicked to us. "Elana."

The name landed like a blow. It echoed inside my skull. I couldn't say why—but it did. Something about her face tugged at a thread buried deep in memory. I didn't know if it was the name or the way she looked at us.

Or didn't.

Not really.

Joshua had stopped breathing.

Gillie's jaw tensed. "You twisted her," she spat. "That's not salvation. That's control."

Marcus smiled faintly. "She made a choice. As you all will, eventually. The swamp demands allegiance, Gillie. It demands sacrifice.

And those who refuse . . . well." He gestured lightly. "It has other ways of taking what it's owed."

Joshua flinched. His eyes locked on Elana, then flicked to Marcus. "She's not..." His voice caught on the words. "This isn't right."

Marcus turned toward him slowly, voice coated in mockery. "Right? You speak of *right* and *wrong* like they mean anything here. Like the swamp cares about your fragile little morality."

His hand lifted slightly. The figures behind him shifted—like smoke trying to take form.

"It doesn't. It thrives on power. On strength. And those who refuse to adapt..." He glanced to Elana with something like admiration. "Are consumed."

The shadows around him grew darker, stretching at the edges of the clearing, and the whispering intensified—no longer passive. Hungry.

"You have a choice," Marcus said, quieter now, but firmer—deadly with certainty. "Stand with me. Step into what's coming. Or cling to what's already lost."

His gaze slid to Gillie.

"You think you're different? You're already unraveling. Every step forward tears something else loose. And you—"

His eyes shifted to Joshua. "You've felt it. The pull. The promise. You're not fighting the swamp anymore. You're bargaining with it."

Joshua's breath hitched, his jaw tightening. He didn't respond. But he didn't deny it either.

"Don't listen to him," I said, stepping between them before Marcus could twist the knife further. "He's using her. He's using all of this—to scare us. To divide us."

Marcus's smile curved crueler at the edges. "Divide you? No, no. I'm here to show you what you are."

He turned to me, gaze narrowing. "And you… you already know the truth, don't you?"

I froze as his words dropped, soft and sharp as a blade.

"You carry the blood of betrayal," he said. "You always have. It's in your steps. In the way the shadows listen to you. You think that's resistance?"

He leaned in, voice lowering to a near whisper. "It's memory. It's recognition. You belong to this place more than any of them ever will."

The air around me shifted—tightened. Gillie's stare burned at the side of my face. Joshua's hollow eyes looked at me, uncertain, accusing.

"I don't…" I started, but the words were too slow. Too soft.

Marcus's smile widened.

"You've already given so much," he said, voice velvet-dark. "Your hope. Your certainty. Your *self.* It's only a short slide from there to giving everything. And trust me—"

He looked to the shadows encircling him. "The swamp is more than willing to take what's left."

He stepped back, fading into the mist, the shadowed forms dissolving with him—no footsteps, no sound, just absence. Just cold.

"You'll see," Marcus said one last time, his voice drifting like smoke through the silence.

"In the end… the swamp always wins."

And then he was gone.

The clearing dimmed. The mist closed in. We stood frozen, surrounded by silence that felt like breath held just behind our ears.

"We need to move," Gillie said finally, voice low and clipped. "Before he comes back."

Joshua didn't move. He was still staring—at me, not at the place where Elana had stood.

His eyes were clouded now. Suspicious. Unsettled.

"Come on," I said, placing a hand gently on his shoulder. "We can't stay here."

He stiffened under my touch but didn't pull away. Just nodded, slowly.

We turned back toward the path, though I could no longer be sure which way was forward. The whispers in the mist had quieted—but they hadn't gone. They'd just retreated into the shadows, waiting for the next wound to widen.

We walked in silence.

But the weight of Marcus's words twisted through our thoughts like roots in soil—deep, slow, and impossible to ignore.

The Widening Rift

Marcus's words clung to the air, thick and suffocating, twisting into the silence between us like a splinter buried too deep to reach. No one spoke. We just moved—steps heavy, the quiet stretching—not into relief, but into something taut. Something waiting to snap.

The swamp fed on it, coiling tighter around us, amplifying every doubt, every unspoken thought.

Gillie's movements were sharp. Her strides deliberate. Her fingers hovered near the hilt of her knife, like she was always one breath away from drawing it.

She didn't look at me. She didn't have to. Her anger radiated—thick as heat, coiling between us with every step.

Joshua trudged ahead, shoulders hunched, gaze fixed on the ground.

His silence wasn't absence.

It was judgment.

Then—Gillie snapped.

"You heard him." Her voice sliced through the quiet as she threw a glance over her shoulder. "Marcus knows something about you. About your family. What aren't you telling us?"

The accusation hit deep. I stiffened, swallowing back the sharp unease twisting in my gut.

"I've told you everything I know," I said, forcing steadiness into my voice. But the tremor still slipped through. "I didn't even know who he was until we got here."

Gillie stopped abruptly and turned to face me. Her eyes were sharp, narrowed.

"Really?" The word landed cold. Heavy.

She stepped forward, breath short, her grip tightening on the knife's hilt.

"Marcus—and Raven, for that matter—know you. They know things. That symbol wasn't just for show. Are you seriously standing there and telling me you don't know what it means?"

I held my ground.

"I didn't know." My voice rose. Firmer now. "I've never seen it before. And Marcus? Raven? They've both got their own agenda."

Joshua paused ahead, half-turned, his gaze flicking between us. Quiet. Weighted. Another unspoken accusation.

Gillie's frustration cracked through her voice.

"This isn't a coincidence," she said, louder. Sharper. "Legacies. Names. Shadows. You expect us to believe none of it has anything to do with you?"

"That's exactly what I'm saying," I snapped, frustration rising like heat. "I didn't know Marcus before this. I didn't even know this swamp existed."

Her glare was a blade.

"But you knew something," she said, voice turning bitter. "You knew coming here meant opening doors you didn't want to face. And you dragged us through them."

My pulse pounded. "I brought us here to fix things."

She laughed—dry, sharp, humorless.

"Fix it? You think we can fix anything when we don't even know what we're fighting? And how are we supposed to trust you when every shadow in this place already knows your name?"

Joshua spoke then. His voice was low, but firm. "If we don't trust each other, the swamp will tear us apart. That's what it's waiting for."

Gillie turned on him fast, her voice still hot with frustration. "And Marcus? And Raven? You think they're not part of that?"

Joshua stiffened, but didn't flinch. "It doesn't matter what they want," he said quietly. "What matters is whether we let them win."

Gillie scoffed, shaking her head. "Win? It's already winning. And if you think Raven—or Marcus—aren't part of that, you're fooling yourself."

I stepped between them, trying to keep my voice steady—even as my heart hammered and my breath caught. The mist seemed to press tighter around my throat, like the swamp was waiting for the first crack in our unity.

"That's enough. We don't know what Raven is. Or what Marcus wants. But we do know they're trying to break us. And if we let that happen, the swamp won't need to take us."

Gillie held my gaze a beat longer, then exhaled through her nose. She stepped back. "Fine," she muttered. "But don't think for a second I'm letting this go."

Joshua hesitated. Glanced at me once. Then followed her. His steps were slow. Uncertain.

I lingered, the mist pressing close—closer now, like the swamp itself was listening. Breathing.

And as I stepped forward, I felt it.

The distance between us wasn't just physical anymore.

It was deeper than that.

And with every step, the rift widened.

The Humming Trees

The Luring Melody

It didn't take long before the sound began.

At first, it was barely there—a whisper threading through the air, too faint to catch, too light to name. But as we moved forward, it grew. Steady. Rising. Creeping into the silence like it belonged there.

The path twisted ahead, narrowing as the cold pressed deeper into our skin. The swamp felt tight, the weight of it pressing low against our backs. Waiting. Listening. Holding its breath.

And the sound did the same.

A low, lilting hum—haunting, melodic—rippled through the trees, sinking into the quiet like a lure that refused to let go. It wasn't like the whispers that had followed us before, not like the creaking branches shifting in the mist.

This was different.

Beautiful—but wrong. Too perfect. Too deliberate. It curled deep inside me, weaving between my ribs like something alive.

Gillie stopped abruptly, her head snapping up. "Do you hear that?" Her voice was sharp, low, edged with something uncertain.

I nodded, the sound wrapping tighter now, pressing, pulling, closing in.

"Yeah." My voice came soft, barely above the hum itself.

"I hear it."

Joshua turned slightly, his hollow eyes widening as he stared into the haze ahead. "*It's… beautiful,*" he murmured, his voice trembling. *"Can you feel it?"*

"No," Gillie snapped, her glare cutting. "Don't. Whatever it is… it's not beautiful. It's not right."

The hum deepened, resonating through the air like a string stretched too tight. I could feel it vibrating in my chest. It wasn't just a sound—it was a pull, subtle but undeniable, like an invisible thread winding around my thoughts and dragging me forward.

The trees around us began to change, their twisted and knotted branches giving way to taller, smoother forms that seemed to hum in harmony with the melody. Their bark glowed faintly—pale, luminous—and the air grew colder still as we stepped deeper into the grove.

The ground beneath us shifted, soft and brittle. I froze as I looked down.

Scattered across the soil were fragments of bone, stark against the dark earth.

"This isn't right," Gillie said, her voice tense and clipped. Her hand moved instinctively to the hilt of her knife as she scanned the grove. "We need to turn around. Now."

But Joshua didn't stop. He kept moving forward, his steps slow and deliberate, his eyes fixed on something just beyond the trees.

"*It's not dangerous,*" he said softly, almost dreamlike. "*It's guiding us.*"

"Joshua, stop!" Gillie shouted, grabbing his arm. Her grip was firm, her expression fierce. "It's not guiding us. It's pulling us off course."

Joshua jerked his arm free, his hollow eyes burning with a strange mix of defiance and desperation. "You don't know that," he said, voice rising. "What if it's her? What if she's trying to show us the way?"

Gillie stepped in front of him, jaw tight, blocking his path. "It's not her," she said, her voice low but unyielding. "It's the swamp. And it's trying to kill us."

I took a shaky breath. The hum burrowed deeper into my thoughts, clouding them, twisting them. It was hard to think, hard to focus, as the melody wrapped itself around me—calm and longing and deeply wrong.

I curled my fingers into my palm, pressing into the sharp sting of my own grip, forcing myself to stay grounded in the moment.

"She's right," I said, pushing the words through the haze. "It's the swamp. It's trying to distract us."

Joshua hesitated, his gaze flicking between us and the grove ahead. "But what if it's not?" he said quietly. "What if we're turning away from the only chance we have?"

"Joshua," Gillie said sharply, her voice cutting through the air like a blade. "Look at the ground. Look at the trees. This place isn't safe."

He glanced down. His breath hitched. His eyes widened.

The scattered bones glinted faintly in the dim light, stark against the glowing bark of the trees. For a moment, his resolve faltered. His steps hesitated.

The hum shifted again—louder, more insistent. I felt it tug harder, pulling at my thoughts. My foot slid forward involuntarily. I forced myself to stop, planting my boots against the brittle ground.

"We need to go," I said, my voice trembling but firm. "Now."

Joshua's shoulders slumped. His gaze dropped.

"I thought…" he began, but the words trailed off, lost in the hum.

"Don't think," Gillie snapped, grabbing his arm again and pulling him back toward the path. "Just move."

I followed, the weight of the grove still pressing at my spine. The pull of the melody faded slightly with each step. The trees returned to their twisted forms, their branches clawing at the mist.

And the haunting hum softened—fainter, distant—until it was nothing more than an echo behind us.

But even as the sound faded, its presence lingered, pressing into my thoughts like a splinter. I couldn't shake the feeling that the melody had wanted something from us.

That it had reached for something deeper.

And almost taken it.

We were still walking.

But the swamp was already keeping score.

Visions of the Past

The hum had faded now, but the silence it left in its wake was suffocating.

The air felt thicker here—colder—wrapping around us like a shroud as we moved deeper into the grove. Every breath was heavier, like I was inhaling the swamp's weight. The trees loomed taller than before, their pale, luminous bark casting an unnatural glow that made the mist shimmer like smoke caught in moonlight. Tension hung in the air, pressing against us with an almost physical force, as though the swamp itself was keeping us from moving forward.

Joshua walked ahead, shoulders hunched, his steps hesitant. Gillie stayed just behind him, knife still in hand, her posture tense and ready. I lingered a few paces back. The path beneath my boots was brittle and uneven. Each step felt like an act of defiance against a presence that didn't want us here.

Then the air shifted.

Subtle at first—like a breeze that wasn't really there—but it grew stronger, heavier, pressing against us in slow, suffocating waves. I froze mid-step, my chest tightening as the trees around us began to warp and twist. The pale bark rippled like water, and the shadows at their bases writhed, stretching unnaturally as if they were alive. The mist thickened, coiling with intent, and a familiar unease clawed at the edge of my thoughts.

Joshua stopped abruptly, his breath shallow and uneven. "*Do you feel that?*" he murmured, voice trembling.

"Feel what?" Gillie snapped, her tone sharp. Her knuckles whitened on the hilt of her knife, her body rigid, bracing for something she couldn't see. "It's just the swamp trying to get in your head. That's all it does."

"*It's not just the swamp,*" Joshua whispered, his hollow eyes fixed on something in the mist. "*There's… something else.*"

My pulse quickened. The air grew denser, threading through my chest and mind like strands of silk. Then I saw it—a shape flickering in the haze, faint at first but sharpening with every breath. The figure stood still, its edges blurred like it had stepped out of an old photograph and into the fog. My breath caught. A chill twisted deep in my spine.

"Do you see him?" I asked softly, unsure if I was speaking to them or myself.

Joshua faltered, his hands trembling at his sides. *"I see him,"* he whispered, voice cracking faintly.

Gillie spun toward him, her glare sharp. "What are you talking about?" she demanded. "See who? There's nothing here but tricks."

But there was something there—and it wasn't just a trick. The figure grew more defined. Angular features. Piercing eyes. A strong jawline. Familiar. Too familiar. Something tugged at the edges of memory like a splinter I couldn't quite reach.

"That face," I murmured. "I know that face."

Gillie's attention snapped to me. "You what?" she said, suspicion flaring behind her eyes.

I shook my head faintly, the ache in my chest twisting deeper as the figure sharpened further. His posture was commanding. His expression—stern, yet once welcoming. I'd seen him in old photographs, yellowed and faded, tucked away in archives and records I'd never wanted to revisit. He was important. He was tied to legacy. To history. To choices I'd tried to forget.

But something about him was wrong now. The familiarity was slipping, giving way to something darker.

"I've seen him in pictures," I said, voice trembling despite my effort to steady it. "But he didn't look like this."

The figure's face began to change. Sternness curdled into cruelty. Sharp eyes hardened into something cold and inhuman. Shadows clung to him now, wrapping like smoke, warping the dignified into the monstrous.

Gillie scoffed, grip tightening on her knife. "This swamp doesn't care about your pictures," she snapped. "It's in your head—twisting everything into something it can use."

"It's not just twisting," Joshua said, barely audible. "It's… showing."

The shadows around the figure grew darker, thicker, dragging him deeper even as he stood perfectly still. The cold smirk spreading across his face sent a jolt through my chest. Whatever he had been—whoever—I didn't recognize him anymore.

"What is it showing you?" Gillie asked sharply, her voice slicing through the thickened air.

I couldn't answer right away. My breath hitched as images flared in my mind—hands gripping the edge of a desk, wood worn smooth by habit. Papers scattered across its surface, sealed with red wax. A crest I recognized but never wanted to name. The shadows pressed closer around the memory, suffocating it. Twisting it into something I didn't want to see.

"It's…" I swallowed hard. "It's pulling at something. Something old. Something I don't want to remember."

Gillie's glare sharpened. "That's convenient," she said bitterly. "The swamp plays tricks, and suddenly you're seeing ghosts? What are you not telling us?"

I clenched my fists, nails digging into my skin. I needed to feel something real. The coin in my pocket pressed cold against my side, grounding me. But the figure didn't move. He just stared. Smiling. Pressing deeper into my thoughts like poison.

Joshua flinched, voice shaking. "*He's not just a ghost,*" he murmured. "*He's… something left behind.*"

The words struck hard. Too hard. The figure flickered—and vanished into mist.

But the shadows remained.

They lingered, threading through the grove like vines. Wrapping around my mind. Refusing to let go.

Joshua moved suddenly, quick and tense. "We have to keep moving," he said, breathless. "It doesn't want us to stop. If we stop, it gets worse."

Gillie hesitated. Her jaw clenched tight as she stared at where the figure had been. She exhaled sharply, then turned back to the path. "Fine," she muttered. "But don't think this swamp isn't trying to break us."

I lingered a moment longer. The shadows coiled tighter, watching, whispering.

Whatever the swamp had shown me—it wasn't just memory.

It was a warning.

And it wasn't done.

The Strength to Resist

The weight hit fast.

Shadows twisted and surged, jagged edges blurring the line between reality and the chaos clawing through my mind. They weren't just flickering—they were alive, shifting like breath, curling at the edges of thought, pulling at fears I couldn't name.

The mist wasn't content to surround us anymore.

It was inside.

Threading beneath my skin. Coiling through memories I couldn't recognize as mine.

I reached for something—anything—to steady myself, but the ground felt impossibly distant, like I was slipping into something I couldn't climb out of.

Then… the voice.

"You feel it, don't you?"

It wasn't Marcus. It wasn't Raven. Not exactly.

It felt older. Deeper. Woven into the swamp itself.

"The pull. The weight. It's yours to bear—just as it was his."

The shadows surged again, sweeping through the haze like a storm, and I saw him—Jonah.

His face flickered like flame, shifting between something familiar and something monstrous. Hollow eyes burned into mine, the echo of who he had been lingering long enough to remind me of the fall.

But then the shadows twisted again.

And this time, it wasn't Jonah.

It was me.

I stood where he had stood, the swamp's darkness clinging to my form like a second skin.

"No," I breathed, the word catching in my throat. My heart thundered, and a sharp pressure coiled in my palm—a desperate grip on nothing, a reflex to hold onto something solid.

"That's not me. That's not who I am."

But the shadows didn't care.

They pressed harder.

Threading deeper, embedding splinters of doubt in their wake. Jonah's face still hovered at the mist's edge—watching. Waiting.

Gillie's voice cut through the haze like a blade.

"This isn't real," she snapped, though there was a crack in her voice. "It's the swamp. That's all it does—twist and turn things until we break."

Joshua flinched beside me, his breath shallow, his hands trembling. "*It doesn't matter if it's real,*" he murmured. "*It feels real. And that's enough for it to tear us apart.*"

"It's not enough," Gillie said, stepping forward. Her grip on her knife was white-knuckled, her posture fierce. "It doesn't get to break us. Not like this."

Her words carried a weight I hadn't realized I needed.

I turned toward her. The tension in her frame wasn't just fear—it was resolve. The kind of resolve that refused to ask for permission to survive.

Not just defiance against the swamp.

But against the version of us it wanted to leave behind.

"We can't keep letting it in," I said, my voice trembling. "We have to push back. Together."

Gillie faced me, her glare softening just slightly. "Then stop holding onto it," she said, nodding toward the coin clenched in my hand. "Stop letting it weigh you down."

My fingers tightened around the metal instinctively. The edge bit into my skin.

"It's not the coin," I whispered, unsure if I even believed it. *"It's what it's pulling at. What it's trying to make me remember."*

"Then let it go," she said. No softness now—just truth. "If it's dragging you under, let it go. You don't have to carry it alone."

The words hit hard.

Harder than I wanted them to.

Her challenge slipped into the cracks I hadn't acknowledged—refused to acknowledge.

I turned to Joshua, still unmoving, his hollow eyes fixed on the shifting mist.

"What about you?" I asked, barely audible. "Can you let it go?"

His shoulders sagged. His breath hitched.

"I don't know," he said, voice trembling. "It's been with me for so long. I don't know what's left without it."

"You," Gillie said, sharper than before. "You're left without it. And that's enough."

Joshua flinched like the words had struck something tender. But after a pause, he nodded—faint, uncertain, but real.

It wasn't everything.

But it was something.

I took a deep breath. The ache in my chest pressed harder, but I pushed to my feet.

The shadows didn't vanish. They still hovered, flickering just beyond reach.

But their grip had loosened.

They no longer held me.

Gillie stepped forward, her blade glinting in the light, her steps tense but driven. "We keep moving," she said. "That's how we resist. That's how we fight."

Joshua nodded, his pace unsteady, but the flicker of something—resolve, maybe—burned in his gaze.

I followed. The weight I'd carried wasn't gone—but it had dulled. Manageable now.

The mist still clung to us. Still watched.

But it didn't feel invincible anymore.

The shadows still moved at the edge of the trees.

Deliberate. Slow.

But they didn't have the same power. Not now.

We weren't whole—none of us were.

But we were still together.

And in the end, that was what the swamp couldn't take.

Not yet.

Not ever.

The Tolling Resumes

The grove released us reluctantly, its shadows fading into the mist—but not its weight.

None of us spoke as we stepped back onto the path, the brittle ground crunching underfoot. The silence pressed in heavier than before, steeped in the aftermath of what we'd seen and heard.

It wasn't a reprieve.

It was a warning.

Then the bell tolled.

Faint at first, trembling through the stillness like a sound carried on an invisible breeze. But as we moved forward, it deepened—sharpening into a low, resonant chime.

It vibrated through the mist, through the ground beneath us, through the very air we breathed.

It wasn't mere noise.

It pulled—subtle, but undeniable.

Gillie froze, her hand hovering near the hilt of her knife.

"The bell," she said sharply, voice tight. "It's started again."

Joshua's steps faltered ahead of us.

His hollow eyes turned toward the mist, narrowing as the toll came again—darker, heavier.

He didn't speak.

But his silence felt loud. Charged. Waiting to crack.

The mist shifted.

A whisper curled through the air—soft at first, but insistent. It sliced through the quiet like a blade.

At first, the words were indistinct. Tangled in fog.

But then they clarified.

And the swamp stilled to listen.

"Six months…" the voice hissed—smooth, venomous.

"Six months since you entered this place. And ninety-nine years for him."

Gillie stiffened, her gaze jerking toward the haze.

"What was that?" she demanded, her voice sharp with fear and fury.

Joshua froze completely. His breath caught.

"Ninety-nine years," he whispered. "That's how long I've been here?"

Gillie turned to him fast, her expression darkening.

"What?" she snapped. "What do you mean *ninety-nine years?*"

Ninety-nine years. I couldn't comprehend it. Not really. But I saw the weight of it settle behind Joshua's eyes. Like he'd aged all at once and couldn't remember how.

Joshua half-turned, his shoulders sagging like the swamp's weight was pressing even harder on him than it was on us.

"It doesn't feel like that," he said softly. "It felt like… days. Weeks, maybe. But the whispers… they've been counting."

Ninety-nine years.

"And six months."

Another toll echoed—louder this time. Deeper.

It reverberated through the air like a heartbeat too big for a body.

I tightened my grip on the coin in my pocket.

Its sharp edge bit into my skin.

Grounding me.

"Gillie," I said cautiously. "The voice said *six months for us.* That's how long we've been here."

Her jaw locked. She whipped around to face me.

"Six months?" she repeated, disbelief laced with rage. "You're telling me this swamp's already stolen half a year from us?"

The mist twisted tighter. The whisper came again.

"Half your time gone. Half the year wasted. Six months remain."

Gillie's breath hitched. Her eyes narrowed as the truth landed like a blade.

"Six months left," she muttered bitterly. "That's not enough. Not for this."

Joshua's voice came soft, but it trembled with something fragile.

"It might not matter," he said. "What if we've already lost?"

Gillie turned on him like a storm.

"We haven't," she snapped. "We're still here, aren't we? That means we haven't lost."

Joshua hesitated. His gaze dropped to the ground.

"But how do we know it's enough?" he asked. "How do we know we'll make it?"

Gillie's jaw clenched. Her frustration cracked through her voice.

"We don't," she said bluntly. "But stopping isn't an option. If we stop now, it's over. For all of us."

The bell tolled again—deeper, more final. The mist seemed to ripple with it.

The air pressed harder against us, like the swamp wanted to squeeze the breath from our lungs.

I swallowed the weight in my chest.

"We keep moving," I said. My voice wavered, but it didn't break. "No matter what."

Gillie nodded sharply. Her knife clutched tight.

"Six months left," she muttered. "We don't waste another second."

Joshua lingered behind, his steps reluctant.

He stared into the mist like it might answer him.

But then he nodded—just slightly—and followed, his shoulders bowed like the toll had aged him all over again.

The bell tolled once more—louder with every step.

Its mournful resonance wasn't just sound.

It was time.

The swamp's countdown.

Ninety-nine years for Joshua.

Six months for us.

And with every toll, the weight grew heavier. Closer. Sharper.

But even through the chimes, the humming of the trees returned.

Faint. Constant. Almost melodic.

A background note to the swamp's cruel design.

Not just sound—memory. Pattern. Power.

The hum wasn't gone. It was a tether.

A reminder.

A symphony of lies and truths twisted together—echoing in every breath, in every branch, in every step.

Gillie turned slightly, her gaze flicking toward the trees. Her face had hardened again.

"The humming trees," she murmured. "They're watching. Waiting. Pulling the strings. Don't let them in."

Her words sliced through the thick air, but the hum didn't flinch.

It was still there. Still pressing. Still listening.

It wasn't just sound.

It was the voice of the swamp itself.

Its sentinels.

Its spell.

Its truth.

The Humming Trees

I forced myself to keep moving, the hum scratching faintly at my thoughts.

The swamp wasn't done with us—not yet.

The trees were humming.

And the swamp remembered everything.

The Whispering Paths

Grace's Subtle Guidance

The tension was suffocating. It hung over us like a weight, pressing into every step, every breath. None of us said it aloud, but I felt it—an unspoken dread threading through the silence. Gillie moved ahead of me, her determination palpable, but even she couldn't mask the strain in her rigid posture. Joshua trailed behind, quieter and slower, as though every step took more effort than the last.

The humming was still there. The trees hadn't stopped their song—that low, constant vibration in the air. It had become so much a part of the swamp, so relentless, that after a while, I'd stopped noticing it—stopped really hearing it. But now, with every step heavier than the last, it crept back into my awareness. The sound wasn't just humming; it was alive, waiting for us to falter.

Then it happened.

A shiver in the air, faint but undeniable, like a single breath drawn too sharply in an otherwise still room. It wasn't just something I noticed—it was something I felt, deep and instinctive, clawing at the back of my mind. My pulse quickened as I stopped mid-step, a chill running down my spine. The world had shifted ever so slightly, tilted on some unseen axis. The hair on the back of my neck prickled, and for a heartbeat, it was as if the air itself was holding its breath.

Gillie froze just ahead of me, her gaze darting through the shadows as her hand hovered near the hilt of her knife. "What now?" she muttered, her voice low, edged with frustration.

Then, she appeared.

A figure emerged from the mist, stepping forward as though she had been part of it all along. At first, I wasn't sure if I was really seeing her or if the swamp was playing tricks on us again. But then Joshua froze, his breath hitching audibly.

"*Grace*," he whispered, his voice cracking on the single syllable.

A jolt ran through me at the name, and I knew instantly—he was right. It was her. There was no mistaking it. The weight of her presence was undeniable, as though every story, every whispered fragment about her had taken shape and form before us. She was exactly as I had imagined—yet entirely different.

Gillie stiffened beside me, her voice sharp. "That's… her?" she asked, though it was more a statement than a question.

The figure stepped closer, her movements fluid and deliberate, her form softly outlined in a dim, flickering glow. She was luminous yet fragile, shaped by the mist itself, and her eyes carried a depth of sorrow that rooted me to the spot. Her tattered shawl clung to her shoulders, and the faint outline of a dress beneath it bore the weight of years that should have broken her—but hadn't.

"*It's her*," Joshua murmured, his voice trembling. "*It's Grace*."

Gillie shot him a sideways glance, suspicion flickering across her face. "How do you know for sure?" she demanded, though I could hear the hesitation in her tone.

"I know," Joshua said, his hollow eyes fixed on the figure. "I just… know."

Grace's gaze moved between us, steady and searching. When her eyes landed on Joshua, her expression softened, her sorrow deepening. "You can't continue this way," she said, her voice low and resonant. It wove through the stillness like a thread of light, carrying strength beneath its sorrow. "The path ahead leads to ruin."

Gillie frowned, her grip tightening on her knife. "What kind of ruin?" she asked sharply. "Be specific."

Grace turned her gaze to her, calm but unyielding. "Even the lost may find their way," she said, her words deliberate, each one cutting through the air, "but only if they choose it for themselves."

Gillie's scowl deepened. "Are you saying he can be saved?" she pressed, gesturing toward Joshua.

Grace's faint glow flickered, her gaze dipping for just a moment. The sorrow etched into her face deepened, and I could feel the weight of it pressing against the air around us. Whatever she carried, it was heavier than any of us could imagine.

"Salvation is a gift," Grace said softly. "Freely given. Costly to refuse. But the gift is life."

Joshua stepped forward, his breath shaky. "Grace," he said, her name a plea. "Why are you here? After all this time—why now?"

Her eyes met his, and for a moment, her expression seemed to falter. The glow around her dimmed slightly, flickering like a candle caught in a gust of wind.

"I'm here to guide," she said softly, her voice steady and clear. "I can guide you, but the choice is yours. It has always been yours."

Grace's gaze lingered on Gillie as the mist shifted around them, her expression serene but weighted with something deeper. There was a stillness about her that felt like it could hold the entire swamp at bay, even if just for a moment. She stepped closer to Gillie, her movements quiet yet deliberate.

"You've carried that knife for so long," Grace said softly, her voice steady but laced with meaning. "A blade without purpose can cut only shadows. But a blade given light… can change everything."

Gillie's grip tightened slightly around the hilt of the knife, her brows furrowing. "What's that supposed to mean?" she asked, her tone sharp, as if refusing to admit she'd let Marcus's words about the knife linger in her mind.

Grace's serene smile didn't waver. She reached out, her touch featherlight as her fingers brushed the edge of the blade. A faint glow rippled across its surface—subtle, fleeting, but undeniably there. It wasn't overpowering, but it was enough to quiet the doubts curling through the air.

"I can't make this choice for you," Grace said, her gaze steady and unyielding. "But I can guide you. And I can offer this knife a new purpose—not to fight against the darkness, but to cut through it. Where shadows grow strongest, light must follow."

Gillie looked at the knife, her grip firm but thoughtful as the glow faded, leaving the blade as it had been before—but something about it felt different. It was still hers. She had carried it this far, through the swamp, through the shadows, through the lies. But now it felt as though it had been joined by something else—a fragment of resolve, an echo of the light Grace spoke of.

For once, she didn't look like she wanted to fight. She looked like she wanted to believe.

Gillie didn't say anything at first. Her sharp gaze flicked back to Grace, wary but unwavering. Finally, she nodded slightly, slipping the knife back into its sheath.

Grace stepped back, her attention shifting to us. Her glow softened once more, her voice carrying a quiet strength.

"The light is never gone," she said. "It waits… for those who choose to let it in."

Her gaze lingered for a moment longer, turning toward Gillie as her tone grew firmer. "Guidance isn't the same as answers," she added. "The swamp doesn't allow shortcuts."

She didn't raise her voice—but the silence that followed said enough. We weren't going to be handed a map. Just a choice. And maybe that was worse.

Gillie's jaw tightened, her frustration brimming just below the surface. "You keep saying that," she snapped. "Guide us where? Toward what? If you're here to help, then just say it."

Before Gillie could argue, Grace's form flickered violently, the glow around her dimming further. She turned her gaze back to Joshua, and her voice softened. "You must choose your path carefully," she said. "The swamp… it doesn't forgive mistakes."

Then, like the mist itself, she faded. One moment she was there, luminous and haunting, and the next, the haze swallowed her whole. The path ahead remained shrouded in shadow, the silence now heavy with her absence.

Joshua stood frozen, his hands trembling slightly as he stared at the spot where she had been. Gillie let out a sharp breath, turning toward me.

"We need to talk about this," she said, her voice low but fierce. "We can't just take her at her word."

"She's real," Joshua said suddenly, his voice quiet but firm. He didn't look at us—his hollow eyes remained fixed on the mist where Grace had vanished. "She's real, and she's trying to help."

"That's not the point," Gillie snapped, stepping toward him. "The point is, we don't know what she's really after. We don't know if we can trust her."

Joshua turned to her, his expression hardening. "I trust her," he said simply.

"Maybe you shouldn't," she fired back, her voice icy. "Not until we know more."

I stayed quiet, my thoughts tangled. Grace's presence had felt— undeniable. But Gillie wasn't wrong. The swamp was a master of manipulation, and nothing here was ever as it seemed.

Even the lost may find their way, but only if they choose it for themselves.

Her words echoed in my mind as we stood there, the tension between us thickening. And for the first time since entering the swamp, I wondered if choosing our way would be enough.

As the mist hung heavy around us, Gillie's voice cut through the stillness. "Joshua, you can't seriously believe her," she said, her frustration bubbling to the surface. "She shows up glowing, talking about gifts and salvation—and we're just supposed to take her word for it?"

Joshua's hands trembled as he clenched his fists at his sides. "I felt something," he said quietly, his voice raw with conviction. "She's real."

Gillie's laugh was sharp, cutting through his earnestness. "Real? You think Marcus wasn't real too? We thought he was helping us, and look what that got us. You don't know what she wants—or even who she really is."

Joshua turned away, his jaw tightening, but her words hung between us, drawing us back into memories neither of us wanted to revisit. The swamp had felt different when Marcus had appeared, alive with the promise of something better. We'd been desperate—and desperate people make dangerous choices.

"You wish for a shorter journey," Marcus had said, his smooth voice flowing like the river current. "I can grant that. But every gift comes at a price."

"What kind of price?" Gillie had demanded, her eyes narrowed. Her frustration, her exhaustion, had made her sharper than usual—but beneath her sharpness, there had been fear.

"Something small," Marcus had replied, his smile smooth, unfaltering. "A memory. One you won't even notice is gone."

Joshua had hesitated, the tension in his shoulders palpable. Gillie had frowned, her grip tightening on her knife. But I—I did not follow. I did not hesitate.

The coin had already made the choice for me. It had shifted in my palm, its weight settling—heavy, certain, insistent. The pull was there, silent yet commanding, threading through my thoughts, turning instinct into action.

By the time I stepped forward, I realized I had never truly considered refusing. That possibility had been swallowed before it could take shape.

We had given Marcus what he asked for, each of us willing to sacrifice a piece of ourselves for a shortcut through the swamp.

Now, in the aftermath of Grace's appearance, the weight of what we'd lost lingered like a shadow. I couldn't remember what Marcus had taken—but I could feel its absence, like an ache in my chest. And judging by the way Gillie's gaze darkened, she felt it too.

"Even the lost may find their way, but only if they choose it for themselves." Grace's words echoed in my mind, elusive but persistent. Her message had felt different—less transactional, more profound. And yet, Gillie's doubts clung to me like the swamp mist itself.

"I don't trust her," Gillie said, breaking the silence. Her voice was steady, cutting, as though she was forcing herself to stay rational. "We've been fooled before. The swamp doesn't forgive mistakes. It doesn't give second chances."

Joshua turned to her, his eyes hollow but resolute. "Grace is different," he said. "Marcus wanted something from us. Grace is giving us something—if we choose to accept it."

Gillie scoffed, shaking her head. "You don't know that. She didn't even tell us what's ahead. She's cryptic, just like Marcus. Nothing here is ever what it seems."

Her words mirrored my own doubts, though I wasn't ready to voice them. The swamp had been a place of illusions since the moment we entered. Grace's presence felt undeniable—but trust, in this place, was a dangerous thing.

"Maybe," I said quietly, drawing their attention, "she's right about one thing. There are no shortcuts here. We might need to figure out what we've already lost before we decide who to trust."

Gillie frowned, her expression conflicted, and Joshua's gaze lingered on the mist where Grace had vanished. None of us spoke, the weight of our choices pressing down like the swamp's heavy air. And as silence wrapped around us, I wondered if salvation—like the path ahead—would come at a price none of us were ready to pay.

Elana's Manipulation

We walked in silence, each step heavy with the weight of Grace's words. The choice was ours—that was what she'd said. But the thought lingered in my mind, refusing to settle, a quiet storm of doubt and possibility. The gift she spoke of felt both near and distant, like it was waiting just out of reach.

I glanced at Gillie ahead of me, her rigid posture betraying the same unspoken tension that gripped us all. Even her sharp remarks, the ones she used to keep the fear at bay, had been replaced by silence.

Joshua trailed behind, his steps dragging, his face pale and hollow. He didn't say anything, but the way he moved—the way the swamp seemed to cling to him—it spoke louder than words. None of us dared to break the stillness. None of us dared to voice the questions swirling in our minds.

And then, through the haze, a figure began to take shape.

At first, it was just an outline—a flicker of light cutting through the gloom. But as the mist shifted, the figure stepped forward with a quiet grace that felt unsettlingly familiar. The faint glow that surrounded her was unmistakable, illuminating the edges of her tattered shawl and serene expression. My breath caught in my chest.

It was Grace—or so it seemed.

Gillie froze, her eyes narrowing. "You again?" she muttered, but her tone lacked its usual edge. There was a tremor in her voice, one I hadn't heard before.

Joshua's reaction, on the other hand, was immediate and visceral. He straightened, his posture suddenly alive with hope as he stepped toward her. "You're back," he said softly, his voice trembling.

Grace—if it was her—met his gaze with what seemed to be genuine warmth.

Something about her felt off. Too smooth. Too sure. But I didn't want to see it—not yet.

"I had to return," she said, her voice low and steady, weaving through the silence like a thread of light. "There was one more thing I needed to tell you."

Gillie's hand hovered near her knife, her suspicion as sharp as ever. "And what's that supposed to be?" she asked. "More cryptic riddles to string us along?"

Grace ignored her, her focus entirely on Joshua. "You have the strength to do what must be done," she said, her tone gentle but weighted. "But you must choose the right path. Even the smallest hesitation could doom us all."

Her words settled heavily in the air, and for a moment, even Gillie seemed unsure. I felt the tension in my chest ease slightly, relief creeping in despite myself. Maybe it really was Grace. Maybe she had come back to help.

But then she laughed.

It started softly—a quiet chuckle that built into something louder, crueler, until the sound filled the clearing and wrapped around us like the mist itself. Grace's form began to shift, the glow around her dimming and twisting, and the face we thought we knew distorted into something sharper, more mocking.

"Of course you believed me," she said, her voice laced with venomous delight. The kindness in her eyes vanished, replaced by a gleeful malice that twisted her features. "You'll believe anything, won't you?"

Joshua staggered back, his expression one of utter devastation. "*No*," he whispered, his voice trembling. "*It can't…*"

"Oh, but it is," she cut in, grinning. Her tone dripped with condescension as she took a step toward him, her movements fluid and predatory. "Did you really think I'd waste my time helping you? You're nothing more than Marcus's playthings—tools to keep the swamp entertained."

Gillie's knife was in her hand before I'd even realized she'd drawn it. "Who the hell are you?" she snarled, her voice steady despite the fury flashing in her eyes. "What do you want?"

The figure stopped, her grin widening. "I'm hurt," she said, mockingly pressing a hand to her chest. "You've forgotten me already?"

As she spoke, her form shimmered, and the glow vanished entirely, leaving behind a familiar figure cloaked in shadow: Elana.

Gillie tightened her grip on her knife, her jaw clenching. "You," she spat. "I should've known."

Elana's expression softened—just slightly—and she raised her hands in a gesture of mock surrender. "Don't look at me like that," she said, her tone now dripping with false remorse. "Marcus made me do it. You know how he is."

"You expect us to believe that?" Gillie shot back, her voice cold as ice.

Elana sighed dramatically, her shoulders sagging as she cast her gaze to the ground. "I didn't have a choice," she murmured. "You don't know what it's like to be under his thumb. I didn't want to trick you—I swear. I'm… I'm sorry."

The silence that followed was heavy, charged with uncertainty. I could feel the tension shift slightly as her words hung in the air, and I glanced at Gillie, who seemed to waver for the briefest of moments.

Joshua, his hollow eyes filled with confusion, stepped toward her hesitantly. "He made you do it?" he asked quietly.

Elana looked up, her expression mournful. "Yes," she said softly. "He forced me. I didn't have a choice."

Joshua hesitated, his jaw tightening as he struggled to reconcile her words with what he had seen. "I… I understand," he said finally, his voice low. "It's not your fault."

And then she laughed again.

The sound was sharp and cruel, echoing through the clearing as her sorrowful expression twisted into one of pure delight. "Fools," she sneered, her voice dripping with mockery. "You actually believed me."

It felt like Grace had died twice. Once when she vanished. And again now, in Elana's grin.

Gillie was on her in an instant, her knife flashing in the dim light. But Elana melted into the mist, her laughter lingering as her form dissolved, leaving nothing behind but the faint echo of her voice.

"We're not done yet," she called, her tone singsong and taunting. "Marcus sends his regards."

The mist swirled violently in her wake, pressing closer around us, and for a long moment, none of us moved. Gillie's breathing was sharp and ragged as she lowered her knife, her knuckles white from the grip. Joshua stared at the ground, his face a mask of anguish, and I felt the weight of Elana's words pressing down on us like an iron hand.

"Is it her?" Joshua finally asked, his voice hollow. "The Grace we saw before—was that even her?"

Gillie didn't answer. She glanced at me, her expression dark and unreadable, and I could see the doubt twisting behind her eyes. The swamp had always been a master of deception, but now it felt like we were grasping at shadows, unable to trust even the faintest glimmer of light.

My thoughts flicked to the truth I carried, steadying me, anchoring me in the chaos. It was the one constant, the reason I was here, the thread that held me together when everything else threatened to unravel.

"We keep moving," I said quietly, though my voice wavered. "Grace or not, we have to keep moving."

And so we did. The path ahead stretched into the haze, shrouded in mist that clung to the air like something alive. The silence pressed down on us, heavy and oppressive, broken only by the faint echoes of Elana's laughter—a sound that lingered far longer than it should have, twisting through the stillness like a cruel reminder.

But then the whispers came.

They didn't creep in slowly, nor did they announce themselves with subtlety. They hit all at once, crashing through the quiet like shards of splintered glass, slicing through thought and tearing into places no blade could reach.

A sharp pressure built behind my eyes, relentless and suffocating. My chest tightened, each breath a struggle against the pulse that throbbed deep within. The sensation dragged through my ribs, twisting and burrowing into my skull like something alive—something invasive, tightening and tearing with every passing moment.

Joshua stumbled beside me, his breath uneven, his shoulders trembling as his fingers twitched against his sides. Gillie stiffened, her jaw locking, her knuckles white as she gripped her knife with a force that seemed to defy the pain.

The whispers were invasive sensations that altered thought, rewrote memory, and made reality feel fragile. The swamp itself seemed to resist us, its presence growing heavier, more oppressive, as though it sought to consume us entirely.

I gritted my teeth, forcing my focus back to the truth I carried—the one thing that steadied me, unchanging, a reminder of what was real. This wasn't fear. It wasn't uncertainty. It was violation, pure and unrelenting, a force that sought to strip away everything I held onto.

"We have to move," Joshua said, his voice strained and thin, barely audible against the weight of the mist.

Gillie nodded sharply, her resolve unshaken despite the tension radiating from her. There was no hesitation, no doubt. They didn't need to discuss it anymore.

They already knew.

Marcus Sends His Shadows

As we started moving again, a welcomed silence settled over the path, pressing into the space where the whispers had been, easing the weight that had curled against my thoughts.

The mist deepened around us, the air growing colder with every step. The oppressive hush of the swamp stretched endlessly, broken only by the faint sound of our footsteps crunching against brittle ground.

Joshua walked ahead, his shoulders hunched, his hollow eyes fixed on the path. I lagged slightly, the thought lingering in my mind—a quiet presence, steady and unshifting—as I scanned the edges of the trail. Gillie stayed close behind Joshua, her knife loose in her hand, though her grip tightened every time the shadows shifted in the corners of her vision.

It was subtle at first—a flicker of movement at the edges of the mist, like shadows cast by an unseen flame. I stopped, my breath hitching as I tried to focus on the shifting shapes. But the moment I turned my gaze directly toward them, they vanished, dissolving back into the haze like smoke.

Gillie noticed my hesitation and glanced back. "What is it?" she asked sharply, her voice low but tense.

"I thought I saw…" I trailed off, shaking my head. "It's nothing."

But it wasn't nothing.

The shadows were there—watching, waiting. And as we moved forward, their presence grew more apparent. They danced at the edges of the mist, shifting in rhythm with our steps, keeping their distance but never truly disappearing. Each flicker sent a shiver down my spine, the hairs on the back of my neck standing on end.

Gillie stopped abruptly, her hand darting to her knife as her sharp gaze scanned the shifting haze. "I see them too," she said, her voice hard. "They're following us."

Joshua didn't stop. He kept walking, his movements mechanical, his head bowed. "*They're always watching*," he murmured, his voice barely audible.

Gillie frowned, turning to him. "Joshua," she said, her tone firm. "We need to talk about this. If you know something about them, now's the time to share."

"They're his," Joshua said quietly, his voice trembling. He didn't look at her, didn't look at me. "They're Marcus's."

The name sent a chill through the air, sharper than the cold of the swamp.

Gillie's expression darkened, and she stepped closer to him, her knife glinting faintly in the dim light. "What do you mean, *his*?" she asked, her voice edged with suspicion.

Joshua hesitated, his hands trembling at his sides. "He sends them to watch," he said finally. "To follow. To make sure we—remember."

"Remember what?" I asked, my voice tight as unease twisted tighter in my chest.

Joshua stopped walking then, his hollow eyes meeting mine for a brief, unsettling moment.

"That we don't belong here."

Before any of us could respond, the shadows moved.

They surged closer, their forms flickering and twisting like smoke caught in a storm. They didn't step into the light—didn't solidify—but their movements were faster, bolder, and the oppressive weight of their presence pressed against my chest.

Then came the whispers—soft, sibilant voices threading through the air like ghostly currents, their words indistinct but chilling.

Gillie spun around, her knife raised. "Enough of this!" she snapped, her voice cutting through the murmurs. "Show yourselves!"

The shadows hesitated, their flickering shapes pausing just beyond the edge of the path. For a moment, I thought they might retreat. But then, the whispers grew louder, their hissing tones resolving into something clearer—sharper.

Marcus's voice.

"You don't have to fight this," the voice said, smooth and resonant, threading through the air like silk. "You don't have to suffer. All you have to do is turn back."

Gillie's jaw tightened, her knuckles whitening around the hilt of her knife. "Not a chance," she growled, her gaze darting between the shadows.

The voice chuckled, low and cruel. "Oh, Gillie," it said, her name dripping with mockery. "Always so stubborn. Always so blind."

"Get out of my head," she snarled, her voice trembling with rage. "You don't know anything about me."

"Don't I?" Marcus's voice purred. The shadows flickered closer, the whispers twining around us like invisible chains. "You're tired. You're angry. You think you can save him, but you know the truth, don't you? Deep down, you know it's already too late."

Gillie took a step forward, her knife poised. "Shut up," she snapped. "You're nothing but a coward hiding in the dark."

The shadows surged again, their movements jagged and chaotic, and the air grew colder still. The voice shifted then, its attention sliding away from Gillie and toward me.

My mouth went dry. It was like his voice had found something buried—and twisted it. The truth I'd been clutching felt suddenly fragile, like it could slip through my fingers with one more breath.

"And you," Marcus said, his tone turning softer, more insidious. "Carrying the weight of a legacy you didn't choose. Trying so hard to be something you're not. Tell me, do you really think you're strong enough to finish this?"

"Still carrying that coin?" he added, voice curling like smoke. "Still pretending it's just a token?"

It felt like he'd touched a wound I didn't know was open.

I swallowed hard, my thoughts pressing against me like a lifeline, steady and unrelenting.

I tightened my grip on the coin in my pocket. It bit back. Good. I needed something to hold onto.

"I don't have to be strong," I said, my voice steadier than I felt. "I just have to keep moving."

The chuckle returned, colder now, more distant.

"Oh, but you'll see," Marcus said. "Soon enough, you'll see."

The shadows began to retreat, dissolving back into the mist, though their presence lingered like a stain in the air. The whispers faded, and the cold lessened, but unease remained—twisting in my chest like a knife.

Gillie lowered her knife, her breaths sharp and uneven. "We need to keep moving," she said, her voice tight. "And we need to stay sharp. He's not done with us."

Joshua said nothing, but his hands trembled at his sides as he started walking again, his steps slow and unsteady.

I followed, the weight of Marcus's words settling over me like a shadow, pressing against my thoughts with every step.

The swamp was never silent. Not truly.

And as the path wound deeper into the mist, I couldn't shake the feeling that the shadows were still watching, waiting for their moment to strike.

The Bell's Echo

The air grew heavier as we pressed onward, the path winding through the deepening mist. The silence of the swamp seemed to thrum with an undercurrent of tension, and every shadow felt closer, more alive, than before. My chest felt tight, and every breath carried the metallic tang of damp decay.

Then it came—the sound that cut through the stillness. Faint, distant, but unmistakable. The tolling of a bell.

It was low and melodic, carrying an unnatural resonance that seemed to vibrate in my chest rather than echo in the air. It was beautiful. And it was wrong. Like hearing your name whispered by something that had no mouth. I froze mid-step, the sound sending a shiver down my spine. It wasn't just a noise—it was a pull, subtle but undeniable, as though the bell's call had reached something deep within me.

Gillie stopped next, her posture stiffening as her head snapped toward the sound. "Tell me I'm not the only one who heard that," she said, her voice sharp but hushed.

Joshua was already walking forward. His hollow eyes gleamed with a faint light I hadn't seen in months, something that might have been hope—or desperation. His movements were slow but deliberate, each step carrying an unspoken urgency. "*It's her,*" he whispered, his voice trembling.

"No," Gillie said flatly, stepping in front of him to block his path. "It's the swamp. And you know it."

Joshua didn't even seem to hear her. "I can feel her," he said, his tone distant but resolute. "She's calling me."

"Joshua, stop," I said, my voice shaking. "We don't know what's out there. That sound…it's not her. It can't be."

Another toll echoed through the swamp, louder this time, deeper. The vibrations carried through the air like the beat of a massive, unseen heart. The mist coiled tighter around us, thickening with every step we took, obscuring the edges of the path.

Gillie swore under her breath, gripping her knife tightly. "This isn't right," she muttered. "We shouldn't be following that sound."

But Joshua had already slipped past her, his focus entirely on the distant pull of the bell. I exchanged a glance with Gillie, her expression dark but determined, and we followed, our steps hesitant as the sound grew louder.

The bell tolled again, its haunting resonance filling the air with a heavy weight. The mist seemed to part slightly as we reached a clearing, and for a moment, the sound was accompanied by something else—light. Faint and flickering at first, but growing brighter until a familiar figure stepped into view.

Grace.

She stood at the edge of the clearing, her luminous form outlined by the pale glow of the mist around her. Her gaze swept over us, steady but filled with something heavy and unspoken. I felt my breath hitch as I took in the sight of her, so much more fragile now than before, her glow dimmed, almost flickering like a dying flame.

"Your time is slipping away," she said, her voice soft but clear, cutting through the stillness like a blade. Her tone carried an urgency that made my chest tighten. "Each toll binds the living and the dead."

Her words twisted through the air, settling over us like a shroud. Gillie stepped forward, her expression hard. "What does that mean?" she demanded. "What are you talking about?"

But Grace didn't answer. Her gaze lingered on Joshua for a moment, and the sorrow in her expression deepened, her light dimming further. I opened my mouth to speak, to plead with her to stay, but before the words could escape, she flared—then vanished. Like a candle in wind.

The mist surged back in her wake, heavier and colder than before. The bell's toll came again, fainter now, as though it were retreating into the distance. I felt the weight of her words settle into my chest, the cryptic warning gnawing at the edges of my thoughts.

"What the hell was that supposed to mean?" Gillie muttered, her grip tightening on her knife. She glanced at me, her eyes hard. " 'Binds the living and the dead'? What does that even mean?"

I shook my head, my hands trembling as I tried to steady my breathing. "I don't know," I admitted. "But we need to avoid the whispers. We need to keep moving."

Joshua didn't say anything. His hollow eyes stayed fixed on the spot where Grace had vanished, his expression unreadable. For a long moment, none of us moved, the weight of the swamp pressing down on us like an iron hand.

Finally, Gillie broke the silence, her voice low but sharp. "Let's go," she said firmly, gesturing for us to follow. "We've waited too long already."

Reluctantly, we turned back to the path, the bell's toll fading into the distance as we walked. But Grace's warning stayed with me, twisting through my mind like a splinter I couldn't remove. Each toll binds the living and the dead.

I clenched my fingers, the sting sharp and grounding. The mist thickened, the path darkened—but we moved. We had to. The bell still echoed, and time was bleeding away.

The Field of Shadows

Meeting the Bellmaker

The bell's faint resonance pulled us through the mist, each toll vibrating in my chest like an unspoken command. The weight of the sound and looming shadows made conversation impossible.

The swamp shifted as we moved, the familiar trees giving way to something colder, emptier. The air here was sharper, biting, and carried a metallic tang that clung to the back of my throat. The path ahead widened slightly, revealing a clearing shrouded in an even thicker haze. And there, in the center, we saw it.

The air rang—not loud, but constant—like a tension wire vibrating just beneath hearing. Something was waiting. Or watching.

A figure stood surrounded by fragments of shattered and tarnished bells, each one lying broken and rusted in the grass like remnants of a long-forgotten war. The bells varied in size—some as small as a child's fist, others towering over us, their cracked surfaces dull and lifeless.

The figure itself was spectral, its form faintly glowing with a dim silver light. It was hunched, its shape draped in what looked like layers of torn and tattered cloth, the faint ring of a bell emanating softly from somewhere within its folds.

Gillie stopped abruptly, her hand instinctively going to her knife. "*What is that*?" she whispered, her voice sharp but hushed.

Joshua froze in place, his breath catching audibly. His wide eyes fixed on the figure, unblinking, and he took an unsteady step forward. "*The Bellmaker*," he murmured, almost reverently.

The name struck something in the air, an electric charge that rippled through the clearing. The figure tilted its head slightly, as if acknowledging the title. Its face—if it could be called that—was obscured by shadow, only faint glimmers of light reflecting off the edges of what might have been features.

"The Bellmaker?" Gillie repeated, her voice skeptical. She didn't lower her knife. "Another one of this swamp's tricks?"

But Joshua's voice trembled with something else—something between awe and fear. "It's not a trick," he said quietly. "It's real. I've… I've heard the toll before."

Gillie turned to him, her expression sharp. "What do you mean you've heard it before?" she demanded. "What aren't you telling us?"

Joshua exhaled shakily, his gaze locked on the Bellmaker. "The swamp whispers about him," he said, his voice low. "The one who binds the living and the dead."

His words hung in the air, and I felt a chill crawl down my spine. It wasn't just the weight of what he was saying—it was the way he said it, like someone describing a ghost they thought they'd never meet.

Joshua's breathing quickened, his gaze dropping as the Bellmaker's toll echoed through the clearing. His face twisted with an emotion I couldn't quite place—grief or longing, perhaps both—and his fingers curled at his side as though reaching for something just out of his grasp. His posture had shifted. He looked small, weighed down by something unseen—no longer with us, lost in the haze.

"Joshua?" I stepped closer, lowering my voice. "Are you okay?"

He didn't answer right away. His jaw tightened, and his chest rose and fell unevenly. I thought he might shake his head or brush me off, but instead, his gaze remained distant, his voice raw when he finally spoke. "It's the toll," he said softly, almost trembling. "It… it reminds me of her."

"Her?" I frowned, leaning slightly closer. "What do you mean?"

Joshua swallowed hard, his eyes flickering with emotion. "Olivia. The day she was born—I didn't know I could feel so much light. I didn't know I could—hold something so pure."

His voice faltered, and he exhaled shakily, his hands clenching at his sides. "Her first cry—it cut through everything. It was like nothing else mattered, just her. Just that moment. I thought I'd carry that with me forever."

The silence hung heavy between us. Then Gillie's voice broke it, quiet but sharp with emotion. "Grandma," she said softly, the weight of the word hanging in the air.

Joshua turned toward her, his face etched with something that might have been sorrow or gratitude. The toll seemed to linger between them, a shared ache that neither could put into words.

The Bellmaker lifted a hand—long fingers, bearing the unmistakable signs of advanced decay, with bone showing through softened flesh, emerging from the tattered cloth. Its movement was slow, deliberate, and as it gestured, the faint toll of a bell echoed through the clearing. The sound wasn't harsh or sharp—it was mournful, resonating with a deep sorrow that seemed to fill the space between heartbeats.

"Who are you?" I asked, my voice trembling despite my attempt to sound steady.

The Bellmaker's head tilted again, and when it spoke, its voice was soft but layered, as though many voices spoke in unison. "We're the keepers of the toll," it said. "The makers of sound that binds."

Gillie frowned, her grip tightening on her weapon. "Sound that binds what?" she demanded.

The Bellmaker's hand moved, gesturing toward the broken bells scattered around it. "Each toll marks a sin," it said slowly, its voice reverberating like the echo of a distant chime. "Each chime binds the living to the dead. And when the God Forsaken Bell tolls its final note, the binding will be complete."

A chill crawled down my spine, the weight of its words sinking deep into my chest. "What does that mean?" I asked quietly. "What happens when the binding is complete?"

The Bellmaker paused, its form flickering faintly as though it were struggling to remain solid. "The swamp will consume the living and the dead," it said simply. "The dark will grow heavier, but the light will endure."

The silence that followed was heavy, the air pressing down on us like a physical weight. Gillie's jaw tightened, and she took a step forward, her knife glinting faintly in the dim light. "Why are you telling us this?" she asked sharply. "What do you want from us?"

The Bellmaker's gaze—or what I assumed was its gaze—settled on her. "You follow the toll," it said. "You seek the God Forsaken Bell. You must understand what it is you chase."

Joshua's voice broke the silence, trembling but determined. "Can we stop it? The last bell... can it be stopped?"

The Bellmaker tilted its head, the faint chime of its movements filling the air. "Stopping the bell isn't the question," it said cryptically. "The question is whether you'll stand when it tolls."

Gillie's frustration bubbled over, and she stepped closer, her voice sharp. "Enough riddles," she snapped. "If you know something, just tell us. What are we supposed to do?"

The Bellmaker didn't flinch at her tone. Instead, it lifted a hand and pointed toward the path ahead. "Follow the sound," it said simply. "Understand its weight. Only then will you know what must be done."

Another toll echoed through the clearing, louder this time, sharper. The Bellmaker's form flickered violently, and the sound of the bell seemed to tear through its shape, leaving only fragments of light behind. Within moments, it was gone, leaving us alone among the broken bells.

The silence that followed was deafening, and I realized I had been holding my breath. Gillie let out a frustrated huff, lowering her knife but not putting it away. "More riddles," she muttered bitterly. "Great. Just what we needed."

Joshua's gaze lingered on the empty space where the Bellmaker had stood, his expression haunted. "*Each toll binds the living and the dead*," he murmured, repeating the Bellmaker's words. "It wasn't lying. We've felt it."

"And we'll feel it again," I said, my voice heavy. "We have to keep moving."

Gillie nodded reluctantly, and together, we turned back to the path, leaving the broken bells behind. But the Bellmaker's warning stayed with me, twisting in my thoughts like a thread pulled too tight. The God Forsaken Bell wasn't just a sound—it was an ending. And we were chasing a sound that might destroy us. And the bell was getting louder.

Distorted Reflections

The memory of the Bellmaker lingered, heavier than the mist clinging to the air around us. Every step forward felt weighted with the echoes of his voice, the strange resonance of his words still carving their way into my thoughts.

There was something unsettling about him—something beyond the obvious. He wasn't like Grace; his presence didn't inspire warmth or hope. He was a herald of something darker, something that felt inevitable. I couldn't shake the feeling that his tolling bell marked more than time—it marked us.

Gillie walked ahead of me, her grip on her knife tight, her focus sharp and unyielding as if refusing to let the bellmaker's words follow her. Joshua's steps were slower, dragging, his shoulders slumped as though the weight of the swamp had finally seeped into his bones. None of us spoke, but I knew we were all thinking the same thing. The bellmaker had changed something. We just didn't know what.

The air shifted.

At first, I thought it was just my own nerves fraying under the lingering tension, but it was more than that—something subtle yet deliberate, like a ripple cutting through still water. My breath caught as I stopped mid-step, my pulse quickening.

The shadows came without warning.

At first, I thought it was just the mist playing tricks on me—shapes flickering at the edges of my vision, indistinct and fleeting. But then I saw it clearly: a figure mirroring my steps, its movements deliberate and calculated. It wasn't Gillie, and it wasn't Joshua. It was me.

I froze, my breath catching as the figure tilted its head. Its features were warped—stretched too far, its body elongated and grotesque. Its hollow eyes burned faintly like embers, and its twisted sneer sent a shiver down my spine.

"Keep walking," Gillie said sharply, her voice cutting through my frozen thoughts. But when she turned, her expression hardened. The shadows hadn't just come for me. They were following her, too.

I glanced over and saw her reflection—a warped, exaggerated version of Gillie that moved in perfect sync with her steps. Its knife gleamed in its hands, its sharp edges catching flickers of light that didn't exist. The figure's face was a mockery of her own, twisted into something cruel. I saw the strain in Gillie's posture as she clenched her knife tighter, her breaths quickening.

Joshua noticed last. His steps slowed as his reflection emerged from the mist—a shadowy version of himself moving with unnerving precision. Its hollow eyes seemed darker than his, sharper, and its expression carried a weight that was almost unbearable to look at. Joshua didn't speak. He couldn't.

The shadows didn't stop at mirroring us. They began to change, their forms twisting and warping into something worse.

I stared at mine, my pulse racing as it began to speak, its voice a distorted echo of my own. "You're just like him," it hissed, its sneer widening. "You'll fall the same way. You're already on the edge—you just don't see it yet."

My chest tightened, the weight of its words pressing into me like a physical force. "*Stop*," I whispered, though my voice trembled and felt small against the looming presence of the shadow.

It laughed—a cruel, hollow sound that seemed to vibrate through the very air around us. "He didn't fall because he was weak," it continued, circling me slowly. "He fell because he was hungry. And you—you carry that same hunger. Don't you feel it?"

I clenched my fingers, the pressure sharp against my skin as I tried to steady myself. The shadow didn't stop. It circled me, its voice cutting deeper.

"You carry everything he left behind—his hunger, his mistakes," it said, its tone dropping lower, more pointed. "You carry his shadow. You'll fall, just like he did."

My gaze flicked to Gillie, desperate to escape the weight of the words pressing into me. Her shadow spoke, too, its voice laced with venom.

"You failed them," it spat, circling her like a predator. "Olivia trusted you, and you let her down. You let all of them down. They broke because of you."

"Shut up," Gillie snapped, her voice trembling but sharp. "You don't know anything."

"Oh, I know plenty," the shadow sneered. "I know how they look at you. I know the way they blame you—you see it every time you look in their eyes. You don't need them to say it, do you? You already know it's true."

Gillie's grip on her knife tightened further, her breaths coming quicker as the shadow's words cut into her. But she didn't move. She just stood there, her jaw clenched, as if trying to will it away.

Joshua's shadow was the last to speak. Its voice was low and mournful, yet cruel. "You abandoned her," it said, circling him slowly, deliberately. "You promised her, and you failed."

"*No*," Joshua whispered, his voice breaking. "*I didn't…*"

"You did," the shadow hissed, unrelenting. "You failed her, and you know it. That's why you're here. That's why you can't leave. Because you know you don't deserve to."

Joshua's hollow eyes darkened, his hands trembling at his sides as the words pressed against him like the weight of the swamp itself. "Stop," he muttered weakly, his voice cracking. "Please stop."

But the shadow only laughed, its twisted grin widening as it circled him. "You think she'll forgive you?" it sneered. "She won't. She can't. And you know that."

The shadows pressed closer, their voices rising and mingling into a cacophony of whispers that drowned out the sound of our breaths. The air grew colder, sharper, the weight of their words wrapping around us like chains.

Gillie's jaw tightened. Her hands shook—but she didn't back down.

"Enough!" Gillie's voice cut through the noise like a blade, sharp and commanding. She stepped forward, her knife raised, her expression hard. "You don't get to define us," she said, her voice steady despite the tremor in her hands. "You don't get to tell us who we are."

The shadows hesitated, their movements faltering as Gillie pushed closer, her knife glinting in the faint light. "We're still here," she said firmly. "We're still fighting. And you can't take that away from us."

The whispering quieted. The shadows retreated slightly, though their presence lingered like a weight in the air. Gillie turned to Joshua, her voice softening. "Joshua," she said gently, "this isn't her. These shadows— they're nothing but tricks. Don't listen to them."

Joshua's shoulders sagged as his gaze darted between Gillie and the distorted reflection of himself, the weight of the moment crushing him like the swamp's oppressive air. His hands trembled at his sides, and for a moment, I thought he might collapse.

He took a slow, unsteady breath, pulling what courage he could from someplace fragile. When he finally nodded, it was stiff, reluctant, but deliberate. "I… I know," he said, though the tremor in his voice betrayed his fear.

My thoughts latched onto the truth I carried—solid, anchoring me against the chaos threatening to pull me under. I stepped forward, fingers tightening until the pressure imprinted into my skin. "They're not us," I said, voice sharp, cutting through the haze. "They're shadows. That's all they are."

The whispers wavered at the mist's edge, testing the strength of my words. Their venom softened, receding slightly, but not disappearing. The shadows lingered, faint flickers at the periphery, waiting. Their presence weighed heavy, sharp, unrelenting—but the tension loosened just enough for breath.

As the whispers faded, their ache remained, burrowed deep like a splinter in thought. The air lifted, but it wasn't relief—it was the eye of a storm gathering strength. I could still feel them watching. Gillie exhaled sharply, lowering her knife but keeping it close. "We need to keep moving," she said, firm. "Before they come back."

Joshua didn't answer, but he followed, steps hesitant as we turned back to the path. The shadows lingered, watching, waiting. Their voices had quieted, but their words stayed, twisting through my thoughts like smoke I couldn't clear.

But we hadn't broken. Not yet.

Grace's Anchor

The silence of the Field of Shadows was broken only by the faint echoes of the distorted reflections, their cruel whispers lingering in our ears long after their flickering forms had receded into the haze. Each step felt heavier, as if the swamp itself were trying to drag us under.

Gillie's grip on her knife remained tight, her knuckles white against the hilt. Joshua walked ahead of us, his shoulders hunched, his steps slow and uneven. None of us spoke. The weight of what we had just endured hung over us, sharp and unrelenting, threatening to press us into the ground.

The silence broke with a flicker of light.

At first, it was faint—a soft, dim glow barely visible through the mist. But it grew brighter as we approached, cutting through the haze with a warmth that felt out of place in the cold, oppressive swamp. The glow steadied, and a figure emerged at the edge of the clearing.

It was Grace.

She flickered into view, her light dim and trembling, but there. She stood beyond the edge of the field, looking at us intently. There was sorrow in her expression and a sense of profound sadness. However, there was also strength—a quiet but firm resolve.

Joshua stopped in his tracks, his breath catching audibly. "*Grace*," he whispered, his voice trembling.

Gillie stepped forward, her knife still in hand, her eyes narrowing. "Is it really her this time?" she muttered, suspicion laced in her words.

The glow around Grace wavered slightly, as though in response to Gillie's doubt, but her expression remained steady. "You carry a heavy burden," she said softly, her voice low and resonant, wrapping around us like the faintest chime of a distant bell. "It'll only grow heavier if you let the shadows win."

Gillie stiffened, her jaw tightening as she slid her knife back into its sheath. "What are you trying to say?" she asked, her voice sharp, though there was a flicker of vulnerability beneath the edge.

Grace turned her gaze to Gillie, her luminous eyes filled with unfathomable sorrow. "You don't have to fight the darkness alone," she said gently. "But you must believe that the light is stronger. Even here."

Joshua took a small step closer, his hollow eyes wide, filled with something fragile—hope, or perhaps desperation. "You told me I could choose my path," he said, his voice shaking. "But what if I don't know how? What if I've already… already chosen wrong?"

Grace's light dimmed faintly, her expression softening as her gaze lingered on him. "Every step forward is a choice," she said. "And every choice matters. But it's never too late to listen for the echoes of the light."

Her words hung in the air like a lifeline, fragile yet unyielding. I tightened my grip on the coin in my pocket, its edges biting into my palm as I stared at her. "What about Raven?" I asked cautiously, my voice quieter than I intended. "Is there any part of him left that can… hear the light?"

Grace turned to me, her gaze piercing yet heavy with something I couldn't name. "Raven carries the weight of many choices," she said, her voice even but firm. "Some his own, and some not. He is dangerous—make no mistake. But even those lost in darkness can hear the echoes of the light, if you believe."

Her words sent a chill through me, not because of their weight, but because of what they implied. Raven was lost—but not beyond reach. Hope twisted in my chest, fragile and almost unbearable to hold onto. Was she saying there was still a chance? That something within him could still be saved?

Gillie's expression darkened, her shoulders tensing as she stepped closer. "How are we supposed to believe in anything here?" she asked, voice tight. "I don't even know what's mine anymore."

Grace's sorrow deepened, but her light grew brighter, steady and unwavering. "The swamp is full of shadows," she said calmly, her voice resonant. "But where there's shadow, there's also light. You must remember that."

The mist began to surge around her, pulling at the edges of her form like tendrils trying to reclaim her. She flickered violently, the glow around her dimming as though the swamp itself was fighting to drag her back into its grasp. Her gaze lingered on us, her expression unreadable, and then she spoke one final time.

"Don't let the shadows define you. You're more than the darkness you carry."

And then she was gone. The light vanished, swallowed by the mist, leaving us alone in the oppressive cold of the clearing. The silence that followed was deafening, sharp and unyielding.

Gillie let out a sharp breath, her hand instinctively returning to the hilt of her knife as she glanced at me. "Do you believe her?" she asked quietly, her voice tight. "About Raven?"

I hesitated, the weight of Grace's words still heavy in my chest. "I don't know," I admitted, my voice barely above a whisper. "But I think... I think we have to."

Joshua didn't speak. He stood motionless, his gaze fixed on the space where Grace had stood, his hollow eyes filled with something I couldn't decipher. For a moment, I thought he might finally say something, but then he turned and began walking again, his steps slow and unsteady.

Gillie glanced at me once more, her expression guarded, before following him. I stayed close behind, steadying myself as we returned to the path. Grace's words echoed in my mind, her voice a fragile but haunting melody: Even those lost in darkness can hear the echoes of the light, but only if you believe.

The shadows pressed closer as we moved, their movements silent and watchful, but I forced myself to hold onto that thread of light. It was faint, fragile, but it was enough.

We weren't done yet.

The Bell's Authority

The distorted reflections loomed at the edges of the mist, their flickering forms lingering even as their voices faded. Their presence, though momentarily subdued, left an indelible mark on the air around us. I could still feel the weight of their accusations pressing against my chest, their words coiling through my thoughts like smoke.

Then, the bell tolled.

The sound tore through the field, loud and commanding, vibrating through the ground beneath our feet. It wasn't the faint, distant resonance we had followed before—it was immediate, visceral, shaking the very air around us. My breath caught as the toll reverberated through my chest, sharp and relentless, shattering the fragile silence.

The shadows reacted instantly. Their forms flickered violently, the edges of their shapes dissolving as if the bell's sound burned them. The whispers rose into a cacophony of hisses and cries, fragmented and chaotic, before falling silent altogether. One by one, the reflections dissipated, their jagged outlines evaporating into the mist like smoke caught in a windstorm.

The field transformed. The mist, which had pressed so closely around us, seemed to recoil, pulling back as though the bell's resonance had pushed it away. For the first time in what felt like hours, I could see beyond the immediate stretch of path ahead. The twisted trees at the edge of the field came into view, their brittle limbs reaching into the dim light like fractured remnants of something long abandoned.

Gillie let out a sharp breath, lowering her knife as her shoulders sagged slightly. "What the hell was that?" she muttered, though her voice trembled ever so slightly.

Joshua, too, seemed frozen in place, his hollow eyes wide with something I couldn't quite place—fear, awe, or maybe both. He didn't speak, but his trembling hands told me enough. The toll had reached him, the same as it had reached me, and neither of us could shake its weight.

"It was the bell," I said finally, my voice breaking the silence. My words felt heavy, as though speaking them made the moment more real. "It drove them back."

Gillie glanced at me, her expression wary. "For now," she said firmly. "That doesn't mean we're safe."

The air was still charged, humming faintly with the bell's lingering echo, and I couldn't shake the feeling that we were being watched. But for the moment, the oppressive pull of the shadows had lessened, giving us a sliver of clarity in the chaos.

And then, as if on cue, the faint glow appeared.

At the far edge of the clearing, the light flickered into existence, soft and fragile against the encroaching haze. Grace stepped forward, her luminous form faint but steady, cutting through the mist like a beacon. Her presence, though fragile, carried the same weight it always did—an anchor in the ever-shifting uncertainty of the swamp.

Joshua's voice trembled as he whispered, "*It's her.*" He took a hesitant step forward, but Gillie's hand shot out, gripping his arm tightly.

"Wait," she said, her tone sharp. "We don't know if it's her. Not for sure."

Grace's gaze shifted to us, her sorrowful eyes landing on Gillie first, then me. Her glow pulsed, dimming and brightening with the rhythm of her words. "The bell has given you time," she said softly, her voice weaving through the air like a thread of light. "But it's not endless. Time will slip away if you let it."

Gillie's grip loosened—but just barely. Her expression didn't soften. "What are you talking about?" she demanded. "What time? What does the bell mean?"

Grace's gaze lingered on her for a moment before turning to me. "Each toll binds the living and the dead," she said, repeating the Bellmaker's warning. "It's a thread—a connection. But when the final toll comes, the thread will break."

Her words sent a chill down my spine, the weight of them pressing against my chest. "What happens when it breaks?" I asked quietly, though I wasn't sure I wanted to know the answer.

Grace's expression darkened, her sorrow deepening. "The end," she said simply. "For the swamp. For you. For all."

The mist began to swirl around her, pulling at the edges of her form as though the swamp itself was trying to reclaim her. She flickered violently, her light dimming further. "Do not linger," she said, her voice barely audible above the rising whispers of the mist. "You must keep moving."

"Grace, wait," Joshua called, his voice breaking. "What do we do? How do we stop it?"

But she was already fading, her glow swallowed by the haze, her presence reduced to a faint glimmer before vanishing entirely. The clearing grew dim once more, the mist pressing closer, heavier, as though it sought to erase her entirely.

Gillie cursed under her breath, her knife glinting faintly in the dim light as she turned to Joshua. "You need to stop running to her every time she shows up," she snapped. "It's getting us nowhere."

Joshua flinched, his shoulders hunching as he muttered, "She's trying to help us."

"She's trying to help?" Gillie snapped. "Then maybe she should try staying longer than two sentences."

I stepped between them, my chest tight with the weight of Grace's warning. "She said we have to keep moving," I said, my voice steady but strained. "The bell's giving us time, but not much. We can't waste it."

Gillie hesitated, her jaw tightening as she glanced between me and Joshua. Her frustration was palpable, but something else flickered in her expression—an edge of doubt, or maybe unease. "She also told us there are no shortcuts," she said sharply, her voice low but insistent. "So what is it? The bell is giving us time? Is that a shortcut?" She shook her head slightly, as though trying to piece together a puzzle. "I don't like it."

Joshua didn't respond. His gaze lingered on the spot where Grace had stood, his hollow eyes clouded with doubt and lingering pain. Finally, he started forward, his steps slow and unsteady, his shoulders slumping under the weight of it all.

Gillie turned back to the path, her grip tightening on her knife. "Fine," she muttered. "But if the next thing we run into is another one of Marcus's tricks, I'm blaming both of you."

I followed, the weight of Grace's words twisting through my thoughts like a splinter. Each toll binds the living and the dead.

The bell's authority had cleared the way, if only temporarily. But the path ahead remained uncertain, and the echoes of the toll hung in the air like a haunting refrain. Gillie's question lingered too, pressing against my chest like a weight. The bell was giving us time—but at what cost?

The path wasn't clear. But the bell had tolled. And the toll doesn't lie.

Games of Deception

Raven's Revelation

The echoes of everything we'd faced tangled in the mist, clinging to me like damp air—heavy, suffocating, impossible to shake. The Field of Shadows had stripped away our defenses, exposing truths too raw to face. Grace spoke of light, fragile and fleeting, slipping through our fingers like dust. And the bellmaker, with his relentless toll, had left his mark deep beneath my skin, a weight I still couldn't name.

Step after step, the swamp pressed closer. The shadows thickened, twisting through the fog, clutching at our feet like grasping hands. Joshua staggered, his shoulders hunched, his movements sluggish, as if the ground was dragging him down. Gillie marched ahead, her knife catching faint light, a glint of defiance. She said nothing, but her silence carried more weight than anything she could have spoken.

I followed, every step heavier than the last. The swamp's grip was tightening, and what I carried coiled around me, a tether to something I couldn't let go.

Then… the mist rippled.

A shift in the air. Subtle at first, barely there. Then it grew, thickening, billowing, wrapping around us like a suffocating veil.

Joshua halted, breath sharp, freezing mid-step.

Gillie spun, her hand flashing toward her knife, her gaze cutting through the haze ahead. "What now?" she muttered, voice low, tense, ready.

The ground beneath me shifted. My foot sank suddenly, not into the swampy soil, but into emptiness—a hidden hollow that hadn't been there a moment before. I stumbled forward, catching myself on the twisted root of a tree that arched out of the ground like a trap waiting to spring. Behind me, Joshua cursed, his balance faltering as the mist thickened, clinging tightly around his legs as though trying to trip him. Gillie swore as her knife slipped from her grasp, vanishing into the shadows underfoot.

The mist rippled again, but this time, a sound came with it—a low hum vibrating through the air. It reminded me faintly of the resonant hum of the trees we'd passed earlier, but this was different. It carried a darker, heavier tone, each pulse pressing into my chest like a warning. The rhythm was unnatural, filled with malice, and it seemed to wind itself into the very air, drawing the shadows closer.

Then came the laughter.

It started low, barely distinguishable from the hum, before it swelled, sharp and chaotic. The sound fractured and distorted, splintering into a mockery of voices overlapping in wild, jarring cadence. It was everywhere at once, weaving through the mist and clawing at my senses. The shadows twisted with it, darting and flitting just out of reach, playing a cruel, teasing game.

Something tugged hard at my jacket, nearly pulling me backward into the muck. I spun around, my breath catching, but there was nothing behind me—only the swirling mist and the sound of laughter growing louder, sharper, more unhinged.

Gillie dropped to her knees abruptly, her hands plunging into the muck below her feet. The swamp sucked at her fingers, thick and unyielding as she searched blindly for the blade. Her breath came unevenly, frustration flashing across her face as the knife remained elusive. The laughter echoed around her, mocking and sharp, but she didn't look up—her focus stayed locked on the ground.

Finally, her fingers closed around the hilt, and she yanked it free with a sharp tug, the blade slick with grime and damp. She stood swiftly, wiping the knife against her sleeve, her movements deliberate and forceful. Straightening, she tightened her grip on the weapon, her jaw clenching as her gaze darted across the mist.

"It's him," Gillie said, her voice heavy with recognition and anger. "That laugh. I'd know it anywhere."

Joshua tensed beside her, his breath hitching. "Raven."

The laughter peaked, a sickening, mocking crescendo that sent chills racing down my spine. The mist shivered one last time, the shadows parting violently.

And then Raven stepped forward.

The mist clung to him, coiling and writhing. It was like the swamp itself could barely contain him. He moved with a fluidity that felt unnatural, his form shifting with each step.

At first, he appeared human—gaunt and pale, his hollow eyes burning with an eerie, unsettling light. But his shape rippled, bending seamlessly into something darker, more primal. His sharp, predatory grin stretched unnaturally wide before his features warped again, twisting into the jagged outline of a beast. Each transformation was chaotic yet deliberate, embodying the disorder and madness that clung to him.

The laughter still echoed in the air, haunting and sharp, as Raven circled us in the mist. His shifting form flickered at the edges of my vision, never fully solid, his presence more of a suggestion than a reality. He didn't need to step closer to unsettle us—his games were more than enough. The swamp itself seemed to bend to his will, drawing us deeper into his chaos.

Something about the way he moved, the way he laughed, tugged at my thoughts. He wasn't just toying with us—he was planting seeds, twisting truths into something darker. I thought back to the last time we had seen him, how he spoke in riddles, dropping pieces of a puzzle I couldn't quite put together. His words then had hinted at something—something I hadn't wanted to believe.

But now, his games felt familiar.

I tried to push the thought aside, but it clung to me, persistent. The way he manipulated the swamp, the way he toyed with us—it was like a story I'd heard once, long ago. A story about Jonah. Jonah, with his silver tongue and his endless tricks. Jonah, who could talk his way into your trust and then vanish with the ground beneath your feet.

"Raven," I muttered under my breath, watching his shadow flicker through the mist. My fingers brushed against the coin in my pocket, its weight grounding me as the pieces began to slide into place. This was more than trickery—this was Jonah's kind of madness. The schemes, the mockery, the cruelty. Jonah would've relished in chaos like this.

And yet, it didn't make sense. Jonah was gone. He'd been lost to the dark years ago, vanished without a trace like so many others whose stories faded into whispers and shadows. But the thought wouldn't leave me—couldn't leave me. I heard my own voice, soft and unbidden, break the silence: "Jonah."

The laughter stopped abruptly.

Raven turned toward me, his flickering form solidifying just enough for me to see his grin widen. His hollow eyes burned with a cruel, predatory light as he stepped forward, his voice layered and resonant, as though the swamp itself spoke through him.

"Jonah is dead," Raven said finally, his voice layered—less a voice, more an echo of the swamp itself. It wasn't just him speaking—it was the swamp, the shadows, and something far greater. "But Raven remains."

The name struck like a hammer, forcing the air from my lungs. My chest tightened, my vision blurred, and for a moment, I felt like the ground beneath me had disappeared. The words repeated in my mind, jagged and relentless. Jonah is dead. Raven remains.

I staggered, gripping the coin in my pocket harder, but even its grounding weight wasn't enough. Everything I had tried to push aside, all the doubts I'd buried, came rushing back in a torrent I couldn't stop.

The truth was unraveling, sharp and unstoppable. I'd wondered so many times. Every moment Raven had spoken of legacies, bloodlines, and burdens—those veiled accusations I thought were meant for Gillie's family, or anyone but me—I'd felt it creeping in, that gnawing suspicion. And every time, I'd forced myself to look away. To tell myself it wasn't possible. That it couldn't be true.

But it was true.

The fragmented memories flooded back, each one sharper than the last: the way his gaze lingered too long, too knowingly. The way he'd twist his words, making them cut deeper than I thought possible. All those moments when I thought he was referring to Gillie's family, when I thought his accusations weren't meant for me. And yet, deep down, I'd known. I'd felt the weight of it in his words, in the way the swamp seemed to twist around him like it was his to command.

I staggered under the weight of it all, the enormity of what I hadn't allowed myself to see. Raven watched me, his hollow eyes burning with cruel delight as he took a deliberate step forward. He didn't need to say anything—he could see it. He could see the truth sinking in, ripping through me with the force of a storm.

"You've known all along, haven't you?" Raven said, his hollow gaze locking onto mine. His sneer widened, sharp and mocking, and his voice twisted through the mist like smoke threading its way into my lungs. "Why you're here. Why the swamp called you."

I opened my mouth, but no words came. My throat felt tight, as though the air itself was closing in on me. All the things I'd tried not to believe—the truths I'd turned away from—were flooding in now, unstoppable.

"*Say it*," Raven murmured, his tone dropping into something low and taunting. He tilted his head, his hollow eyes gleaming with cruel amusement. "Say the words. You've been holding them back for so long, haven't you?"

I shook my head weakly, my breaths coming in shallow gasps. My chest felt like it was going to collapse under the weight of everything I was carrying, everything I couldn't let go of.

Raven took another step forward, his form flickering, shifting into something darker, more jagged. "Say it," he repeated, his voice cutting through the air like a blade. "Let it out. Let us hear it."

The mist felt like it was pressing into me now, suffocating and cold, forcing me to confront the truth I couldn't avoid any longer. My grip on the coin tightened further, the sharp edges cutting into my skin until I felt the sting of blood.

"I…" My voice cracked, the words breaking apart before they could fully form. I swallowed hard, forcing myself to speak again. "I'm here because…"

The shadows around Raven twisted, curling tighter around his form as his grin widened into something monstrous. "Because we called you," he said, cutting me off. His voice was sharp, triumphant, dripping with malice. "You're here because you belong to us. Because you carry him with you—every mistake, every failure, every piece of him that you tried so hard to deny."

"*No*," I whispered, my voice trembling.

"Oh, yes," Raven said, his laughter cold and hollow, echoing through the clearing like the toll of a bell. "You've felt it, haven't you? That hunger gnawing at the edges of your soul? That pull dragging you deeper and deeper into the swamp? It's his. And now it's yours."

"I'm not him," I said, louder this time, though my voice cracked under the weight of my own doubt.

Raven leaned closer, his jagged form flickering violently as he tilted his head. "Aren't you?" he hissed. "The swamp knows the truth. It sees you for what you are. And so do we."

The words twisted through me like a knife, cutting deeper than I thought possible. My legs buckled, and I fell to my knees, the weight of his presence pressing harder against my chest with every second.

Raven sneered, his hollow eyes gleaming with delight as he watched me crumble. "*That's it*," he murmured, his tone almost tender in its cruelty. "*That's the truth you've been running from. And now it's here, staring you in the face.*"

I squeezed my eyes shut, my breaths shallow and ragged. My chest burned with the ache of realization, with the full weight of everything I didn't want to believe crashing down at once.

"I'm not him," I said—not with strength, but with everything I had left.

Raven's laughter grew louder, his form flickering violently as he began to retreat into the mist. "You can keep telling yourself that," he said, his voice fading into the haze. "But the swamp knows. And so do you."

And then he was gone.

The mist collapsed in behind him, closing like a wound that had never been opened.

The silence he left behind was suffocating, heavier than the mist itself. It sank into my chest, twisting through my thoughts like a wound that wouldn't heal.

Gillie's steps slowed as she turned back toward me. Her sharp gaze softened, her grip loosening on the knife she still clutched. I felt her eyes on me, studying the way I knelt there, broken under the weight of what Raven had just revealed. Her posture changed, and the tension in her shoulders melted into something unfamiliar—sympathy.

For a moment, neither of us spoke. The silence stretched between us, heavy with the gravity of everything that had unraveled. When she finally broke the stillness, her voice was quieter than I'd ever heard it.

"I didn't know," she said softly, as though the words were meant to hold me steady, to pull me back from the edge. "I didn't know you didn't know. That you didn't see it coming."

I couldn't lift my head. The ache in my chest twisted deeper, raw and unbearable. "*I didn't know*," I whispered, though my voice trembled. "*Not until now.*"

Her steps brought her closer, deliberate but slow, as though she didn't want to startle me. "*You weren't lying*," she murmured, more to herself than to me. "*You weren't keeping anything from us.*"

I glanced up at her briefly, searching her expression for the mistrust I'd grown used to. But it wasn't there anymore. Instead, there was something I hadn't seen in her before—understanding. She lowered the knife slightly, her knuckles no longer white from gripping it.

"You didn't know Jonah had become Raven," she said plainly, her voice steady but softer than I expected. "And now that you do—you know what it feels like."

I nodded faintly, my chest tightening further as her words sank in. "It's the same thing you've carried your whole life," I said quietly. "The weight. The pain. The fear."

Her gaze didn't waver, but it softened further. "It doesn't make it easier," she said. "But now... I see you."

The words hung in the air, and for the first time since we entered the swamp, I felt something shift between us. Her anger had always burned sharp and unyielding, but now it had twisted into something else entirely— a quiet acknowledgement, a shared burden.

She let out a sharp breath, lowering her knife completely as she stepped closer. "You okay?" she asked quietly, her voice softer than I'd ever heard it.

I couldn't answer. My chest felt hollow, my thoughts tangled in the storm Raven had unleashed. "Let's just keep moving," I said finally, though my voice barely felt like my own.

Joshua didn't speak. He started walking, his steps slow and uneven, his hollow eyes darker than before. Gillie hesitated for a moment before following him, her expression guarded as she glanced back at me. I trailed behind them, the coin digging into my palm like a lifeline—but even that couldn't hold back the ache twisting in my chest.

Jonah is dead. Raven remains.

The swamp seemed darker now, its presence heavier, more oppressive, as though it knew the truth had already begun to destroy us.

A Dangerous Deal

The mist curled tighter around us as we pressed forward, its tendrils clinging to the air like something alive. Every step felt heavier, the swamp itself seeming to resist our progress. The oppressive silence was broken only by the soft crunch of leaves beneath our boots, but even that sound felt swallowed by the haze.

Then, out of the quiet, a voice slid through the air—soft, almost soothing. "You've come so far," it said, wrapping around us like silk. "But the hardest part is yet to come."

Gillie stopped first, her knife already in her hand, her sharp gaze cutting through the mist. Joshua froze beside her, his hollow eyes widening as the figure emerged from the fog.

Elana.

Her appearance was different now—less overtly threatening, more restrained. The shadows still clung to her like a second skin, but her expression was soft, almost kind. She raised her hands in a gesture of mock surrender, her dark eyes gleaming with something unreadable. "I come as a friend," she said softly. "Or, at least, as someone who can help."

"Help?" Gillie scoffed, her tone sharp. "That's rich, coming from you."

Elana's lips curved into a faint smile, and she tilted her head. "I know you don't trust me," she said, her voice low and measured. "But the path ahead will destroy you without guidance. I can give you that. I can show you the way."

Gillie's grip on her knife tightened, but it was Joshua who spoke first. "What way?" he asked, his voice shaky, uncertain.

Elana turned to him, her gaze softening as she stepped closer. "The way forward," she said, her tone almost tender. "The answers you've been seeking—the truth you've been chasing. It doesn't have to be this hard, Joshua. You don't have to keep suffering."

Her words hung in the air like a lullaby, and for a moment, Joshua seemed to falter. His hollow eyes flicked to Gillie, then back to Elana, doubt twisting across his face. "You know the truth?" he asked quietly, his voice trembling. "About the bells? About Grace?"

Elana nodded slowly, her smile deepening. "I know everything," she said. "And I can help you—if you let me."

Gillie moved between them, her knife glinting in the dim light. "Don't listen to her," she snapped, her voice cutting through the tension. "She's trying to play you. She's working for Marcus. You know that."

Elana's gaze shifted to Gillie, and the softness in her expression hardened ever so slightly. "And what has your stubbornness gotten you so far?" she asked, her tone sharp now. "Pain? Loss? You think you're protecting them, but all you're doing is dragging them further into the dark."

Gillie's jaw tightened, and she took another step forward, her voice rising. "Grace told us the swamp doesn't allow shortcuts," she said firmly, her words cutting through the mist like a blade. "You're lying. You're trying to twist this, just like you always do."

Elana's smile didn't falter, but her eyes gleamed with something sharper now—something dangerous. "Grace," she said softly, almost mockingly. "She was wise, yes. But she didn't tell you everything, did she? The swamp doesn't allow shortcuts for those who don't know the way. But I do. I've walked this path before. I've seen what lies ahead. And I can guide you through it."

Joshua hesitated, his gaze flicking between Gillie and Elana, uncertainty etched across his face. "What if she's telling the truth?" he asked, his voice barely above a whisper.

"She's not," Gillie snapped, her grip on the knife tightening. "She's trying to manipulate you. Don't fall for it."

Elana sighed dramatically, shaking her head. "Your pride will be your downfall," she said, her voice quiet but firm. "You think you're strong, Gillie, but you're not. None of you are. And when this swamp devours you, you'll wish you'd taken my offer."

"Enough," Gillie snapped, her patience clearly wearing thin. "Get out of our way, or I'll make you."

"Gillie, wait," Joshua said suddenly, stepping between them. "What if she's telling the truth? What if she really can help us?"

Gillie's expression darkened, and she turned to him, her tone fierce. "She's not here to help us, Joshua. She's here to manipulate us. That's what she does."

Elana smiled faintly, a hint of mockery in her gaze. "Perhaps," she said softly. "But manipulation is only effective if there's truth in it. Isn't that right, Joshua?"

Joshua hesitated, his hands trembling at his sides as doubt flickered in his hollow eyes. Gillie saw it—felt it—and she stepped forward, blocking Elana's view of him. "You don't get to do this," she said, her voice low and dangerous. "You don't get to twist him against us."

Elana's smile widened, a flash of amusement in her dark eyes. "Twist him?" she repeated, her tone mocking. "Oh, Gillie, I don't need to twist anyone. Your faith in each other will be your undoing."

The words sent a chill through the clearing, sharp and unrelenting. Gillie didn't wait for Elana to say more—she lunged, her knife flashing in the dim light. But Elana was faster. She melted into the mist just as Gillie's blade cut through the air, her laughter echoing like the toll of a bell.

"Remember my words," she called, her voice fading as her form disappeared. "The darkness is patient. And so are we."

The mist surged back in her absence, heavier and colder than before. Gillie let out a sharp breath, lowering her knife as she turned to Joshua, her expression hard. "You can't keep hesitating like that," she said, her voice sharp but not unkind. "She's trying to tear us apart."

Joshua didn't respond. His gaze lingered on the spot where Elana had vanished, his hollow eyes clouded with confusion and doubt.

"Let's go," I said finally, breaking the tense silence. The weight of Elana's warning twisted in my chest, her words echoing through my thoughts like a shard under the skin. "We can't let her distract us."

Gillie nodded reluctantly, and we started forward again, the path ahead darker, heavier. But her words lingered, hanging in the air like smoke.

Your faith in each other will be your undoing.

The Shadows Close In

The path ahead felt heavier, each step pressing deeper into the damp earth, but none of us spoke at first. Elana's words hung in the air, twisting through my thoughts like an echo that refused to fade. Your faith in each other will be your undoing. It was a warning—or maybe a challenge—and it struck a nerve I couldn't shake.

Gillie broke the silence first, her grip tightening on the knife she'd just retrieved from the muck. "She doesn't know anything about us," she said firmly, her voice cutting through the tension like a blade. "Our faith in each other is why we're still here. It's why we've made it this far."

Joshua hesitated beside her, his hollow eyes flicking between the mist ahead and the spot where Elana had vanished. "*What if she's right?*" he murmured, his voice quiet, almost trembling. "*What if trusting each other makes us weaker?*"

Gillie spun toward him, her expression hard but not unkind. "No," she said sharply. "That's what she wants you to think. She's trying to break us apart, Joshua. If we start doubting each other, we'll fall right into her trap."

Her words were steady, resolute, but there was an edge to her tone—a frustration she couldn't quite hide. Joshua's doubt seemed to weigh on her, pressing against the determination she was clinging to. "Look at what we've been through," she continued, her voice softening slightly. "We've faced Marcus, the swamp, Raven—all of it. We haven't fallen yet. That's because we trust each other."

I glanced at Joshua, his shoulders slumped, his gaze clouded with uncertainty. I could see the weight of Elana's offer pressing on him, twisting through his thoughts like a vice. "She wants us to turn against each other," I said quietly, speaking into the space between them. "But she's wrong. Faith in each other isn't a weakness—it's our strength. It's the only thing keeping us from falling apart."

Joshua looked at me, and for a moment, there was something in his eyes—a flicker of understanding, maybe even hope. "You really believe that?" he asked, his voice barely above a whisper.

"Yes," Gillie and I answered in unison, the force of our conviction filling the silence that followed.

The tension between us eased, just slightly, but the weight of Elana's warning lingered. It wasn't something we could simply brush aside—not with the path ahead growing darker, heavier.

And as the mist thickened around us, a flicker of movement caught Gillie's attention. She stopped abruptly, her knife glinting faintly in the dim light as her sharp eyes darted between the shadows. "They're back," she said grimly, her voice steady, but her posture tense.

Joshua froze beside her, his hollow eyes widening with fear. I clenched my fingers, the sharp sting cutting through the haze as the shadows began to close in around us. There were more of them this time, their movements bolder, more aggressive, as though emboldened by something unseen.

The first toll of the bell came then, loud and commanding, cutting through the mist like a blade. The sound reverberated in my chest, sharp and relentless, disorienting me for a moment. The shadows surged forward in response, their jagged forms flickering violently as they advanced.

"Stay together!" Gillie shouted, stepping in front of Joshua and raising her knife. Her voice cut through the chaos, firm and unyielding, but the tension in her posture betrayed the fear she was trying to suppress. "Don't let them separate us!"

The shadows didn't hesitate. They lunged toward us with an aggression we hadn't seen before, their movements erratic and chaotic. Gillie met the first one head-on, her knife flashing in the dim light. But this time, something was different. The blade glowed faintly as it struck, a sharp, radiant edge cutting through the shadow like it was tearing apart smoke. The creature recoiled with a distorted hiss, its form flickering violently before dissipating into the mist.

Another toll rang out, louder and more resonant, as though the bell itself was drawing nearer. The sound rattled through my skull, throwing off my balance, and I stumbled backward just as one of the shadows darted toward me. I barely managed to raise my arm in time to block its swipe, the force of the impact sending a sharp jolt through my body.

"Hold your ground!" Gillie yelled, slashing at another shadow as it lunged for her. Her movements were precise, calculated, and the knife—now imbued with Grace's light—seemed to cut through the darkness itself. For every shadow she drove back, two more seemed to take its place, but the blade's glow didn't falter.

Joshua was frozen, his eyes locked on the shifting figures as though he couldn't look away. "Joshua!" I shouted, my voice cutting through the cacophony. "Move! Don't just stand there!"

But he didn't move. The shadows pressed closer, their flickering forms surrounding him, and for a moment, I thought they would consume him entirely. Then another toll echoed through the clearing, shaking the very ground beneath our feet, and the shadows recoiled slightly, their shapes flickering with an unnatural light.

Joshua staggered back, his breaths shallow and rapid, but he still didn't speak. Gillie darted to his side, her knife slashing through the air as she drove the shadows away from him. The blade's glow flared with each strike, the light cutting through the darkness like a beacon. "Snap out of it!" she barked, her tone fierce. "We can't protect you if you don't move!"

The bell tolled again, louder this time, its resonance twisting through the air like a physical force. The sound made my head spin, disorienting me as the shadows surged forward once more. They moved in unison now, their aggression more coordinated, as though responding to an unseen command.

"They're working together," I said, my voice strained as I dodged another attack. "It's Marcus. He's controlling them."

Gillie let out a sharp breath, slashing at a shadow that had crept too close. The knife's light flared again, and the shadow dissolved into the mist with a guttural hiss. "We figured that out already," she snapped, though her tone lacked its usual bite. "Any ideas on how to stop him?"

The shadows pressed closer, forcing us into a tight circle as we fought to hold our ground. Their distorted forms flickered and shifted, their attacks relentless. The tolling of the bell grew louder with each strike, its sound pounding in my chest like the beat of a war drum.

And then, amidst the chaos, Marcus's voice slid through the air like a whisper wrapped in silk. "You're unraveling," he said, his tone smooth and mocking. "Your trust is fragile. Your resolve is breaking. It's only a matter of time before you turn on each other."

The words sent a chill through me, sharper than the cold of the swamp. I glanced at Gillie, her jaw clenched as she slashed at another shadow, and then at Joshua, his hollow eyes clouded with fear. The tension between us was palpable, Marcus's influence winding through it like a poison.

"Don't listen to him!" I shouted, my voice rising above the toll of the bell. "He's trying to tear us apart!"

The shadows hesitated for a moment, their movements faltering as though responding to my defiance. But the bell tolled again, louder and more resonant, and they surged forward with renewed aggression, their shapes twisting into jagged, chaotic forms.

Gillie raised her knife higher, the faint glow of Grace's light reflecting in her determined eyes. "We're not done yet," she said fiercely, her voice cutting through the chaos. "We keep moving. We don't stop. Not for him. Not for anything."

Her words were enough to pull me back from the edge. I tightened my grip on the coin, its sharp edges grounding me as I stepped forward, striking out at the nearest shadow. Joshua hesitated for a moment longer before finally following, his movements slow and uncertain but deliberate.

The shadows pressed closer, their attacks relentless, and the tolling of the bell grew louder, reverberating through the air with a weight that threatened to crush us. But Gillie didn't falter. Her knife cut through the darkness, its faint glow defying the chaos surrounding us. I followed her lead, each step driven by the determination in her voice, the quiet strength in her resolve.

Joshua moved cautiously, his steps unsteady but deliberate, as though something deep within him had begun to stir. The swamp seemed to pull at us with every breath, but we didn't stop. We couldn't stop. Whatever lay ahead, we would face it—together.

The sound of the bell faded into the distance, replaced by the steady rhythm of our footsteps. The shadows receded, retreating back into the mist like smoke dissipating into the air. For a moment, there was silence. But it wasn't peace—it was the calm before something far greater. The swamp wasn't done with us.

And neither, it seemed, was Grace.

Grace's Quiet Pain

The aftermath of the attack left us shaken and battered. The shadows had retreated, dissolved into the mist, but their presence lingered like a cold stain on the air. The tolling of the bell had faded into silence, yet its resonance still hummed faintly in my chest, like an echo that refused to leave.

Gillie leaned against a tree, her knife still in hand, its edge smeared with the remnants of whatever substance the shadows left behind. She let out a sharp breath, glancing at Joshua, who stood a few paces away, his shoulders hunched and his gaze locked on the ground. He hadn't said a word since the shadows withdrew.

"Joshua," Gillie said quietly, her voice softer than usual but edged with concern. "You okay?"

He didn't answer. The hollow look in his eyes had deepened, as though the weight of everything—the swamp, the shadows, the tolls—was finally crushing him. Gillie sighed, a quiet curse slipping from her lips, and turned to me, her frustration barely masked. "He's worse than before," she said flatly. "Whatever Elana or Marcus did to him, it's getting to him."

I didn't have a response. My chest felt tight, the echoes of Marcus's mocking voice still twisting through my mind. Before I could gather my thoughts, the mist shifted again.

A soft glow flickered to life at the edge of the clearing, faint at first but growing steadier. Grace stepped forward, her luminous form fragile yet unyielding, her presence cutting through the haze like a fragile beacon. She moved with the same quiet grace as before, her sorrowful gaze sweeping over us.

Gillie stiffened, her hand moving instinctively toward her knife. "Is it her?" she muttered under her breath, though she didn't sound as doubtful as she usually did.

"*It's her,*" Joshua whispered, his voice barely audible. His eyes widened, the hollow darkness in them flickering for the briefest moment.

Grace stepped closer, her sorrowful gaze landing on Joshua first. Her expression softened, but the sadness in her eyes seemed deeper, heavier. "You've endured much," she said quietly, her voice weaving through the stillness like a thread of light. "But your path is far from over."

Joshua's gaze faltered, and his hands trembled at his sides. "Why does it have to be this way?" he asked, his voice cracking. "Why does it feel like—like I'm walking this path alone?"

Grace flinched slightly at his words—so subtle it might have been missed, but it was there. Her glow dimmed just a little, and she hesitated before speaking. "*You were never meant to walk it alone,*" she murmured, her voice so soft it was almost swallowed by the mist.

The words lingered, heavy and unspoken, as she turned her gaze to the rest of us. "Your bonds must hold," she said, her voice steadying slightly. "You may stumble, you may fall, but only together can you stand again."

Gillie closed the distance, her tone cautious but firm. "And what about him?" she asked, nodding toward Joshua. "Is he supposed to carry everything for the rest of us?"

Grace's gaze lingered on Gillie for a moment before shifting back to Joshua. She didn't answer Gillie's question directly. Instead, she stepped closer to Joshua, her hand hovering near him but never quite reaching. "You carry more than your share," she said softly, her light flickering as if straining against an unseen force. "But strength doesn't come from bearing it alone."

Joshua didn't respond, but his shoulders hunched further, his breath trembling as though her words had struck something deep inside him. Grace's sorrow deepened, her glow dimming further.

The mist began to swirl around her, pulling at the edges of her form. She looked back at us one last time, her expression unreadable but heavy with meaning. "You must hold on," she said, her voice growing fainter as the haze started to reclaim her. "The swamp takes everything—but it cannot take what you refuse to give."

And then she was gone, her light vanishing into the mist like a whisper carried off by the wind. The clearing felt darker, colder in her absence, the silence pressing down on us like a weight.

Joshua didn't answer. But his jaw clenched, just slightly, and his fingers twitched at his side—like something inside him was beginning to stir, even if he didn't know what to do with it yet.

Gillie let out a sharp breath, running a hand through her hair as she turned to me. "Well, that was… cryptic," she muttered, though her voice lacked its usual edge. She glanced at Joshua, who still hadn't moved. "You think he's going to be okay?"

I didn't answer right away. Grace's words echoed in my mind, twisting through my thoughts like a splinter. He was never meant to walk this path alone. My fingers curled against my palm, the pressure sharp, grounding me as I tried to steady myself.

"He'll have to be," I said finally, though the words felt hollow. "We all will."

Joshua turned then, his movements slow and hesitant, his gaze fixed on the path ahead. Without a word, he started walking, his steps uneven but deliberate. Gillie and I exchanged a glance before following him, the weight of Grace's quiet pain lingering in the air like a shadow.

Purgatory's Reflections

Olivia's Beauty

The swamp shifted as we trudged onward, its oppressive grip on the air momentarily easing. The thick mist parted slightly, revealing a clearing bathed in a faint, ethereal glow. The clearing felt—different. The weight of the swamp lessened here, replaced by an almost peaceful stillness that felt out of place amidst the chaos.

Gillie hesitated, her steps faltering as the glow intensified. It seemed to draw her in, tugging at something deep within her—a memory, a feeling she couldn't name. The air itself seemed to hum softly, almost soothingly—carrying the impossible scent of sun-drenched linen and baking stone, like the porch of a house that never existed. The faint outline of a figure began to form in the center of the light.

"Gillie," the voice called, soft yet unmistakable. It carried a warmth that cut through the swamp's cold, a voice she thought she'd never hear again. The figure solidified, and there she was. Olivia.

Her grandmother's presence was as Gillie remembered—poised, graceful, her sharp eyes twinkling with wisdom. She stood amidst a vision of lush fields that stretched endlessly, their vibrant greens swaying gently under a sun that seemed impossibly warm. A crystal-clear river ran through the scene, its water sparkling like glass, and the sky above was a tapestry of endless blue and shimmering stars, even in the daylight.

Gillie's breath caught in her chest as she took a halting step forward, her knife lowering as her resolve softened. "*Grandma?*" she whispered, her voice trembling.

Olivia turned toward her, a small, knowing smile gracing her lips. "It's been a long time, Gillie," she said, her voice steady and full of warmth. She gestured to the field around them, her movements slow and deliberate. "Do you remember? This is the world we had before The Fall."

Gillie swallowed hard, her throat tightening as memories she had buried for so long surged forward. The stories Olivia had told her as a child—the tales of a world untainted by ruin, of a time when rivers weren't choked with ash and the skies weren't darkened by decay. She had clung to those stories as a child, even when reality seemed to render them impossible.

"It was beautiful," Gillie said softly, her voice barely above a whisper. Her gaze flickered to the river, the fields, the stars above, each one stirring something in her chest she hadn't felt in years—hope.

Olivia's expression grew wistful, her gaze lingering on the river as if she could see the memories reflected in its surface. "It was more than beautiful," she said. "It was a promise. A glimpse of what could be, if we fought for it. If we believed in it."

Gillie's jaw tightened, her grip on her knife tightening slightly. "That world's gone now," she said bitterly. "The Fall took it. The swamp took it."

Olivia turned to her, her sharp eyes meeting Gillie's with a quiet intensity. "Perhaps," she said gently. "But redemption is never beyond reach. Even here, in the darkest places, the light can still shine."

The words settled heavily in the air, twisting through Gillie's thoughts like a thread she couldn't unravel. She looked back at her grandmother, her gaze searching. "Why are you here?" she asked, her voice cracking. "Why now?"

Olivia stepped closer, reaching out as though to touch Gillie's cheek. The gesture was fleeting, her hand stopping just short of contact, but the warmth it radiated was undeniable. "Because you needed to be reminded," she said softly. "The fight you're waging—it's worth it. The world may not look as it did, but its beauty isn't gone. It's waiting. It's waiting for someone strong enough to find it again."

Gillie's breath hitched, her chest tightening as tears pricked the corners of her eyes. She looked away, her jaw clenching as she tried to steady herself. "It's too much," she said finally, her voice strained. "We've lost too much. And I'm not strong enough."

Olivia smiled, her expression both tender and resolute. "You're stronger than you know, Gillie," she said. "You've faced the worst this world has to offer, and yet you stand. That is strength. That is hope."

The clearing began to shimmer, the vision of the fields and rivers rippling as though caught in a breeze. Olivia's form flickered, her glow growing fainter, but her voice remained steady, unwavering. "Promise me," she said softly, "that you'll keep fighting. That you'll carry the promise of this world forward."

Gillie's grip on her knife loosened, and she nodded slowly, her voice quiet but firm. "I promise."

Olivia's smile deepened, the light around her glowing with warmth as the lush fields and vibrant sky held steady, untouched by the swamp's darkness. Gillie stood rooted to the spot, her gaze fixed on her grandmother and all the beauty around her, absorbing every word, every nuance of the moment. There was a strength in her now—a quiet, growing resolve that Olivia seemed to nurture with her presence.

"Remember this," Olivia said gently, her voice steady and sure. "The world's beauty isn't gone. It's waiting—for you to find it again and bring it back."

Gillie hesitated, her grip tightening on the knife as her gaze flicked between Olivia and the idyllic landscape surrounding them. The warmth of the vision was a refuge, a balm against the darkness she'd been battling for so long. But the weight of Olivia's words pressed heavily on her, pulling her in opposing directions.

"I…" Gillie started, her voice faltering. She looked back at Olivia, her uncertainty written plainly across her face. She wanted to move forward, to find the strength Olivia saw in her—but something held her back, a doubt she couldn't shake.

The pause stretched, and Olivia's expression shifted subtly, her smile thinning. "Gillie," she said, her tone soft yet edged with urgency. "You must go. Time is running out. If you don't act now, this beauty—the promise of what the world could be again—may never return."

But Gillie couldn't bring herself to move, her boots planted firmly in the lush grass. The vision seemed to shimmer faintly, almost imperceptibly, as if responding to her hesitation. Joshua and I exchanged a glance, the tension in the air twisting like a thread pulled too tightly.

"I can't," Gillie whispered, her voice barely audible. "What if I fail? What if I can't bring this back?"

Olivia's Disappointment

The lush fields surrounding them flickered once, twice—and then began to darken. The vibrant greens dulled to gray, the river slowed to a murky trickle, and the stars above flickered out one by one. The air thickened, colder and heavier, as shadows pressed in from every side. Olivia remained where she stood, but the glow surrounding her dimmed, her radiant form growing sharper, harder.

Gillie staggered back as the warmth seeped away, the idyllic vision crumbling into shadow. "*Grandma?*" she whispered, her voice trembling. "*What's happening?*"

Olivia turned to her, and Gillie's breath caught sharply in her chest. The softness in her grandmother's eyes was gone, replaced by a piercing gaze that seemed to strip away every layer of her defenses. Olivia's expression hardened, her features etched with disappointment.

"What's happening?" Olivia echoed, her tone sharp and cutting. "That's what I'd like to ask you, Gillie."

The words hit like a blow, sharp and unforgiving. Gillie blinked, her grip on her knife faltering as she took a step back. "What do you mean?" she asked, her voice cracking.

Olivia gestured to the withering landscape around them, her movements deliberate and unrelenting. "Look at what's become of our world," she said, her tone harsh but steady. "The Fall took so much, but it didn't take everything. The promise of redemption remains, yet you…" she paused, her gaze hardening further "you've done nothing to break the curse that holds us."

Gillie flinched, the weight of the accusation pressing down on her like an iron hand. "That's not fair," she said, her voice low but strained. "You don't know what it's been like… what we've been through."

"I know more than you think," Olivia countered, her tone icy. "I know that promises without action mean nothing. What good is a promise, Gillie, if it doesn't save anyone?"

The words twisted in the air, cutting through Gillie's defenses with a precision that left her reeling. Her chest tightened, and she looked away, unable to meet Olivia's piercing gaze. "I'm trying," she said weakly, her voice barely above a whisper. "I'm trying, but it's… it's too much."

"Trying isn't enough," Olivia snapped, her voice rising. "You carry the weight of our family, of everything we've lost, and yet you hesitate. You doubt. You fail to act when it matters most."

Gillie's hands trembled at her sides, her grip on the knife faltering further. "I'm not strong enough," she admitted, the words spilling out before she could stop them. "I can't… I don't know how to fix this."

Her knees threatened to buckle, a tremor rippling through her limbs like the earth itself had turned on her.

Olivia stepped closer, her presence towering despite her slight frame. "Strength isn't about knowing how," she said sharply. "It's about refusing to let the darkness win. It's about choosing to fight, even when it feels impossible. You've forgotten that, Gillie. You've let the swamp's lies get to you."

The clearing shimmered again, the withered fields crumbling further into shadow as Olivia's form flickered. Her voice softened slightly, though the sharpness never left it entirely. "I believed in you," she said quietly, her tone heavy with unspoken emotion. "But belief alone isn't enough. You have to believe in yourself. Do you?"

Gillie's breath hitched, her chest twisting painfully as her grandmother's words bore into her. She opened her mouth to respond, but no sound came out. The doubt twisted tighter, coiling around her resolve like a vice.

The vision began to dissolve, Olivia's form fading into the mist as the clearing darkened completely. The last thing Gillie saw was the disappointment etched into her grandmother's face, the sharpness of her words lingering like a wound.

And then she was gone.

Gillie stood frozen, the knife slipping from her hand to the ground as the swamp reasserted its grip on the clearing. The oppressive mist closed in once more, and the warmth of Olivia's vision was replaced by a numbing cold that seeped into her bones. Her breathing was shallow, her gaze locked on the ground where her grandmother's form had disappeared, as though she could will Olivia back by sheer force of will.

"Gillie," I said softly, stepping closer, my voice low and steady. "Are you okay?" I hesitated, unsure if she could even hear me. "You've been the strongest of us—you've kept us together through all of this. If you break…" I trailed off, the weight of my own words hanging heavily in the air.

She didn't respond. When she finally lifted her head, her expression was unreadable, her eyes clouded with something I couldn't quite name. "I'm fine," she said flatly, her voice hollow and distant. But her words felt like a lie, heavy with doubt that seemed to grow darker with every passing moment.

The oppressive silence between us deepened as we started forward again, the bell's faint, mournful toll echoing through the mist. Each step felt heavier than the last, as though the swamp itself had tightened its grip on us.

The bell tolled again, louder this time, reverberating through the air like a distant warning. The mist coiled thicker, colder, pressing against my skin with an almost sentient weight. I stopped, curling my fingers against my palm, the sharp pressure cutting through the haze as a shiver ran down my spine.

The world shifted around me.

The swamp fell away, its oppressive atmosphere replaced by something altogether different. The mist transformed, tightening into dense, shadowy coils that dragged at the edges of my thoughts. The cold deepened, seeping into my bones, and the silence became deafening.

Jonah's Curse

And then it began.

The fragments came first—splintered moments, chaotic and disjointed, flashing like shards of a broken mirror. The swamp was gone, replaced by flashes of something distant yet unnervingly close. Jonah was at the center of it all, his silhouette sharp against the backdrop of fragmented memories.

It was as though the stories I'd heard had come to life. Jonah, the clever and cunning man, the one whose tricks were as famous as his courage. I'd been told of his strength, his resolve in the face of impossible odds, and now, I could see it. His posture was straight, his expression calm yet fierce, his eyes alight with purpose. He carried himself with the kind of quiet confidence that demanded respect, a stark contrast to the chaos and despair I associated with Raven.

I saw him kneeling beside a river, his hands cupped to carry water to his lips. The sun caught his features, illuminating the lines of his face in a way that made him seem almost ethereal. But the moment fractured before I could hold onto it, giving way to something darker.

The river turned to black sludge, the sun disappeared, and the peaceful expression on Jonah's face twisted into something unrecognizable. His hands, once steady, trembled violently, clawing at his chest as though he could tear away what was consuming him. His hollow eyes—Raven's eyes—

burned into mine as his form shifted and twisted. I could feel his agony, his desperation, like it was my own.

The scene shifted again. Jonah stood alone in a vast, unyielding expanse—a place stripped of color and shape, where the ground beneath his feet wasn't firm but felt like it would give way if he moved. The air hung thick and still, pressing down like a weight on his chest, suffocating yet silent.

With each breath, the air slid down his throat like cold oil—coating, clinging, refusing to be swallowed.

The horizon was an endless void, neither light nor dark, a realm of muted tones that stretched infinitely in every direction. It was a space that wasn't alive, but it wasn't empty either. It felt watching—waiting.

There was no sound but Jonah's labored breaths, each one loud against the oppressive quiet, as if the space itself devoured anything louder. He looked around, frantic, his movements disjointed, as though searching for a boundary that didn't exist. His face was twisted in anguish, rage, and grief—the emotions warring within him as the void pressed in from all sides, tightening its hold on his resolve.

And then Marcus appeared.

He emerged from the void like a shadow given form, his presence towering and all-encompassing. The air seemed to ripple around him, bending to his will as he approached Jonah with slow, deliberate steps. Marcus's smile was sharp and cruel, a predator savoring its prey. He stopped just short of Jonah, his gaze piercing and unrelenting, before leaning in close.

The silence deepened as Marcus whispered something in Jonah's ear, his voice low and serpentine. The words were inaudible, but their effect was immediate. Jonah flinched violently, his knees buckling as though the weight of the whisper was too much to bear. His hands clawed at the empty air, his face contorted in a mix of agony and fury. Whatever Marcus had said, it was tearing Jonah apart, unraveling him piece by piece.

But it wasn't just pain Marcus had planted—it was something darker, something insidious. The torment in Jonah's eyes shifted, his grief twisting into something far more dangerous. The light in his gaze dimmed, replaced by a shadow that seemed to consume him from within. His posture straightened, his movements steadied, but the man he had been— the man of clever resolve and fleeting peace—was gone.

The void around them seemed to pulse, alive with the transformation. Jonah's expression twisted into something sharp and predatory, his features hardening into a mask of cruelty. His voice, when it came, was no longer his own—it was layered, resonant, and filled with a malice that echoed endlessly in the empty expanse.

Marcus stepped back, his smile widening as he watched the transformation complete itself. Jonah's form flickered, his silhouette shifting and warping as though the void itself was reshaping him. The torment was gone, replaced by something far worse.

Raven was born.

His form contorted, his features sharp and jagged, his posture hunched like he was carrying an unbearable weight. I watched as his rage consumed him, twisting his movements into something erratic and animalistic. His voice fractured, splitting into overlapping tones as he screamed, the sound reverberating through the vision and piercing through my thoughts.

I staggered back, my chest tightening as the vision continued to fragment. I saw Grace then, stepping through the haze. Her presence was faint, her glow dimmed, but her sorrow was tangible, radiating from her like heat from a dying fire. She knelt beside Jonah—or was it Raven now?— her hand reaching toward him, though she never quite touched him. Her expression was heavy, her gaze filled with an aching grief that twisted my stomach.

"Raven remembers too much and too little," she said softly, her voice echoing in the fractured space. Her words carried the weight of a warning, sharp yet filled with sorrow. "You must understand this, or you will not reach him."

Before I could respond, before I could ask her what she meant, the vision dissolved around me. The fragments of Jonah's life, his transformation, and Grace's sorrow crumbled into mist, leaving me standing in the oppressive cold of the swamp once more.

I steadied my breathing, forcing back the unease clawing at my chest. The weight of what I'd seen pressed against me like a vice. Jonah wasn't just lost—he had been broken, twisted by the swamp and by Marcus's influence. But Grace's words lingered, their cryptic warning refusing to leave my thoughts.

Raven remembers too much and too little.

I swallowed hard, my pulse racing as I tried to make sense of it. How could someone remember both too much and too little? What was left of Jonah beneath the chaos of Raven, and how could I confront him knowing the pain that had shaped him?

"Are you okay?" Gillie's voice cut through the silence, pulling me back to the present. She stood a few feet away, her knife in hand, her eyes sharp as she scanned the mist for threats. "You looked… off."

I nodded, though my movements were slow, hesitant. "I'm fine," I said, though my voice was hollow, the words feeling false even as I spoke them.

Gillie frowned, her gaze lingering on me for a moment longer before she turned back to Joshua, who was standing silently, his shoulders hunched. The tension between us felt heavier than ever, the fractures Marcus had been exploiting threatening to widen with every step.

As we started forward again, the weight of the vision twisted in my chest like a blade. Grace's words repeated in my mind, a haunting refrain that refused to let go. I didn't know what they meant—not fully—but I knew one thing for certain.

Confronting Jonah wouldn't just be about fighting Raven. It would be about facing the man he used to be—the man he might still be, somewhere beneath the chaos. And I wasn't sure if I was ready.

The Bell's Demand

The mist thickened, the weight of Olivia's disappointment and Jonah's torment pressing down on us like an unseen hand. The air felt heavier, colder, and every breath carried with it the metallic tang of the swamp's damp decay. The silence that followed the visions was unnerving, a stillness so absolute it felt as though even the swamp itself had paused.

Joshua lingered a few paces behind, his shoulders hunched, eyes downcast as though the weight of everything threatened to fold him in on himself. But something in the air shifted—faint, almost imperceptible—and his head lifted. Just slightly. Like he heard a voice no one else could.

Then, the bell tolled.

Its sound was different now—deeper, louder, and far more commanding. The thunderous vibration tore through the air, rattling through the trees and driving straight into my chest. It was no longer the distant, mournful chime we'd followed before. This was something immediate, urgent, suffused with an authority that demanded attention.

Gillie staggered slightly, her hand flying to her knife as her gaze darted through the haze. "What was that?" she muttered, though the tremor in her voice betrayed her attempt at composure.

Joshua froze, his hollow eyes snapping to attention as though pulled by the resonance of the toll.

For the first time in hours, he looked like he was ready to move forward—not because he wasn't afraid, but because he was finally choosing not to be.

His hands trembled at his sides, and for a brief moment, I thought he might collapse under the weight of it. Instead, he straightened, his gaze sharpening with a clarity I hadn't seen in days. He didn't speak, but the lines of hesitation etched into his features began to shift into something else. Resolve.

The bell tolled again, the sound even heavier this time, reverberating through the ground beneath my feet. I steadied myself against it, the sharp pressure cutting through the chaos as I tried to hold my ground. My heart raced, the echoes of the bell twisting through my mind like a song I couldn't escape. But beneath the disorientation, a strange steadiness began to take root.

"It's closer now," I said, my voice cutting through the tense silence. "The bell. Whatever it is, we're closer than we've ever been."

Gillie glanced at me, her expression hardening as she nodded. "Good," she said firmly, her grip tightening on her knife. "Because I'm done playing games. If Marcus wants to throw every shadow and trick at us, let him. We're still standing."

Her defiance sparked something in me, a flicker of determination pushing back against the weight of doubt Olivia's vision had left behind. I glanced at Joshua, his hollow eyes still locked on the path ahead, his breathing shallow but steady. Whatever he'd taken from Grace's warning—and Jonah's shadow—it was clear he wasn't going to let it stop him.

The bell tolled a third time, its resonance sharper now, cutting through the haze like a jagged blade. The sound seemed to pull the mist closer, as though the swamp itself was tightening its grip around us.

But instead of faltering, we moved.

Gillie took the lead, her movements sharp and deliberate, her determination radiating with every step. Joshua followed close behind, his gait unsteady but purposeful. I trailed just behind them, the coin in my pocket grounding me as the weight of the bell's demand pressed against my chest.

The echoes of Olivia's accusations lingered, twisting through my thoughts, but I held onto the promise of her earlier words—the memory of a world worth fighting for. Grace's cryptic warning about Raven circled my mind as well, its meaning elusive but urgent, like a puzzle piece just out of reach. The tolling bell seemed to embody all of it: the weight of the past, the chaos of the present, and the uncertainty of the future.

As we walked, the swamp shifted around us, the shadows at the edges of the path growing darker, more defined. The mist carried with it a tension that crackled in the air like a storm waiting to break. And yet, amidst the darkness, our resolve grew.

The bell's thunderous call was both a challenge and a reminder.

Whatever waited ahead would not defeat us—not without a fight.

The next toll rang out, louder and more foreboding than before.

This wasn't a warning.

It was a demand.

And we answered.

The Watchman's Test

Ezekiel's Warning

The swamp's silence shattered—a faint sound in the distance. Soft, deliberate footsteps pressing through damp undergrowth.

Gillie's hand darted to her knife, sharp eyes cutting through the mist. I tensed, scanning for movement. Joshua stood still, his hollow eyes locked ahead.

Then, the figure emerged.

He stepped from the fog as if he had always been there—an older man, gray streaks through his hair and beard. His sharp gaze flicked between us, cautious and worn. A long staff rested in his grip, knuckles white against the wood.

"Stop right there," he said, his voice gruff, tinged with an accent I couldn't place. His gaze swept over us, his hand tightening on the staff. "You've come farther than you should."

Gillie took a step forward, her knife raised slightly. "Who are you?" she asked, wary but steady. "And what do you mean, 'farther than we should'?"

The man tilted his head, his expression unreadable. "Ezekiel," he said simply. "And I mean you don't belong here. Nobody does." He gestured around us with his staff, the motion deliberate and slow. "The swamp doesn't let people walk free—not without a price."

"We're not turning back," I said, stepping up beside Gillie. My chest felt tight, but I forced my voice to stay steady. "Not after everything we've been through."

Ezekiel let out a bitter laugh, shaking his head. "You think that matters?" His tone was sharp. "The swamp doesn't care about your determination or your stubbornness. You think it's going to let you waltz in, get what you're after, and walk out unscathed?" He leaned on his staff, his gaze boring into mine. "It doesn't work that way."

Joshua finally stirred, his hollow voice breaking the tension. "Then why are you here?" he asked quietly, his tone careful. "If the swamp doesn't let people walk free, how are you still standing?"

Ezekiel's expression hardened, and for a moment, something flickered across his face—regret, maybe. Guilt.

"I'm not free," he said flatly, his voice carrying a quiet weight. He straightened, his grip on the staff tightening, his knuckles whitening against the wood. "I walk, I breathe, I speak… but I'm not free. This place is in me, wrapped around me like chains I can't break."

He glanced away, his gaze momentarily distant, as if looking at something none of us could see.

"Every step I take, every word I speak, it's like this place is watching—listening. Sometimes, it's as though it's pulling the strings, deciding how much control I get to keep. And when it doesn't like what I do…" He trailed off, his voice heavy with unspoken dread, before adding bitterly, "It reminds me who's really in charge."

Gillie took a step closer, her knife still in hand but her gaze softening slightly. "Why you?" she asked, her tone edged with suspicion but tinged with curiosity. "Why would it keep you like this?"

Ezekiel exhaled sharply, a mirthless smile flickering across his face.

"Maybe I'm penance," he said bitterly. "Maybe I did something to deserve this. Or maybe it just enjoys watching me try to save people when I know I never can. The swamp doesn't give second chances. It takes, and it keeps taking, until there's nothing left. That's the only truth here."

He squared his shoulders again, his grip on the staff tightening once more.

"I can't leave. I can't die—not the way you think. I'm bound here, stuck between being alive and being something else. And I'll keep patrolling, trying to stop others from making the same mistakes, knowing full well it's not enough."

"And what happens to them?" Gillie pressed, her grip firm around her knife, her gaze unrelenting.

"They stay," Ezekiel said bitterly. "Or worse, they become part of it. This place takes what it wants and leaves nothing behind."

His words settled heavily in the air, twisting through my thoughts like a warning I didn't want to hear. I steadied myself, pushing back against the doubt creeping in, refusing to let it take hold.

"We're not staying," I said finally, my voice resolute. "We're not giving up."

Ezekiel snorted, shaking his head. "You think you're special? That you're different from all the others who came before you?" He stepped closer, his sharp gaze locking onto mine. "You don't know what you're walking into. You don't understand what this place can do."

Gillie squared her shoulders, her voice cutting through the tension like a blade. "Then explain it to us," she said, fierce and unwavering. "If you know so much, tell us what we're up against."

Ezekiel hesitated, his weathered face unreadable. For a moment, I thought he might actually answer, but then he shook his head, his expression darkening.

"It won't make a difference," he said quietly. "You've already made your choice. And the swamp—it doesn't let go."

His gaze lingered on us for a moment longer, the weight of his warning pressing heavily against my chest. Then, without another word, he turned to walk away, his staff tapping faintly against the damp ground. As the mist began to close around him, his voice cut through the heavy air, steady and deliberate.

"I'll be watching," he said. "Watching as the swamp takes what it always does."

Gillie watched him go, her eyes narrowing at his retreating figure until he was just a shadow in the haze.

"Let him watch," she said, her voice firm, cutting through the lingering silence. "He doesn't get to decide for us."

She turned to Joshua and me, her grip tightening as her jaw set with determination.

"He can watch us all he wants," she said, her voice sharp and resolute, "but he'll be watching us succeed where everyone else failed."

Joshua didn't say anything, but his hollow gaze lifted slightly, his hands trembling less as her words hung in the air.

I swallowed hard, Ezekiel's warning still twisting in my chest, but Gillie's resolve seemed to push us forward.

The faint toll of the bell echoed again, deeper and more resonant than before, pulling us into the swamp's heart.

We followed its call, our steps heavy yet deliberate.

Humanity's Failings

Ezekiel's staff struck the ground as he turned to face us, his expression unreadable, his weariness carved deep into his features. It was the look of a man who had seen this same choice play out too many times before, who had long since stopped expecting anyone to listen.

His gaze settled on each of us, the weight behind his stare like the years pressing into his spine.

"I warned you," he muttered, shaking his head. "You don't listen. None of you ever do."

Joshua shifted uneasily, his shoulders tightening, his hands twitching at his sides. His gaze flicked toward the mist beyond Ezekiel, lingering just a little too long. As if he expected something to step through. Or someone. His jaw clenched, and his breath hitched once—then he blinked hard and looked away.

Gillie, unyielding, stepped forward. "You talk like you know how this ends," she said, voice sharp. "Like you know us."

Ezekiel let out a short, mirthless chuckle. "I know enough." He gestured vaguely to the mist swirling around us, voice edged with something dark. "I've seen them—people clawing their way through this place, desperate for an escape, convinced they could fight their way out. People who thought strength, wit, sheer willpower would be enough to defy the swamp."

His voice dropped, just above a whisper.

"You know where they are now?"

He leaned forward slightly, the movement deliberate. "Gone. Some twisted into something unrecognizable, their purpose erased. The others?" His eyes flickered toward Joshua, gaze heavy.

"They suffered the same fate as him."

His grip tightened on the staff, shoulders stiffening, his tone growing colder. "There is no escape. No freedom. The swamp takes what it wants, and if you fail…" He exhaled, the sound slow, bitter. "You don't die. You burn. Stripped of everything you once were. A living death, one breath at a time."

Ezekiel's eyes swept over us again, and the weight of his words pressed heavily against my chest. "You don't walk free from this place," he said bitterly. "You either endure its flames and rise again—or you burn forever."

His words hung heavy in the air, twisting through the oppressive silence like smoke. The weight of his despair was suffocating, and I forced myself to hold steady, pushing back against the doubt creeping in.

"You think humanity deserves saving?" Ezekiel continued, his tone cutting. "Look at what we've done. The Fall wasn't an accident. It was a reckoning. We tore this world apart, and now you think you can just—fix it?" He laughed again, bitter and hollow. "You're more foolish than I thought."

"That's enough," Gillie snapped, her voice slicing through the tension. She stepped forward, her grip on her knife firm, her gaze blazing. "You don't get to stand there and judge us like that. You don't know what we've been through."

Ezekiel's eyes flicked to her, unimpressed. "You think your suffering makes you special?" he asked, his tone cold. "Everyone's suffering. That's all that's left now."

Gillie's jaw tightened, but instead of snapping back, she took a breath, her voice steadying. "You're right," she said. "The world's a mess, and maybe we're part of the reason why. But you standing there, telling us we're doomed, that we're not good enough—how's that any better? What's the point of surviving out here if you've already given up?"

Ezekiel didn't respond immediately. His grip on his staff tightened, and for a moment, something flickered in his expression—guilt, perhaps, or a memory he didn't want to relive. "I'm not here to fix anything," he said finally, his voice quieter now. "I'm here because someone has to watch. Someone has to warn people like you."

"Well, thanks for the warning," Gillie said sharply. "But we're still going."

His eyes narrowed. "Why?" he asked, his voice almost curious. "What makes you so sure this is worth it?"

Gillie hesitated for only a moment before answering, her voice clear and unwavering. "Because I believe in her," she said, nodding toward Joshua. "I believe in the promise she made. And I believe that promise is worth fighting for. That's enough."

Ezekiel's gaze lingered on her, and though his expression didn't soften, he didn't argue. "Belief doesn't mean anything to the swamp," he said bitterly. "It'll take everything from you, belief or not."

"Then it can try," Gillie fired back. She didn't flinch, didn't waver, her resolve as sharp as the knife she carried. "But we're not stopping."

Ezekiel let out a long sigh, his shoulders sagging slightly as he planted his staff firmly into the damp ground. "You're a fool," he said simply, his voice tinged with quiet resignation. "But at least you're consistent."

He didn't move after that. He remained at the swamp's edge, his gaze locked on us with a heavy, unwavering intensity. His expression was hard to read, but there was something about the way his eyes narrowed— not just in disapproval, but in a lingering sense of pity—that made my chest tighten. It felt as though he wasn't looking at us, but through us, already seeing the end of a story we hadn't lived yet.

The silence stretched unbearably as we stood there under his scrutiny. Joshua shuffled uncomfortably, his hollow gaze flicking to the mist around us. "Why's he just standing there?" he muttered quietly, his voice strained. "Like he's already decided."

"Because he has," Gillie shot back, her tone sharp but low. Her knuckles whitened as she gripped her knife, though she didn't draw it again. "He thinks he knows how this ends."

"And maybe he does." The words spilled out before I could stop them, a bitter thought I hadn't realized I was holding. The tightness in my chest grew worse as Ezekiel's gaze lingered, his silence cutting sharper than anything he could have said. It wasn't contempt—not entirely. It was the absence of hope, like he'd already given up on us before we'd truly begun.

Gillie turned her head sharply toward me, her eyes flashing. "He doesn't get to decide that," she said fiercely, her jaw set with determination. She turned back toward Ezekiel, her stare locking with his for a brief moment. "He can stand there all he wants, watching us, judging us—but he'll be watching us succeed where others failed."

Joshua shifted uneasily again, casting a glance back at Ezekiel, whose figure stood unmoving against the haze. "Why does it feel like he's already burying us?" he muttered under his breath, barely loud enough for me to hear.

"Because he's afraid," Gillie replied, her voice firm but tinged with something deeper. "Afraid we might prove him wrong."

She sheathed her knife with a sharp motion, turning away from Ezekiel entirely. "Let's go," she said, her tone leaving no room for argument.

Joshua and I hesitated for a moment longer, the oppressive weight of Ezekiel's gaze still pressing against us. It made the air feel colder, the mist heavier. But when Gillie started walking, her steps deliberate and unwavering, we followed. The swamp seemed darker somehow, heavier, but her resolve burned like a fragile flame cutting through the shadows.

As we moved forward, the sensation of Ezekiel watching us lingered—his presence at the swamp's edge was inescapable, a shadow in the periphery. We could feel him still, his silent judgment trailing after us like a specter.

Grace's Challenge

Ezekiel stood at the swamp's edge, his staff planted firmly in the mud as his gaze stretched out across the mist. The weight of years spent walking these cursed paths was visible in his slouched posture, the weariness in his eyes. The echoes of his bitter words lingered in the air like a fog he couldn't clear.

"You can warn them all you like," he muttered to himself, his voice low and rough. "But they never listen. They never survive."

The mist shifted behind him, so subtly at first that he didn't notice. The faintest glow began to grow, cutting gently through the haze. Then, with a presence so quiet it was nearly imperceptible, Grace stepped forward.

"Ezekiel," she said softly, her voice carrying warmth and calm like a light breeze in the cold.

He stiffened but didn't turn. "Another ghost," he said bitterly. "The swamp likes to torment me with those."

"I'm no tormentor," Grace said gently, stepping closer. Her glow was faint, fragile, but it seemed to radiate a quiet strength that pushed against the darkness around her. "I've come because you need to hear what I have to say."

Ezekiel let out a dry laugh, shaking his head. "Do I? And what could someone like you possibly say that I haven't already heard a hundred times before?"

Grace tilted her head slightly, her sorrowful gaze resting on him. "Perhaps nothing. But perhaps something you've forgotten."

He sighed, finally turning to face her. His eyes narrowed as they settled on her glowing form, his skepticism clear. "You're like them, aren't you? The ones who think they can fix this place. The ones who think they can change what can't be changed."

Grace's expression didn't falter. "I'm not here to fix the swamp," she said simply. "I'm here to remind you of what's worth fighting for."

Ezekiel's grip on his staff tightened, his jaw clenching. "Hope's a fool's game," he said sharply. "I've seen where it gets people. It's not worth it."

Grace took another step closer, her glow brightening slightly. "Hope might fail," she said, her voice calm but firm. "But giving in to despair never saves anyone."

The words seemed to strike something in him, and for a moment, his hardened expression wavered. He looked away, his gaze drifting back toward the swamp. "You don't know what it's like," he muttered. "The things I've seen—the people I've lost. Hope didn't save them. It just made it worse."

Grace's sorrow deepened, but she didn't look away. "I know loss," she said softly. "I know despair. But I also know that the darkness only wins when we let it." She paused, her voice carrying more strength now. "*The fight isn't about survival, Ezekiel. It's about redemption—for those we've lost and for those who are still trapped here.*"

His shoulders sagged, the weight of her words pressing down on him like the years he carried. "And what would you have me do?" he asked quietly, his voice tinged with something that sounded almost like regret. "I'm one man. I can't change anything."

"You can stand with us," Grace said, her gaze unwavering. "You can be part of something greater than yourself. This isn't a fight we win alone— it's a fight we win together."

Ezekiel turned back to her, his expression torn. The bitterness in his eyes had dimmed, replaced by a flicker of something uncertain, something hesitant. "And if I say no?" he asked. "If I stay here?"

Grace's glow brightened, her sorrow giving way to quiet determination. "Then you let the swamp win," she said simply. "But I believe you're stronger than that, Ezekiel. I believe you want something more than just survival."

He stared at her for a long moment, the silence between them heavy with unspoken thoughts. Finally, he let out a heavy sigh, his shoulders lifting and falling as though he were shrugging off a burden he'd carried for too long.

"All right," he said reluctantly, his voice low. "I'll help you. But don't expect me to start preaching hope and light."

Grace's smile was soft, her glow warm and steady. "I don't ask for perfection," she said. "Only that you try."

Ezekiel grunted, shaking his head as he hefted his staff. "You're a strange one, Grace," he muttered. "But I guess it's better than doing nothing."

Grace's light glowed brighter as we moved, her presence steady even as the weight of Ezekiel's doubts lingered in the air—like a distant drumbeat beneath the quiet, or the scrape of memory against stone. His steps were slow, measured, as if each one carried the weight of a decision he wasn't entirely sure he'd made. But he was walking with us now. That meant something.

Still, the swamp had shifted—subtle at first, but undeniable. It wasn't just watching anymore. It was waiting.

A Haunting Threshold

The deeper we pushed, the heavier the air became. The sharp chill pressed into my lungs, my breath visible in the dim light—white, fleeting—yet sweat clung to my skin, damp and unrelenting. My body couldn't decide whether it was freezing or burning.

Grace's glow, once a beacon, began to fade, swallowed by the thickening darkness.

Gillie moved ahead, her grip firm on her knife, her gaze cutting through the shadows as if sheer force of will could reveal what lay ahead. Joshua trailed behind her, quieter than before, his hollow eyes unfocused, lost in something I couldn't name.

I stayed close behind, refusing to let the suffocating air drag me down.

The swamp had changed. It wasn't just hostile—it was restless.

The whispered movements at the edges of my vision had grown bolder, louder. Branches creaked and groaned under the weight of something unseen, skeletal limbs reaching toward us like grasping fingers. The shadows, once passive, now pulsed with intent, shifting ever closer but never quite touching.

Then, faint but unmistakable, the sound came.

It wasn't the bell's thunderous toll—it was quieter, fragmented. A resonance lingering in the air, broken and incomplete, like the remnants of a melody left unfinished.

It drifted through the cold, haunting and dissonant, pulling at the edges of my thoughts.

Joshua stopped abruptly, his breath hitching as he strained to listen. "*The bells,*" he murmured, his voice trembling. "*They're... not whole.*"

Gillie frowned, her grip tightening on her knife. "It's a warning," she said flatly, though there was an unease in her voice she couldn't quite hide. "Or a trap. Either way, we don't stop."

The sound grew faintly louder as we pressed on, each note twisting through the air like a thread pulling us deeper into the swamp's grasp. The darkness grew heavier, the mist swirling with an almost sentient malice. My chest tightened as I forced myself to focus on the path ahead, the weight of what we were walking into pressing down like a vice.

Gillie's voice broke the silence, sharp and commanding. "Stay close," she said, glancing over her shoulder to make sure we were still with her. "Whatever's waiting for us—Raven, Marcus, whoever—it's not going to catch us off guard."

Her determination cut through the oppressive atmosphere, grounding us even as the swamp seemed to push harder against us. But her words couldn't erase the creeping sense that we were being not just followed, but hunted. The shadows pulsed again, shifting closer, their movements now deliberate, purposeful. My pulse quickened, the sharp sting of instinct pressing into me—an unspoken warning I couldn't ignore.

The faint resonance of the bells continued, but this time, there was something different—something more unsettling. It wasn't just the incomplete melody twisting through the silence; it was what followed. At first, it was faint, so faint that I thought I had imagined it. But then it came again, cutting through the mist like a jagged blade.

Laughter.

Low and hollow, it rose from somewhere distant, echoing as if it were carried on the mist itself. The sound wrapped around us, cold and insidious, sinking into my chest and twisting my resolve. It was unmistakable. Raven was coming.

Gillie stiffened at the sound, her grip on the knife tightening as her eyes narrowed. "*His laugh,*" she murmured, her voice quiet but firm. She glanced over her shoulder, her gaze lingering on each of us. "*He's close.*"

Joshua shuffled uneasily, casting a glance toward the shadows pressing in around us. "How many times can we do this?" he asked, his voice brittle. "How many times can we make it through?"

The tension in my chest tightened further at his words. I wasn't sure I could do it again—face the madness, the traps, the torment that Raven always brought with him. My legs felt heavy, my breath uneven, and my thoughts began to spiral until Gillie's voice cut through.

"Focus," she said sharply, her eyes steady. "We've made it this far. That's more than most."

Before I could respond, the swamp shifted again, the ground beneath us softening as shadows writhed along the edges of the path. The air thickened, heavy and damp, forcing us forward until the path abruptly ended.

In its place, a dark, tangled maze rose from the ground—its walls not built, but conjured. Twisted branches and warped stone spiraled upward like something grown in a nightmare, pulsing faintly with a cold, wrong energy. Mist coiled at the edges like skeletal fingers, eager to pull us inside. The swamp closed in behind us, shadows pressing tightly together, forming a barrier that left no other options.

Gillie's gaze fixed on the maze entrance, her expression hardening. "This is it," she said, her voice steady but with a sharp edge. "Raven's games. He always sets the stage."

Joshua shook his head, his hands trembling at his sides. "We're walking straight into a trap," he said, his voice shaking. "There's no way out of that."

"There's no way out of this," Gillie countered, gesturing around us. "The swamp isn't giving us a choice."

The shadows pressed closer, curling around the maze entrance like smoke drawn to flame. And somewhere within them, a whisper slithered free:

"In here, the path doesn't lie. You do."

I froze.

The voice was Raven's—intimate, wrong, like a breath pressed to the back of the neck. He didn't just want to stop us. He wanted Joshua to fail. I could feel it in the air, thick and coiled like hunger. He fed on that failure, that unraveling—whatever was left of Jonah twisted into something that only felt *alive* when it broke others down. Especially him.

I swallowed hard, my chest tightening as I stared at the maze ahead. Its dark, twisted walls loomed like something alive, pulsing faintly with an energy I couldn't name. My instincts screamed to turn back, to run, but there was nowhere to go. The laughter echoed again, louder now, reaching through the air like an unseen hand pulling us forward.

Joshua hesitated, then took a step toward the maze, his shoulders hunched but his movements deliberate. Gillie followed, her knife in hand, her pace unyielding.

I stood frozen for a moment longer, the weight of my fear anchoring me in place. But as the moment stretched, something steadied me—just enough to take the first step forward.

The maze loomed before us, dark and foreboding, its twisted walls seeming to shift and breathe.

And as we stepped into it, Raven's laughter followed—low and echoing, like the breath of something ancient exhaling in delight.

The Price of Hope

The Maze of Doubt

The swamp's oppressive weight deepened as we entered the labyrinth, the lingering echoes of Raven's laughter winding through the air like a cruel melody. It was faint now, a ghostly remnant that seemed to weave through the mist, but its presence was inescapable. With every step, the paths around us twisted and shifted, warping unnaturally as though the swamp itself had breathed life into the maze.

The fog thickened, swallowing the space around us until it felt as though the shadows themselves were closing in, cutting off any hope of retreat. The ground beneath us rippled faintly with each step, unstable and pulsing as though alive, as though the swamp reveled in every uncertain move we made.

Gillie led the way, her knife raised, her posture rigid and deliberate. Even so, I could see the strain in the set of her shoulders, the stiffness in her movements. Joshua trailed just behind her, his hollow eyes darting from one shifting shadow to the next. His shallow breaths were loud in the pressing silence, an audible reminder of the fear we all shared. I brought up the rear, feeling the weight of the moment as it bolstered my resolve against the mounting anxiety within me.

Raven's laughter surged again, louder now, rising from somewhere deep within the labyrinth. It echoed in layers, fractured and cold, wrapping around us with a malice so palpable it felt like a touch. My steps faltered as the sound chilled me to the core, and then his voice followed, slithering through the air like venom.

"We built this place for you," he said, his tone dripping with mockery and glee. "Every twist, every turn, every riddle. It's all for you. Do you like it?"

The words reverberated through the twisting corridors, carried by a voice that seemed to come from everywhere and nowhere all at once. Gillie froze mid-step, her grip on the knife tightening until her knuckles whitened. Her sharp gaze swept the shifting mist ahead as though she could will Raven to reveal himself.

"Where are you?" she demanded, her voice cutting through the laughter with sharp defiance. "Show yourself!"

The laughter deepened, echoing louder. "Why should we?" he said, and the voice seemed to double—one familiar, one distorted. "This is our game. You're just pieces on the board."

I glanced at Joshua, his face pale and stricken, and tried to steady myself. The maze felt alive, twisting and pulsing with every word Raven spoke. The paths around us rippled again, the ground shifting subtly, and the shadows at the edges of the mist flickered, moving as though they were waiting.

"You're trapped," he continued, his tone light and mocking, almost playful. "And the only way forward is through us. Every riddle, every choice—it's all part of the game. *You'll break. Let's find out when.*"

The first riddle came then, carried on the air like a whisper wound from shadows.

"What can run, but never walks; has a bed, but never sleeps; has a mouth, but never speaks?"

The silence that followed was oppressive, the weight of the question pressing down like a physical force. I racked my brain, but the twisting paths and Raven's voice made it almost impossible to think clearly.

"It's a river," I said finally, my voice trembling. "The answer is a river."

For a moment, the ground beneath us rumbled faintly, and the mist seemed to pull back, revealing a sliver of a clearer path ahead. Raven's laughter returned, tinged with mock approval.

"Impressive," he commented, with a hint of amusement in his voice. "Perhaps you're not entirely hopeless. But don't get too confident—the maze doesn't like to be solved."

The shadows surged again, the paths twisting into new, incomprehensible shapes as the labyrinth reasserted its grip. The mist grew heavier, colder, and Raven's voice followed, harsher this time.

"Next question," he said. "What belongs to you, but others use it more than you do?"

Joshua spoke this time, his voice quiet but firm. "Your name," he said.

The labyrinth rumbled, shifting slightly, but this time the mist didn't part as much. The faint path ahead was murkier, and Raven's laughter echoed louder, filled with cruel delight.

"Oh, very good," he said. "But you'll find that cleverness only delays the inevitable. The maze always finds a way to take what it's owed."

The oppressive weight of his words settled over us, and the cracks in our resolve began to show. The shadows pulsed at the edges of the mist, and I could feel the labyrinth feeding on every hesitation, every doubt.

"You think you're strong," he sneered, his voice cutting through the air with precision. "You think your faith will carry you. But trust us—it won't. We've seen so many just like you, and they all break in the end."

The riddles continued, each one sharper and more personal than the last, digging into fears we tried to keep buried. Every wrong answer sent the paths spiraling into chaos, reshaping the labyrinth into something darker, deeper, and more hostile. Raven's taunts never ceased, his voice a constant presence that wound through the air like poison.

"We see you," he whispered, his voice low and cruel. "We see every doubt, every failure, every crack. And we'll wait. We're very good at waiting."

Despite the weight of his words, we kept moving. The faint resonance of bells echoed in the distance—haunting and incomplete—but their discordant chime gave us something to hold onto, no matter how fragile. The maze stretched ahead endlessly, twisting and shifting as Raven's voice lingered, mocking and patient.

The Price of Freedom

The labyrinth twisted and shifted, the paths warping unnaturally with every step. The mist pressed closer, thick and suffocating, and the weight of Raven's presence was suffocating. His voice curled through the air, sharper now, cutting into the silence with cruel precision.

"Freedom comes at a price," he said, his tone both mocking and measured. "Tell us, little wanderers, what are you willing to pay?"

Gillie's footsteps faltered, her knife flashing faintly in the oppressive gloom. "We're not giving you anything," she said sharply, though the tension in her voice betrayed her unease.

"Oh, but you are," Raven purred, his voice wrapping around us like a vice. "The swamp has already started taking from you what you haven't already given away. Can't you feel it? Your faith. Your strength. Your memories. They all slip away, little by little. But if you're willing to let go, we might just help you move forward."

The shadows flickered at the edges of the path, their movements more deliberate now, like predators circling their prey. Then, with a surge of mist, an object appeared on the ground ahead of us. It was small and unassuming—a box, worn and weathered, with edges frayed from years of use.

Gillie froze, her breath hitching audibly. Her knife lowered slightly as she stared at it, her expression tightening. She took a slow step forward, her gaze fixed on the box as though it were a living thing.

Raven's voice softened, his tone almost gentle. "That's yours, isn't it?" he asked, his words laced with faux empathy. "A tie to her. To the stories she told you. To the beauty of the world before it crumbled. But you've carried it long enough, haven't you? Perhaps it's time to let it go."

Gillie knelt slowly, the mist enveloped her as her trembling hands hovered over the box. Her jaw tightened, her breaths uneven as she brushed her fingers against its worn surface. "*What do you want?*" she whispered, her voice barely audible.

"Leave it behind," Raven said simply. "Cast it into the darkness, and the path ahead will open."

Her shoulders tensed, her knife shaking faintly in her other hand. "No," she said, her voice growing steadier. "I'm not giving this up. Not for you. Not for anything."

The Price of Hope

The mist swirled violently, and the box dissolved into shadow as Raven's laughter echoed through the labyrinth. It was cold and cutting, a sound that seemed to ripple through the ground beneath us. "How predictable," he said. "You think your attachments make you strong, but we know better. The swamp always takes what it's owed."

The path ahead shifted, the air growing colder, heavier, and the shadows pulsed with renewed energy. Raven's attention turned to me then, his voice sharper as he said, "And what about you? You've been clutching something, haven't you? Something tied to him. To Jonah. To us. Let's see if you're strong enough to let it go."

My chest tightened, and I felt the coin in my pocket grow impossibly heavy. Its edges pressed into my palm with a weight that felt sharper than ever before. Raven didn't need to say what he wanted—I already knew. The coin wasn't just a memento. It was a tether, a connection to the man Jonah used to be and the choices that had led him to become Raven. Letting go of it felt unthinkable.

"We see how tightly you hold it," Raven said, his voice curling around me like smoke. "But does it really keep you grounded? Or does it weigh you down, pulling you deeper into the darkness?"

My hand trembled as I drew the coin from my pocket, its surface cold against my skin. The echoes of Grace's warning twisted in my thoughts. Raven remembers too much and too little. What would this choice mean— for me, for him, for everything we were fighting for?

I stared down at the coin in my palm, its dull surface gleaming faintly in the suffocating haze. The shadows at the edges of the labyrinth pulsed impatiently, like they were alive, waiting for me to falter. The oppressive silence pressed down harder, and I could feel Gillie's gaze on me—steady and sharp, though she said nothing.

The coin felt heavier than ever, as though it carried the weight of every choice, every failure, every consequence that had brought me here. I didn't want it—not anymore. I wanted to drop it, to let it vanish into the mire of the swamp and pretend it had never existed. But I couldn't. The weight of it wasn't something I could simply abandon. It clung to me, demanded to be borne, whether I wanted it or not.

My fingers tightened around the coin, the sharp edges biting into my skin like a cruel reminder. "No," I said at last, my voice quiet and strained, the resolve in it born not of defiance, but resignation. "This isn't yours to take."

The mist recoiled and snapped back around us, lashing the air like a whip as Raven's laughter rang out again, colder and sharper than before. It cut through the silence like a blade, sending a shiver down my spine.

"Pathetic," he sneered, voice curling with mockery. "You think clinging to that makes you brave? That it gives you power?"

His laughter fractured—each note a splinter of glass in the air. "The maze doesn't reward sentiment. It feeds on it."

The shadows twisted tighter, the labyrinth shifting in protest, reshaping into something more suffocating, more intimate in its malice. The air closed in like a fist, pressing against my ribs.

"You'll splinter," Raven hissed, his voice sliding through the fog like a blade. "They always do. One crack at a time. And when you break—oh, how it devours."

His voice lingered for a moment longer, before fading into the swirling fog. The suffocating silence that followed was heavier than before, and for a moment, I wasn't sure I could move. My legs felt anchored, my chest tight. I hadn't realized my hand was still gripping the coin until the sharp edges bit deeper into my palm, breaking through the haze of my thoughts.

Gillie's voice brought me back, cutting through the fog. "We're not stopping here," she said firmly, though her tone was softer this time—less sharp, more steady. "Not now."

The bell tolled again, distant but clearer now. It wasn't a call—it was a countdown. And I was running out of time.

Joshua said nothing, but his hollow gaze met mine briefly. There was something unspoken in his look—fear, perhaps, or a fragile understanding. Slowly, he turned, his steps tentative but deliberate as he followed Gillie forward.

The path ahead was darker, the mist heavier, but we kept moving. The weight of the coin pressed against me with every step, its edges a constant reminder of what I couldn't let go. And though Raven's voice lingered in the air like a cruel refrain, taunting us with every choice we'd made, we didn't stop.

The Fading Connection

The faint resonance of the bells grew sharper as we moved deeper into the labyrinth, their dissonant chimes slicing through the heavy silence like shards of broken glass. With each step, the labyrinth altered its form, with the paths twisting and contorting in an unnatural manner. The air itself seemed to twist around us, pulling and pressing as though it had a will of its own. It tugged at us, dragging us in different directions until the spaces between us began to stretch.

The ground beneath my feet rippled faintly, unsteady and unpredictable. The mist thickened, swallowing the faint outlines of my companions, while the shadows moved nearer with each breath. I opened my mouth to speak—to call out to Gillie and Joshua—but the words dissolved into the suffocating weight of the fog.

It wasn't until I stumbled forward, reaching for what I thought was Gillie's shape, that I realized we were no longer moving together. The swamp had done what it always intended—it had separated us. One by one, we were drawn into the maze's grasp, the paths pulling us further apart, severing the fragile thread that held us together.

Gillie faltered, her steps slowing as the mist thickened around her. The path ahead was obscured by swirling shadows that seemed to breathe, pulsing faintly with a life of their own. Her grip on her knife tightened, her sharp gaze sweeping the darkness for any sign of the others. But the silence around her was crushing, broken only by the faint sound of her own breathing.

Joshua, too, found himself alone. His hollow eyes darted from shadow to shadow, his pace faltering as the air grew colder and heavier. He whispered something—a name, maybe, or a plea—but the mist swallowed it whole, leaving him with nothing but the sound of his footsteps.

I was the last to realize I had been left to my own path. The weight in my hand seemed to burrow in, a cold ache blooming just beneath the skin, as if reminding me I was never meant to let go. My chest tightened as I glanced behind me, the faint hope of seeing Gillie or Joshua fading into the consuming fog. The shadows around me danced and writhed, their movements taunting, as though they knew I was finally alone.

And through it all, the bells tolled faintly, their chimes fractured and distorted, echoing endlessly through the labyrinth. They sounded like a countdown, or perhaps a warning, as the trials waiting within the maze began to close around us.

Gillie stalked forward through the rising haze, her blade a cold glint in the gloom. The mist thickened until it silenced everything around her. No voices. No movement. Just the thud of her own pulse and the memory of footsteps she could no longer hear.

The silence pressed down like a weight, thick and suffocating, broken only by the faint sound of her breathing. It was the absence, the stillness, that gnawed at her. She hadn't realized how much she'd relied on hearing the shuffle of Joshua's movements or my occasional murmurs until they were gone.

Her grip on the knife tightened as her gaze darted again to the surrounding mist. "Where are you?" she muttered under her breath, her voice clipped but laced with frustration. The swamp had separated them—that much was clear. But the intent behind it felt darker, more deliberate. This wasn't just isolation—it was a trap.

Gillie exhaled sharply, her free hand brushing against her side, and narrowed her focus on the shifting shadows ahead. Her instincts screamed at her to keep moving, to stay alert, to trust in her own strength. Whatever was waiting for her here, she wouldn't meet it passively. But as the haze shifted, a faint movement caught her eye—a figure emerging from the fog, walking toward her with a steady, deliberate pace.

She froze, her heart catching in her chest as the figure grew clearer through the mist. At first, she thought it might be Joshua or even me, but as her vision sharpened, the truth settled heavily into her chest. This wasn't either of us.

It was Olivia.

Her grandmother's presence was unmistakable, but there was something wrong. Olivia's face was solemn, her piercing gaze heavy with disappointment. The warmth Gillie remembered was absent, replaced by a coldness that cut deep.

"You've come so far," Olivia said softly, her voice carrying an edge that made Gillie flinch. "But what have you accomplished, really? Has your promise been kept?"

Gillie swallowed hard, her grip on her knife faltering. "I'm trying," she said, her voice trembling but firm. "I haven't given up."

Olivia's expression darkened, her disappointment deepening. "Trying isn't enough," she said sharply. "You swore to fight for something greater, to carry forward the light we lost. But all I see is someone stumbling through the darkness, clinging to the past."

Gillie's chest tightened, the weight of Olivia's words pressing down on her like a vice. "I haven't failed," she said, her voice breaking. "I… I won't fail."

But Olivia didn't respond. Her form flickered, fading into the mist, leaving Gillie alone with the echo of her words. The path twisted ahead, darker and more treacherous, and Gillie forced herself to move forward, her resolve shaken but not broken.

I found myself alone, the swamp pulling me deeper into its suffocating embrace. The shadows pressed closer, their flickering forms twisting at the edges of my vision. The faint sound of the bells grew louder, their dissonant chime resonating in my chest like a warning I couldn't ignore.

And then he appeared.

Raven stepped from the mist with an unnatural fluidity, his hollow eyes burning as his form shifted faintly in the dim light. He moved with eerie poise, his expression sharp and predatory as he approached.

"We've been waiting for you," he said. "You've come so far, haven't you? But do you even know why you're still walking?"

I clenched my fists, the coin in my pocket digging into my palm. "I know why," I said firmly, though my voice trembled. "I know what we're fighting for."

Raven's grin widened, cruel and mocking. "Do you?" he asked. "You clutch that little coin like it makes you strong. But it doesn't. It's a crack we can dig into. A rot we can feast on."

His words struck harder than I expected, twisting through my thoughts like a blade. "You don't know that," I said, my voice shaking.

Raven laughed coldly, his voice layered and resonant. "We know him better than you ever could," he said. "We're him. And we're more. Jonah is gone. Raven remains. Tell us, wanderer—what are you really trying to save?"

I stared at him, my chest tightening as the echoes of Grace's warning twisted in my mind. Raven remembers too much and too little. The words felt heavier now, their meaning more elusive and urgent. But I forced myself to hold his gaze, refusing to let him see my doubt.

"You're wrong," I said quietly, though the words felt fragile. "He's not gone. He's still in there, somewhere."

Raven's grin faded, his expression hardening as his form flickered violently. "Fool," he hissed, his voice colder now. "You hold onto hope like it'll save you, but it's already slipping through your fingers."

The mist thickened around him, swallowing his form as he disappeared. The path ahead twisted again, and I staggered forward, the weight of his words pressing against my chest like a stone. But I didn't stop. I couldn't.

Joshua stood still as the mist coiled around him, thick and suffocating, muffling the world in every direction. His breaths came shallow and uneven, his chest rising and falling as though even the act of breathing had become a burden. The oppressive silence pressed down on him, more consuming than the shadows shifting at the edges of his vision.

For a long moment, he didn't dare turn, didn't dare move. He clung to the hope—fragile and fleeting—that if he just stayed still, they'd come back. Their comforting presence walking behind him would remind him that he wasn't alone.

But no voices came. The fog only thickened, and the labyrinth twisted in ways his mind couldn't follow. Joshua's throat tightened, panic swelling in his chest as the realization set in. They were gone. Somehow, without him even noticing, they'd slipped away, leaving him stranded in the suffocating grip of the swamp.

"Gillie?" he called out, his voice breaking. It was barely louder than a whisper, hoarse and trembling, but it echoed unnaturally through the mist, warped and hollow. He tried again, louder this time. "Hey! Where are you?"

The silence devoured his words. The mist swirled in response, taunting him with its suffocating stillness. His hollow eyes darted around the shifting darkness, his mind clawing at the edges of his memory. Had they ever been here at all? Had he truly seen them, walked beside them, or had this all been some cruel illusion? A bad dream, so vivid it had tricked him into believing, only to snatch it away?

Joshua's knees threatened to buckle, his trembling hands grasping at nothing. "*No,*" he whispered, his voice shaking. "*No, you were real. I saw you. I… I know I did.*"

But the swamp whispered differently, shadows creeping in and twisting his thoughts. The doubt crept in, sharp and merciless. What if this had all been a lie? What if he'd conjured them out of desperation, imagining the companionship, the hope, just to keep himself moving forward? And now that hope was gone, as fleeting and fragile as the glow of a dying flame.

His breath hitched, his chest tightening further as his mind twisted under the weight of the possibilities. He squeezed his eyes shut, trying to push it all away, to hold onto the memory of them—Gillie's unyielding determination, the presence of another steady figure grounding him when he faltered. But the mist crawled closer, wrapping itself around him, whispering the truth he didn't want to face.

"*This can't be real,*" he murmured, his voice cracking. His hands trembled as he pressed them to his head, trying to steady himself against the crushing wave of guilt and doubt. "*They were here. I know they were…*"

The mist pulsed, and suddenly, through the suffocating haze, a figure emerged. Joshua's breath caught in his throat as he froze, his hollow eyes widening as the shape became clearer. It wasn't Gillie or the comforting presence he longed for—it was someone else entirely.

Grace.

Her glow was faint, almost fragile, but steady, pushing back against the swirling shadows with an ethereal warmth. Her sorrowful gaze locked onto his, and Joshua felt his legs threaten to give way under the weight of his emotions. She stepped toward him slowly, her movements deliberate, her voice soft and gentle.

"Joshua," she said, her tone carrying both warmth and sadness, like a lullaby that tugged at memories he couldn't quite grasp. "You've carried so much."

His lips trembled as he struggled to find the words, his voice catching in his throat. "*Grace,*" he whispered finally, his voice shaking as tears threatened to spill. "*I… I'm so sorry.*"

She lifted her hand, her delicate fingers hovering just shy of touching him. Her sorrow deepened as she met his gaze. "You've nothing to be sorry for," she said gently. "You've done everything you could."

But then her expression shifted, a flicker of something darker passing through her sorrow. Her voice, too, changed—still soft, but with an edge of something colder beneath it. "Have you truly been carrying this alone?" she asked, her tone almost gentle, but laced with sharpness. "Are you sure there's been anyone else, or are you afraid to face the truth that it's only been you all along?"

Joshua flinched, his hollow eyes searching hers in desperation. "What… what are you talking about? I wasn't alone. I…."

Her glow flickered faintly as though the swamp itself was reshaping her. "You've been alone, Joshua," she said, her tone almost soothing, but edged with cruelty. "The swamp takes everything, little by little, until there's nothing left but you. Isn't that what you've been feeling? Isn't that what you've been afraid to admit?"

The doubt surged like a wave, crashing against him with brutal force. Joshua staggered back, shaking his head as her words threatened to tear apart the fragile threads he'd held onto. "No," he said, his voice trembling. "No, I know they're real."

Her glow wavered, flickering violently before surging back. But her expression grew colder, her sorrow twisting into disdain. "The swamp sees your guilt," she said, her voice biting now, colder than before. "It knows your fear. And it will use it to break you."

Her glow dimmed entirely, her form dissolving into the mist as she faded from view. Joshua reached out instinctively, his hand grasping at nothing as the oppressive silence rushed back in around him. He stood trembling, his chest heaving as the weight of her words settled heavily in his mind. But even as the doubt clawed at him, something deeper burned—a defiance, however fragile.

"*They're real*," he murmured to himself, his voice raw but certain, as though saying it aloud could hold the truth in place. "*They're real.*"

Alone once more, Joshua's hollow eyes turned to the path ahead. It was faint, barely visible through the swirling haze, but there was no other way forward. The guilt clung to him like a shadow, twisting his thoughts with every step he took into the darkness.

The Price of Hope

The swamp grew darker as we pressed on, our fragile bonds fraying under Raven's riddles and lies. Every step forward felt like a step deeper into the labyrinth's grip, the shadows pressing tighter, the paths twisting further out of reach. The resonance of the bells grew louder, their incomplete chimes echoing through the mist like a haunting melody that clung to the edges of my thoughts.

The swamp's hold on us wasn't just physical—it was something deeper, something that gnawed at the fragile bonds we had shared. Alone, the weight of Raven's words and the oppressive silence cut sharper, planting seeds of doubt and fear that twisted with each passing moment. Whatever waited ahead wasn't just testing our resolve—it was testing our faith in one another.

Somewhere in the swirling haze, I thought I caught echoes of their voices—Gillie's firm tone, Joshua's wavering murmur. But the swamp distorted everything, twisting sound and sight alike into cruel illusions. The shadows pulsed and writhed, alive with malice, and I couldn't tell anymore what was real and what was another trick meant to break me.

For a fleeting moment, I thought I felt something—a pull, a flicker of connection, a tether that hadn't yet been severed. But it was gone almost as quickly as it came, leaving me standing alone in the choking mist. The weight of the swamp bore down like it wanted to bury me where I stood, and yet, somehow, I pressed forward, each step heavier than the last.

The bells rang again, louder now, their dissonant chime cutting through the suffocating silence. Whatever waited ahead was calling us deeper, and I knew we would have to face it—together or alone.

The Bells Call

The labyrinth released us as abruptly as it had consumed us. The twisting paths that had separated us straightened, the oppressive mist thinning just enough to reveal the clearing ahead. One by one, we stumbled into the open space, the swamp's grip loosening slightly but refusing to let go entirely.

Gillie emerged first, her shoulders squared as if bracing for another fight, but her eyes told a different story. There was a heaviness in her expression, the kind of weight that came from bearing too much alone. The tension in her jaw and the tight grip on her knife hinted at the encounter she wasn't ready to speak of.

Joshua was next. He stumbled through the haze, his hollow gaze darker than before, his steps unsteady. His breathing was shallow, every movement stiff as though the swamp had tried to crush him completely. His eyes darted to Gillie, then to me as I stepped into the clearing last, his expression flickering with something fragile, unspoken.

I was the last to arrive, every part of me aching from the trials I couldn't yet bring myself to acknowledge. The clearing wasn't a reprieve—it was another pause in the swamp's relentless torment—but the sight of them, standing there, was enough to cut through the suffocating weight, if only for a moment.

We didn't speak. The silence was thick, not just with the aftermath of what we had faced, but with everything we didn't know how to say. Relief simmered under the surface, unspoken but undeniable. For a moment, we simply stood there, each of us catching our breath, glancing at one another without lingering too long.

Joshua's lips parted slightly, as though he wanted to say something, but he hesitated. He shifted on his feet, his gaze lowering to the ground. He'd nearly convinced himself he was alone—that we were nothing more than figments conjured by the swamp to taunt him. Now, seeing us here, real and solid, left him unsure what to do with the flood of emotions he didn't dare express.

Gillie broke the tension first. She sheathed her knife with deliberate precision, her posture stiff but controlled. "We've wasted enough time," she said, her voice firm but quieter than usual. She glanced at us, the corners of her mouth tightening almost imperceptibly before she looked ahead. "Let's move."

We fell into step without argument, the weight of the swamp pressing down on us as the mist wreathed tighter. The sound of the bells grew louder, pulling us forward with their haunting, incomplete melody. And though the cracks Raven had left in each of us felt wider now, harder to ignore, we moved as one. For now, that would have to be enough.

Then, the bell tolled again.

Louder. Closer.

Not a call—

A countdown.

And the end was waiting.

It wasn't the dissonant chime we'd heard within the labyrinth—it was something vast and commanding, a presence that seemed to emanate from all around us. My chest tightened as the toll reverberated, a pressure that seemed to echo through my spine.

Gillie flinched but recovered quickly, her grip tightening on her knife. "It's louder now," she muttered, her voice steady despite the tension in it. "Closer."

Joshua didn't speak. His shoulders sagged, his head bowed as though the sound itself was pulling him down. I steadied myself against the force of the bell, its resonance pressing sharply against me, threatening to unravel the fragile hold I had left.

The sound rolled through the swamp in waves, its echo flattening the silence into something brittle. We didn't speak. Even the swamp held its breath. For a moment, the oppressive atmosphere seemed to ease, the mist pulling back slightly, as though even the swamp itself was cowed by the bell's authority. But the reprieve was brief, and as the toll faded, the weight of our experiences settled over us once more.

"Does it ever stop?" Joshua finally asked, his voice barely above a whisper. There was a rawness to his tone, a weariness that made it clear how much the swamp had taken from him.

Gillie's gaze shifted to him, her expression softening, but she didn't answer. Instead, she turned her attention back to the path ahead, which remained as shrouded and uncertain as ever. "It doesn't matter," she said firmly. "We keep moving. We don't have time to stop."

Her words carried a sharpness that wasn't just determination—it was a defense, a way of keeping the doubt Raven had sown at bay. But even as she spoke, I could see the strain in her posture, the weight of Olivia's haunting words clinging to her like a shadow.

The swamp seemed to hum faintly, its presence a constant reminder of how close we were to something greater, more dangerous. The faint resonance of the bells lingered in the air, their echo growing softer but no less commanding. They were a reminder of our dwindling time, a warning that the trials ahead would only grow harder.

I glanced at Gillie, her unwavering grip on the knife, and then at Joshua, his shoulders heavy but his steps steady. Despite everything, we were still here—battered, yes, but still moving. The trust between us was fragile, stretched thin by Raven's manipulations, but it hadn't broken. Not yet.

As the mist began to close in around us once more, the shadow of Raven's games lingered in my thoughts. His taunts, his riddles, his relentless attempts to tear us apart—they weren't just tests. They were warnings. And though we had passed his trials, I couldn't shake the feeling that he wasn't done with us.

The path ahead remained uncertain, the darkness pressing closer with every step. But the bell had called, and we would answer.

The Whisperer and the Silent Child

The Whisperer Awakens

The swamp stretched endlessly ahead of us, its mist thickening with every step we took. The faint resonance of the bells—our constant companion since entering this cursed place—had faded into an oppressive silence. The stillness laced the air with dread, heavy as smoke in our lungs. Then, cutting through the quiet, came the first whisper.

It was soft at first, indistinct, like a distant murmur threading through the fog. But as we pressed forward, the voices grew clearer, sharper, each word carving into the air with purpose. I knew almost immediately that these voices weren't just noise. They were aimed at us.

Gillie was the first to react, her fingers tightening around the handle of her knife. She glanced warily over her shoulder, her sharp gaze cutting through the mist. "Do you hear that?" she said, her voice low, tense.

Joshua didn't respond. He walked stiffly ahead, his shoulders hunched as if the weight of the swamp had finally begun to crush him. Then I saw him falter, his steps slowing as his head tilted slightly to the side.

"Joshua," came a voice, soft yet filled with sorrow. It was Grace's voice, though twisted, unfamiliar in its sharpness. "*You've failed me,*" it whispered, the words carrying the weight of accusations that seemed to press against him like a physical force. "*You abandoned me. You'll abandon them too. That's all you've ever done.*"

"*No,*" Joshua muttered under his breath, his voice breaking. "*That's not true. I'm trying…*"

"Trying?" the voice cut him off, harsher now. "Trying isn't enough. You fail. That's who you are."

He tightened his fists, his head bowing lower, but before I could say anything, Gillie stumbled to a stop just ahead of him. She straightened her back, her posture stiff as though bracing for something unseen.

"*What good is a promise if it saves no one?*" a second voice whispered, this one cutting through the air like a blade. It was Olivia's voice, sharp and cool, each word a carefully placed wound. Gillie's expression didn't change, but I saw her flinch, her knuckles whitening as they tightened around her knife.

"I've done my best," she said, her voice taut with an edge I rarely heard in her. "I haven't given up."

"Haven't you?" Olivia's voice resonated with clarity, navigating through the mist with precise articulation. "You hold onto it like it's enough, but what has it saved? Who have you saved? You've failed them, Gillie. You've failed all of them."

Gillie's sharpness faltered. She didn't respond this time, her jaw locking as she pressed forward, as if moving faster could drown out the sound.

And then I heard it.

It was colder than the other voices, darker, carrying a familiar weight that sank into my chest like a stone. Raven. "You carry our blood," he said, his voice smooth and mocking, wrapping around me like smoke. "You think you're different? You're not. You'll fall, just as we did. You're already so close."

My hand moved instinctively to the coin in my pocket, clutching it tightly. "*I'm not like you*," I whispered, though the words felt small, fragile against the tide of his voice.

Raven's laughter followed, low and cutting, as if he could sense the doubt lingering at the edges of my resolve. "We know you better than you know yourself," he said, his tone almost amused. "And the swamp? It doesn't lie. It shows the truth."

The whispers surged again, louder, sharper, relentless. Their chaotic hum seemed to come from everywhere and nowhere at once. Each word sliced through the air with cruel precision, layering over one another until they were a jagged symphony of malice. I could feel them burrowing deeper, twisting into my thoughts like roots digging into the cracks I'd tried to seal. They weren't just speaking to me—they were invading me.

Joshua's head hung lower as the weight of the whispers pressed against him, his shoulders sagging under the force of their words. "Grace," he muttered, his voice trembling. "No… I didn't abandon you… I'm trying…"

Gillie's movements turned stiff and uneven, her sharpness faltering as the voices clawed at her resolve. Her knuckles whitened around the hilt of her knife, but even she couldn't shake the weight pulling her down. "You're wrong," she hissed through gritted teeth, though her voice cracked. "I haven't given up…"

The whispers didn't care. They grew louder, their words folding over one another, twisting into cruel shapes that echoed endlessly. "Failure. Coward. Useless. Weak. Liar." Their venom cut sharper than blades, slicing through the fragile bonds that tethered us together.

"Focus!" Gillie barked suddenly, her voice sharp as she turned to Joshua. "If you've already given up, just say it. Stop dragging this out."

Joshua snapped his head up, his hollow gaze flicking toward her with a flicker of desperation and anger. "I haven't given up," he shot back, his voice rising. "I'm not the only one hearing things. Don't act like you're holding us together!"

The tension between them tightened like a noose, twisting tighter with every word. The whispers surged again, feeding on the fractures, pressing harder against the fragile space between us.

"Enough!" I said, my voice strained, though I forced it through the chaos. The weight of the moment pressed against me, steadying me just enough to speak. "Fighting each other isn't going to help. It's what they want."

But even as I spoke, I could feel the words falter under the weight of the whispers, their cruel symphony drowning out everything else. The swamp seemed to shiver, restless and alive, as though it was watching, waiting for us to break.

"Keep moving," Gillie muttered finally, though her voice had lost some of its edge. She turned away, her steps deliberate but heavy, her knife held tightly at her side. "It's the only thing we can do."

I followed, forcing my legs forward, though every step felt slower than the last. Joshua lingered for a moment before stumbling after us, his head bowed as the voices carved into his thoughts.

The whispers didn't stop. They pressed harder, louder, their venom seeping into the mist, into the air, into everything. And with each step forward, it felt as though the swamp was closing in tighter, pulling us deeper into its grasp.

The Weight of Silence

The whispers rose to a fever pitch, cruel and chaotic, their words overlapping and splintering until they became impossible to distinguish. What had begun as cutting accusations turned into a cacophony of venom, each voice carving relentlessly at the walls we'd tried to build around ourselves, peeling back the layers of who we were, exposing every doubt, every fear.

And they were loud. Not in volume, but in presence. Each word was a whisper, soft and intimate, but together they grew, expanding, filling every corner of the swamp. It was as if the very air was being spoken into submission. The whispers pushed and pulled, overlapping, becoming a jagged symphony that clawed at our thoughts. My own mind seemed to fracture under the weight of it, the voices too many, too sharp to ignore.

"Useless," one hissed, the word slicing through the fog like a dagger.

"You can't fix this," another sneered, its tone like smoke.

"Failure. Coward. Liar."

The words were no longer directed solely at us—they were at everything. At the swamp, at the air, at the space itself, growing louder and louder until it felt like the whispers might tear the entire place apart. Gillie staggered but didn't stop, her face set like stone, though her eyes flicked nervously to the shadows, her grip tightening on her knife as if the blade could cut through what we couldn't see.

Joshua's head bowed lower, his breathing shallow and uneven. His lips moved faintly, though I couldn't hear what he was saying. It looked like he was arguing with them—or maybe pleading—but whatever he whispered back was drowned in the rising storm of voices. I wanted to reach out, to tell him to keep going, but I could barely move. The sound—

no, the force—of the whispers wrapped around me like chains, pressing into my chest, my thoughts, my very breath.

And yet, even as they grew louder, something else began to change. It was like something older than the swamp itself had begun to stir.

The mist thickened, swirling with a strange urgency, but beneath the chaos of the whispers was something else—a silence. At first, it was small, faint, like a subtle shift in the air, but it grew quickly, pressing outward with an intensity that made my ears ache. It didn't come like sound or movement; it simply was, a presence that emerged without warning or invitation.

The whispers faltered. Not all at once, but in jagged, uneven bursts, like a symphony gone suddenly off-key. "No," one hissed, the word filled with an edge of something new—fear. "Not yet."

The silence pushed deeper, growing heavier, stronger, until it wasn't just in the air but in the ground beneath our feet, in the very space around us. The swamp reacted too—shadows that had lingered at the edges of the mist recoiled as if burned, pulling back toward the places where light couldn't reach. The whispers fought against it, rising in pitch, each word growing more frantic, more desperate.

"Stop this," one voice growled, sharp and guttural.

"You don't belong here," another hissed, breaking into a panicked snarl.

But the silence didn't stop. It pressed further, filling the spaces the whispers had dominated just moments before. The stillness wasn't empty— it was charged, alive, a force that carried weight beyond anything I had ever felt. It didn't suppress the whispers; it erased them, replacing them with something colder, more resolute.

The whispers began to twist, their once—coherent venom splintering into fragmented echoes, like glass shattering under immense pressure. I couldn't see them, but I could feel their agony—something primal in the way they recoiled, shrieking against the silent force that bore down on them. One by one, the voices dissolved into strained murmurs, their jagged edges blunted until they were little more than static on the edges of my mind.

Gillie's jaw tightened as the tension in the air shifted, the oppressive noise retreating into strained pockets of sound. Her knife dipped slightly in her hand, though she didn't lower it completely, her sharp gaze darting to the mist as though searching for whatever force had silenced the swamp's tormentors.

Joshua's chest rose and fell in uneven bursts, his hollow eyes darting from shadow to shadow. The fear etched into his face had deepened, but beneath it was something else—something lighter, more uncertain. Relief, maybe, though he wouldn't show it.

And me? My fingers tightened, but I didn't focus on the pressure—I couldn't. My attention was on the silence itself. It wasn't comforting; it wasn't freedom. It was heavier than the whispers had been, suffocating in its magnitude. The air felt fragile, like it might shatter if any of us spoke, though none of us dared try.

The whispers weren't gone. I could still hear them at the edges of my mind, faint and flickering, but they no longer clawed at us with the same desperate malice. They sounded strained, pained, as though something stronger was bearing down on them. The silence pressed further, pushing them into the corners of the swamp like a tide forcing out debris, and the weight of it felt overwhelming.

And just for a breath—maybe less—I thought I felt something else. Not the child. Not the whispers. Something gentler. Like a breeze that didn't belong. Like the air remembered something older than the swamp.

For a long moment, nothing happened. The swamp held its breath, the mist frozen in place, and the silence stretched taut around us. I felt my pulse pounding in my ears, unnatural in the absence of anything else. The air was so heavy, so thick, it felt like I was drowning in it, and yet I couldn't bring myself to fight it.

Gillie shifted first, her shoulders squaring as she broke through the tension enough to take a single step forward. She said nothing, but the gesture was enough to pull me back into myself, to remind me that we were still here, still moving. Joshua didn't speak either, his gaze flicking briefly toward me before returning to the shadows ahead.

And then, deep within the silence, there was movement.

The Silent Child Appears

The clearing stretched before us, a pocket of stillness surrounded by the dense, restless swamp. The air here felt different—thin yet heavy, like it had been drained of the swamp's oppressive weight but hadn't quite let us breathe freely. The mist, ever-present and alive, seemed to hesitate at the edges of the space, curling lazily as though unwilling to intrude. For a moment, none of us spoke. The sound of the whispers had been unbearable, their venom carving into us mercilessly, but their abrupt absence left a strange void that we didn't know how to fill.

It wasn't freedom, not exactly. The silence wasn't empty; it pressed against us, humming faintly with something I couldn't name. It wasn't the suffocating stillness of the swamp—it was something else. Something deliberate. And then we felt it.

The silence deepened, heavier and colder, rolling outward from the far edge of the clearing like a ripple in water. I felt it before I saw anything— a subtle shift in the air, the weight of it pressing gently against my chest. It wasn't oppressive, not like before, but it was undeniable. It seemed to reach into the spaces the whispers had filled, not replacing them but claiming them. It was power, and it was coming from somewhere near.

That's when we saw them.

The child appeared at the edge of the clearing so suddenly it was as though they had always been there, shaped from the mist itself. They were small, their frail figure wrapped in tattered, faded clothing that clung to their thin frame. Their hair was dark and messy, falling in uneven strands across their face and obscuring most of their features. They didn't move—not toward us, not away. They stood there, utterly still, their presence impossible to ignore.

The silence surrounding us unfolded slowly, like a blanket drawn over the swamp, muffling even thought. It wasn't suffocating, but it wasn't comforting either. It wrapped around us like an invisible shroud, muting everything else in the clearing. My breath hitched as I felt it press against my chest, sinking into my lungs with each shallow inhale.

Gillie's voice was the first to break through, sharp but strained. "Is that…?" she started, her words trailing off as she tightened her grip on her knife. Her gaze was locked on the child, her body tense as though expecting an attack at any moment. "What the hell is that?"

"It's a kid," Joshua said, his voice trembling. He took a shaky step closer to me, his hollow eyes wide as he stared at the figure. "It's… just a kid. What's a kid doing out here?"

"It's not just a kid," Gillie snapped, her tone harsh but quieter than usual. She didn't take her eyes off the child, her knuckles white around the hilt of her blade. "Nothing here is just anything."

We stood frozen, caught in the intensity of the silence emanating from the child. It wasn't just an absence of sound—it felt alive, pulsing outward from them in steady, unrelenting waves. I could feel it pressing into me, filling the space the whispers had occupied only moments before. My pulse quickened, and when I glanced at Joshua, I saw him trembling.

Joshua's lips parted slightly, his breath uneven as he found his voice. "Was it you?" he asked, his words fragile and soft. "Did you stop the whispers?"

The child didn't respond. They didn't move. But their silence was an answer in itself, woven into the air and pressing against us with quiet certainty. It was so unspoken yet so loud that I felt my chest tighten, my hands shaking slightly at my sides. I could see the realization dawning on Joshua's face—whether he wanted to believe it or not, he already knew.

"*You did*," he whispered, his voice catching. He clenched his fists, his hollow eyes fixed on the child. "*You stopped them.*"

Still, the child remained silent. Their stillness felt deliberate, as though their presence alone carried everything they needed to say. Joshua's shoulders stiffened, his gaze faltering as though the quiet itself was forcing him to confront something deeper—something buried.

"I know them," he said suddenly, his voice trembling. He turned slightly away from us, his head bowing. "I've seen them before. Not here. Not like this. But I've seen them."

Gillie frowned, her sharp gaze darting between Joshua and the child. "What are you talking about?" she asked, her voice laced with suspicion. "What do you mean you've seen them?"

Joshua's breathing quickened, his hollow eyes flicking back to the child. "It was... an accident," he said slowly, the words faltering. "I didn't mean for it to happen. They were just... in the wrong place, at the wrong time."

"What are you saying?" I asked, though the question came out quieter than I intended. My own chest felt tight, the silence pressing into my thoughts like it wanted to tear them apart.

Joshua clenched his jaw, his voice breaking as he continued. "I was trying to fix something. I thought… I thought I could make things right. But I didn't see them until it was too late. It happened so fast, I didn't even… I didn't even realize…" He trailed off, his fists trembling at his sides.

Gillie's gaze snapped toward the child, her expression hard but uncertain. "They got hurt because of you?" she asked bluntly, though her voice had lost some of its sharpness.

Joshua flinched at her words, his breath hitching. "I didn't mean to," he said, his voice cracking. "But it doesn't matter, does it? It doesn't change what happened."

The silence around the child seemed to grow heavier, deeper. It wasn't accusing—it wasn't anything at all. It just was. And yet, it pressed into Joshua like a physical weight, forcing him to face what he couldn't ignore.

"I didn't know their name," he admitted, his voice barely audible now. "I didn't even look back to see if they were okay. I just… kept going. And now…" He swallowed hard, his hollow eyes fixed on the child. "Now they're here."

The child didn't react, didn't speak. Their silence remained steady, unwavering, but it carried an undeniable gravity. Joshua staggered back slightly, his breaths uneven, as though the quiet itself was suffocating him.

Gillie shifted uncomfortably, her knife lowering slightly. "Why are they here now?" she asked, her voice quieter but still tense. "What do they want?"

"*Maybe… Maybe they want me to remember,*" Joshua whispered, his voice trembling like a fragile thread stretched too thin. The weight of his words hung in the air, heavy and unresolved, as if even speaking them had cost him something.

Again, the child said nothing. They didn't need to. The silence that radiated from them wasn't empty—it pulsed faintly, alive in a way that defied explanation. It pressed outward, filling the space around us with an unspoken resonance that made my chest tighten and my thoughts falter. There was no malice in it, no accusation, but it carried a weight that settled into our bones. It felt like an answer all on its own—one we weren't equipped to understand but couldn't deny.

Joshua's shoulders sagged slightly, his hollow eyes fixed on the ground. The tension in his posture didn't release; it shifted, drawing inward as though the silence itself was forcing him to confront what he had long tried to bury.

Gillie's voice cut through the quiet, sharp but laced with something unsteady. "What the hell are we dealing with?" she asked, her knife still poised in her grip, her gaze flicking back to the child.

I glanced at the child, my thoughts clouded by the strange pull of the quiet surrounding them. My pulse quickened, and I swallowed hard, trying to push down the mounting tension. "I don't know," I said finally, though the words felt hollow against the charged air. "But it's… something. Definitely something."

"Great," Gillie muttered under her breath, lowering her knife just slightly but keeping her stance guarded. "This just keeps getting better."

The child didn't move—not toward us, not away. Their stillness was unnerving, but it wasn't threatening. It was almost—patient. They stood there as though they had been waiting for this moment, waiting for us to notice what they wouldn't—or couldn't—say. The air around them felt charged with meaning, though none of us could grasp what it was supposed to be.

And then, slowly, deliberately, they lifted their arm. Their movement was so measured it felt calculated, as though every inch carried purpose. They pointed to a path on the far edge of the clearing—one we hadn't noticed before. The trees framed it like a dark, beckoning archway, and the mist thinned just enough to suggest it was the way forward. Their gesture hung in the air, silent but commanding, leaving no doubt that this was their intention.

"They're showing us something," Joshua said quietly, his voice carrying a strange mix of reverence and unease.

"Or leading us into another trap," Gillie countered, her grip tightening on her knife. Her knuckles were white, and I could see the tension rippling through her stance like a coiled spring. "I don't trust this."

"What do we do?" I asked, glancing between the child and the path. My voice wavered slightly, the uncertainty clear in my tone. The feeling of unease increased with each passing second, affecting my thoughts and causing hesitation. "We don't know if they're helping us or…"

"Exactly. We don't know," Gillie cut me off, her tone sharper now. "So why the hell should we follow them?"

"Do we have another option?" Joshua asked, his voice rising slightly, tinged with a desperation that hadn't been there before. He glanced at her, his hollow eyes flickering with something raw. "We're going in circles. The swamp's playing with us, and now we've got someone—something—pointing the way. What if it's the only way out?"

Gillie's jaw tightened, and her gaze narrowed as she turned back to the child. "And what if it's the fastest way to get us killed?" she shot back. "You don't just trust something because it looks innocent."

"I'm not saying I trust them," Joshua replied, his voice trembling. "I'm just saying… we're stuck. What else are we supposed to do?"

Gillie didn't answer right away. She stared at the child for a long moment, her expression unreadable as though trying to find the hidden threat in their small, unmoving frame. "They're too calm," she said finally, her voice quieter now. "It doesn't make sense. Why aren't they scared of us?"

"Maybe they're not here to hurt us," I said tentatively, the words sounding uncertain even as I spoke them. The swamp wasn't exactly a haven of kindness or safety, and I wasn't sure I believed my own suggestion. But the silence radiating from the child didn't feel hostile—it felt like something else entirely, something I couldn't name.

Gillie shook her head, but she didn't argue further. Her grip on her knife loosened slightly, though her hand didn't leave the hilt. "Fine," she said grudgingly. "We'll follow them. But if this goes sideways, don't say I didn't warn you."

The child didn't wait for us to decide. As Gillie spoke, they turned and began to walk down the path they had pointed to. Their movements were slow, deliberate, each step measured as though they knew the way perfectly. For a moment, none of us moved. Then, without a word, Gillie started after them, her steps cautious and her posture stiff with unease. I followed close behind her, my heart pounding as the darkness of the trees began to swallow us.

Joshua trailed after me, his steps hesitant, his gaze flicking back toward the clearing as though expecting it to vanish behind us. "Do you think they're leading us to safety?" he asked softly, his voice barely more than a whisper.

"I don't know," I admitted, my grip tightening. The pressure was heavier now, sharp enough to steady me. "But we're about to find out."

The silence that followed us felt different. It wasn't the oppressive weight of the swamp, crushing and all-consuming. It was thinner, quieter, leaving room for the sound of our footsteps and the faint rustle of leaves underfoot. Still, it carried an unease I couldn't shake. The child moved ahead without hesitation, never looking back, their small frame an unsettling guide through the gloom.

Gillie's eyes darted between the child and the shifting mist surrounding us, searching for threats that weren't there—at least, not yet. "I don't like this," she muttered under her breath. "It's too quiet."

"It's quieter than before," Joshua said, his voice carrying a faint, shaky hope. "That has to mean something, doesn't it?"

Gillie shot him a sharp look, but she didn't respond. She kept moving, her knife still in her hand. The child remained just ahead, leading us deeper into the swamp, their pace unchanging.

I couldn't shake the feeling that we were stepping into something we didn't understand—something that could either save us or destroy us. For now, though, we had no choice but to follow.

A Flicker of Light

The path ahead was narrow, weaving through twisted trees and shallow pools of stagnant water. The Silent Child led us with steady, deliberate steps, never hesitating, never glancing back. Their small frame moved through the mist like it belonged to the swamp itself, yet there was an unnatural stillness about them—no crunch of leaves beneath their feet, no sound at all to mark their passing.

I glanced at Joshua as he followed closely behind me, his expression a mixture of fear and hope. His lips moved faintly, as though he were whispering something to himself, but I couldn't make out the words. Gillie walked further ahead, her hand still resting on the hilt of her knife. Every muscle in her body seemed tense, ready to spring into action at the slightest provocation.

"This is a bad idea," Gillie said under her breath, though her voice carried in the oppressive quiet. "We don't know what they are or where they're taking us."

"We don't know much of anything," I replied, though I kept my voice lower, wary of being overheard by something lurking in the shadows. "But so far, they're the only one—or thing—that hasn't attacked us outright."

"Yet," Gillie muttered. She shot a glare over her shoulder at Joshua. "And you're just fine with this, huh? Following some ghostly kid into who knows what?"

"What choice do we have?" Joshua said, his voice rising faintly. "Do you want to turn around? Go back to where the Whisperer's voices were clawing at us? Because I don't."

Gillie's eyes narrowed, but she didn't argue further. She turned her attention back to the child, who had just stopped at a fork in the path. For a moment, they stood perfectly still, head slightly tilted, as though listening to something only they could hear. Then, without a word, they turned left and continued walking.

"Do you think they're leading us out of here?" Joshua asked me, his voice quiet now, almost reverent.

I hesitated, my fingers brushing against the coin in my pocket. "I don't know," I admitted. "I don't know if they're leading us out or leading us deeper."

"You think it's a trap?" Gillie asked, her voice hard and suspicious.

"I think," I said carefully, "it doesn't matter. We don't have any other way forward."

Gillie didn't respond, but the sharpness in her movements told me enough. She didn't trust the child. Neither did I. But we had to follow. The alternative was staying lost in the swamp, circling endlessly until something worse found us.

The further we walked, the quieter the swamp became. The wind that had whispered faintly through the trees earlier had stilled entirely. Even the water, which usually gurgled and rippled with unseen movements, was silent. It was unnatural, this stillness, and it made every step feel heavier, more deliberate.

Joshua broke the silence after a while. "*Do you think they're, like… human?*" he asked, his voice tentative. "*Or something else?*"

Gillie let out a bitter laugh. "Look at where we are, Joshua. Nothing here is human anymore."

"That's not what I meant," he said, his voice defensive. "I mean, do you think they were like us once? Someone trapped here who… I don't know, lost themselves?"

Gillie didn't answer, her attention fixed on the child ahead, but her silence carried weight. Joshua fell quiet again, his expression troubled as he stared at the child's back.

The path twisted and narrowed further, the trees closing in around us like barricades, their branches forming a canopy that seemed to block out any light from above. The mist pressed closer, thickening at our sides, yet the child moved with the same steady pace, unbothered by the swamp's choking grasp. I found myself focusing on the faint movements of their frame, the way they walked without hesitation, as if they knew exactly where they were going.

And maybe they did.

Gillie slowed suddenly, holding up her hand to stop us. "This doesn't feel right," she said, her voice low. "The air's too still. It's like the swamp's holding its breath."

"Maybe that's a good thing," I offered, though I didn't fully believe it. "The swamp's been trying to kill us at every turn. Maybe this is… I don't know, a safe moment."

Gillie gave me a sharp look. "There's no such thing as safe here."

I didn't argue. She wasn't wrong.

The child stopped again, turning their head slightly as if listening. There was no sound that I could hear—no whispers, no wind, no movement—but the way their head tilted made it seem like they were hearing something we weren't. After a moment, they pointed to another path, this one narrower than the last, with shadows pooling at its edges.

"This is where it gets worse," Gillie muttered, her grip tightening on her knife.

"Or it gets better," Joshua said quietly, though there was a tremor in his voice that betrayed his doubt.

I glanced back at the path behind us, barely visible now through the encroaching mist. There was no going back, not without facing the Whisperer and whatever else the swamp had waiting for us. Forward was the only option, whether it led to safety or something far worse.

The Silent Child started walking again, and we followed.

Each step forward sank us deeper into uncertainty. Still, the child moved, and we followed.

Maybe it was their calmness, their lack of hesitation. Or maybe it was the faint flicker of hope they carried, no matter how fragile or ambiguous it was.

For now, it was enough.

The Silent Child's Guidance

Shifting Paths

The Silent Child led the way, their movements slow but assured, as though they were traversing a path only they could see. We followed at a distance, each step dragging us deeper into the swamp's tangled and unyielding grasp. The mist thickened again, swirling erratically as the terrain underfoot shifted with a strange, unsettling fluidity. What once seemed like solid ground rippled beneath our feet, the earth groaning and rolling like waves on a restless ocean.

Gillie stopped abruptly, her hand darting out to steady herself against the trunk of a tree. "Did the ground just move?" she asked sharply, her voice tinged with alarm.

"It's been moving," I said, my gaze fixed on the Silent Child as they continued forward without hesitation. "We're not on solid ground anymore."

Joshua took a cautious step forward, the waterlogged earth beneath him sinking slightly under his weight. He looked down, his expression twisting with unease. "*It's like we're walking on the back of something alive,*" he murmured. "*Are we sure we should keep going?*"

"Do you want to turn around?" Gillie snapped, though the sharpness in her tone betrayed her own unease. "Because I don't see anything better behind us."

Joshua flinched slightly at her words but didn't argue. I kept my eyes on the child, who moved effortlessly across the shifting terrain. Each step they took seemed to stabilize the path ahead, only for it to dissolve and ripple again after they passed. The swamp was changing around us, as though it was actively resisting our progress.

The silence stretched between us, broken only by the faint squelching of our boots in the muddy ground and the occasional groan of shifting earth. The trees loomed closer, their branches reaching out like claws, and the mist churned with an almost sentient malice. Every so often, the Silent Child would pause, tilting their head as if listening for something, before pointing down an indistinct path and continuing forward.

Gillie let out a frustrated sigh as she sidestepped a patch of ground that bubbled ominously, nearly slipping in the process. "This is ridiculous," she muttered. "This path doesn't even make sense. It keeps twisting back on itself."

"It's not supposed to make sense," I said, though the words offered little comfort even to me. "This place… it changes. We have to trust the child."

Gillie spun around to face me, her expression tight with irritation. "Trust them? Are you serious? We don't even know what they are. What if they're leading us into one of those pits we keep almost falling into?"

"They haven't yet," Joshua said hesitantly, his voice faint but steady. "If they wanted to hurt us, wouldn't they have done it already?"

Gillie turned her glare on him now. "Or maybe they're waiting. Waiting until we're too far in to turn back."

"Do we even have a choice?" I interjected, cutting through the argument. I gestured vaguely to the swamp around us, the endless mire and mist that stretched in every direction. "It's this or wander aimlessly until the swamp gets us."

Gillie looked like she wanted to argue, her jaw tightening as her eyes flicked back to the Silent Child, who was now several paces ahead, waiting patiently for us to catch up. After a tense moment, she muttered something under her breath and continued forward, her steps sharp and deliberate.

As we followed, the terrain grew even more unstable. Pools of dark water appeared where there had been dry ground moments before, and thick roots coiled out of the earth like serpents, writhing and shifting as though alive. The Silent Child navigated it all effortlessly, their slight frame moving gracefully across the treacherous landscape. But for us, every step became a gamble.

Joshua nearly lost his footing when the patch of ground beneath him gave way, sinking into a shallow pool of murky water. He caught himself on a nearby root, his breaths coming quick and shallow. "This place is alive," he said, his voice trembling. "It's like it's trying to swallow us."

"Keep moving," Gillie barked, her voice cutting through the rising tension. She reached out and pulled him upright, her grip firm but unkind. "If you fall, you're dead weight. Don't make me carry you."

Joshua nodded mutely, his face pale as he steadied himself. I glanced at the Silent Child, who had paused again, their head tilted slightly as if listening to the swamp itself. Then they pointed to a new path, narrower than before, cutting through the thickest part of the mist.

"What if that's not even a path?" Gillie muttered, but she didn't stop walking. Her knife was out now, gripped tightly in her hand as though it could cut through the swamp's growing hostility.

The Silent Child moved forward again, their footsteps quiet and assured. I followed, the weight of the shifting ground underfoot making every step feel like walking on the edge of an abyss. The swamp seemed to close in tighter with every passing moment, the trees and mist conspiring to press us into darkness.

But through it all, the child kept leading us.

And for reasons I couldn't explain, we kept following.

The Return of the Whisperer

The mist thickened around us again, the swamp folding in on itself like a labyrinth alive with malice. The Silent Child continued ahead, their pace unchanging, their small frame moving without hesitation. But the rest of us were faltering. The shifting paths, the bubbling ground, the lingering unease—it had worn us down, and now the Whisperer's voices were back, louder than ever.

Joshua was the first to react. His steps slowed, his shoulders hunching as Grace's voice reached through the air again, weaving its way into his thoughts. "You always abandon the people who need you," the voice accused, sharper than before. "You abandoned me. You abandoned yourself. Why are you even here?"

Joshua froze, his breathing uneven as the weight of the words pressed against him. "*I didn't… I didn't mean to,*" he murmured, his voice trembling. "*I tried to….*"

"Try?" Grace's voice snapped, cutting him off like a whip. "Trying isn't enough. You know that. You failed me. You'll fail them too."

Gillie turned sharply at the sound of his voice, her expression tight with frustration. "What is wrong with you now?" she snapped. "You keep muttering. Can you focus for five seconds?"

Joshua didn't respond, his gaze fixed on the ground. The trembling in his hands was faint but visible, his knuckles whitening as he clenched his fists.

"Joshua," the voice cooed again, softer this time, but no less cruel. "You'll always abandon them. It's who you are."

Gillie scoffed and turned away, but then I saw her stumble slightly, her eyes narrowing as her shoulders stiffened. I knew immediately that the Whisperer had found her again.

"You think you're strong," Olivia's voice said, low and bitter. "You think holding onto your promise makes you better than them. But what good has it done? What good are you to anyone?"

Gillie let out a sharp breath, her hand tightening around the hilt of her knife. "I haven't failed," she hissed, though the edge in her voice betrayed her uncertainty. "I won't fail."

"You've already failed," Olivia's voice pressed. "You just don't want to admit it. That's what you do—you lie to yourself. You're no better than anyone else here."

Gillie spun around, her eyes flashing with anger. "And what about you?" she shot at me, her voice cutting through the growing tension. "You think you're better? You think you're not hearing things too?"

I didn't answer her immediately, Raven's voice unraveling through my thoughts, twisting tighter with every passing second. He was louder this time, his tone colder, more assured. "You carry our blood," he said, mocking and cruel. "You think you're different? You're not. You'll fall, just as we did. And you'll take them down with you."

It sounded like Grace. Like Olivia. Like Raven. But the more I listened, the more I wondered—was that really them? Or just echoes of the worst things we already believed?

"*I'm not like you,*" I whispered, though the words felt fragile under the weight of his voice.

Raven laughed quietly, the sound enveloping me like smoke. "We're in you," he said simply. "You can feel it, can't you? The swamp knows the truth. It always does."

"Are you going to say something?" Gillie demanded, her voice sharp and cutting as it forced its way through the oppressive air. Her anger wasn't just directed at me—it was at everything. At the swamp, the whispers, the child, the silence itself. "Or are you just going to keep staring at the ground like him?"

"I'm dealing with it," I said finally, though my voice lacked any strength. It barely sounded like me, as if the swamp had robbed me of even that.

Gillie scoffed, her frustration radiating from her as she turned away. She stepped toward the Silent Child, who stood just ahead. Their figure remained still, untouched by the chaos around us—the relentless whispers clawing at the edges of my mind and the silence pressing against my chest like it wanted to crush me. The child didn't react, their calmness unwavering, and yet it felt heavy, sharp, as though their silence carried a power that was pushing us to the brink.

They watched everything but never flinched. Like they didn't see what we saw. Or maybe they couldn't. Maybe they'd died before they ever learned what cruelty really was.

"What is this kid even doing?" Gillie muttered under her breath, her knife held tightly in her hand, though her grip trembled faintly. "They're just standing there. Watching. Why aren't they helping?"

The whispers surged again, rising in intensity—not in volume, but in presence. Their words were cruel and cutting, their venom twisting deeper into the cracks they'd already opened. I could hear them layering over each other, overlapping like a cacophony of broken truths that were louder than sound itself. At the same time, the silence pressed outward, steady and unyielding, filling the spaces the whispers left behind. It wasn't just one or the other—it was both, suffocating us from every direction. The swamp had trapped us in a deafening paradox, and there was nowhere to go.

Joshua stumbled closer, his breathing uneven and shallow, his gaze darting between Gillie and the child. "Are they ignoring us?" he asked, his voice shaking. "Why won't they say anything? Why won't they stop this?"

They never even turned their head when the voices tore through us. Maybe they didn't hear them. Maybe that's what innocence really is—not ignorance, but silence in the face of suffering.

I looked at the child, their small frame so still it was almost painful. Their limp hand hung loosely at their side, their head tilted faintly toward the mist as though listening to something far beyond us. Their silence pressed into me as heavily as the voices themselves, leaving a bitter taste in the air. It wasn't comfort, it wasn't protection—it was relentless, forcing us to endure the weight of both forces colliding at once.

"Maybe they can't," I said quietly, my throat dry and my voice brittle. "Or maybe they won't."

Joshua let out a shaky breath, his hollow eyes fixed on the child. His lips moved faintly as if he were trying to say something more, but his voice faltered. When he spoke again, his tone was low and fractured. "*It's like before*," he murmured. "*When they… when I….*"

Gillie turned sharply, her expression hard but curious despite the tension in her posture. "What are you talking about?"

Joshua's voice cracked, trembling as he forced himself to speak. "When they were alive," he whispered, his gaze still locked on the child. "When they were suffering, I didn't say anything. I didn't do anything. I just stood there. Just like they're doing now."

The words hit like a blow, reverberating in the silence that wrapped around us. The air felt charged, suffocating not because it was loud, but because of its weight. I could see the strain in Joshua's posture, the way his fists clenched tightly at his sides, his shoulders trembling under the oppressive force pressing down on us.

"I could've done something," Joshua said, his voice breaking. "But I didn't."

They watched him fall apart. Watched him cry and scream and shake. But they didn't step closer. Maybe they didn't know they should. Maybe they never learned what it meant to help someone hurting.

Gillie exhaled sharply, her knife trembling in her grip before she forced it steady again. "This isn't helping," she muttered, though her voice lacked its usual sharpness. "Whatever happened back then, it doesn't change what's happening now."

She turned away, her focus shifting back to the narrowing path ahead. "If they're not going to do anything, then standing around is pointless," she added, her frustration bleeding through every word.

I lingered for a moment, staring at the Silent Child as they remained unmoving. Their calm presence was unnerving, their silence cutting through me more sharply than the whispers ever could. The weight of it pressed deep into my thoughts, forcing me to wrestle with questions I didn't want to answer. "Why won't you say anything?" I asked, though the question felt hollow even as I said it.

The child didn't respond. They didn't turn, didn't flinch, didn't even acknowledge that I'd spoken. Their silence stretched across the clearing like a shadow, unbroken and unyielding, filling the space between us and the whispers with a deafening tension. I couldn't tell if they were holding back or simply didn't care.

Gillie's voice came from further down the path, sharp and impatient. "Are you coming, or what?"

I hesitated, my gaze lingering on the child. Their stillness felt deliberate, but it offered no answers, no assurance. It left us stranded between the suffocating whispers and the crushing silence, with nothing to guide us but the weight of both.

Reluctantly, I turned and followed the others. The mist thickened as we stepped forward, the whispers fading but still holding us tightly. Their weight remained, pressing into every crack they'd carved in us, while the silence dug even deeper, filling the spaces they hadn't yet claimed.

The Silent Child followed, silent and unyielding, their presence as enigmatic as ever.

Moments of Isolation

The swamp began to splinter around us, the path narrowing and twisting until the mist seemed to devour everything beyond a few feet. The air grew colder, sharper, biting at my skin as though the swamp itself wanted to seep inside. The Silent Child's quiet footsteps followed closely behind, a steady but unsettling rhythm amidst the oppressive stillness. But then, without warning, they passed us.

Their movement was slow, deliberate. They didn't turn, didn't pause, didn't acknowledge us in any way as they stepped ahead, their small frame disappearing into the shifting mist. Their silence had weighed on us before, but without them behind us, the air collapsed—pressing in, relentless.

Raven's voice came next, slithering through the air like smoke, smooth and insidious. "*You're alone now,*" he murmured, his tone soft but no less cutting. "*Just like we were. Do you see it yet? It doesn't matter how hard you try. You can't outrun what's in you. You'll fail, just as we did. It's inevitable.*"

"I'm not like you," I said aloud, though the tremor in my voice betrayed me. The mist tightened around me, and the whispers seemed to grow louder, feeding on Raven's words. "I won't let myself become you."

Raven's laughter followed, deep and ominous, drawing nearer with each breath. "You already are us," he said, his tone taunting, his words cutting deeper. "We see it, even if you don't. You're one misstep away from falling. And when you do, they'll leave you. Just like everyone else."

The mist pulled tighter, the suffocating stillness pressing against my chest until breathing felt like an impossible task. My pulse pounded in my ears, and my steps faltered as the swamp itself seemed to push against me from all sides. Raven's words echoed endlessly in my thoughts, sharp and invasive, each one carving deeper into the spaces I had tried to keep hidden.

Somewhere ahead, I thought I saw a flicker of movement—the Silent Child's shape blurred through the haze, still walking, still silent. But I couldn't call out to them. The weight of Raven's voice was too much, dragging me down into the doubts he knew were buried deep within me.

Gillie's voice broke through the mist, sharp and angry. "What do you want from me?" she snapped, though I couldn't see who—or what—she was talking to.

"You think you've held onto your promise," Olivia's voice replied, colder now, as though the warmth Gillie associated with her grandmother had been stripped away. "But what have you done with it? What good is a promise if it saves no one? You're clinging to a memory, not a mission."

Gillie's footsteps were heavy, her anger evident in every stomp. "I've done everything I can!" she shouted. "Don't stand there and tell me I've failed. I'm still here, aren't I? I haven't stopped."

"Not yet," Olivia's voice said, softer, almost pitying. "But you will. You know you will. When it matters most, you'll fail them—just like you failed me."

"I didn't fail you!" Gillie yelled, her voice cracking. "I won't fail them!" But her words faltered as the mist thickened, cutting her off from us.

Joshua's voice was barely audible through the fog, trembling as though he were speaking through gritted teeth. "I didn't abandon her," he said, his tone quiet but desperate.

"Didn't you?" Grace's voice replied, its sorrow sharp enough to draw blood. "I was right there, Joshua. I needed you, and you let me fall. How many more will you abandon before you're done?"

"I'm trying," Joshua said, his voice breaking under the weight of the whispers. "I'm still trying."

"Trying isn't enough," Grace's voice cut through the haze, dark and cold. "It never was. You'll leave them too. You'll leave everyone, because that's who you are."

His breathing grew louder, more ragged, but his footsteps didn't stop. "*You're wrong,*" he whispered, though there was no conviction behind his words. "*You're wrong about me.*"

The mist shifted abruptly. It pulled back—not smoothly, but as if torn away by unseen hands, the swamp briefly exposing what had been hidden. Shapes emerged from the dense fog—Gillie ahead, her tense shoulders rigid with fury, Joshua pale and trembling behind me.

And between us, standing motionless where there had been nothing before, was the Silent Child.

I lurched back instinctively, barely managing to stop myself from staggering outright. They hadn't walked forward. They hadn't stepped through the mist. They had simply appeared, like they had always been there, like the swamp had decided, for just this moment, to let us see them again.

Their head tilted slightly, their stillness unnatural, unnerving. I had no doubt they had been listening the entire time.

Gillie cursed under her breath, cutting the silence with a sharp snap of frustration. "What the hell is wrong with this place?" she demanded. Her glare flicked between Joshua and me, narrowed with suspicion. "You two look like you've seen ghosts."

"*Maybe we have,*" Joshua murmured, his voice barely more than a breath. He was staring at the Silent Child, his expression tangled in something I couldn't fully decipher—fear, desperation, maybe even a sliver of hope. "*You watched them die,*" Joshua whispered—not accusation, but confession. "*And I let you.*"

The child didn't respond. They didn't react. They just watched, with that same unsettling stillness.

Gillie stepped toward them, her knife still in her grip, though not raised—yet. "I'm talking to you," she said, her voice taut, edged with something close to fury. "We've been walking behind you, following whatever path you lead us down. And for what? You just stand there and watch while this swamp tears us apart. Why won't you say anything?"

The child tilted their head again, a fraction of movement, their dark hair shifting over their face like a veil. Still, they said nothing.

Gillie's grip tightened on her knife, her breathing uneven, frustration spilling into the space between us like a physical weight. But instead of pressing further, she exhaled sharply, shaking her head. "This is useless," she muttered, turning away abruptly, cursing under her breath.

Joshua wiped his hands on his shirt, as though trying to rid himself of the suffocating tension pressing into his skin. His voice came out small, barely audible. "Why won't they help us?"

I had no answer.

The Silent Child slowly turned, their movements unhurried, deliberate, and then they began walking forward again, leading us deeper into the swamp. Whatever they were, whatever they wanted—it remained locked behind their eerie, silent presence.

We followed because we had no other choice.

When they were alive, they never told anyone. Now they don't even notice. It's like their silence has swallowed the pain so completely, they've forgotten it was ever there.

But the mistrust between us had thickened, tangled into something raw and unspoken. It lingered in every glance, every hesitant movement, pressing against us like an unseen force. The swamp was breaking us, piece by piece, and the Silent Child's silence—steady, unyielding—offered no solace.

Only more questions.

A Narrow Escape

The swamp roared to life around us, the stillness replaced by a violent upheaval that felt like the swamp itself had turned against us. The mist churned in thick, chaotic waves, blurring everything beyond our immediate surroundings. The once-twisting paths now crumbled into gaping pits, shadows spilling out and clawing at the air.

The ground beneath my feet trembled as if ready to collapse, rippling like water but with the jagged, unnatural pull of something alive. Gillie stumbled to the side, her knife out, though there was nothing tangible to strike at. "What the hell is happening?" she shouted, her voice rising over the chaos.

Joshua barely managed to keep his footing, his wide eyes darting between the shifting ground and the looming shadows that surged and retreated like waves crashing against an invisible shore. "It's like the swamp's breaking apart," he said, his voice high with panic.

"It's pulling us in," I shouted back, struggling to stay upright as the ground buckled beneath me. "We need to move!"

Ahead of us, the Silent Child stood motionless, their small frame untouched by the chaos erupting around them. The fog swirled gently at their feet, a stark contrast to the violent currents dragging at ours. For a moment, they seemed like a figure carved from the storm, their calmness unnerving in the face of everything collapsing around them.

Gillie pointed her knife at them, her breath ragged and sharp. "Do something!" she yelled. "Why are you just standing there?"

The Silent Child raised their arm slowly, their movement deliberate, unaffected by the trembling earth beneath them. They pointed to a narrow opening ahead—barely visible through the haze of mist and shadows— where a faint glimmer of light flickered in the dark.

"Is that a way out?" Joshua asked, his voice filled with desperate hope.

"Doesn't matter!" Gillie shouted back, pushing forward toward the opening. "If it's a way forward, we're taking it!"

The Silent Child remained still, their arm outstretched, guiding us toward the faint glimmer. I forced myself to move, my feet slipping on the unstable ground as I followed Gillie's sharp strides toward the path. Joshua stumbled behind me, his breathing loud and labored, his panic evident.

The shadows surged again, curling like claws around the edges of the opening, threatening to swallow it whole. The mist pressed harder, as though it were trying to pull us back, to drown us in its chaos. The Silent Child remained behind, watching as we ran, their presence both a witness and a guide. I wanted to look back at them, to understand why they had shown us this path, why they refused to help beyond pointing the way. But there was no time.

Gillie reached the opening first, her movements quick and deliberate, her knife ready in case the swamp tried to fight her. She turned back, her eyes wide and wild. "Move faster!" she yelled, grabbing my arm and pulling me forward as the ground shifted violently beneath us.

Joshua stumbled just as he reached the opening, falling to his as the mist enveloped his legs like tendrils. I reached out, grabbing his arm and yanking him upward. "Don't stop!" I shouted, pulling him through the narrow space. "Just keep moving!"

The shadows behind us roared, their movements erratic and desperate as though trying to claw their way forward. The opening began to close, the mist thickening into a wall of opaque white that threatened to swallow us whole.

Gillie grabbed Joshua's other arm, dragging him forward with the strength of someone who refused to lose anyone else. "Don't you dare fall now," she muttered through gritted teeth.

We stumbled out of the collapsing path onto firmer ground, panting and trembling as the chaos of the swamp began to recede behind us. The shadows pulled back, retreating into the mist like an angry tide, and the trembling earth stilled enough for us to catch our breath.

Joshua sank to his knees, his hands pressed against the ground as he gasped for air. "What was that?" he asked between breaths, his voice trembling.

Gillie paced, her knife still gripped tightly in her hand. "The swamp," she said simply, her tone hard. "Whatever it is, it wanted us dead."

I turned to look behind us, searching for the Silent Child.

They were gone.

The spot where they had stood was empty, swallowed by the mist that had turned calm once again. Their absence was sudden, absolute—almost as if the swamp itself had erased them the moment we no longer needed them. And yet, I couldn't shake the feeling that they had chosen to disappear.

"Where did they go?" I asked aloud, though I wasn't sure who I was asking.

Gillie snorted bitterly. "Of course they disappeared," she muttered. "We follow them to the edge of hell, and they just vanish. Figures."

Joshua glanced back at the path, his face pale and drawn. "Do you think… do you think they were trying to help us?"

Gillie hesitated. Her jaw tightened, frustration flickering into something else—uncertainty, maybe even regret. "Doesn't matter," she said finally, though her voice lacked its usual sharpness. "We're alive. That's all that counts."

But I couldn't let it go. The Silent Child had guided us, stood firm amidst chaos, pointed toward escape without asking for anything in return. And now they were gone, their silence lingering in the air but no longer shaping the swamp around us. Why had they left now, just as the world around us shifted again? Had they abandoned us, or had their purpose simply ended?

A cold weight coiled in my gut. The swamp had stilled, but something else—something worse—was beginning to wake.

The Rise of Marcus

Elana's Descent

The swamp twisted with every breath Marcus took, reshaping itself in quiet obedience, bending beneath his will as if it had never known resistance. The stillness that followed the Silent Child's departure wasn't relief—it was an invitation, a void lingering in the absence of its former occupant, waiting for someone strong enough to fill it. And Marcus stepped into that space without hesitation.

He had been watching. Waiting.

From the shadows, his presence pressed against the mist, stretching outward, coiling through the bones of the swamp like ink bleeding into water, saturating every unseen corner until there was nothing left untouched by his influence. This place had always carried whispers of him, remnants of his growing dominion threading themselves into the fabric of its existence. But those whispers had given way to certainty. There was nothing left to resist him now.

The Silent Child was gone.

And so, Marcus rose.

He inhaled deeply, deliberately, letting his satisfaction roll through the air like a tide, slow and inevitable, drawing everything into its current. A quiet chuckle emerged from his throat, permeating the dense fog and blending into the surrounding stillness.

"*Do you see now?*" he murmured, his tone laced with triumph. "They were never meant to stay. They were never meant to win."

The mist shifted, pulling inward, tightening its grip on the space around him like unseen fingers closing around a throat.

Marcus took another step forward, the ground firm beneath him—not trembling, not uncertain, but steady, unyielding. There was no resistance beneath his feet, no hesitancy in the world shaping itself to his command.

"They left because they had no power to wield," he said, tilting his head slightly, the movement subtle, thoughtful. "No real influence. If they did, don't you think they would've stopped me?"

I swallowed hard. The words pressed into the silence with a weight that demanded acknowledgment, a truth that crept into the spaces I wasn't ready to fill.

I wanted to deny it.

But the swamp remained silent.

Marcus exhaled, shaking his head, the idea amusing him.

"They stood there," he continued, voice gentle, almost coaxing, as though the conversation were merely an exchange of logic, a discussion of inevitabilities. "They watched. And then they disappeared. Not because they saved you. Not because they chose to leave. But because they were never strong enough to fight me to begin with."

The swamp shuddered, responding to his words, the mist thickening at his feet, pulling inward, dragging itself deeper into the framework Marcus had built for it.

And then… it shifted.

The swamp had never been empty.

The lost souls had always lingered here, unseen, forgotten, caught in the tightening grip of Marcus's influence, suspended in the quiet spaces beyond perception. They were remnants—fragments of lives pulled beneath the surface, held in place by forces beyond their understanding. But now…

Marcus's power solidified.

The mist moved, revealing what had always been hidden, peeling back the layers of illusion that had veiled them in secrecy. It wasn't just the swamp that was changing. Reality itself was bending, shaping itself beneath Marcus's will, folding to his design.

Elana moved through the mist with quiet grace, unaware that she was leading them exactly where Marcus wanted them to go. She believed she was guiding them toward salvation, ushering them toward peace, carving out a path that would free them from the weight pressing upon their existence. But the truth was far darker.

Marcus's grip had ensured they could no longer remain unseen.

Joshua, Gillie, and I watched as the souls emerged, their forms flickering like shadows caught in fractured light. The swamp itself breathed, pressing against our skin, entering the borders of our thoughts, seeping into the gaps where uncertainty lay.

Joshua's breath hitched, his hollow eyes wide, his voice barely more than a whisper.

"*They were always here,*" he murmured, the words brittle in the stillness. "*We just couldn't see them.*"

Gillie's grip tightened around the hilt of her knife, her gaze darting through the mist, searching for movement, for answers, for any sign that reality could still be trusted.

"Marcus is showing us what he wants us to see," she said sharply, voice edged with urgency, cutting through the weight pressing against us. "He's controlling everything."

Marcus took another deliberate step forward, watching as the lost souls were drawn into the open, watching Elana guide them with quiet certainty, watching them inch toward a fate they didn't yet understand.

She still believed she was leading them toward light.

Marcus knew better.

Elana turned slightly, her glow flickering in the mist, her presence warm, soothing, filled with the kind of confidence that made others follow without question.

"This is the way," Elana would tell them, her voice wrapping around them like reassurance, her hand outstretched in quiet certainty. "Follow me, and you'll find peace."

And they believed her.

They always did.

But Marcus was waiting.

His shadow stretched unnaturally through the mist, lurking just behind her, watching as she gathered them, as she led them straight into his hands.

And when they reached him…

Marcus smiled, the expression slow, deliberate, steeped in certainty. His voice, when he finally spoke, wrapped around them like a noose, tightening with quiet command, pressing into every hesitation, every lingering doubt.

"Welcome," he said, his tone smooth, unwavering, drenched in the assurance of inevitability. "You've made the right choice. With us, you'll never have to suffer again. Together, we'll rise."

The lost souls trembled, but it wasn't fear that mutated within them—it was hope, twisted and reshaped into something darker beneath Marcus's gaze. There had been resistance once, a flicker of uncertainty, a question left unspoken in the depths of their consciousness. But Marcus did not leave room for hesitation, did not allow space for doubt to breathe. He wove his promises around them, sculpted them into something that felt safe, felt absolute, felt unchallenged.

And Elana watched.

She watched as Marcus unmade them, as the swamp devoured them, twisting their forms, hollowing them out piece by piece. She saw what she had done—felt the weight settle into her bones, pressing against her ribs, demanding acknowledgment.

But she didn't stop.

Because this was her descent.

She had joined Marcus not out of belief, but out of desperation, clinging to the illusion that power meant salvation, that it could erase the fractures within herself, could make her something whole again. In the beginning, she had convinced herself that helping Marcus build his army was a sacrifice for something greater—that there was purpose in what they were doing, that the choices she made had reason beyond destruction.

But the truth stood before her now, undeniable.

She saw the way Marcus hollowed them out with his words, how his lies reshaped them until they were little more than echoes of what they had once been.

And yet—she continued.

The threads of Marcus's influence were wound too tightly around her mind, binding her body, ensnaring her purpose. Even as understanding seeped into her consciousness, even as realization threatened to tear through the illusion, she didn't step away, didn't question aloud what she knew in silence.

Alone in the swamp, Elana paused, staring down at her reflection in the dark waters pooling beneath her feet.

The face staring back at her was her own.

But not her own.

Hollowed. Haunted.

Her fingers twitched at her sides, nails pressing lightly into her palms as she studied the image before her, searching for something familiar, something she could recognize as her own. But nothing remained.

"*This isn't what I wanted,*" she whispered, the words cracking as they left her lips, too fragile, too raw, too real. "*This isn't what I was supposed to be.*"

The swamp didn't answer.

It didn't shift, didn't murmur reassurance, didn't react as if it understood her distress. It knew her, but it did not respond—not yet.

Instead, something else stirred.

A voice curled at the edges of her mind, threading into the space between her thoughts, smooth, rich, drenched in amusement.

"*You're doing exactly what you're meant to, Elana,*" Marcus murmured, his tone settling into the quiet with a satisfaction that made her breath hitch. "*You're helping me. And together, we'll become unstoppable.*"

Her fists clenched, her fingers tightening sharply, nails digging into her skin, pressing deep enough to leave crescent—shaped imprints against her palms. Her body shook—not from fear, but from the force of her own doubt, from the weight of uncertainty pressing its full gravity upon her.

And yet—she couldn't leave.

Marcus had tied her fate to his, had woven his influence into her decisions, had shaped her movements into something aligned with his vision. Even as resentment coiled beneath her ribs, even as recognition clawed at the edges of her thoughts, she couldn't see a way out.

Not yet.

For now, all she could do was move forward.

Behind her, the mist coiled, restless, waiting, shifting as if sensing the hesitation buried within her mind.

Marcus tilted his head slightly, his gaze flickering across the space, his awareness sharp, attuned to the smallest changes in the air.

The swamp trembled, quiet, subtle—but something else stirred beneath the surface.

Something always watching.

Marcus allowed himself a knowing grin before speaking, his voice cutting through the darkness with quiet command, effortless in its certainty.

"Raven."

The name settled into the air, sinking into the murky depths, absorbed by the swamp as if it understood exactly what was coming.

This wasn't a summoning.

This was inevitability.

Marcus wasn't calling Raven—he was pulling the strings, setting the stage, maneuvering the moment into place with the patience of someone who had already secured his victory. And the swamp responded, twisting in anticipation, adjusting to the narrative Marcus had already carved into reality.

The mist moved inward with a steady, measured flow—like a beast waiting to pounce, ready but unhurried, certain but deliberate.

And Marcus smiled.

Not at the gathering mist.

Not at the tremor in the air.

But at the reaction unfolding before him.

At the swamp itself, preparing the game that had already begun.

Raven's Manipulations

The swamp felt the shift—the subtle pull, the whispered recognition that Raven had arrived. But he hadn't been summoned. Raven did not come when called. He never had, and he never would. His presence wasn't one of obligation, nor of necessity. No, he arrived only when it suited him, when the moment had ripened to his liking, when the pieces had aligned precisely enough for him to weave his influence into the cracks of control.

The mist swirled unnaturally at his presence, thickening, pressing inward, shifting as though uncertain whether to welcome him or recoil. His arrival bled into the air like ink spilling into water, slow and deliberate, expanding until every breath carried his weight. There was nothing accidental about how he moved, how his presence folded into the silence, how the very space around him seemed to shift under the gravity of his arrival.

Marcus's smirk did not falter. He had expected this.

"*There you are,*" Marcus murmured, his tone smooth, expectant, carrying no trace of surprise. He spoke as if Raven's presence had been inevitable, as if this meeting had been scripted long before either of them set foot in the swamp.

Raven's laughter was soft, moving through the mist like smoke—amused, effortless, carrying the same confidence that had never once betrayed him. "You called, Marcus," he mused, voice edged with satisfaction, with knowing. "That means we arrived exactly when we meant to."

Marcus did not blink, did not shift, did not acknowledge Raven's attempt to twist the moment. Instead, he rolled his shoulders, relaxed, letting the mist coil tighter around him, unfazed by its movement. "You flatter yourself," he said, his voice calm, assured, carrying the weight of certainty. "But you play my game, whether you admit it or not."

Raven's smirk stretched slightly, but beneath it lay something sharper—something edged. "Your game?" His voice slipped through the mist, smooth as a blade finding its mark. "And yet, here you stand, needing us to lead them."

Marcus exhaled slowly, deliberately, amusement glinting at the edges of his expression. "Needing you?" he echoed, the words more observation than inquiry.

Raven stepped forward, the mist shifting around him, adapting, bending beneath his movement. "If you truly held them, if they were wholly yours, you wouldn't require us at all." His head tilted slightly, his gaze unwavering. "But you do."

Marcus remained still, watching.

Raven's attention flicked toward the others.

"*Look at them,*" he murmured, his voice laced with deception, but not recklessly so—no, his words were designed to root themselves into the cracks, to thread into the minds that hadn't yet fully yielded. His gaze shifted, landing on Joshua, on Gillie, on the uncertain faces still lingering at the edges. "They still fight, Marcus. They still resist. And you know why?" His tone held no expectation of an answer. He did not need one. "Because they see what's happening. They see through it."

Joshua's fingers clenched instinctively at his sides, a movement that did not go unnoticed.

"They were always meant to stay," Raven continued, his voice threading through the air, winding between them like mist searching for purchase. "But you? You fight for something meaningless. Resistance is fleeting, Joshua. And Marcus knows it."

Joshua flinched at the words but remained still.

Raven's smirk deepened as he leaned in slightly, as if the space between them had tightened just enough for the weight of his voice to press directly into Joshua's mind. "You feel it, don't you?"

Marcus let the silence linger, allowing the moment to stretch beneath Raven's influence. Then, finally, he spoke.

"I won't argue with that."

Joshua stiffened.

Raven's grin widened.

"And Marcus knows better than anyone," Raven said smoothly, turning toward him now, letting his amusement sharpen at the edges. "That all things end in submission." His voice was edged now, pressing, testing Marcus's patience. "Isn't that right?"

Marcus tilted his head slightly, watching Raven with effortless amusement.

"I suppose that depends," Marcus mused, voice light, untroubled, as if Raven's words were merely something to be considered, not something meant to provoke him. He let the silence stretch just enough before continuing, just enough for Raven to believe he had settled into certainty. "Some things break. Others bend. And some…" His gaze settled directly on Raven then, sharp, focused, calculating, a subtle reflection of the amusement Raven himself had wielded moments before. "—never realize how deeply they've already fallen."

The mist tightened—not chaotically, not unpredictably, but deliberately. It did not shift at Raven's command. It did not recoil in response to his words.

It was waiting.

Raven's laughter continued, resonating through the thickened air, but beneath it—beneath the amusement, beneath the control—something flickered, small and imperceptible to anyone but Marcus.

"You think you hold them," he mused, his tone light yet edgy, deceptively careful. His gaze flickered toward the lost souls—not with possession, but with certainty. "But they're not yours, Marcus. Not yet. They cling to you because the swamp allows it, because they have yet to see what waits beyond your promises."

The mist shifted, rolling thick through the space between them, but it did not move toward Raven. It pressed tighter against Marcus, firmly withing the boundaries of his control.

Raven remained unshaken. If anything, the moment only deepened his amusement.

"You believe control is the same as devotion," he continued, tone coaxing, deliberate, each word measured as if he were testing for weaknesses. "But devotion is earned, Marcus. And we have seen how easily things slip from your grasp."

Marcus exhaled slowly, evenly, no trace of hesitation weaving into his expression. He let Raven speak, let him believe, let him edge closer to the illusion of certainty he had so carefully crafted for himself.

"And what do you believe, Raven?" Marcus asked, his voice effortlessly smooth, his posture unmoving.

Raven took the bait.

His smirk deepened, sharpened. He stepped forward, his movements fluid, each shift deliberate, as though he were weaving his words into the space itself.

"*We believe control is fragile,*" he murmured, his voice threading into the mist, laced with confidence that hadn't yet wavered. "*That even the strongest ruler is vulnerable when doubt begins to settle.*"

Marcus tilted his head slightly, watching, listening, calculating—not reacting, merely observing. He let Raven work, let him press forward with conviction, let him carve himself deeper into his own words.

For a moment, the lost souls lingered—hesitant, caught between Marcus's stillness and Raven's promises.

And then…

They moved.

Not toward Raven.

Toward Marcus.

Raven's amusement faltered—not visibly, not outwardly, but Marcus saw it, felt it, held it like a blade between his fingers.

Marcus let him linger in the moment.

Let him taste the false victory.

And then Marcus spoke.

"You're right, Raven," he murmured, his voice calm, unhurried, weighted with something final. "Control is fragile. Doubt can shift it. You understand that better than most."

Raven's confidence flickered. Barely. But Marcus noticed.

"You've given them doubt," Marcus continued, his tone agreeable, effortless, precise—offering Raven the illusion of a win, feeding his belief that he was swaying the tide. "You've made them hesitate. You've played your role well."

Raven's smirk returned, triumphant, sharpened with the expectation of victory, the belief that Marcus was slipping, faltering, considering his words.

And then Marcus shifted.

His tone moved like silk, steady, controlled, unbreakable.

"*But you forget,*" Marcus murmured, quieter now, softer, yet somehow heavier than before. "*That it does not matter.*"

The mist tightened.

The swamp answered.

The lost souls chose.

And they pressed—fully, completely, undeniably—toward Marcus.

Raven exhaled, slow and measured, his amusement intact at the edges, but something had changed. Something had cracked.

Marcus saw it.

And he smiled.

"*You see now?*" Marcus murmured, his words a whisper of certainty, smooth, effortless, final. "*They were never yours to take.*"

And Raven did not answer.

Not because he couldn't.

But because Marcus had already won.

Grace's Quiet Resistance

Silence stretched through the swamp under Marcus's command, his victory sinking like a stone into deep, unmoving waters. He felt it—the weight of certainty pressing into the mist, threading through his dominion's fabric, locking every thread of resistance. The lost souls had chosen, their surrender complete, final, undeniable.

Raven had played his part, unwittingly, inevitably. The game had never been his, though he had danced within its confines, shaping words with care, believing, for a moment, he wove something beyond Marcus's control. But the truth had waited, circling just out of reach, patient in its inevitability.

Obediently, the haze folded, settling into the rhythm Marcus dictated, swirling exactly as it should.

Then, a stirring.

Not rebellion. Not force. Just a whisper.

"You can still endure."

The words didn't force entry; they didn't demand attention. Instead, they slipped between the mist, threading gently through the stagnant silence, careful, patient. They were alien here, misaligned with the tide formed by Marcus's rule.

Yet, they reached their target.

Joshua inhaled sharply, freezing mid-movement. A sudden jolt of pulse beneath his skin, his breath caught in his throat, held by something unseen. His gaze darted through the mist, searching for what lay beyond his sight, something unaccounted for, something Marcus hadn't contained within his dominion.

"Grace."

The name barely escaped his lips, but it sufficed.

The swamp responded.

The mist coiled, not in hesitation, but in angry twists, writhing at the intrusion, pressing against itself, resisting an indefinable presence, something that shattered its constructed certainty. Marcus felt the pull, the friction tightening his grip as he hardened his hold.

And then…

Grace whispered again.

"You don't belong to him."

Quiet. Soft. Barely a ripple in the heavy air.

But Marcus felt its impact.

Some of the lost souls flinched—a shudder, a sharp intake of breath, the smallest, most imperceptible movement toward something other than Marcus.

Joshua clenched his fists, his voice breaking through the silence, urgent, thin. "You hear her, don't you?"

Marcus exhaled, slow and controlled, pressing his command deeper, sinking it further into the mist, forcing every thread of resistance beneath the weight of certainty.

"Silence," he murmured, his voice threading into the swamp, shaping it, reinforcing its foundation. *"There's nothing left but certainty."*

The mist obeyed.

It tightened, pressing around the souls, dragging them forward, closing the gap between hesitation and submission, driving them toward Marcus's rule. Most followed without question. Most didn't dare resist.

But some hesitated.

Grace's voice wove through the mist again—soft, unwavering, delicate yet unbroken.

"You are still yours."

The swamp shuddered.

Not violently. Not chaotically. But with something unexpected beneath Marcus's control.

Small. Fleeting.

But Marcus felt it.

And so did Raven.

They stood slightly apart, Raven observing Marcus with careful, sharp amusement. He saw it—the shift, the flicker, the fracture in Marcus's seemingly unbreakable foundation. Subtle, barely visible to others. But Raven knew.

A slow smirk tugged at his lips.

Marcus was losing control. Not entirely. Not enough for a challenge. But enough to be felt. Enough to be noticed. Enough for doubt to linger.

Yet, beneath Raven's amusement, unease settled, creeping at the edges, threading into his ribs like an encroaching mist. He had fought

Marcus. He had lost. And now—something else had introduced a factor beyond even his influence.

Marcus felt the weight of the shift.

Immediate fury surfaced.

The mist lashed through the swamp, snapping back into place, sealing the cracks, crushing hesitation, forcing obedience back into submission.

"Fix this," Marcus snarled, sharp and cold, his gaze cutting toward Elana, toward Raven. His patience had vanished, stripped away by the lingering flicker of defiance. "Fix this!"

Elana didn't hesitate.

Her voice wove into the mist—steady, suffocating, sharp with command.

"You do not resist."

The words sank deep into the swamp, pressing into the space where doubt had begun to root, reinforcing Marcus's grip, strengthening the certainty he had forced.

Raven sighed, amusement fading into resignation.

"You were always meant to follow," he murmured, his tone drifting between the souls, threading into their minds, locking them into silence. *"You were always his."*

And just like that, resistance fractured.

One by one, the lost souls pressed forward, surrendering again, hesitation smothered beneath Marcus's rule, doubt swallowed before it could take hold.

The swamp settled. Not because it was calm, but because Marcus had forced it into submission.

His smirk returned, slow, triumphant.

Grace exhaled softly.

She didn't move. She didn't whisper again.

But she had seen it.

She had seen doubt.

And doubt—once planted—could not be erased.

The Swamp's Transformation

The last whisper had faded, dissolving into the thick air, swallowed by the mist that curled obediently under Marcus's command. Grace was gone, leaving nothing behind—not a trace, not a lingering defiance, not even a hesitation to suggest she had been here at all. What had flickered for just a moment, that fragile crack in Marcus's grip, had been sealed over with ruthless precision. Any chance of resistance had been suffocated before it could fully form.

The swamp exhaled, but it didn't breathe with the same restless energy it had carried before; it didn't twist or react with anything resembling independent will. Instead, it collapsed into Marcus's grip, pressing itself into submission beneath the weight of his will. The mist coiled, not as an unruly force bending under pressure, but as something smooth, fluid, perfect in its obedience. It no longer hesitated, no longer wavered between chaos and control—there was no longer anything left within it that had the capacity for disobedience.

Marcus had shaped it into something else entirely.

Joshua's breath was uneven, shallow, like the air itself had thickened, like inhaling required more effort than before. The swamp had always been unpredictable, had never fully committed to Marcus's rule, had always held onto something feral, something untamed just beneath the surface. But now, that unpredictability was gone, wiped away with a precision that was unnatural.

Gillie whispered, barely audible, yet her voice carried weight, pressing against the silence with the only thing left that resembled defiance. "*It's… wrong.*"

She wasn't shaking, but her voice wavered, fragile in a way that suggested she was resisting the urge to let fear take hold.

I felt it too—that shift, the heavy, suffocating weight pressing in from all sides. I didn't know if it was the swamp itself or just the way it had folded so entirely into Marcus's command, but the sensation was crushing, like the space around us had shrunk, like it had closed itself off from any possibility of escape.

Marcus wasn't simply controlling the swamp. He was rewriting it, molding it into something entirely his own.

The shadows didn't coil unpredictably; they bent into their places as if they had been sculpted to fit within them. The mist didn't pulse erratically; it flowed with seamless precision, every movement calculated. Even the ground beneath us felt too steady, too unnatural in its stillness, as if it had been locked in place, forced to obey even in its existence.

Joshua exhaled sharply, shaking his head, the movement small but filled with frustration, his breath uneven as he tried to process what had just happened. His gaze darted between Gillie and me, searching desperately for some unspoken reassurance that we could still fight back, that this wasn't as final as it seemed. But nothing in our faces, nothing in the suffocating air around us, nothing in the way the swamp had settled completely beneath Marcus's grip suggested that there was anything left to grasp onto. When Joshua finally spoke, his voice wavered, brittle beneath the weight of surrender that none of us wanted to accept.

"I thought…" He swallowed hard, his throat working against the words, as if some part of him refused to say them aloud. "*I thought she could change something.*"

Grace.

He meant Grace.

For a moment, her presence had shaken something, had created a shift, had cracked the illusion of Marcus's absolute control just enough for doubt to slip through the fractures. It hadn't been resistance, not in any clear, forceful way, but it had been something—a whisper in the dark, a breath of hesitation from the lost souls, a break in the suffocating silence that had begun to settle like stone.

For a moment.

For a breath.

But Marcus had been faster, sharper, more deliberate.

He had crushed that flicker of uncertainty before it had time to root itself, before it could spread, before it could turn into anything that resembled a challenge. His dominion was precise, total, a force that reshaped not just the swamp but the very air we breathed, twisting it into something unnatural, something perfected. Every movement of the mist, every curl of shadow, every inch of the ground beneath our feet had bent entirely to his will, and there was no chaos left, no unpredictability, no openings in which we could escape.

Joshua's voice dropped lower, barely above a whisper, as if saying it quietly might lessen its impact, might make it hurt less.

"I really believed she could stop him."

Gillie, who had been silent up until now, finally spoke, though her voice was hollow, distant, as if she had already accepted what we refused to.

"We all did."

Her words didn't feel like comfort. They felt like defeat.

Marcus had rewritten the swamp, had carved out every imperfection, had taken whatever wild remnants had refused to conform and forced them into silence. The mist didn't pulse unpredictably. The shadows no longer shifted with uncertain movements. Even the ground beneath us had become unnervingly still, no longer shifting under our weight, no longer reacting as if it had any will of its own. Everything obeyed Marcus perfectly, seamlessly, as if it had never known anything else.

Grace had barely left a mark.

The realization settled deeper, locking itself into the pit of my stomach, pressing against my ribs, heavy and suffocating, closing in around me like the swamp itself had turned into something sentient, something aware of how final this was.

Joshua didn't speak again. Neither did I.

Gillie wiped her hands against her arms, as if trying to shake off the weight of the moment, but it didn't work. It wouldn't. There was nothing to shake off. There was nothing to escape from. This was no longer a place we could fight in—it had been turned into something too structured, too controlled, too perfectly aligned with Marcus's command to allow for anything else.

The silence stretched, thick and unyielding, swallowing us whole.

Marcus watched.

Waiting.

And then…

A shift.

Not chaos. Not resistance. But something else.

A presence.

It didn't announce itself. It didn't shatter the mist. But I felt it. A pulse—low, steady, not mine, not Marcus's. Something older. Something untouched. It moved through the stillness, threading past Marcus's grip like it had always known how to avoid him. And for the first time since the swamp fell silent, I breathed like I meant it.

Joshua felt it too, sharp and sudden, his breath catching as his pulse jolted against his ribs, his body reacting before his mind had even begun to process what had changed.

Gillie stiffened, her fingers clenched, her posture rigid, as if bracing for something she didn't yet understand.

I inhaled, waiting, my senses tuned to whatever had just disrupted the perfection of Marcus's dominion, searching for the crack, the mistake, the anomaly that should not have existed in a place Marcus had made entirely his own.

Marcus noticed it too.

He didn't react outwardly, didn't shift his stance, didn't let the control in his expression falter, but something about him had changed, tightened, just slightly—just enough to be seen, just enough to be felt.

Redemption wasn't impossible.

It had just arrived.

The Redeemed

The Unyielding Presence

The swamp responded to Marcus's dominion with a thick, tangled breath held within the mist, a heavy stillness blanketing the land. Through the silence, he felt the pulse of his authority, a presence woven into the air and stretched across every surface, indistinguishable from the world itself. Every inch of this place had yielded, folding under his command without question, sculpted into obedience with absolute precision.

Without hesitation, the lost souls had surrendered, pressed into the inevitable with the certainty of those who knew no other path. At Marcus's feet, the mist shifted and coiled, anticipating his desires and molding itself to his will. The swamp mirrored him, an extension of his being, entirely governed by his dictated rhythm. Within it, no force remained that was not his, no space unclaimed, no breath existed outside his command.

And yet . . . something new had arrived.

The Redeemed

Initially, the disturbance was a mere whisper, an impression slipping into the quiet with an impossible awareness. Unlike the others, it wasn't shaped by established expectations, didn't move within set boundaries, and refused to bend to his will. It existed outside his rule, untouched by inevitability, defying the rhythms he had designed.

Marcus narrowed his gaze, intently observing this newcomer, anticipating its eventual collapse into familiar defiance. He had witnessed this before: the brief hesitation of those who believed they could resist the predetermined, the futile struggle of minds too weak to accept their fate.

But this presence did not flicker. It showed no tremor of submission, no wavering beneath the oppressive air. It did not regard Marcus as a force of inevitable destruction, nor did it stand as a temporary defiance before surrender.

It simply stood, as if Marcus's authority held no meaning, his dominion no weight, arriving with the inherent knowledge that it would not yield.

This defied the established order. The swamp was his. Everything within it belonged to him.

Marcus inhaled slowly, a sharp smirk holding steady on his lips, unreadable. His expression betrayed no uncertainty, acknowledging only the absolute control he had always known. Tilting his head, he watched and waited, his voice resonating with effortless command through the thickened air. *"You don't belong here,"* he murmured, his tone deliberate, sinking into the silence with absolute certainty. *"The swamp has chosen. You will, too."*

The presence offered no response. Marcus allowed the silence to stretch, expecting the inevitable collapse into submission. Yet, the presence remained still, unbending, offering no acknowledgment. A subtle twitch betrayed Marcus's composure—small, almost imperceptible, but present in his fingers at his side.

"Elana," he commanded, his voice a cold steel wrapped in velvet, edged with purpose. "Fix this."

Elana moved with slow, deliberate grace, her body a sinuous dance. The mist yielded before her, as if instinctively knowing better than to touch. Every movement spoke of intent: the roll of her hips, the relaxed set of her shoulders, the curve of her spine painting seductive promises in the air.

Heat gathered in her wake, and the golden glow of her presence bled softly into the haze, intimate as candlelight on skin. Her gaze locked onto the figure, lashes low, eyes dripping with purpose. A knowing, sultry smile touched her lips. She was no longer merely a woman; she was a storm cloaked in silk.

"You do not resist," she purred, her voice a honeyed lure with a dark undercurrent.

The words were not a request, but a seduction woven with magic. She closed the distance, each step dissolving space and unraveling reason. Her hand grazed her breast, a deliberate draw to his gaze. Her fingers trailed down her thigh as she passed, a slow, teasing caress, marking places of imagined touch. The air thickened, charged with her magnetic heat. She reached, her breath a trespass against his skin, yet not quite touching.

Still, the presence remained unmoved.

Marcus watched, his stance as sharp as a drawn bowstring. "Deeper," he commanded. "Make him feel you."

Elana's smile widened, sharpened. She tilted her head back, exposing the vulnerable curve of her throat. Her fingers danced to her collarbone, a slow drag over skin shimmering with the mist's dampness. "*Tell me what you want,*" she whispered, her voice soft and smoky. "*I'll give it to you. I'll take you apart.*"

Nothing. The presence stood unyielding.

A flicker of something beyond desire touched Elana's movements, a subtle falter born not of doubt, but of the cold weight of his silence—a silence that drowned out her allure. She leaned in, her lips a breath away from his ear. "*Break*," she whispered, the word a plea disguised as command.

The presence remained. He looked through her, into her, and past her, as if she were no more substantial than the mist.

Marcus exhaled, his patience fraying beneath a controlled expression. His gaze flicked toward Raven. "Take care of it."

Raven hesitated. Not from fear, not from doubt, but because Marcus had miscalculated.

This was beyond their control.

And then . . . the bells tolled.

The sound carved through the mist, deep and resonant, a force alien to Marcus's dominion, pressing into the air. It rang through the silence, an intrusion that shifted the atmosphere into something heavy, unnatural, impossible. Marcus did not command these bells. Yet, they rang. He did not falter, though. He smirked, shaking his head, dismissing the sound as belonging to others, not to him.

And then . . . the bells tolled again.

Marcus stiffened, a barely perceptible reaction, but visible nonetheless.

Then came the whisper. "*Three months.*"

Marcus's gaze flickered, a small, imperceptible movement, but Raven saw it. Elana saw it. Joshua felt it. Marcus released a slow breath, rolling his shoulders, attempting to restore the moment's certainty. This was a game. This was nothing. "*Is that all?*" he murmured, his tone layered with unbothered amusement.

The bells tolled again. This time, Marcus's smirk faltered, just for a moment, but it was enough.

Then, the presence stepped forward, emerging from the mist with quiet certainty, steadily closing the distance in a way Marcus could not command.

He didn't walk in. He arrived. Like he'd always been there, waiting.

Joshua inhaled sharply, his pulse hammering against his ribs, his breath caught in his throat. He knew him. But he didn't know why.

The words escaped Joshua before he could stop them, breathless and uncertain. "I know you."

The presence offered no reaction. The others turned toward Joshua, the atmosphere thickening with tension and discomfort. Gillie's voice was sharp and cautious. "What do you mean?"

Joshua opened his mouth, then closed it, his heartbeat a thunderous echo in his ears. "I . . . I don't know." The silence stretched, pulling at the edges of something unknown, precarious, impossible. Gillie stepped closer, her expression urgent. "Joshua, how do you know him?"

Joshua's hands fisted tightly at his sides, his pulse erratic, his thoughts fracturing into incomprehensible pieces. "I don't . . . I just. . . ."

The presence watched him, unmoved, unbothered, untouched by the unraveling moment. Joshua shook his head, frustration flickering in his voice. "I don't know."

The Unbreakable Light

The haze twisted at Marcus's feet, thick and obedient, threading itself through the swamp, pressing inward, constricting like a living force bound to his command. It folded effortlessly under his rule, settling into the rhythm of his dominion, coiling around the lost souls as if sealing them into place. His victory had already taken shape—woven into the silence that lingered after resistance had crumbled, carved into the bones of the swamp itself, etched into the air with certainty.

There was no longer space for doubt. No breath left for rebellion. No fractures in the control he had meticulously constructed. And yet…

The presence remained.

It didn't fold. It didn't submit. It stood. Steady. Unyielding. Untouched.

Marcus exhaled slowly, deliberately, as if drawing amusement from the moment, letting the edges of his smirk sharpen against the quiet. He tilted his head slightly, watching, waiting, expecting the inevitable surrender.

"You're wasting your breath," Marcus murmured, his voice blending into the surrounding mist, threading through the silence with quiet finality. "There's nothing to save."

The presence didn't flinch. It didn't look at Marcus. Instead, its gaze found Joshua.

"You used to hum that song when we were stationed at the outer post," he said quietly. "Off-key, always. And louder when you were afraid."

He didn't smile. He didn't need to. "We were together when it all began. We fought side by side. We did terrible things."

The words landed with weight, slipping between the mist, settling into the space between past and present.

Joshua inhaled sharply. His throat tightened. His pulse pounded against his ribs in something near panic.

Marcus smirked. He could use this.

"You remember now, don't you?" Marcus pressed, stepping forward, his voice sliding through the tension like silk. "You remember the choices you made. You remember how easily you followed."

Joshua wavered, his breath faltering. But before he could speak—before Marcus could twist that moment of hesitation into something deeper, something useful—the presence stepped forward, his voice cutting through the thickened air.

"I am The Redeemed," he said, his voice steady, saturated with unshaken conviction. "Redeemed in the light that you seek now."

Gillie scoffed under her breath, folding her arms, skeptical. "You seriously call yourself that? That's a title, not a name. Who even decides to go around calling themselves The Redeemed?"

The Redeemed turned to her, unbothered, unaffected by the weight of her challenge. His expression did not shift, did not flicker, did not acknowledge her doubt as anything worth engaging.

"*I am what I am,*" he murmured, his tone calm but resolute, layered with something unbreakable. "*It's a badge I wear with honor.*"

He did not elaborate further. Did not offer justification. Did not attempt to convince her. The truth of his name was unchallenged, because it was simply fact—not a declaration, not an argument, but something already settled.

His gaze did not waver. Did not hesitate. Did not shift beneath Marcus's looming presence.

"It's within your grasp. Nothing is lost while the light remains."

Marcus stepped forward, slow, deliberate, letting his presence pull at the space between them, letting his voice settle in the thickened air with quiet certainty.

"This is who you are," Marcus murmured, his tone shaped into something smooth, persuasive, dangerous. "This is what you were meant to become. You were never meant to escape this. You were never meant to be saved."

The Redeemed did not react.

Marcus's words slid off him like rain against stone, finding no weakness, no opening, no place to take hold. His presence remained unchanged, as if Marcus was nothing more than a passing shadow in a world already illuminated.

"I was there," The Redeemed said, his voice steady, smooth, untouched by the poison curling at the edges of Marcus's smirk. "I was with you when we abandoned the Silent Child. I saw what we did. What we allowed. We let the devil turn us into monsters."

The admission came without hesitation. Without shame. Without the weight of regret pressing into his bones.

For a moment, something in his voice hit too close. Gillie looked away before anyone could see it.

Joshua sucked in a sharp breath, his lungs tightening, his pulse hammering violently against his ribs. He felt it—the truth settling in, raw and unforgiving.

Marcus leaned in, his presence stretching forward, pressing against Joshua, against the moment, against the hesitation that lingered at the edges.

"You followed me once," Marcus said, his tone soft, coaxing, sharpened at the edges with quiet triumph. "You obeyed. You were just like him—just like all of them."

Joshua froze. The Redeemed did not move.

"And then I was free."

Marcus's smirk faded. Just slightly. Just enough for Raven to see it. Just enough for the mist to shift, unsettled, uncertain, responding not in perfect obedience but with something smaller—something fragile beneath the surface.

Marcus hated this. He hated the calm. The certainty. The immovable presence before him, standing in defiance, untouched by his influence, immune to his control.

He pressed forward, sharp and cold, his voice slicing through the moment like a blade.

"You're lying to yourself," Marcus said, his voice lowering, stretching through the mist. "You're still the same. You're still mine."

The Redeemed did not acknowledge him. Marcus felt his fury rise, thick and immediate, clawing at the edges of his patience. He needed submission. He needed control.

"You think you can escape this?" Marcus hissed, his voice a twisted echo of the past. "You think you can find redemption? There's no redemption for you. There's only darkness. Only the void."

Joshua's heart pounded in his chest, each beat a painful reminder of his own fragility. He wanted to believe The Redeemed, wanted to grasp onto the hope that flickered like a distant star in the night. But Marcus's words were like a poison, seeping into his mind, clouding his thoughts with doubt and fear.

But The Redeemed only turned to Joshua, his voice unwavering.

"You can be free," he murmured. "I chose redemption. You can, too."

Joshua swallowed, his thoughts spiraling, unraveling beneath the weight of everything pressing into him—the past, the truth, the possibility.

The swamp seemed to hold its breath, the mist enveloping Marcus's feet, as if sensing the tension that crackled in the air. The silence stretched, heavy and oppressive, pressing down on Joshua's shoulders, making it hard to breathe. He could feel the weight of Marcus's gaze, the cold, calculating eyes that seemed to see right through him, stripping away the layers of his soul until there was nothing left but raw, exposed nerves.

"You'll never escape what you are." Marcus's voice slithered through the mist like a serpent, cold and deliberate. "It's written into your bones, carved into your very existence. You can pretend. You can fight. But it will always be there—waiting."

His tone sharpened, tightening around Joshua's hesitation like a noose. "Redemption's a myth that can never be found. It's a lie told to the weak, a false hope clung to by fools who don't understand the truth."

He stepped forward, his presence stretching, pressing, suffocating. "And the truth is simple—you're beyond saving."

Joshua's heart pounded in his chest; each beat a painful reminder of his own fragility. He wanted to believe The Redeemed, wanted to grasp onto the hope that flickered like a distant star in the night. But Marcus's words were like a poison, seeping into his mind, clouding his thoughts with doubt and fear.

The Redeemed stepped forward, his presence a beacon of light in the suffocating darkness. "You're stronger than this, Joshua," he said, his voice steady and unwavering. "You have the power to choose your own path. To break free from the chains that bind you."

Marcus's eyes narrowed, his smirk fading into a snarl. "You're nothing," he spat, his voice dripping with venom. "You're weak. You're a coward."

Joshua's breath hitched, his chest tightening with the weight of Marcus's words. But The Redeemed's gaze never wavered, his eyes filled with a quiet, unshakable determination.

"You're not alone," The Redeemed said, his voice a soothing balm to Joshua's frayed nerves. "I'm here with you. We can face this together."

The mist seemed to pulse with a life of its own, swirling around Marcus like a living entity, feeding off his anger and hatred. But The

Redeemed stood firm, his presence a shield against the darkness that threatened to consume them all.

"You'll never be free," Marcus hissed, his voice a twisted echo of the past. "You'll always be mine."

Joshua swallowed, his thoughts spiraling, unraveling beneath the weight of everything pressing into him—the past, the truth, the possibility.

Marcus stood there—watching, waiting—his presence heavy, suffocating.

But The Redeemed did not yield.

And Marcus could do nothing about it.

Lessons of Redemption

The mist seemed to wrap itself inward, sluggish in its movements, as though carrying the weight of something unseen, something fractured beneath the surface. It had always bent seamlessly to Marcus, had always slithered into his grip without hesitation, had always been an extension of his dominion—a silent confirmation that the swamp belonged to him, that nothing within its grasp could truly resist.

And yet…

Now, it hesitated.

It did not rebel, not entirely, but there was a subtle shift beneath its obedience, a trembling in its presence, a faltering in its certainty. The movement was slight, almost imperceptible, but Marcus felt it, nonetheless. It pressed against the edges of his command, threading through the air with something dangerous, something wrong, something that should not have been possible.

The moment stretched, long and heavy, thick with an unfamiliar uncertainty that threatened to unravel at the seams. Marcus's jaw tightened, his fingers curling slightly at his side, his breath measured as he willed himself to ignore it. Whatever this was—whatever illusion of resistance was pressing its weight into the swamp—it didn't matter.

Because he still held Joshua.

Marcus inhaled slowly, carefully. His smirk remained in place, the edges sharp and deliberate, sculpted into something that would not falter, would not break. His eyes flickered toward Joshua, watching the way his breath hitched, the way his shoulders tensed, the way his pulse drummed violently against his ribs, which was exactly what Marcus wanted.

Marcus saw the crack forming.

He could use this.

He stepped forward, each movement smooth, controlled, calculated. The mist moved around his feet as he walked, adjusting to his movement and the gravity of the situation.

"Do you see it now?" Marcus murmured, his voice passing through the thickened air, sliding between the hesitation settling into Joshua's frame. *"Do you see who I've always been? Who you've always been?"*

Joshua's breath trembled, uneven, caught somewhere between denial and reluctant understanding. His jaw tightened, a hard line forming as he seemed to grapple with the intangible: the empty space between past and present, the remnants of choices he had long abandoned but had never truly outrun.

Marcus pressed further, his tone layered with quiet triumph, coaxing, threading through the tension with ease.

"You are the shape of this place," The Redeemed murmured, his voice steady, swirling through the mist like something woven into its very fabric, a truth that had long existed but had only now been spoken aloud. *"It's carved in your reflection, bound to you as shadow is bound to light. You move, it moves. You break, it fractures. You fall, it remembers."*

Joshua inhaled sharply, uncertainty flickering in his gaze.

"You were never apart from it," The Redeemed continued, quieter now, as if the words themselves didn't need force to carry weight. "This is no land forged by fate. It wasn't conjured from nothing. It's an echo, a song long sung, a testament to what you were before time unraveled you into this."

Joshua swallowed, his pulse uneven, his thoughts spiraling between recognition and refusal.

"You think you walk through it, but you don't." The Redeemed's voice pressed into him, light yet unwavering. "You're not passing through its boundaries—you're looking in a mirror. This place isn't a prison, not a battleground, not a lesson to be learned."

His gaze did not waver, did not break, did not soften.

"It's simply what remains."

Joshua exhaled—ragged, unsteady, as if the world had suddenly tilted beneath him.

The Redeemed did not move.

"You were never meant to leave it behind."

Joshua inhaled sharply, his gaze flickering, uncertain, searching.

And then…

The Redeemed turned to Marcus.

The shift was immediate.

Not slow, not hesitant—it was inevitable.

There was no warning, no build-up, no gradual recognition. It was pure certainty, unshaken, absolute.

"You mistake power for control."

The words did not lash outward, did not claw through the silence with aggression. They were not loud, were not forceful, were not shaped to wound.

They simply existed.

And Marcus cowered.

The reaction was small—so small it could've been overlooked. But Raven saw it. Gillie inhaled sharply. Joshua's pulse jumped against his ribs.

Marcus forced a breath past his teeth, rolling his shoulders, tilting his head slightly, crafting an expression of amusement, as though it meant nothing, as though it did not weigh upon him at all.

But it wasn't convincing.

And The Redeemed continued—unbothered, untouched by Marcus's attempts to recover, immune to his influence.

"You believe that because the swamp bends to your will, you own it," The Redeemed said, his voice steady, unwavering. "You believe that fear gives you dominion over those who stand beneath you. That because they don't resist, they belong to you."

Marcus inhaled slowly, deliberate, but not deliberate enough.

Gillie stepped forward, her voice sharp, suspicious. "What does that mean?" she demanded, eyes narrowing. "What are you saying?"

The Redeemed did not turn to her. His attention remained locked on Marcus.

"And yet," The Redeemed continued, as if Marcus's presence meant nothing, "true freedom doesn't come from the force of one's will. It doesn't come from dominance or submission. It comes from surrendering to grace."

The mist wavered—small, slight, but enough to catch.

Enough for Gillie's suspicion to deepen.

Enough for Joshua's breath to break against his chest.

Joshua shook his head, the breath leaving him uneven, caught somewhere between understanding and refusal. "That…" He swallowed, his throat dry, his voice brittle. "That's not possible."

The Redeemed turned to him fully, his expression soft but absolute.

"It is," he murmured. "Grace doesn't measure worthiness. It doesn't demand perfection. It doesn't ask that you arrive whole—it simply asks that you arrive."

Joshua sucked in a sharp breath, his thoughts spiraling, colliding, unraveling beneath the weight of everything pressing into him—the past, the truth, the possibility.

Gillie scoffed under her breath, folding her arms, skepticism thick in her voice. "And you expect us to just believe that?"

The Redeemed did not answer her.

Instead, he watched Joshua.

Joshua's fingers clenched at his sides, his voice breaking against the edges of something too big to hold onto.

"But I…" His voice cracked at the edges, his grip tightening, struggling to steady himself. "I can't be redeemed."

The mist shuddered, pulling inward, folding in upon itself, resisting the declaration.

Marcus felt his own breath hitch—small, imperceptible, but Raven saw it. Gillie saw it.

Marcus felt the moment slipping from his grasp.

"No." His voice lashed against the silence, sharp and cold. "No, this isn't how it works."

But The Redeemed did not turn.

Did not yield.

Did not acknowledge Marcus's words.

"I was lost once," The Redeemed said, his voice layered with something unbreakable, something whole. "Just as you are now. I believed I had no path forward. That my choices had taken me too far, that I was bound to the darkness I had created for myself."

Joshua's breath was shallow, his pulse uneven, his gaze darting, searching.

Marcus reeled—his stomach tightening, his chest constricting, his mind screaming.

The Redeemed looked at Marcus for a long moment, his gaze steady, unwavering. He had denied Marcus the recognition he craved, refusing to acknowledge him, refusing to play into the illusion of control Marcus had carefully cultivated. And now, standing before him, there was no reverence, no hesitation—only indifference.

"You hold no power over me."

The mist recoiled, the swamp twitched, as if something ancient had shifted beneath its surface, sending a ripple outward, unseen but undeniable. It struck Marcus with a force so subtle it might have gone unnoticed had he not stumbled—just slightly, just enough to betray the instinctive recoil, the momentary fracture in control.

Gillie saw it.

Joshua saw it.

Raven did not move, watching, waiting.

Marcus swallowed hard, the burn in his chest sharpening, his pulse quickening. The Redeemed held his gaze, unshaken, unwavering, his presence cutting through the thick air like something absolute. And then, with unnerving certainty, he took a slow step forward, closing the space between them with a patience Marcus did not understand.

Marcus stiffened, but he did not move away.

"Your games mean nothing to me," The Redeemed said quietly, his voice carrying through the mist like something far older than Marcus, something unafraid. "You twist, you manipulate, but in the end, you only prey on the lost. You cannot touch me."

Marcus had always commanded attention, had always been seen. No one had ever denied him like this—not outright, not with certainty. The mist moved around his feet, changing in response to something beneath the surface that Marcus was aware of but could not clearly identify. He swallowed hard, his smirk gone, his amusement dimmed. And then—his body stiffened just slightly—an instinctive reaction to something he could not control.

The Redeemed smiled, just barely, just enough for Marcus to know—he had never mattered. Not truly.

Marcus exhaled sharply, his chest rising unevenly, and for the first time in longer than he cared to remember, he did not know what to say. He had always been acknowledged, feared, treated as inevitable.

And now, standing before The Redeemed, he was simply dismissed.

Without another word, he took a step backward into the mist. The shadows swallowed him whole.

The Redeemed watched the spot where he had disappeared, lingering—not long, just enough to let the weight of his presence settle into the air, into the silence Marcus had left behind. Then, as though hearing something beyond us, he turned toward the mist at the edges of the clearing.

Joshua's breath hitched, his fingers trembling at his sides. The Redeemed's gaze found his once more.

"You can be free," he whispered. "If you only choose to be."

And then, like the mist itself, he vanished.

His absence settled over us, thick and profound, and for a brief moment, the swamp felt… different. Lighter, though not freed.

But not everyone had disappeared.

Shadows Watching

Raven seized the moment, his presence growing more insidious as he stepped forward from the shadows. His voice slithered through the air with quiet malice, aimed straight at Joshua. "*They'll leave you behind,*" he whispered, his tone soft but insidious, the kind of whisper that burrowed deep and stayed there. "*You already know it, don't you? The looks they give you, the hesitation in their voices. They don't trust you. They never have.*"

Joshua stumbled, his steps faltering as his breath hitched audibly. His shoulders slumped forward, his body folding under the weight of Raven's words. "*That's not true,*" he muttered, his voice almost too quiet to hear. "*That's not true.*"

Raven tilted his head, watching Joshua with an expression steeped in mockery, a slow, deliberate amusement curling at the edges of his smile.

"You think they'll stay?" Raven mused, his voice smooth but sharpened, threading through the mist like something inevitable. "You think they won't leave you behind? You'll see, Joshua. We've seen it before. It's always the same. They'll keep you around as long as you're useful, as long as you're not a liability. But when the time comes—when it matters most—they'll save themselves. And you? You'll be left to rot."

Joshua flinched, his breath uneven, but he didn't look away.

Raven's eyes gleamed, his smirk widening ever so slightly.

"Just like The Redeemed did," he murmured, his voice layered with cruelty. "He didn't care about you when he needed to save his own ass."

Joshua stiffened, his fingers tightening, a sharp, instinctive reaction. He shook his head quickly, his voice edged with something desperate, something raw.

"He came back," Joshua said, louder now, as if trying to force certainty into his words. "He didn't abandon me. He came back. You don't get to say he didn't."

Raven's expression didn't change, only deepened, the amusement never fading, never wavering.

"We know everything," he said, his words laced with venom, with certainty, with something far worse. "We've seen it, lived it. You already feel it, don't you? The way they look at you. The way they hesitate. They'll leave you, Joshua. Just like you left her."

Joshua froze, his breaths growing heavier, more uneven, and I saw his fists clench at his sides. "You're lying," he said, louder this time, though his words lacked conviction. "It's not true."

"Joshua!" I called out, stepping closer to him, my voice cutting through the eerie quiet. "Don't listen to him. He's trying to break you— don't let him win."

Joshua looked at me, his eyes wide and unfocused, filled with doubt that Raven had so effortlessly planted. "What if he's right?" he asked, his voice trembling. "What if I really am a burden? What if you'd be better off without me?"

Gillie turned back sharply, her knife flashing faintly in the dim light. "Don't start with that," she snapped, her voice a mix of frustration and urgency. "We're not leaving anyone behind. But we sure as hell can't stop moving just because you're having a crisis."

"You see?" Raven's voice came again, soft and insidious, weaving through the air like a toxin. "She doesn't care, Joshua. She needs you to keep moving, to play along. But the moment you falter, the moment you're no longer useful…"

"That's enough!" I shouted, my voice cutting through the air like a blade. My pulse hammered, my muscles coiled tight with the force of the words. "You don't get to do this, not to him, not to any of us."

I felt his attention shift, his shadow brushing against the edges of my thoughts. "We know you," Raven said, his voice directed at me now. "We know your failures, your fears. You think you're helping him, but you're only delaying the inevitable. He'll fall, and it'll be your fault."

I pressed forward, my steps deliberate, my voice steady. "You don't know anything about me."

Raven's laughter rippled faintly through the air, low and mocking. "Oh, but we do. We're in you. You carry us in your blood, in your bones. The swamp knows it, feels it. You can't outrun what's inside you."

Gillie's voice cut sharply through the tension. "Enough talking!" she barked, her movements deliberate as she slashed at a root snaking too close to her boots. "You don't get to stand there and listen to him. He wants us to crack, to fall apart. Don't give him the satisfaction."

Joshua straightened slightly, though his hands were still trembling. The mist thickened around us, coiling tighter, heavier, pressing into the spaces between the tolling bells. It wasn't subtle this time. The whispers came suddenly, sharp and invasive, threading through thought, digging into bone, twisting behind the ribs like something alive.

Joshua gasped, his breath uneven, his hand shooting to his temple as if trying to crush the sensation, force it out. Gillie flinched beside me, her jaw tightening, her fingers twitching against the hilt of her knife.

She exhaled sharply, her breath hitching, her voice strained and uneven. "It's starting," she managed, her words breaking as though the effort to speak was too much. "We can't stay. We have to move."

The whispers didn't relent. They sank deeper, pulling at memory, pressing into the cracks Raven had carved, feeding on hesitation, on doubt, on the weight of everything we couldn't escape.

"We keep moving," I said firmly, forcing my voice to cut through the thick air, ignoring the sharp pulse behind my eyes. "Now. Together. No one's stopping."

Gillie nodded sharply, her movements deliberate, her grip steady on the knife. "Let's go," she said, her voice clipped but resolute. "The longer we stand here, the worse it gets."

Joshua hesitated, his gaze flicking toward the shifting shadows, but then he took a deep, shuddering breath and followed. I stayed close to him, keeping pace, forcing my legs to move even as the whispers pressed harder, threading deeper, pulling at the edges of thought like something trying to take hold.

The pain didn't fade as we walked. It lingered, sharp and unrelenting, threading through muscle and thought, refusing to fully release its hold. The swamp wanted us still, wanted us vulnerable, wanted us broken.

But we kept moving.

And slowly—step by step, breath by breath—the whispers loosened their grip. The tension didn't vanish, but it thinned, unwinding in slow retreat, unraveling at the edges of thought. They didn't tighten. They didn't deepen. They only watched, reluctant to release completely, but unable to hold on with the same cruel force.

The silence stretched between us, tense and uneasy.

Grace's Revelation

A Quiet Moment

Joshua's breaths were uneven, and Gillie's grip on her knife never loosened. The weight of what had just happened clung to us, unspoken but undeniable, and though none of us said it aloud, we were all wondering the same thing—had The Redeemed truly escaped this place? Or was it just another trick?

Then, ahead of us, something shifted. The mist thinned—not completely, but enough that the shadows receded just a little. The air felt different, less oppressive, as though we had stepped into a pocket of quiet untouched by the swamp's grasp.

And for the first time since the whispers had seized us, the pain didn't return.

Joshua inhaled slowly, almost cautiously, as if testing the air, expecting the sharp sting to creep back in. But it didn't. His steps steadied slightly, his shoulders straightened, bracing against something unseen.

"They're… not holding on," he murmured, uncertain.

Gillie exhaled, a slow, deliberate breath, testing the space as if waiting for the weight to press in again. But it didn't.

"They can't reach us now," she said, her voice quiet but certain. "Not while we keep moving."

She was right.

The whispers only held power when we hesitated, when doubt festered, when uncertainty left us open. But now… now we were moving, and the swamp did not grip us, did not press in.

For the first time in hours, maybe longer, the air felt lighter.

And there it stood—a towering oak tree, its branches sprawling wide and its ancient roots disappearing deep into the earth.

The sight of it stole the breath from my chest. It wasn't just a tree— it was something unshaken, something enduring. Though the swamp pressed from all sides, its chaos seeping into everything, the oak stood untouched, its massive form resolute against the creeping corruption. It did not belong to the swamp—it stood beyond it, apart from it, stronger than it.

Joshua stopped walking, his eyes fixed on the tree. His expression softened as if, for a fleeting moment, the weight of the swamp had eased from his shoulders. "*That tree…*" he murmured, his voice barely more than a whisper. "*It feels… different.*"

"It doesn't belong here," Gillie said, her tone tight, though her grip on her knife seemed looser than before. "Nothing this solid survives in a place like this. So why is it still standing?"

Grace stepped forward, her gaze steady, her voice calm. "Because its roots run deeper than the swamp," she said quietly. "Deeper than the darkness, deeper than the chaos. This tree is older than the swamp, older than the storms. It was here before they began, and it'll remain long after they're gone."

Gillie frowned, glancing between Grace and the tree. "You sound pretty sure of that. How do you know?"

Grace didn't answer right away. She kept her eyes on the oak, her expression softening. "You don't need to see the roots to know how deep they go. You can feel it. It's why the swamp hasn't touched it—can't touch it. This tree is a marker, a reminder that no storm, no darkness, lasts forever."

I felt the truth of her words settle over us, wrapping around us like a fragile shield against the swamp's relentless pull. The oak's presence was undeniable, its strength so absolute it felt as though the swamp itself had no choice but to give it space.

Joshua took a step closer, his voice unsteady. "It's like it's watching us," he said. "Like it's waiting for something."

Grace turned to him, her expression soft but firm. "It's waiting for you."

Then her gaze shifted to me, her eyes holding a knowing look. "And this place… this quiet here… it holds more than just peace. There are roots here that go deeper than we can see, and sometimes, the greatest strength lies hidden, waiting for the right moment to be revealed."

The oak seemed rooted not just in the earth, but in something far deeper, something ancient and unchanging. Its presence felt timeless, as though it had been there before the swamp's corruption, before the storms began their ceaseless assault. It wasn't just a tree. It was a truth, a strength, a symbol of something greater. Something that had endured long before the swamp and would endure long after.

Joshua shifted uneasily beside me, his expression conflicted. "Why is it here?" he asked, glancing between Grace and the tree. "Why does it matter so much?"

Grace turned to him, her gaze calm but piercing. "The oak represents a truth the swamp can't corrupt," she said simply. "Its roots hold fast against the storm because they run deeper than anything the swamp can reach. It's unshakable, eternal. And now, it's calling you forward—to face what's coming."

Joshua stared at the tree, his shoulders slumping slightly under the weight of her words. "So we're supposed to go there? To face… whatever the swamp has left for us?"

"Not yet," Grace said firmly, holding up a hand as though to stop him. "Not like this. You're all carrying too much—fear, doubt, exhaustion. The swamp is relentless, but you can't fight it if you're already broken. We need a moment to breathe. To prepare."

Gillie let out a sharp breath, crossing her arms. "You really think pausing here is a good idea? The swamp doesn't exactly give us timeouts. That thing—Raven, the shadows—the whispers—they're always watching, always waiting. And if we stop, they'll sink back in."

"They are," Grace agreed, her tone steady. "But they can't take what you don't give them. Right now, you're giving the swamp your doubt, your pain. It's using it against you. If you don't take this moment, it'll only take more."

Gillie opened her mouth to argue, but then she hesitated, her jaw tightening as though swallowing her next words. She looked toward the tree again, her expression unreadable.

I glanced back at the group, at Joshua's trembling hands and Gillie's unyielding grip on her knife, at the weight each of us carried in silence. Grace was right. The swamp had taken so much from us already—our hope, our unity, our faith in ourselves. But here, in this quiet moment with the oak tree standing tall against the mist, there was a chance to take something back.

"All right," I said, my voice firm. "We'll pause. Just for a moment."

Gillie raised an eyebrow, but she didn't argue. Instead, she sank down onto a fallen log, her knife resting loosely in her lap. Joshua stayed standing, his eyes locked on the tree as though trying to understand something too vast to grasp.

Grace didn't move, but her presence felt more grounded than ever, as if she were drawing strength from the oak itself. The swamp pressed against us, its mist lingering at the edges, but for the first time in what felt like forever, it couldn't reach us. Not here.

The oak tree stood tall, its roots deep, its branches wide. It felt eternal, unshaken, unyielding—a symbol of something far greater.

For now, the shadows and the whispers stayed at bay, and we allowed ourselves a moment to breathe.

The Deepest Roots

The mist settled, the oak tree's towering form standing steady against the swamp's chaos, its branches reaching out like quiet arms offering shelter. We stayed there for a moment longer than we had planned, none of us speaking—until Grace broke the silence. Her voice was calm, but it carried a weight that demanded attention.

"I've been here long enough to understand what this place does to people," she said, her gaze fixed on the tree, not on us. "Long enough to see how it holds them, how it changes them."

Joshua shifted uneasily, his shoulders hunched as though the weight of her words pressed against him. "You mean... this swamp?

Purgatory?" His voice trembled slightly as he said it, the word cutting through the quiet like something forbidden.

Grace nodded, thoughtful. "This place twists what you carry, turns your burdens into chains. But it's also a choice. We decide, ultimately, what we hold on to and what we let go."

Gillie, perched on a low root, crossed her arms, her knife resting on her thigh. "So you're saying you chose to stay here? Why would anyone do that?"

Grace turned to her, her gaze steady but gentle. "Because redemption is worth waiting for. And because Joshua wasn't ready to walk this alone."

Joshua blinked, his brow furrowing. "You stayed here… for me?"

Grace didn't answer immediately. She watched him, her expression soft but unwavering. "When I first came here, I didn't know if you would follow. I didn't know if you would ever make it this far. But I stayed because I saw the weight you carried, and I knew you couldn't face it alone."

Joshua looked away, his shoulders slumping further. "I don't understand," he said, quieter now. "Why me? Why would you wait for me? I'm not strong enough to make it through this, and I've already messed up so much. What's the point?"

Grace stepped closer, her movements deliberate but unassuming. "The point," she said gently, "is that redemption doesn't depend on how strong you think you are. It doesn't depend on how many mistakes you've made or how far you've fallen. Redemption is about surrendering to grace—to the truth that you can't carry the weight alone. That you don't have to."

Joshua shook his head, rubbing at his face with trembling hands. "I don't know if I can do that," he admitted. "I don't even know where to start."

"You already have," Grace said simply. "You kept walking. You kept moving forward, even when everything inside you told you to give up. That's where it begins—with one step."

Gillie leaned back slightly, her arms still crossed but her posture less tense. "So what do you do, Grace?" she asked, her tone quiet but pointed. "You just wander around helping people? Waiting for them to figure it out?"

Grace smiled faintly, though there was sadness in it. "I guide," she said. "I listen. I plant seeds that might one day grow into something stronger than the doubts and fears that bind them. I can't make anyone change—can't force anyone to let go of what holds them here. But I can offer light where there's darkness. Hope where there's despair."

Joshua stared at her, his eyes searching for something in her expression. "How do you know this will work? That I can actually walk out of here?" His voice was unsteady, filled with doubt.

Grace glanced at the oak tree. Its towering form pulsed with quiet strength, its branches stretching into the mist as if carving space away from the swamp itself.

"This tree has stood against the storms, against the darkness, and yet its roots remain—deep, unmoved, unbroken," she said, her voice calm but firm. "There's something greater here, something eternal, that runs deeper than the swamp's reach. Like the roots of this oak, nothing can uproot the truth that stands against the flood."

Joshua swallowed hard, staring at the tree, his breath uneven.

"For so long, you've believed the swamp can take everything from you," Grace continued, turning toward him. "But the deepest roots don't break. They endure. They hold. And they'll hold you, if you choose to stand."

She hesitated then, her gaze drifting beyond the tree, deeper into the mist, as if searching for something unseen.

"This oak… It's strong," she murmured, almost to herself. "But It's only a reflection—a shadow of something greater. The foundation deeper than any of us, the truth that has always been, that will always be."

Joshua frowned, his gaze flickering between her and the towering tree. "What are you talking about?"

Grace exhaled, shaking her head slightly, as though dismissing a thought before it could fully form. "You'll see," she said finally. "When the time comes."

For a moment, none of us spoke. The oak tree loomed over us, its roots disappearing deep into the earth, its branches wide and unwavering against the mist's creeping darkness. Grace's presence, her words, felt like the echo of that strength—a reminder of what this place couldn't take away.

Reactions to the Truth

Grace's words lingered in the air, settling like a gentle but unrelenting weight on all of us. The oak tree loomed above, its steady presence a reminder of everything Grace had just said—about redemption, grace, and the choice to keep walking, no matter how heavy the burden.

Gillie's expression shifted as she stared at the tree, the hard lines of her face softening for the briefest moment. Her grip on her knife loosened, her fingers brushing against the hilt absentmindedly as though she was somewhere far away.

"I know what you're saying," she said finally, her voice quiet but steady. "What you're talking about… it's what Olivia used to try to teach me. She always told me that promises only matter if you hold to them when it gets hard. That it's not about being perfect—it's about showing up, about doing the work." Her voice wavered slightly as she said the last part, but she straightened her shoulders, gripping the knife more firmly now. "I made a promise, and I'm not breaking it. No matter what the swamp throws at me."

She glanced at Grace, her expression less guarded than usual. "What you said—about roots running deep. That's what Olivia was to me. My roots. I didn't get it back then, but… maybe I do now."

Grace nodded gently, her smile soft but filled with understanding. "Roots are what keep us standing in the storm," she said. "And promises, when they're rooted in love and truth, can withstand anything."

Gillie didn't respond, but there was a flicker of something in her eyes—something stronger, steadier. She turned back to the oak tree, her jaw set with renewed resolve.

For me, the weight of Grace's words settled differently. The pressure pressed against me, sharp but steady, grounding me in a way I couldn't explain. My thoughts drifted, unbidden, to the betrayal that had brought me here—the choices my family had made, the paths they'd walked that had broken us apart. Raven's whispers of shared blood, of inevitable failure, echoed faintly in my mind, but now, they felt quieter. Distant.

Grace's words cut through them, sharper and truer than anything Raven had ever said. "Redemption is about surrendering to grace—to the truth that you can't carry the weight alone."

I had been carrying the weight of my family's betrayal like armor I never wanted and chains I didn't know I still wore, letting it shape every step I'd taken. But standing here, beneath the unwavering oak, I realized that the only way forward wasn't to carry that weight—it was to let it fall. Not to erase what had happened, but to choose something different. To make amends. To prove, even if only to myself, that I could be more than what Raven claimed.

The weight didn't ease entirely—it couldn't, not yet—but I felt a spark of determination kindle in its place. A small, flickering light that felt like a beginning. And looking at the towering oak, I wondered if even the smallest seed, planted in the right ground, could hold the potential for such enduring strength.

Joshua, meanwhile, hadn't moved. He stood slightly apart from the group, his eyes fixed on the tree but unfocused, as though he wasn't seeing it at all. His hands trembled at his sides, and I could see the conflicting emotions warring across his face—guilt, hope, doubt, all colliding in a way that made him look as though he might shatter.

"I don't know if I can do it," he said softly, his voice breaking the silence. "I want to… I want to believe everything Grace said. But I don't know how to let go. I've been holding on to my guilt, my fear, for so long. It feels like it's part of me. Like if I let it go, I won't know who I am anymore."

Grace stepped closer to him, her presence calm and steady. "Letting go isn't about losing yourself, Joshua," she said gently. "It's about finding who you are beneath the weight. And you don't have to do it all at once. Even the smallest steps matter."

"But what if I fail?" Joshua whispered, his voice trembling. "What if I can't… what if it's not enough?"

Gillie glanced at him, her tone softer than usual as she spoke. "We've all failed," she said. "Over and over. The only thing you can do is keep going. Falling doesn't matter as long as you get back up."

Joshua looked at her, his expression torn. "But what if I can't get back up next time?"

"You will," Grace said firmly, her voice carrying a quiet conviction. "You've made it this far. That's proof enough."

Joshua nodded slowly, though the doubt didn't leave his eyes entirely. He turned back to the tree, his gaze lingering on its unyielding form. "I want to believe that," he said quietly. "I just don't know if I can."

"Belief isn't always a feeling," Grace said. "Sometimes it's a choice. One step forward, even when you're not sure. That's all it takes."

For a while, we said nothing more. The oak tree stood tall, a silent witness to the unspoken struggles that lingered in each of us. But as we began to move forward again, the weight felt slightly different—not gone, but less suffocating. Grace's words, the strength of the oak, and the flicker of hope they had planted carried us just a little farther.

The Last Crossing

Beneath the sprawling branches of the oak, we had found something we hadn't dared to hope for—safety. The swamp hadn't reached us here. The whispers had fallen silent. The relentless pull of doubt, the suffocating weight of its grasp, had loosened for the first time.

The air beneath the tree felt different, untouched by the darkness pressing in from all sides. It was the first place we had rested without fear. But this wasn't where we were meant to stay.

Beyond the mist, beyond the grasp of the swamp, stood another tree—larger, darker, older. The Ancient Oak.

It was waiting for us.

Gillie exhaled slowly, rubbing at her arm, her expression distant. "We should keep moving," she muttered, though there was hesitation in her voice, a reluctance that hadn't been there before.

Joshua's gaze lingered on the towering branches above us. *"Why do we have to leave?"* he murmured, more to himself than to any of us. *"We're safe here. If we go back out there...."*

I understood what he meant. The swamp was relentless, and stepping forward meant walking back into its grasp. We had finally escaped it—but only for a moment.

Grace's voice cut through the quiet, sharp and unwavering.

"You have to go. Now."

Joshua turned toward her, his brow furrowing. "Why?"

"Because this place isn't meant to hold you," she said simply. "The oak gives shelter, but not permanence. You're meant to move forward, not hide. If you stay, it'll become another chain—and chains are what keep you here."

Gillie stiffened, her jaw tightening, but she didn't argue. The truth of it weighed between us, pressing into the silence.

Joshua turned back toward the tree, his expression conflicted, but then… through the mist, just beyond the reach of this shelter—the Ancient Oak appeared.

Gillie's voice broke the silence, firm and certain. "The Ancient Oak. That's where we have to go."

The decision was made. We stepped forward.

The swamp lashed out.

The moment we crossed the threshold, the mist surged in, thickening like something alive, wrapping around our legs, our arms, tightening like grasping fingers. The silence shattered—the whispers crashed back into place, rising in a violent crescendo that made my skull ache.

Joshua stumbled, his breath hitching, his body locking up as the pressure sank into him. He squeezed his eyes shut, gripping the side of his head, his movements jerky and uneven. "It wasn't like this before," he gasped. "It wasn't this strong…"

The ground shifted beneath us, unstable, pulsing, like something breathing beneath the surface. My balance faltered for just a moment before I forced my feet forward. If I stopped—if I hesitated—the swamp would take hold.

Gillie cursed under her breath, her steps quick and sharp, every movement precise and deliberate. But I could see it—the temptation pulling at her, the weight of the swamp pressing against her resolve.

We had all felt it. The urge to go back.

A few steps. That's all it would take. Just a few steps back, and the quiet would return. The whispers would silence. The weight would ease.

We had been safe there. We hadn't been touched there.

Joshua's breath came fast and uneven, and I could see the fear in his eyes, the hesitation creeping in.

I turned back, gripping onto that last shred of safety. The oak still stood behind us, its towering form unmoved, untouchable against the creeping mist. But Grace was vanishing.

She was fading, dissolving into the thickening haze, as though the swamp itself was drawing a curtain between us.

But her voice came through the mist, steady and firm.

"It's time for the final test," she said. "The swamp won't give you another chance after this. It'll do what it does best—it'll press against your fears, force your choices, and make you wonder whether you've chosen the right path at all. But you can't stop. You can't doubt. You have to keep moving forward."

The mist clawed at us harder, the ground shifting violently beneath my feet. I forced my steps forward, swallowing against the tension in my chest.

Joshua clenched his jaw, his fists shaking at his sides. He didn't want to move. None of us did. But I saw the moment he made his choice—the moment he took the step that carried him beyond the oak's reach, fully into the storm.

The swamp roared in fury.

Then the bells tolled.

A deep, thunderous resonance swallowed the air, reverberating through the ground, rippling through the mist like an unseen force pressing down on our chests. The sound wasn't just a warning—it was a signal. A command. The echoes rolled outward, stretching into the storm, and something answered.

The shadows shifted.

First, it was subtle—a ripple in the darkness, a shudder beneath the mist. Then, movement. Sharp. Precise. Calculated. The swamp wasn't just alive—it was responding, reacting, unleashing.

We did not turn back.

And as the mist swallowed us whole, the oak behind us remained standing, untouched, unwavering—a silent witness to what came next—still as stone, older than fear, and rooted in a truth the swamp could never reach.

The Final Test

The Army Awakens

The air shook with the tolling bells, each strike crashing against the ground, vibrating through our bones. The sound wasn't just noise—it was weight, crushing down on us, stealing our breath, forcing the storm into something greater, something unavoidable.

The swamp had come alive.

The mist writhed in violent currents, the ground trembled beneath our feet, and the shadows moved with purpose. They didn't lurk at the edges anymore—they were shifting, gathering, preparing.

The bells split the sky. I flinched before I knew I'd moved.

It wasn't sound anymore—it was presence. It was warning. It was war.

"They're not waiting anymore," Gillie said, her voice strained as she tightened her grip on her knife. She scanned the shadows, her eyes darting toward every flicker of movement. "They're coming. All of them."

"They're not just shadows anymore," I said, my voice barely audible over the deafening roar of the bells. "They're his army. Marcus is here."

Joshua's breathing was uneven, his hands trembling as he stared at the churning darkness. "I don't think I can do this," he said, his voice shaking. "It's too much. I'm not strong enough."

We had been fighting against the swamp's grip since the moment we stepped into it, pushing forward despite every force trying to drag us under. And now, it was unleashing everything.

Grace's words echoed in my mind, steady despite the chaos: The swamp will throw everything it has at you now. It will try to break you, to make you turn back. You can't let it.

I swallowed hard, gripping the coin in my pocket. You can't let it.

Joshua clenched his jaw, his uncertainty flickering in his eyes.

Gillie took a sharp breath, glancing toward the towering oak in the distance. "Here we go," she muttered under her breath. "Grace told us this was the last test… just one more."

The ground beneath us trembled violently, cracks splintering through the earth as dark tendrils of mist began to rise, coiling around our feet like shackles. The shadows surged closer, their movements sharper, more deliberate.

And then, for the first time, we saw them—figures emerging from the swirling darkness.

Marcus's Army of the Dark.

Twisted forms of lost souls bound to his will. Their eyes glowed faintly in the dim light, their movements unnaturally fluid as they formed a circle around us, cutting us off from the oak tree.

Marcus's voice broke through the roar of the bells, smooth and commanding, carried on the wind like a taunt. "You've come so far," he said, his tone laced with mockery. "But did you really think it would be that easy? That you could reach the end without facing the cost?"

Then, quieter—too quiet for anyone but me to hear: "*I gave everything for this.*"

Gillie raised her knife, her stance defensive. "Show yourself, Marcus!" she shouted, her voice defiant even as the air grew colder around us. "If you're so powerful, why are you hiding behind them?"

His laughter rippled through the swamp, low and resonant. "Why waste my energy when my army will do the work for me? You're already breaking. I can feel it. And soon, you'll fall."

The bells tolled again, louder than ever, the force of the sound knocking us back a step. The shadows of Marcus's army surged forward, their movements chaotic but purposeful, their hollow eyes fixed on us.

"We have to move," I said, my voice shaking but firm. "If we stand here, we're done."

"Toward the tree," Gillie said, her voice steady despite the growing tension. "It's the only place they can't touch. If we make it there, we'll see the truth. We'll face what we've been running from."

Joshua hesitated, his eyes darting between the looming army and the towering oak in the distance. "And if we don't make it?"

"We will," Gillie said sharply, grabbing his arm and pulling him forward. "We have to."

We ran.

The mist tore at us like grasping hands. The bells hammered our skulls. The ground split beneath our feet. The army of shadows surged toward us from all sides, pressing closer, trying to force us back.

But the oak stood ahead, unmoved, unwavering, a beacon against the storm.

Confronting Raven

The storm raged, its fury threatening to tear the swamp apart. The tolling bells pounded against the sky, each strike reverberating through my skull, shaking the ground beneath my feet. Shadows closed in, pressing against the mist, Marcus's army pushing forward, relentless in their pursuit.

We ran, but the swamp didn't just pull at our bodies—it pulled at our minds, twisting through our thoughts, forcing doubt into every breath. The wind screamed, the ground fractured, the shadows warped around us, shifting with unnatural precision.

Then the air changed.

The mist tightened, constricting inward like a hand closing around my throat. The storm bent—not breaking, but shifting—contorting into something colder, sharper. It wasn't Marcus's army.

It was something worse.

The bells stretched into something hollow, a sharp, lingering sound that rang between the thunder. And as the mist rolled aside, Raven stepped forward, his presence cutting through the chaos like a blade.

Marcus's army didn't stop, their footsteps pounding against the trembling earth, their movements syncing with the storm. They were still coming—always coming.

But Raven wasn't with them. He didn't need numbers, didn't need weapons or brute force.

He was the storm itself.

His presence bent the chaos inward, folding shadows against the wind, pressing weight into the space around us. My lungs strained against the suffocating pressure, and yet my feet kept moving, pushing forward, pulling the others with me.

"You've fought so hard to leave us behind," Raven said, his voice slicing through the storm, cutting through the noise like it had been built to own it. "But we're still here. Watching. Waiting. You thought you could outrun us? Escape us? We've always been with you."

Marcus's army pressed closer. Their movements never slowed, their pace unbroken, closing the gaps, forcing us toward the only place left to go.

I thought of the weight I had carried long before entering this place. A choice I wasn't sure had ever truly belonged to me. A burden that had shaped every step forward, whether I realized it or not.

"You don't know anything about me," I said, forcing my voice steady even as the storm threatened to break me apart. "You're not with me."

Raven tilted his head slightly, the movement small, calculated—predatory. "Not with you?" he murmured, his voice soft but sharpened. "We're in every thought you try to push away. In every doubt you carry. You feel it, don't you? No matter how fast you run, how far you go—you carry us with you. Because you can't outrun what's in your blood."

"You've always run," he said, his voice dropping low. "Even before the swamp. Even when it was just that field, that night, the candlelight, the guilt."

Behind him, something lurched in the mist—a flicker of movement, a ripple in Marcus's army. Their pace shifted, tightening their hold, adjusting their approach. They weren't waiting anymore.

They were preparing.

I clenched my teeth, forcing my steps forward even as Raven's voice bore against my ribs, pressing into the edges of my resolve.

"You don't define me," I said, sharper now, though my voice still wavered. "I'm not you."

Raven laughed, the sound wafting through the air like smoke. "Oh, but you are," he said, taking a slow step forward. His form flickered, the mist pulsing against his presence. "You carry everything we were—our guilt, our failures, our pain. It's all there. You've tried to bury it, but it's always been there. And it always will be."

Marcus's army was still moving, threading through the storm, pressing closer with each second.

"You're wrong," I said, though the words felt fragile against the weight of him. "*I carry your mistakes, yes. But I'm not you. I'm something more.*"

His smile darkened. His eyes narrowed, his voice dropping to something colder. "*You think carrying us makes you stronger?*" he asked, his words threading through the wind, wrapping around my pulse. "It doesn't. It makes you weak. And when you fall—and you will fall—it'll be because of us. You'll never be rid of us. We are in you."

The bells screamed, shaking the swamp beneath us. Marcus's army moved in tandem with the sound, their figures shifting in the mist, their pace unbroken.

I forced my steps forward, locking eyes with Raven, meeting the weight of his presence without stopping.

"You're right," I said, my voice quieter now but steadier. "I can't get rid of you. I can't change the fact that your blood is in my veins. But that doesn't mean you define me. It doesn't mean I have to give in to you."

His expression flickered, his smile hesitating for the briefest moment.

Then the storm fractured around him, his shadow rippling violently, his form twisting in the chaos.

"You think carrying us differently changes anything?" he asked, his voice rising, edged with quiet fury. "You're already falling. And when you hit the ground, you'll see—you were never different from us. Never."

The shadows tore through the mist, feeding off his words, pulling the storm tighter. Marcus's army hadn't broken stride, their movements syncing with the chaos, their presence pressing in from all sides.

I kept moving.

I didn't falter.

And through the storm, through the writhing mist, the shadows, the chaos, I saw it…

The ancient oak.

Still standing.

Still waiting.

Marcus's army hadn't stopped—the storm had grown, had tightened.

But I didn't stop either.

Raven's form shattered like glass, dissolving into the mist, his shadow bleeding into the swirling darkness. But even as he disappeared, the weight of his presence lingered, heavy and unyielding.

The storm raged on. The bells tolled louder than ever. Marcus's army hadn't stopped—their pursuit was still relentless.

They moved like a tide with purpose—no faces, no names, only direction.

And I ran.

Raven's blood might flow through my veins. His pain, his failures, his choices were part of me. But they weren't all of me.

I could carry them without letting them consume me.

And that was something he—and they—could never take away.

Elana's Sacrifice

The storm surged forward, unrelenting. The tolling bells hammered against the air, the mist writhing as Marcus's army closed in, their movements tightening, adjusting, hunting. We ran, but the swamp twisted against us, forcing the maelstrom into something more merciless, more calculated.

Then Elana stepped from the shadows.

Her glow flickered—weak, barely holding. She stood in our path—tense shoulders, hesitant steps. Her gaze darted toward the mist, toward the shifting army pressing closer, but not with fear.

She was watching. Waiting.

Joshua's voice cracked against the storm, raw with confusion, maybe even hope. "Elana! We have to keep moving—are you coming with us?"

Gillie didn't slow. She didn't hesitate.

She tightened her grip on her knife, eyes sharp, voice sharper. "Move," she snapped. "Now, Elana. Or get out of our way."

Elana didn't move.

"*I… I wanted to help you,*" she whispered, her voice thin, swallowed almost instantly by the torrent. "*But he won't let me.*"

Gillie laughed, but it wasn't amusement—it was sharp, bitter.

"Of course he is," she said. "And you're helping him again. You always help him. You never cared about us, never once."

Elana flinched, but she didn't argue.

"He promised me power, purpose," she murmured. "He promised I could make a difference. But all I've done is…." Her voice cracked.

I pushed forward, heart pounding, watching Gillie's stance as much as I watched Elana. Marcus's army hadn't slowed. We didn't have time for hesitation.

"Elana, if you want to fight him, then fight him," I said, my voice urgent, pressed against the weight of the storm. "But we're moving forward."

Gillie didn't ease up, didn't soften.

"You don't understand," Elana murmured, her voice barely holding. "He's in my head. In my heart. I can't escape him."

Gillie's voice came fast, clipped. "Then why are you here?"

Elana hesitated too long, just long enough that the mist tightened.

Then she whispered, "He's coming. He's using me to bring you to him."

Gillie snorted, shaking her head. "Obviously." She stepped forward, knife still in hand. "That's what you do, Elana. You play the innocent while leading people straight to him."

Elana winced, but didn't deny it. "*I didn't want to,*" she whispered, voice rising slightly, desperate. "*But he… he has power over me. I couldn't…*" Her voice cracked. "*But I can't let him win. Not completely.*"

Joshua hesitated, his expression torn. "Elana, we can help you…."

"No," Gillie cut him off. "She's stalling. She's always stalling."

Elana shook her head, a faint, bitter smile crossing her lips. "You can't help me. Not anymore. But I can help you."

Gillie's grip tightened on her weapon. "Why should we believe that?"

Elana didn't flinch now—instead, she held her ground, gaze steady despite the tremble in her voice. "Because it's the only way to stop him. He expects me to trap you before you reach the oak. But if I break free, even for a moment, it'll be enough."

Gillie didn't move, but something flickered in her expression—something uncertain.

Marcus's army pressed closer—the mist tightened, the tempest writhed, preparing for the inevitable moment it would strike.

Elana turned toward the darkness, her shoulders squaring.

"Go," she said, firm now, unyielding. "Get to the oak."

Joshua reached for her, desperation clinging to his voice. "Elana, please. You don't have to do this alone."

She didn't flinch this time. "Yes, I do," she said quietly. "But it's okay, Joshua. This is my choice. And for the first time, it's mine alone."

Marcus's army shifted—their hesitation was ending.

Before we could stop her, she stepped into the shadows.

A ripple of movement rushed through the mist—the army lunging forward, their dark forms converging around her. But then, with a burst of light, she pushed them back, her voice cutting through the chaos.

"Marcus!" she screamed, her voice splintering through the gales. "You wanted me to lead them? Then let's see if you can follow."

The light surrounding her flared brighter. The shadows recoiled. The chaos twisted violently, the mist unraveling into something wild, something uncontrollable.

Marcus's voice roared through the swamp, filled with fury. "Elana, you fool! You think you can defy me?"

She didn't answer.

Instead, she turned back to us one last time, her glow pulsing, flickering between strength and collapse.

"Run," she said softly.

And then she was gone, consumed by the light and the storm.

Marcus's army screamed, the mist writhing violently, but her sacrifice had created an opening—a path to the oak tree, clear and unobstructed.

We didn't have time to mourn.

We ran.

The Final Choice

The storm devoured the swamp, collapsing inward, its grip tightening with each step we took. Tolling bells crashed through the sky, rolling over the wind, pressing into my ribs, stealing my breath.

Beneath the weight of Marcus's unseen army, the ground trembled. Their forms shifted like a single, calculated entity moving through the mist. They weren't scattered forces; they were unified, deliberate, unstoppable.

Lightning shattered the mist, briefly illuminating dark forms closing in. Their movements threaded through shadows, pressing forward, sealing our escape.

The swamp wouldn't release us.

Marcus's grip intensified, and with it, the storm's violence, its intent.

No escape route formed, no path opened; we weren't running toward safety. Instead, we were directed. Pushed. Guided toward something unseen.

That realization burned, coiling around my pulse.

Then, whispers. Not spoken, not shouted, simply present. *You're too close to see it, aren't you?* A ripple of unease crawled up my spine.

Raven. His presence wasn't sudden but inevitable, wrapping around us, threading into the cracks of our fear, dragging itself into the disturbance as if it belonged there. No entrance needed, no announcement given; he had always been waiting.

Joshua slowed. His breathing was uneven as the mist swirled around us—not an attack, not a trick, just an oppressive presence. Watching. Listening.

His grip tightened on his belt, fingernails digging into the leather. This was a desperate, almost unconscious attempt to ground himself against the encroaching dread.

But unwelcome words whispered at the edges of his mind, refusing to dissipate:

What if Marcus isn't lying?

That uninvited, toxic seed of doubt had been silently circling since their last harrowing encounter. It was a persistent hum beneath the surface of his resolve.

Gillie shot Joshua a sharp, tense glance. Her stance was coiled and more defensive than usual. Her senses were acutely attuned to the subtle shifts in the atmosphere and his demeanor. "You okay?" Her voice was low, laced with a concern that bordered on suspicion.

Joshua's hesitation stretched for a fraction of a second too long. It was a beat of uncertainty that did not go unnoticed. Gillie's gaze sharpened. "Joshua." He exhaled sharply, shaking his head as if to physically dislodge the intrusive thought. He rubbed his temple with a weary hand. "I just… he talks like he knows something we don't."

Frustration twisted Gillie's features, her skepticism evident. "That's manipulation, Joshua. That's him. You think for one second he's telling the truth?" Joshua's delayed answer hung in the charged air. The silence itself was a damning indictment.

Marcus's voice, like a tendril of intrusive smoke, wound its way through Joshua's thoughts. It was a venomous whisper designed to erode his certainty: "*You think you know the truth, Joshua? Tell me—if you're so certain, why does the swamp still hold you? Why haven't you escaped? Why haven't you won?"*

His pulse hammered against his ribs, a frantic, erratic rhythm. It mirrored the turmoil in his mind. He'd pondered those very questions before. They were a shared, unspoken burden they all carried.

The swamp held them by its own inscrutable will. That was Gillie's unwavering belief, Grace's insistent truth, ingrained since the very beginning of their desperate struggle. But Marcus held his own insidious certainty, a counter-narrative that gnawed at the edges of their collective faith.

Joshua's breath hitched, a sudden intake of air. "What if…" He swallowed hard, his gaze flickering with a hesitant uncertainty toward Gillie. "What if… what if we're the ones refusing to see something?"

Gillie's blade sprang into existence. It moved with a swift, lethal grace. A sharp metallic scrape cut through the electrically charged air. "No," she snapped, her voice tight with conviction. "That's his game, Joshua. Doubt planted. The fight blurred. He wins before we even swing."

Joshua's jaw clenched involuntarily. A knot of anxiety tightened in his stomach. "You don't *know* that, Gillie." Gillie's posture stiffened. Her shoulders drew back with a rigid defensiveness.

Regret, sharp and immediate, pulsed through Joshua. He registered the impact of his words, the subtle fracture in their unity. There was no shout, no outright accusation. Just a slow, weary headshake. Frustration laced her voice, raw with exhaustion and a deeper, unspoken fear. *"I do know, Joshua,"* she murmured, her gaze unwavering. *"And deep down, you do too."*

The gusts magnified as Raven moved, his presence bending the wind inward, drawing the mist unnaturally at his feet, suffocating the air like an invisible hand.

"You think she saved you?" Raven's voice, dominant, owned the chaos. "She didn't. Merely delayed the inevitable." Joshua's breath caught again.

I forced my steps forward, refusing to yield. "You don't know that," I bit out. "You don't know anything about us."

Raven's slow, sharp laugh threaded through the mist, a sound that had already decided the outcome. *"Not about you,"* he murmured. *"But her? Oh, we know her too well. Fought for you? Lied for you? Never. Always herself."*

Gillie pushed ahead, her expression ice-cold, but a flicker of hesitation betrayed her; Raven's words weren't unnoticed. The poison had found its cracks, seeping beneath the surface.

"She didn't lead them away," Raven continued, his soft voice creeping inward. "She led you forward. You ran into the trap willingly, trusting the one who always knew how to make you hesitate. Do you see it now?"

The ground fractured. The storm pressed, trying to slow us, to force us to listen. *They don't see it.* The unbidden thought wove through my pulse.

Then the mist ripped apart. Elana stepped forward, half-formed, her glow flickering weakly against the darkness. Slow, uncertain movements, her body trembling against unseen forces.

A raised hand—not a greeting, but a halt. The wind whipped violently, the force peeling apart the silence.

Joshua's voice cracked. "Elana! We have to keep moving—are you coming?" Her gaze darted toward the mist, the waiting army, and her hesitation chilled me.

Gillie, ever vigilant, noticed it first. "Why are they waiting?" she demanded. Her knife was gripped white-knuckled. Her voice was sharp with suspicion. "They've never hesitated before. Why no attack?" Elana flinched visibly. Her eyes were wide with a trapped fear. "They… Marcus… he's watching."

Not enough.

Gillie stepped forward, unreadable. "Did he tell you to stop us?" she asked, her voice unnervingly steady. Elana's headshake was too slow. "No. I…"

"You led him straight to us," Gillie said coldly, the truth exposed. Marcus's army shifted, pressing closer, as if sensing the moment was breaking.

Gillie moved toward Elana, breath sharp, eyes narrowed. "Then why haven't they moved?" Elana's glow flickered. "I…"

Suddenly, Raven's low, knowing chuckle pierced the air. "Of course she's stalling," he said, irony lacing his voice. "Brilliant, really. If you fail, Elana's plan wins. Distraction. Just long enough for Marcus. You already believe her."

The realization hit hard. *No.* I turned toward the mist, toward the waiting army. That was the test. The trap. Marcus didn't need to attack. He was already winning.

Joshua took a shaky breath. "Elana, what did you do?" She looked at him, eyes wide, pleading, as though searching for an answer. But was it real?

The wind screamed through the swamp, the chaos reached its peak, the mist swallowed everything but the untouched oak. I stepped back, heart pounding. "The tree. Move—now."

Gillie's voice was sharp and final. It cut through the storm's roar. "Tell the truth, Elana. Did Marcus send you?" A single, damning moment of hesitation. Gillie didn't wait for the lie. Knife gripped tight, she let out a sharp, decisive exhale. "Run."

Joshua faltered. Elana's pleading gaze met his, waiting—almost as if she knew that single moment of hesitation was all she needed. But I saw it with stark clarity—no reach for us, no step toward the sanctuary of the oak. She wasn't coming. She never planned to.

I grabbed Joshua's arm. My grip was firm and urgent. "Run!"

The storm collapsed inward with a violent implosion. The mist recoiled. The tolling bells screamed a final, deafening lament. Marcus's unseen army surged forward. Their hesitation was shattered. Dark forms ripped through the dissipating haze, lunging with terrifying speed.

We ran, driven by a primal instinct for survival. The ground fractured beneath our feet. The wind tore at us like unseen hands, dragging us back toward the encroaching darkness. Raven's voice, twisted with cruel satisfaction, echoed in the chaos. *This was your test. You failed it the moment you trusted her.*

Marcus's relentless army pressed closer. Their unseen presence was a suffocating weight. Lightning split the sky one last time. It briefly illuminated the steadfast oak, our only hope.

I wasn't running from Raven, or the guilt. Not anymore.

I was running toward something—who I could be. Who I was already becoming.

We didn't look back. We ran toward the light. Toward sanctuary. Toward the truth we could no longer avoid.

The shadows crashed in around us. Marcus's army roared their unseen triumph. The mist collapsed completely—but we made it. We reached the oak. And everything shifted.

The mist broke against the oak like a scream swallowed by silence.

The First Four Bells

The First Bell: The End Begins

The oak tree rose before us, larger than life itself. It wasn't just a tree—it felt eternal, ancient, untouched by the darkness that had gripped every part of the swamp. Its roots stretched wide and deep beneath the trembling ground, weaving through the earth like veins carrying the lifeblood of something far greater. The air around it felt different, charged with something unspoken, something neither the storm nor the chaos had managed to claim.

The storm hadn't followed us here. It churned at the edges, pressing against an unseen boundary, its fury rolling through the mist but never crossing. Beneath it, Marcus's army remained, shifting at a distance, waiting—not attacking, not advancing, simply holding the line in eerie silence. The space surrounding the oak pulsed with an invisible force, pushing back against the storm, against the war itself.

The bark was weathered and smooth, yet beneath its surface, something pulsed faintly—a golden glow, as though light itself resided within, waiting to be revealed. A steady, radiant beam of energy shot upward, piercing the storm above, rising past the mist like it was reaching for something beyond sight, something greater than the battlefield. And for the first time, the swamp was silent.

But silence was never safety.

The air shifted, charged with something heavier, something deliberate. It wasn't relief—it was expectation. The ground beneath us no longer trembled in fear, but in anticipation. The war had reached its threshold, and now, there was only this—standing beneath the oak, breathing in the weight of the moment before the truth revealed itself.

Then came the voice.

"You've come far," it murmured—soft, unrelenting. It wasn't new, wasn't sudden. It existed previously, beneath the storm, moving with the wind while unnoticed. It had waited. It had watched.

"Farther than we expected. But you did not come whole."

The mist thickened, weaving itself into shifting forms, twisting through the space between the roots and branches. The air itself stirred, twisting inward, pressing against my skin like unseen hands threading through the fabric of the world itself. And then Marcus stepped forward, emerging from the mist, his form blurring at the edges, shifting like the swamp itself.

His dark eyes gleamed with quiet amusement as he gestured toward something suspended in the air—small, flickering remnants woven between the golden strands of light.

"There they are," he murmured, tone laced with satisfaction. *"The pieces you lost."*

His fingers twitched slightly at his side, almost absentmindedly, as though testing the weight of his own words.

"The parts of you I stripped away."

The fragments pulsed, flickering above the roots. Their light was soft, familiar—but wrong. Dimmed, fragile, incomplete. Marcus tilted his head, studying them, watching as they trembled, as if caught between existence and oblivion.

Then, his gaze found Joshua.

"Your hope."

The nearest fragment flickered weakly, the glow fragile, fading, struggling to remain. Joshua's jaw tightened, his breath shallow—but he didn't recoil. Didn't flinch.

Marcus watched, waiting. Expecting collapse. Expecting the weight of absence to bury him beneath something irreversible.

But Joshua only exhaled, slow and steady, his shoulders squaring, his stance unshaken.

Something sharp flashed through Marcus's expression, but he didn't stop.

His eyes flicked to Gillie.

"Your fire."

Another piece trembled, struggling to hold onto its light, threatening to collapse in on itself. Gillie's hold on her knife became more secure, with her fingers firmly gripping the handle without any movement. She didn't speak—not with words, not with anything Marcus had expected.

He had anticipated anger. Defiance. A challenge.

Instead, she just stood there, silent, teeth clenched around something unyielding.

His smirk wasn't quite as sharp now.

Finally, his eyes locked onto me.

"Your purpose."

The last fragment shuddered, the glow dimming, teetering on the edge of something irretrievable. My fingers found the coin before I could think about it, pressing it into my palm, gripping it with something that felt more like certainty than desperation.

It was still there.

Marcus let the silence stretch, his gaze flickering between us, searching.

Waiting.

And that was when I felt it.

The absence wasn't just loss.

It was change.

Marcus's smile vanished altogether.

For the first time, he didn't understand what was happening.

He gestured lazily toward the fragments, but the movement wasn't quite as effortless as before. He had been so sure, so assured that whatever he had taken, whatever he had stripped away, would be final. Irreversible.

"You remember them, don't you?" he murmured. "That feeling, just beyond reach?"

The weight of his words settled into my ribs, pressing against something fragile I wasn't prepared to name. Joshua stared at the flickering glow in front of him, unmoving. Gillie tightened her grip on her blade, still silent, still watching, still waiting.

And me—I still felt the weight.

Just differently now.

Marcus stepped forward, his voice lower now, pressing into the charged air, testing it.

"You thought you could move forward unchanged," he said, watching us carefully. "You thought the price wouldn't linger. But the swamp doesn't forget. And neither do I."

The ground rumbled, and the light at the center of the oak pulsed brighter, stretching long shadows across the swamp, bending them in unnatural ways.

"The time has come," Marcus said, his amusement now gone completely. "To reclaim what you've lost—or to let it go forever."

Joshua's voice cracked as he whispered, "*What… what do you mean?*"

Marcus exhaled slowly, tilting his head, the sharp amusement dulling into something unreadable.

"Ah, choices." His tone was flat now. "So tedious, yet so inevitable."

He turned back toward the fragments, his gaze lingering.

"Reclaim them, if you dare." His voice had sharpened, the edge now forced, no longer effortless. "But the swamp won't make it easy. You'll have to face it—all of it. The weight, the regrets, the fear. Everything you buried to survive."

The mist coiled tighter, shifting at the edges of the clearing, pressing inward, crawling toward us with renewed intention.

Marcus's voice remained steady.

Unforgiving.

"Can you confront it?" he asked, the words sinking into the space between us.

"Can you endure it?"

His gaze swept across us, calculating, searching for the cracks, for the hesitations, for the weakness he could exploit. Then, he paused, letting the silence stretch, letting the weight of the moment settle deep into the air between us. When he finally spoke, his voice was softer, but the venom laced the edges of his words, slipping through the stillness like something tangible.

"Or perhaps," he murmured, his tone almost contemplative, almost amused, "you've grown comfortable with your emptiness. Why reach for what's already gone? Let it go. Accept what you've become."

Gillie snarled, the sound sharp, cutting through the stagnant air as she stepped forward, her knife drawn, her stance rigid, unyielding. "And if we don't choose?" she demanded, her voice edged with something final, something unforgiving, her teeth clenched around something that hadn't broken.

Marcus tilted his head, watching her, expression unreadable. Then, with a deliberate slowness, he exhaled. "Then the swamp will choose for you," he said, his voice heavy with finality. "And I assure you—you won't like its answer."

The words had barely settled before the world shattered.

The explosion tore through the swamp, violent and absolute. A detonation of pure sound, rupturing the air, rolling through the mist in unchecked waves, bursting through the ground beneath us. Cracks splintered outward, jagged fractures slicing into the earth, stretching toward the mist as if tearing through the very fabric of the world itself.

The force didn't stop at the ground—it tore through us, pressing into our chests, forcing the breath from our lungs, leaving only pressure, only pain.

Joshua stumbled backward, hands clutching his ears, his voice strangled as he gasped, "It's… it's worse than before! It's in my bones… it's everywhere!"

Gillie gritted her teeth, bracing against the oak's roots, muscles locked against the tremor rattling through her. "It's not just a sound," she shouted over the chaos. "It's a force!"

The swamp shuddered, mist writhing, twisting violently, shrinking back in chaotic waves. The air throbbed with something primal, something living, something neither light nor darkness had controlled before.

Then… the realization struck.

It was one of the bells.

But this chime was different.

And Marcus—he moved.

Not forward.

Back.

His form blurred at the edges, his stance faltered. Breath uneven. Jaw tight. His reaction wasn't fear. It was pain. Real, undeniable, clawing through him like something he hadn't anticipated. The bell's chime was tearing through him, pressing into the spaces where his power had once felt untouchable, forcing into the gaps, cracking the foundations he had once believed were indestructible.

The echo lingered, stretching into a silence thick, charged, alive.

Then, cutting through the ringing, the voice came again.

"Twelve hours."

The words settled heavily, sinking deeper than the bell's toll, more suffocating, more certain.

Joshua turned wildly, searching for an answer, for something, for someone.

The mist parted.

Grace stepped forward.

The air still trembled, the swamp shaking beneath our feet, the bell's fury lingering like an aftershock refusing to fade. The echoes pressed against my ribs, thrumming through the ground, through the mist, through my pulse, threading into the cracks of uncertainty that had yet to be sealed.

Grace's voice cut through the chaos, sharp, unwavering.

"Twelve hours."

Joshua flinched, his breaths uneven as he turned to her. "Twelve hours? What does that mean?"

Grace didn't hesitate. "It means you only have twelve hours before the God Forsaken Bell. When it rings the final time, it'll decide what's left of you."

Joshua's breaths came fast and shallow as his gaze darted toward her, searching for something beyond the words. "And then what?" he rasped. "What are we supposed to do?"

Grace exhaled sharply, but her eyes remained locked on the tree, her pulse steady despite the tremors still rattling the ground beneath us.

"You have to choose," she said. "Now."

Gillie let out an exasperated breath, pacing near the base of the trunk, frustration bleeding through the cracks in her composure. "Decide what?" she snapped, her voice sharp, demanding something solid to hold onto. "We're here. We made it. What else is there to decide?"

Grace turned to her, expression firm, unyielding.

"What you're willing to let go of," she said simply. "What you're willing to surrender."

Joshua's hands shook at his sides as he stared up at the branches, their ends disappearing into the misted sky. "I've been holding onto all of it—my guilt, my fear—because I didn't think I could let go," he said, voice cracking under the weight. "What if I can't? What if I don't know how?"

Grace stepped closer, her voice no longer sharp, but steady. Grounding.

"The tree isn't asking for perfection," she said. "It's asking for truth. For surrender. Only you can decide what that means."

Joshua's gaze flicked to me, then to Gillie, and finally back to the radiant glow of the tree. His breaths came fast and shallow, fear threading through every movement, tightening at the edges of hesitation.

"What if it's not enough?" he whispered. "What if I let go and… there's nothing left of me?"

Grace's expression softened, but her voice held the same weight, the same certainty.

"You are enough," she said firmly, the words resonating as clearly as the bell had moments ago. "You always have been. But now, you have to believe it."

The oak stood steady, its light unwavering, its roots anchoring it against the chaos still lingering beyond its reach. It hadn't faltered. It hadn't bent beneath the storm.

Whatever came next, it would demand everything we had left—and everything we were willing to release.

The countdown had begun.

The Army of Light Gathers

The second bell tolled—sharper, sudden, cutting through the hush like a blade drawn clean through flesh. It cracked against the air, splitting the stillness apart, forcing the swamp to flinch beneath the weight.

The waters rippled violently, trembling beneath the unseen force. The twisted roots buried in the mire strained, bending inward as if the bell's toll had reached beneath the surface, pulling at what had long remained hidden. The mist did not just thicken—it clutched, its edges weaving together in tight coils, suffocating the space around us.

Joshua staggered, one hand clutched against his chest as the vibrations rattled through him, shaking him from the inside out. His breath came sharp and uneven, his voice strained, broken between gasps. *"It's heavier now,"* he murmured, words forced between breaths. *"Like it's driving straight through us."*

Gillie gritted her teeth, bracing against the oak's roots, her grip iron—tight as she fought to stay steady. Her legs trembled under the force, but she did not falter. "It's not just sound anymore," she muttered, voice sharp, strained. "It feels like it's tearing into the ground itself."

The storm shrieked, the ground buckling beneath the pressure, but then—the light struck back.

The golden beam flared, expanding outward with blinding force, flooding the clearing with an intensity that defied the swamp's darkness. The tree wasn't passive—it was reacting, its branches lifting higher, its roots anchoring deeper, answering the bell's violent call with something stronger, something more primal.

The light pulsed, weaving through the air like a living force, forcing the mist back, forcing the shadows to retreat. Marcus's domain was breaking, splintering beneath the presence of something it could no longer control.

And Grace—she stood unmoved, woven into the radiance, no longer just calming but commanding, undeniable, like the tree itself had drawn her into its pulse, threading her presence into the golden strands of power stretching outward.

Joshua stared, the glow washing over his face, digging into his skin like something searching for something inside him. *"Grace,"* he whispered, voice raw with urgency. *"What's happening? What are you doing?"*

She turned to him, her expression firm, unshaken. "It's not just me," she said, her words carrying weight, laced with something vast, something neither of us could fully grasp. *"It's all of us. The ones who chose the light."*

Gillie tensed, her knife still raised. "Others?" she demanded, voice sharp. "Who are you talking about?"

Grace's gaze lifted toward the mist beyond the clearing.

"The lost souls."

Her voice was steady, but there was something heavier beneath it—something that carried years of suffering, of choices that could never be undone. "The ones who refused the dark. The ones who held on, even when everything tried to pull them under."

Then, the golden beam pulsed again, expanding, reaching, calling.

And they answered.

Light threaded through the mist, weaving like strands of gold, touching the edges of the swamp and drawing figures from the darkness.

Joshua stepped forward, watching as the glow stretched across the clearing, its reach undeniable, unstoppable.

They were coming.

At first, it was just a few—silhouettes emerging, faces etched with exhaustion but filled with determination.

Then more.

And more.

Until they gathered, moving as one, drawn to the beam, to the tree, to Grace.

The army of light had arrived.

Gillie's grip on her knife loosened slightly, her gaze darting between Grace and the growing procession. The presence of the lost souls filled the clearing, their movements steady, their resolve unshaken.

But something else moved in the mist.

Not the light.

Not the ones who had chosen to hold on.

Gillie noticed them first—dark figures coiling at the edges, unmoving but watching.

Grace exhaled, barely shifting the air, but her voice carried across the space between us, pressing inward with quiet finality.

"There were others," she said softly. "The ones who gave in."

Joshua's breath hitched, his pulse quickening, his hands tightening into fists at his sides.

Grace continued, her voice measured, deliberate, unflinching against the truth.

"*They followed the darkness. They let themselves be taken. And now—they serve him.*"

The words settled like stone, sinking into the air between us.

"Marcus twisted them," she said, her voice unwavering despite the weight of what she was saying. "He made them believe the light abandoned them. That it betrayed them. That it was never meant for them."

Her gaze flickered toward Joshua, then Gillie.

"So they turned against it. Against everything that could've saved them."

The mist tightened, swirling inward, shifting—not striking yet, but waiting.

"And now," Grace murmured, "they follow him."

Joshua's jaw locked, his fingers clenching slightly at his sides, his breath short, uneven.

Gillie's grip on her knife didn't waver, but her breath did.

The lost souls stood at the edges, their presence cold, unwavering, brimming with something twisted inside them, something shaped by Marcus's hand, something willing.

The golden beam pulsed, stretching outward, pulling the army of light closer, tighter, unified.

And behind them—the mist stirred.

Preparing for something none of us could stop now.

The Shadows Close In

The third bell struck—a pulse, deep and resonant, stretching through the swamp, rattling the hollow space between water and sky. It didn't crack like the second, nor did it hum like the first. It swelled, filling every empty space, forcing its weight into the land.

The stagnant water lurched, sucking at the ground as if something beneath it had stirred. The air thickened, damp and heavy, burning against our lungs with each toll. The swamp was no longer just reacting—it was responding.

But the oak did not bend.

Its roots held firm, threaded deep into the earth without strain, without hesitation. The golden beam at its core blazed against the fury, untouchable, unbroken, defying the force that tried to break it. The light did not falter—it only grew, stretching higher, expanding outward, forcing back the suffocating mist with unwavering strength.

The bell's toll tore through the air, through us, leaving a pressure so overwhelming it was as though the swamp itself had split wide open, as though its very foundation had cracked beneath the weight of this final warning.

But the tree stood—unchallenged, unmovable, absolute.

Joshua clutched his chest, his knees buckling as a strangled gasp tore from his throat. "It's tearing everything apart!" he choked, his voice barely cutting through the immense, resonant echo that still rattled through the clearing.

Gillie stumbled, her knife slipping from her grasp as she clamped her hands over her ears, eyes squeezed shut against the force of the sound. "This is worse than the last two," she shouted, though the words were small against the sheer crashing weight of the bell. "It's like it's trying to crush us!"

Grace stood unmoved.

The glow surrounding her remained steady, radiating through the chime's relentless force. The air still vibrated, the resonance clinging to the ground, threading through the mist, refusing to fade.

Then—her voice cut through the chaos, sharp, unwavering.

"The bell isn't trying to crush us."

She wasn't shaken. She wasn't afraid.

She understood.

"It's a warning."

Her gaze flicked toward the shifting mist, toward the tightening shadows, toward the tremors still rattling the ground beneath our feet.

And then she spoke the words that landed heavier than the bell's toll itself.

"He's coming."

The swamp changed.

The mist, once suffocating, turned sharp, cold, alive. The air thickened, pressing against us like unseen hands, twisting inward, threading into our lungs, forcing itself into the spaces where fear lingered. The ground shifted, buckling, wrenching into something new—something deliberate.

At the edges of the clearing, the shadows stilled.

No longer flickering.

No longer uncertain.

Now, they moved.

Purposeful.

Precise.

Marcus's voice tore through the storm, louder than before, more commanding than ever.

"You think your light will save you?" he taunted, his tone seething with contempt, rich with amusement. "You've clung to your hope, to your foolish faith, but none of it will stand against what's coming. You've brought yourselves to the heart of my domain…"

The mist swelled.

The ground cracked deeper.

And then Marcus declared.

"Now, you will fall."

The oak tree's light flared.

Brighter.

Bolder.

As though answering his challenge.

The golden beam that shot toward the sky expanded, stretching outward in a burst of defiance, pushing against the encroaching mist and shadows. It was no longer just a presence—it was a shield, a defense against the growing storm.

And Grace stood at its center.

Her glow merged with the tree's radiance, intertwining until there was no distinction between them.

And then—the oak did not resist.

It did not fight back.

It did not retreat.

It simply allowed.

The shadows surged.

Their movements were no longer erratic but calculated, synchronized, their forms rippling through the swamp like a living tide. They weren't just shadows anymore.

They were Marcus's forces.

An army of darkness, twisted and willing.

They poured from the mist like a flood—endless, unrelenting, consuming the space between us with their sheer magnitude.

And leading them, towering and suffocating, stood Marcus.

He emerged from the blackness like the embodiment of the swamp itself, his form shrouded in shifting shadows, his presence radiating with raw power. His voice carried over the battlefield, sharp and commanding, clawing into our bones.

"You stand against me with your pitiful light?" he snarled. "You think it'll protect you? You think it'll save you? Look around."

The mist twisted.

The swamp thrived beneath him.

And then Marcus declared, his voice a final blow.

"The swamp is mine. This place is mine."

His gaze settled on us.

"And now—so are you."

The air crackled with tension, thick with inevitability, as the two forces faced off—the golden light of the oak blazing defiantly against the coming storm. The army of light, those who had gathered at Grace's call, stood at the ready, their glow intensifying as they prepared to meet the onslaught. They weren't warriors in the traditional sense.

They carried no blades.

No armor.

But they carried something stronger.

Their hope.

Their faith.

Their refusal to fall.

Grace stepped forward, her presence commanding despite the overwhelming odds.

"Marcus."

Her voice rang clear over the storm.

"You've fought to claim this place, to bend it to your will. But your darkness will never consume the light."

She did not falter.

"It never has."

And then, the declaration that split through the battlefield—unshaken, unbroken.

"It never will."

Marcus laughed.

A low, mocking rumble that rolled through the swamp, through the storm, moving against the golden light.

"You think words will stop me?"

His sneer was sharp, cruel.

"You think your tree, your faith, your light can stand against the storm?"

The mist grew, thickening behind him, swallowing the space where the shadows moved in silence.

"I will tear you apart."

Marcus stepped forward.

"I will devour everything you hold dear."

Joshua hesitated, his fear evident as he glanced at the oncoming army, his breath shallow, his pulse rapid. "Grace," he rasped. "What do we do? How do we fight them?"

Grace turned to him.

Her gaze steady.

Her resolve absolute.

"You don't fight with fear," she said simply.

"You fight with everything the swamp tried to take from you—your hope, your resolve, your faith. The darkness feeds on what you give it."

Her voice pressed into the moment, undeniable, unwavering.

"But it can't touch what you hold onto."

Gillie bent down, her grip firm now as she picked up her knife.

Her stance was resolute.

"Then we don't let it take anything else."

She stepped beside Grace.

Her voice was sharp. Determined.

"If this is where we make our stand, so be it."

The swamp twisted violently as Marcus's forces surged closer, their movements relentless, merciless, unstoppable. The light from the oak expanded again, pushing against the darkness, but the shadows fought back with equal ferocity.

The battlefield was set.

The armies of dark and light stood at the brink of collision.

And as the echoes of the third bell faded into the storm…

The final battle began.

The Fourth Bell: Time Slips Away

The fourth bell was heavier, slower, dragging itself into existence like a force ancient enough to know it did not need to rush. It didn't burst outward. It sank, spiraling into the air, settling deep within the swamp's core, threading its resonance through tangled roots and poisoned water.

The ground buckled, water forcing its way up through cracks in the earth, bubbling, shifting, pulling as though something deep beneath had woken. The mist rolled, folding into itself, no longer spiraling, no longer hiding. It thickened to the point of suffocation, a phantom grip pressing against every surface, waiting, watching.

Above, the golden beam of light surged, piercing the sky, its glow defiant and unwavering. But the air grew heavy, charged with an unspoken force—a pressure coiling at the edges of the clearing, settling into the space between heartbeats. It wasn't just weight. It was something waiting. Something arguing against the moment before it collapsed inward.

And then… the whispers came.

"It's too late."

They were quieter than the bell, but they sunk deeper, twisting into the space beneath skin, beneath thought, beneath resolve.

"You failed."

"There's nothing left to do."

"It's over."

Joshua staggered, breath coming too fast, too shallow, his hands pressing against his ears—but the whispers didn't need sound to be heard. They were inside already, threading into the cracks left behind by every moment of exhaustion, every second of fear.

"I can't," he gasped, voice frayed, cracking. "I can't take this anymore. The bells, the whispers—it's too much. We've fought, we've survived, but now… now I don't even know why we're still standing."

Gillie turned sharply, frustration flaring behind the fear in her eyes. "That's exactly what they want," she snapped, though her voice wavered at the edges. "Marcus needs us to hesitate. He needs us to freeze. That's why the whispers keep coming."

Joshua sank to his knees, hands trembling against the dirt, fingers clutching against the weight driving down on him. "Then what do we do?" His voice was barely more than breath. "We're here, but what comes next? How do we even move forward when we don't know what forward is?"

No one answered.

Because he wasn't wrong.

The weight of time pressed down.

We had faced the swamp's trials, endured its tests, walked the path that led us here—and now, at the heart of it all, the way forward had vanished. The tree did not offer answers. It stood silent, massive, unyielding, its light blazing upward, carving through the sky with power—but it did not speak.

It did not tell us what to do.

Gillie's fists clenched, frustration spilling past restraint. "This is ridiculous," she hissed. "We're out of time. We've done everything we were supposed to do, and now nothing? What was the point of all of this?"

Grace turned to her, gaze steady, patient—but unwavering.

"The tree won't tell you what to do." She spoke quietly, but there was no hesitation in her voice. "Because this isn't about the tree."

Gillie exhaled sharply, running a hand through her hair, breath uneven. "What does that even mean?"

Grace stepped forward, fingertips grazing the tree's glowing bark, the warmth threading into her skin.

"It means the trials weren't about proving you could survive the swamp." She paused, looking at each of us in turn.

"They were about proving you could survive yourselves."

Joshua gripped the roots, his fingers curling tight as though holding onto them would keep him from falling apart.

"I don't know how," he whispered. "I don't know how to let go of something that's been part of me for so long. What am I without it?"

Grace knelt beside him, presence calm, grounding.

"You're more than what hurt you." Her words weren't soft—they were steady. "Those things shaped you, but they don't define you. Marcus wants you to believe you can't be more, that you can't move forward without them. But you can."

The whispers pressed harder.

"You've already lost."

"It's too late."

"You're nothing without your suffering."

But even as they coiled tighter, I felt something shift—a flicker of resolve, faint but steady.

Grace was right.

The whispers only had power if we gave it to them.

The swamp could only take what we refused to release.

My fingers found the coin, pressing it into my palm, its edges digging in like a lifeline, solid against the weight of the voices driving inward.

"We're not done yet," I said, my voice cutting through the whispers, through the noise, through the storm.

Gillie's stare was sharp. "So what do we do?"

I looked at Joshua, at Grace, at the oak tree looming above us.

"We stop fighting to hold onto everything that's breaking us."

Joshua's breath hitched, and for a moment, he looked as though he might collapse beneath the weight of it all.

But then—slowly—he nodded.

His trembling hand reached toward the tree's light.

"*I'll try*," he whispered. "I don't know if I can, but... *I'll try.*"

The oak's light pulsed, answering him.

The fourth bell's echo still lingered, heavy in the air, but it was drowned out by something stronger.

Hope.

The Second Four Bells

The Fifth Bell: The War Unleashed

The fifth bell struck—low, guttural, resonating through the swamp like a pulse buried deep beneath the surface. It did not ring cleanly. It dragged, pulling at the stillness, stretching the sound thin and frayed, forcing the air to carry something heavier than before.

The waters lurched again, this time not as ripples, but as waves rolling outward, pushing, forcing us beyond the confines of our own stagnation. The mud tightened, pulling against our boots, the ground beneath us no longer merely shifting—it was closing, closing around us.

The ground lurched, cracks splintering outward in jagged veins, ripping through the swamp's surface, spreading across the battlefield as if the very earth was protesting the clash between light and dark.

Above, the golden beam surged, stretching higher, unwavering, slicing through the sky with absolute force. It did not hesitate. It did not falter. The pressure thickened, coiling around us, pressing inward, threading through the spaces between heartbeats, between thoughts, wrapping itself into the moment before collision. The light did not retreat. Neither did the shadows.

And then—they revealed themselves.

They did not rise—they spilled forth, pouring from the unseen corners of the world, twisting into impossible shapes, crawling through the cracks of fractured roots, dripping from the sky like ink bleeding into water. They did not rush to strike, did not lash out in desperation. They were waiting. Watching. Encircling the battlefield in calculated silence, pressing into the edges of the clearing like they already knew the outcome.

Marcus stepped forward, his presence stretching outward, too large, too consuming, his body woven into the mist, threaded into the darkness that bowed beneath his command. His army formed behind him, shifting as one, their movements synchronized—not chaotic, not frantic, but precise, poised, steady, waiting for the moment when he would let them loose.

He tilted his head, eyes gleaming—not with anger, but with satisfaction, with amusement, with certainty.

"Look at them," he murmured, gesturing toward the swirling abyss pressing against the clearing's edge. "The storm is listening. The shadows are waiting. They know the truth better than you do."

His gaze flicked toward Grace, settling on her with something sharper now, more dangerous.

"You believe your light is strong?" His voice dripped with mockery, fingers twitching slightly at his side. " It's fleeting. A flicker in the dark. What happens when you let go of it?"

Grace did not flinch. She did not step back.

Instead, she stepped forward.

Her glow intertwined with the golden beam, merging with it, expanding outward, pushing past the mist, pressing against the air like it had always belonged here.

"You misunderstand the light," she said simply.

Marcus's smirk remained—but his eyes sharpened, glinting beneath the storm.

"Do I?"

Grace's presence only strengthened, the radiance growing, threading through the battlefield with undeniable force.

"It doesn't fear the dark," she answered, her voice even, unwavering. "It doesn't flicker. It doesn't fail. It's not something to hold onto. It's something to stand within."

The golden beam pulsed again, expanding—not in retaliation, not in defense, but in response. And beyond the oak's reach—the world answered.

Figures stepped from the shadows, their glow stretching through the mist, cutting through the remnants of the storm, their presence undeniable. They rose across the swamp, moving between shattered trees, drawn toward the heart of the battle—not as soldiers, not as warriors, but as something more.

Marcus's army had not come alone.

Neither had the light.

For the first time—the battlefield was full.

Marcus's amusement vanished. His presence shifted, darkening, growing heavier, the shadows coiling tighter at his feet, feeding off his fury, waiting for the command that had not yet come.

"Enough," he snarled, his fingers twitching.

The mist lurched, shadows pressing inward, creeping closer—but still not striking.

Then, with a single motion—Marcus unleashed them.

A flick of his wrist.

A surge of fury.

And the shadows attacked.

They did not advance—they collided, crashing into the clearing with unstoppable force, rushing toward the light with unrelenting hunger.

The battle had begun.

Joshua staggered, his breath sharp, his pulse pounding against his ribs. He turned wildly, eyes scanning the battlefield, watching the way the darkness swarmed.

"They're everywhere!" His voice cracked under the weight of it. "There's too many—how do we fight this?"

Gillie raised her blade, stance steady, body firm—but her grip was too tight, too rigid, hesitation threading through the instinct to strike.

She wanted to fight.

Survival demanded it.

The storm begged for it.

But Grace turned to us, gaze unwavering, voice calm despite the chaos.

"You don't fight with force."

Joshua's breath hitched—not loudly, not noticeably, but enough for me to hear it, enough for the weight of her words to press against something inside him, something unspoken.

His eyes flickered toward her, sharp, questioning—not challenging, but searching, as if her certainty carried something he had not yet grasped.

Gillie blinked, grip tightening—but she did not move forward.

I felt it too—the instinct to run, to lash out, to carve a path through the violence the way the swamp had taught me to.

But Grace stood against that instinct, against that fear, her presence cutting through it without effort, without struggle.

"You fight by trusting in the light."

Joshua's hands trembled at his sides—not enough to be seen, but enough to be felt.

I didn't know what war had demanded of him before this moment. I didn't know what words Marcus had whispered in his ear, what truths he had twisted, what doubts had been sewn into Joshua's breath before today.

But Joshua did not move.

Not forward.

Not back.

Gillie exhaled sharply, frustration tightening the lines in her expression.

"That's not how war works," she snapped. "That's not how anything works."

Grace did not argue.

She did not raise her voice, did not push back against Gillie's anger.

She only stood.

Rooted.

Expanding.

Merging with the light, until they were one and the same.

Joshua's chest rose and fell too fast—controlled, restrained, outwardly steady but inwardly weighted with something he had not yet named.

And yet—he did not step back.

He did not ask questions.

He did not let the hesitation become doubt, did not let the doubt become action.

The golden beam remained, unchanged, unbroken, pressing outward as shadows crashed against it, but never consuming it.

The darkness was relentless.

But so was the light.

And in the clash between storm and stillness, the light did not flinch.

Elana's Transformation

The sixth bell ruptured the air, its force tearing through the swamp like thunder rolling through fractured sky. The toll wasn't just a sound—it was a force, a pressure, something pushing, pulling, demanding.

The mist convulsed, whipping violently before collapsing in on itself, dragging the air tighter—relentless, breathless. The stagnant water swelled, spilling over the edges of the marsh, rolling in thick waves that did not retreat. The swamp no longer trembled—it writhed.

And the war transformed.

It was no longer just a battle—it was something deeper, something that pressed inward, tightening the battlefield into a single, suffocating moment. The force of the toll did not strike—it infiltrated, weaving through the storm, threading between the warriors locked in combat, sinking into the space where strength and weakness blurred together.

The ground convulsed, darkness surging against light, war breaking apart in violent waves as shadows clawed toward the golden glow that refused to bend, refused to break. The swamp had become something else— something alive, something that no longer merely contained the war, but fed it.

And still—the golden beam remained.

Unyielding. A pillar against the chaos.

But Joshua felt the toll differently.

Not like before. Not like sound, or thought, or doubt. He jerked forward, gasping—not in pain, but in loss, in confusion, in the weight of something pulling at him, something unfamiliar, unrelenting, slipping through his ribs like it had always belonged there.

"I…" His breath hitched, uneven, sharp. "I don't…"

He couldn't finish the thought—because he didn't know what it was. Only that it felt like something slipping away.

The storm pressed harder, lightning fracturing across the sky, shadows coiling tighter, war erupting all around us, consuming everything beyond the tree's reach.

And within that chaos—she emerged.

From the mist. From the storm. From whatever force had summoned her.

At first, she looked like Grace.

Her glow threaded with the golden light, radiating familiarity, settling into the battlefield like she had always belonged there. Her movements were steady, her presence strong, carrying the same kind of certainty that had led us through every trial, every choice.

For a fleeting second—the battlefield stilled.

Beyond the clearing, warriors clashed in a storm of light and shadow, but here, in this space between breaths, something paused.

Joshua inhaled sharply, staring at her, exhaustion pressing forward, closing in around him like something ready to collapse.

"Grace?" His voice cracked, flickering between confusion and hope.

She smiled—softly. Carefully.

"I'm here, Joshua," she murmured, tone steady, unwavering. "You've carried so much. You've fought so hard. It's time to let me take that burden from you."

But something was wrong.

Her voice was Grace's. Her cadence, her presence.

But beneath it—something twisted.

I turned toward the real Grace—the one who stood rigid, her glow brighter, her expression sharp, warning.

"It's not me," she said quietly, urgency pressing into each syllable. "That's not me."

But Joshua didn't hear her.

The sixth bell had done its work, threading into his exhaustion, feeding his longing for an end, for peace, for relief.

He stepped forward.

Just slightly.

"I knew you wouldn't leave us," he whispered, his voice frayed, worn. "I knew you'd find a way to help me."

Beyond the clearing—Marcus's forces pushed harder, shadows pressing against the light, crashing against warriors who refused to retreat. But here—Elana was attacking differently.

Gillie's voice cut through the moment—sharp, desperate, filled with something dangerously close to fear.

"Joshua, stop!" Her tone was raw, urgent. "That's not Grace! Look at her. Really look at her!"

Joshua hesitated.

His gaze flickered between them, uncertainty clouding his features, pressing into his pulse, into the weight of everything still unresolved.

"What are you talking about?" His voice trembled. "It's Grace. It's her. She's here."

"It's Elana."

Grace stepped forward, her glow flaring, pressing against the illusion.

"She's using my form to deceive you. To pull you away. You have to see it."

The false Grace's expression flickered—just for an instant—something cold and sharp twisting behind her eyes.

But then she stepped closer, her tone softening, voice weaving carefully into the air between them.

"Don't listen to them," she urged, voice like silk, smooth, inviting. "They don't understand. They don't see what you've been through. But I do, Joshua. I see you. I believe in you."

Joshua's knees buckled slightly, his hand lifting toward her without thinking.

Beyond the clearing—Marcus saw the hesitation.

His warriors pressed forward, their movements mirroring Elana's deception, sensing weakness, sensing an opening, hunting for the moment when the choice would be too late to undo.

The storm twisted, lightning splitting the sky, shadows coiling through the battlefield, pressing against the defenders who had already sacrificed too much.

But here—Joshua's choice was its own battle.

"I don't... I don't know what to believe anymore." He sounded lost, the words dragging like something pulled from underwater. "I just want to stop carrying all of this."

Her smile widened—unnatural now, stretching too far.

"And you can," she murmured. "Let me take it away."

Beyond the clearing—Marcus commanded his army forward, their weapons of darkness mirroring Elana's whispered temptation, an attack that was more than force—it was persuasion.

Joshua was being pulled into both battles.

"Joshua, no!" My voice shattered through the space, urgent, frantic. "That's not Grace! It's the swamp, it's Marcus, it's everything we've been fighting. Don't let it pull you in!"

The storm screamed, the mist twisting violently, shadows pressing inward.

But the golden light remained.

Grace stepped forward, her glow burning against the lie, challenging its presence, refusing to let it stand.

"You've come so far," she said gently. "Don't stop now. Don't let the swamp steal what you've fought to reclaim. The truth is here, Joshua. You just have to choose to see it."

Joshua froze, caught between the two figures—between the war around him and the war inside him. His hand trembled, fingers tightening toward the illusion, the deception, the temptation.

And then—the oak pulsed.

Its golden light erupted outward, wrapping Joshua in something real, something undeniable.

He inhaled sharply—

And the deception cracked.

The false Grace's expression twisted, her form rippling, shadows surging angrily around her.

"You're a fool," she spat, venom lacing her words. "You think you can save him? He's already mine. You all are."

Grace stepped forward, her glow exploding outward, blinding, burning against the mist.

"You're wrong," she said, voice steady, absolute. "The light will always be stronger. And Joshua is stronger than you."

The oak pulsed again, its golden light blazing upward, forcing the shadows back, pushing the false Grace into sharp relief.

Her form faltered, the illusion fracturing as the light tore through her.

She hissed, furious, recoiling as the mist consumed her, dragging her back into the storm.

Joshua staggered, breath heavy, eyes wide.

"I almost…" His voice shook. "I almost believed her."

"But you didn't," Grace said gently, resting her hand on his shoulder. "And that's what matters."

The light of the oak flared brighter, steadying, as the war around us raged on. The bell's toll had faded, but its shadow lingered—a reminder of how close destruction had come.

And how quickly it could return.

When the Darkness Trembled

The seventh bell tolled, and the battlefield ruptured under its weight.

It wasn't merely a sound—it was a strike so powerful it shook the very marrow of the land. The toll didn't rise and fade—it thundered, stretching long, stretching deep, like the swamp itself had no choice but to absorb it.

The surface of the water churned, something beneath stirring, shifting, awakening. The ground buckled, moisture pulling upward in unnatural rivulets, coiling into the mist like fingers reaching, grasping. Everything was moving now—everything was bending to the sound.

The mist spiraled violently, caught in the force, bending into broken waves, while lightning carved the sky into burning splinters, answering the chaos in violent bursts. The storm itself howled, twisting into unnatural forms as the war tightened, pushing everything toward the edge of collapse.

Shadows poured from unseen depths, flooding across the battlefield like a tide that had finally broken free, twisting unnaturally, jagged figures moving with a hunger that had been kept restrained for too long. Marcus's forces pressed forward, their movements not reckless, not wild, but precise—fed by fury, driven by his command, their pace sharp, calculated, relentless. They did not stumble. They did not hesitate. They were not merely creatures of darkness. They were instruments of his wrath.

And the army of light—they met them without fear.

The warriors stepped into the storm, pressing into the weight of the collision, radiance surging through the battlefield like an undeniable force. They did not retreat, did not shrink beneath the pressure. Their presence remained absolute, pushing back the tide of darkness with each step forward, with every strike, every movement that defied the chaos and refused to yield.

The battle expanded, pushing past its former boundaries, stretching into something larger than before. It was no longer confined—it was unleashed, neither side bending, neither side relenting. The storm was no longer an obstacle—it had become part of the war itself.

Joshua doubled over, his body trembling, breath catching between gasps, his shoulders rigid beneath the weight of the toll. "It's worse," he choked, fingers clutching his chest as if trying to hold himself steady against something unseen, something unbearable. "So much worse…"

Gillie pressed herself against the oak's roots, white—knuckled grip tightening around the hilt of her blade, her breath sharp, uneven, muscles locked in restraint. "We're running out of time!" Her voice cut through the chaos, raw, fierce, laced with frustration, splitting the moment apart. "These bells—each one is worse than the last! And we're standing here! Doing NOTHING!"

Her words hit hard, slamming into the space between us, weighed with the truth we had not yet spoken.

She was right.

The war was slipping past us, moving too fast, crashing into itself, and yet—we were still here, standing inside it, watching, hesitating. Shadows pushed closer, the hesitation feeding their momentum, their movements becoming sharper, more deliberate, sensing weakness, sensing vulnerability. A warrior of light struck an incoming figure, their collision sending a rupture through the battlefield, splitting the storm apart, throwing bursts of energy across the land. The ground beneath us shuddered under the impact—yet we stood still.

Grace did not move. Her glow remained steady, her stance unwavering, but her gaze was closed, her hand pressed against the tree—not as a shield, not as a plea, but as if listening to something beneath the war, something deeper than any of us could reach. Joshua sank lower, his fingers gripping the soil, his pulse uneven, raw exhaustion pressing into every movement. "*We're going to fail,*" he whispered, his voice barely audible, fragile, stretched too thin beneath the weight of uncertainty. "*We're close. Too close. But I still don't know how to let go of this. I don't know what the tree wants.*"

Gillie exhaled sharply, her frustration slipping toward desperation, fingers threading through her hair as she clenched her jaw. "What are we missing?" she asked, the question carrying the urgency we all felt, the answer we could not find.

Grace's fingers shifted against the bark.

She opened her eyes.

She did not hesitate.

She spoke calmly, deliberately, as though the words carried more than meaning—as though they carried weight.

"Truth is always beneath the surface."

The war did not stop. The battle did not slow. But the moment stilled. Something pressed into the space between breaths, something massive, something undeniable.

And then… the golden light pulsed.

Not gently.

Not faintly.

Explosively.

The force detonated outward, rupturing the storm apart, an eruption of brilliance too powerful to contain. It slammed into the battlefield, colliding with darkness in an unrelenting wave, forcing itself into every space, crushing the mist, spreading into the deepest corners where the shadows lurked.

The earth shuddered.

The war convulsed.

Reality itself fractured.

Marcus's army reeled—not by strategy, not by command, but by instinct. They staggered backward, their movements involuntary, shaped by something they had never been forced to feel before.

Fear.

The strongest among them—the figures shaped by Marcus's will, the creatures built from the abyss—hesitated.

Marcus's fury slashed through the battlefield like fire, his presence expanding, suffocating, raw with aggression. He slashed through the chaos with his voice—venomous, seething, a whip across his faltering army.

"ON YOUR FEET!"

Joshua exhaled sharply, his breath uneven, caught somewhere deep in his chest before releasing.

His hands flexed at his sides.

Not clenched.

Not shaking.

Just—uncertain.

For the first time since the war began, I saw something fracture in him.

Not physically.

Not outwardly.

But beneath the surface—beneath whatever resolve had carried him this far.

He had followed Marcus's words for so long. He had heard them, absorbed them, believed them. And yet—here, now, in the space between impact and aftermath, something did not feel the same.

His gaze locked onto the battlefield—not at the war, not at the figures, but at the light itself, at the pulsing glow beneath the tree, at something vast, something undeniable, something that had shaken even Marcus's forces.

And Joshua felt it.

I saw it—in the way his breath caught again, in the way his fingers hovered before closing inward, in the way his weight shifted so slightly it might not have been intentional.

Something had changed in him.

Something had shifted.

But Joshua did not speak.

He didn't betray the realization that had pressed into his ribs, into his pulse, into whatever remained of his belief.

Marcus stepped forward, his presence looming, suffocating, pressing into the shattered silence, his gaze locking onto the forces that had faltered.

Joshua looked at him.

For the first time—not in certainty.

Not in trust.

But in something deeper.

Something questioning.

And then… his fingers curled tighter, his breath steadied, and he moved forward again, following the war, following the chaos, following everything as he always had.

But I saw it.

The hesitation—the way his body had betrayed him, even for a moment, even if no one else had seen it.

Marcus slashed through the battlefield with fury.

"IT'S JUST A LIGHT!"

His voice clawed through the space, crushing the hesitation, demanding obedience.

"NOTHING MORE!"

And Joshua—he didn't argue.

He didn't fight.

He didn't resist.

He just kept moving.

But I had seen enough to know—his belief had cracked.

The shadows convulsed, figures staggering upright, their fear twisting into something sharp, something forced, something shaped by his fury. Marcus would not let them break.

And the war…

Did not stop.

It erupted again—stronger, fiercer, angrier.

Driven not by belief, but by denial.

And yet—the golden light remained, still pulsing beneath the tree, waiting.

Its glow hadn't faded.

Its pulse hadn't stopped.

It had changed everything—and yet, none of us knew why.

Gillie stumbled back, blinking toward the light, her breath uneven, caught between awe and panic.

Joshua stared—consumed by something beyond thought, beyond words, beyond certainty.

I saw the shift in him. Not in his stance. Not in his movements.

But in the way he looked at the battlefield, at Marcus, at the storm itself.

Something about the light had shaken even Marcus's forces.

Something about its presence had made them hesitate, retreat, question—if only for a breath, if only for a fraction of time.

And Joshua felt that hesitation.

I could see it—in the way his fingers flexed inward before releasing, in the way his breath hitched just before stabilizing, in the way his weight shifted ever so slightly before steadying again.

Marcus was furious.

The light had disrupted something deeper than the battle itself— something more than the war, more than the collision between forces.

It had pierced belief itself.

But Joshua moved forward, pressing into the chaos, pushing past whatever had shaken him, keeping his steps sharp, his presence steady.

He buried it.

He pressed it deep.

And yet—I had seen it.

He had changed.

Even if no one else knew it yet.

The war screamed back into motion, forces crashing together, Marcus's army flooding forward, warriors of light meeting them head-on, their collision shifting the battlefield back into unrelenting chaos.

Joshua exhaled sharply, gripping his head, voice trembling between panic and uncertainty.

"What are we supposed to do?"

His question felt suffocating—not because we didn't know the answer, but because we didn't even know what to ask.

The golden light flared again.

Waiting.

We were too lost to hear it.

The Eighth Bell: Reflections of Ourselves

The eighth bell clashed against the world with a force that rang too sharp, too deep, too wrong. The toll split the air apart, ripping through the thickness like a knife drawn through flesh.

The swamp folded inward, mist crashing, twisting violently. The surface of the water fractured, breaking apart into roiling tides that pushed outward with nowhere to go. Something below was fighting. Something below was coming undone.

It was no longer a force imposing its will upon us—it was responding.

It knew.

Something was changing.

And then, as the toll faded, as its echoes drifted into the mist like something lingering, something waiting—the light beneath the oak pulsed again.

Brighter.

Bolder.

No longer just a glow—a beacon. A force that did not demand attention but refused to be ignored. The mist hesitated. It curled away—not violently, not as an attack, but with something closer to fear, shrinking back from the radiance instead of surging toward it.

And within the golden beam—something shifted.

Joshua froze, breath catching. "It's different." His voice was barely above a whisper, threaded with something uncertain, something shaken.

Gillie tightened her grip on her knife, her stance solid, wary. "There are shadows… inside the light."

At first, they were soft. Indistinct.

Then… they took shape.

Faint silhouettes flickered within the glow, hovering like echoes of something familiar—something we should have seen before, but hadn't. And then, slowly, we recognized them.

They weren't strangers.

They weren't distant figures.

They were reflections of ourselves.

Each movement, each flicker of light revealed pieces of us, pieces of our journey, pieces of who we were—who we had always been. Moments replayed—Gillie stepping in front of us, shielding us even when she never admitted she cared. Joshua pressing forward through fear, through exhaustion, never yielding. Grace standing quiet, steady, holding something deeper than guidance, something essential.

The reflections shifted, showing us what we had never seen before—the way we had always been protected, the way the light had always been with us, even when we believed it was gone.

Joshua took a step forward, his breath shaking, his voice barely above a whisper. "All the times we thought we were alone…" His gaze locked onto the figures, his body rigid with emotion. "We weren't."

Gillie lowered her knife slightly, her expression shifting—not defensive, not dismissive.

Uncertain.

Shaken.

Acknowledging something she could no longer ignore.

Grace stepped forward, her presence quiet but unshakable. "The light was never gone," she said gently. "Even in the deepest parts of the swamp, even when the darkness surrounded you, it was there. It always will be. But now—it's time for you to carry it."

The golden light flared again—brighter, sharper, as if responding, as if acknowledging the words as truth.

And beyond the glow—the storm reacted violently.

The mist convulsed, shadows at the edges of the clearing surging forward, clawing toward the light with frantic, reckless force.

They knew.

The swamp knew.

They were close to something.

And Marcus knew it too.

His voice thundered through the battlefield, sharp, venomous, laced with fury. "You think this light will save you?" His words cut through the storm like serrated steel, slicing into the moment, into the breath before the battle could erupt again.

"You think it'll protect you?" His tone carried disdain, contempt—but beneath it, beneath the edge sharpening his words, was something else.

Something raw.

Something close to panic.

"It's NOTHING." His voice escalated, seething, pressing into the shadows like a command—like an attempt to force them into believing the lie he needed them to believe. "A flicker that will burn out before the end."

The shadows thrashed, throwing themselves against the edges of the golden light with ferocity, their movements erratic, wild, as though trying to erase what had just been revealed. The ground trembled violently, cracks deepening, reaching for the beam's core—but the oak stood firm, its branches stretching higher, its glow refusing to bend, refusing to be consumed.

Gillie lifted her knife again, her expression shifting—no longer wary, no longer uncertain, but sharp, solid, unyielding.

"If they want to stop us," she said, voice cutting through the chaos, "they're going to have to try harder."

The golden light pulsed again.

Waiting.

For them to accept it.

The Final Four Bells

The Scroll Unearthed

The ninth bell roared, its weight crushing the last fragments of hesitation, driving through what little space remained untouched. The toll carried deep, too deep, far beyond the surface, far beyond the reach of the living.

The mist shrank, compacting itself into a density it had never held before. The waters heaved, dragged backward, then shoved forward, crashing against the edges of the swamp. The very air tightened, drawing in close, leaving no space to breathe.

The ground heaved beneath us, cracks spiraling outward from the roots of the oak tree, reaching for the golden light as if trying to pull it down, trying to unravel something that refused to be undone. But the glow remained. It shone steady, blazing defiantly despite the weight of the toll, shaking slightly beneath the force of the moment but never retreating, never bending beneath the chaos.

Joshua staggered, his hands flying to his ears, his body trembling as a raw, broken cry escaped him.

"It's too loud!" he gasped, voice splintering under the pressure. "It's like it's inside my head—it's tearing me apart!"

Gillie grabbed his arm, her grip fierce despite the tremors threading through her own hands, despite the war closing in around them. "Stay with me!" she shouted over the roar. "You don't get to give up now, Joshua. Not here. Not after everything!"

The storm howled, a violent scream that stretched across the battlefield, waves of mist slamming inward, throwing themselves against the golden light with reckless desperation. But then… the ground shifted beneath us.

Not just from the tremors.

Not just from the war.

Something beneath the tree reacted.

The golden light pulsed again, stretching outward, pouring into the fractures, illuminating the deep, jagged wounds in the earth—revealing something beneath. Something buried.

I froze, breath catching, pulse hammering beneath the pressure, beneath the sheer weight of the moment crashing into me. The glow beneath the oak wasn't merely illuminating the cracks—it was pointing at them.

At first, the thought barely formed, half—realized, buried beneath urgency, beneath chaos. But as I stared, as the light pulsed steadily, unwavering, drawing its presence deeper into the earth—it hit me.

It was leading us downward.

We had to dig.

My voice escaped before I could fully process it.

"Under the tree," I breathed, barely louder than a whisper. "We have to dig beneath it."

Joshua's breathing was uneven, his gaze locking onto mine, then flicking to the glow, to the cracks, to the fragments of earth shifting with every pulse. Gillie followed my gaze, her expression twisting between disbelief and rising panic. "You've got to be kidding me," she muttered. "Now? When the whole swamp is trying to kill us?"

Grace stepped forward, her glow strengthening, intertwining with the oak's light as though lending it power, solidifying its presence. "The path has led you here," she said simply. "Now you must unearth what it has been waiting to reveal."

The swamp reacted violently.

The mist convulsed, clawing at the golden light, driving into the edges of the clearing like a force trying to smother it before we could act. The ground shook, tremors rolling beneath us—not just from the war, but from the resistance of the earth itself, as if it knew the truth buried within and refused to let it rise.

The battle raged closer, warriors slamming into each other, steel clashing, sparks exploding into the mist, bursts of energy shattering through the space behind us. The war was grinding into reality, pressing into time itself, forcing destruction through every breath. The shadows lunged forward, shrieking, thrashing, their movements wild, erratic, as though they felt the shift, felt the moment slipping away from them.

The golden beam flickered, strained—but held.

For now.

I dropped to my knees, fingers clawing into the dirt.

The earth fought back.

The ground rejected my hands, the soil thick, damp, refusing to yield, resisting as though it had been commanded to keep its secret buried forever. War crashed in on all sides, steel grinding against flesh, screams splintering through the battlefield, the storm forcing against us with suffocating force. Still… I kept digging.

Gillie slammed her hands into the dirt beside me, pulling rough, jagged handfuls away, her teeth gritted, her body rigid with urgency. Joshua hovered for a second longer, his fear visible in the tremble of his hands, in the sharpness of his breath.

But then… he exhaled sharply, shaking off the hesitation, dropping to the ground, his hands joining ours in the frantic race against time.

The mist surged, slamming into the golden light, twisting like claws, trying to bury us beneath it, trying to drag the revelation back into the earth. The ground trembled, rejecting us, shuddering beneath the storm—but the golden light surged, forcing its presence deeper.

The battlefield never stopped screaming.

It tore through reality.

It pressed against time, against space, against breath.

Still… we kept digging.

I ripped away the last handful of dirt—and my fingers brushed against something smooth.

I froze, breath catching, pulse hammering beneath the weight of discovery. Slowly, carefully, I brushed away the remaining soil, hands trembling as I pulled the object free and lifted it into the light.

A scroll.

But this wasn't just any parchment.

It was alive.

Its surface gleamed faintly, catching the golden light, symbols carved into it with a precision too perfect to be ordinary. They pulsed softly, beating in rhythm with the glow itself, as though part of it, as though responding to the storm, to the war, to us.

The golden light surged.

The clearing held its breath.

The shadows quivered, faltered, their movements recoiling, pulling away as though even the presence of the scroll burned them.

For a fleeting instant, it felt as if the light had won.

But the storm did not relent.

The mist coiled tighter, thickening into suffocating waves, moving against the golden light, trying to drown it, trying to drag it back into the chaos. The howl of the storm escalated, no longer just wind, no longer just fury—it was war itself, screaming through the battlefield, splintering reality into combat, into destruction, into carnage.

Figures collided violently, warriors slamming into each other, metal grinding against metal, cries of battle shredding through the air. Shadows swarmed, clawing through the mist, their forms twisting, slamming into warriors of light with bone-shattering force, sending bursts of energy flashing through the clearing.

The war knew what was happening.

And the swamp reacted.

The earth convulsed, roots shuddering, cracks reaching hungrily toward the golden beam, as if trying to consume it, trying to swallow the moment before it could fully emerge.

And then... from the edges of the battlefield—a voice cut through the storm.

Low.

Insidious.

Sharp.

"The truth," it hissed, mocking, contemptuous. "Do you think a mere scroll will save you?"

The Whisperer emerged, their form flickering, twisting through the mist, weaving their voice into the storm like poison.

The scroll pulsed, waiting.

Joshua didn't move.

His fear still lingered.

The clearing darkened.

The battle crushed into the moment.

And yet… the scroll remained.

Waiting.

For a choice to be made.

The Tenth Bell: The Battle for Joshua

The tenth bell did not ring—it detonated. The sound came too fast, too heavy, too overwhelming, filling every hollow space left in the swamp, overtaking the echoes of the tolls before it. It split through the battlefield, tearing into the trees, into the warriors clashing at its edges, shaking the ground beneath us, coiling into the air like judgment itself. The golden light blazing from the ancient oak flickered, strong but strained, battling against the storm that refused to let it stand.

And then—the war surged.

Shadows came first.

Before the armies collided, before the warriors of light clashed against the dark, before the battle screamed through the clearing like destruction incarnate, they came for us. Silent. Jagged. Twisting shapes that carried the weight of everything we tried to hide, bury, deny.

Gillie was the first they reached.

The darkness split open before her, condensing, swirling into something too familiar, too personal. A shadowy figure, identical to her in shape, in stance—but twisted. Mocking. Cruel. It stepped forward, its voice an echo of her own.

"Look at you," it hissed, each word sharper than the last, stabbing into her like blades. "You think you've led them here? You think you're a leader? They've carried you this far. They'll carry you still, while you crumble under the weight of your own failures."

Gillie faltered, her grip tightening around her knife, but her voice wavered.

"That's not true," she said, barely more than breath.

The shadow stepped closer, deliberate, cruel. "You hesitate. You second-guess. You fail. How many times have they saved you because you couldn't save yourself? How much longer before they stop carrying you altogether?"

I saw the tremor in her hands, the way her resolve slipped beneath the weight of its words.

But then—she drew a sharp breath, and her voice hardened. "I've fought too hard to let you win," she snarled. "I've made it this far—not because I'm perfect, but because I don't give up. And I won't start now."

The shadow lunged, its blade meeting Gillie's in a clash that rang through the clearing, their struggle reflecting the battle raging within her—the fight to reclaim herself.

I wasn't prepared when the mist twisted before me, shattering into jagged fragments, pulsing with dim, fractured light.

They weren't whole.

They were pieces.

Pieces of me.

Scattered. Incomplete.

They swirled closer, their voices rising, intertwining, driving into me like splinters of thought.

"You think you're whole?"

"You think you've held it together, but look at yourself. You've been broken since the start. The swamp didn't take anything from you—it only showed you what was already gone."

I flinched, the coin in my pocket biting into my palm—a weight, an anchor, a reminder. But the whispers tightened around me, their grip relentless.

"You're nothing without them. Without this journey. Without the scraps of purpose you've clung to. What's left when this ends? Who are you?"

My breath caught. The emptiness clawed at my chest—a hollow ache, a pressure I couldn't escape. I didn't have an answer.

"*I don't know*," I whispered, my voice breaking beneath the weight of it.

The golden light flared—not violently, not desperately—but insistently. It reached for me, cutting through the shadows' whispers, shattering their hold. One of the fragments floated just ahead, its glow faint but familiar. I reached out, my hands trembling, pulling it toward me. Its warmth pressed into my chest, filling the space the shadows had exploited, sealing the cracks they had tried to break open.

Nearby, Gillie drove her blade through her shadow. It shattered into mist, and her fragment burned brighter, her resolve rekindled. She staggered back, gripping the glowing piece tightly, whispering with breath sharp and unyielding.

"I'm not giving up. Not today. Not ever."

But Joshua. . .

Joshua hadn't moved.

He stood frozen at the center of the clearing, the scroll trembling in his hands. The mist around him thickened, forming faces—hollow, accusing—clawing into him, crowding his thoughts. And then… the Whisperer rose.

It slipped from the darkness, its form flickering, jagged, twisting, as though it were woven from doubt itself. Its voice was soft, coaxing—the kind of softness laced with poison. The kind that didn't strike, but suffocated. That didn't force, but crushed beneath its weight.

"You've carried the burden too long, Joshua," it murmured, threading itself into the storm, pressing into his breath.

"Why must you bear it alone?"

Joshua's breath hitched, his body rigid, his fingers twitching over the scroll. The Whisperer leaned closer, its presence folding into the chaos, sinking into the weight of the war.

"Give it up."

The battlefield screamed—warriors clashing, figures falling, the swamp writhing under the violence pounding into it. But Joshua remained still. His fear had rooted deep. The Whisperer knew it.

"Let it go."

Joshua did not move. He did not speak. He did not fight. He only stood there, breaking beneath its voice, beneath the pressure bearing down on his chest.

The storm tightened around him, the war demanding a choice.

"Do you see them, Joshua?" it murmured. "The ones you couldn't save. The ones you failed. They're all here. Look at them."

Joshua staggered back, his breath catching as the faces pressed closer.

"You left us," one of them hissed.

"You could've saved us," another whispered.

Joshua clutched the scroll tighter, tears streaking his face. "I tried," he said, his voice breaking. "I did everything I could."

"But it wasn't enough," the Whisperer countered. "It'll never be enough. Let it go, Joshua. Let them go."

The oak's light flared again, brighter and steadier, defiant against the storm. Each of us stood at the precipice, our struggles laid bare. Gillie and I had fought, had reclaimed the pieces the swamp had tried to strip from us. But Joshua… Joshua's soul wavered.

The shadows surged closer, jagged edges reaching for Joshua.

But the armies of light stood their ground.

And then… Ezekiel strode into the chaos.

He moved with purpose, his glow burning fiercely, not as someone who had suddenly found resolve, but as someone who had waited for this exact moment. This wasn't hesitation—this was confirmation.

"You held fast," he declared, voice cutting through the battlefield like steel. "Even when the swamp tried to break you. Even when it whispered the doubts you feared the most. You didn't turn back. You didn't fold."

His gaze locked onto Joshua, his presence steady, unwavering.

"This was always the test. The swamp doesn't take the weak—it takes the willing. And you . . . you refused to be taken."

Grace stepped beside him, her glow intertwining with the golden beam from the oak, strengthening the light against the storm.

"You stand because you chose to," she said, her voice carrying through the battlefield—sharp, commanding, undeniable. "And now we fight—together."

The storm raged, propelling violently into the clearing, trying to drown the moment, to erase the resolve standing against it.

And then… Gillie stepped forward.

Her voice rose above the din, crackling like fire, burning with the certainty of what they had endured. "My grandmother taught me to fight for the world we lost . . . for the world we could have again. She believed in peace, and I won't stop until I see it for myself."

Her gaze locked onto Joshua, unrelenting, refusing hesitation. "Joshua, it's time to choose. You have to fight—not for yourself, but for all of us."

The mist thickened at the swamp's edge, gripping tightly, unwilling to let go…

And then… Olivia stepped forward.

She walked with quiet purpose, her eyes fixed on Joshua, her presence cutting through the hesitation, through the weight pressing into him. "Joshua," she said softly, "you've been fighting this for so long. Let us carry it with you."

The battlefield tightened, the storm wrapped into every breath, the war demanding action…

But Olivia's voice held it back.

Just for a moment.

The golden glow reached forward, wrapping around Olivia and Joshua, anchoring them, shielding them against the storm. Olivia's hand rested lightly on Joshua's shoulder, grounding him, pulling him back into something real, something stronger than fear.

The shadows recoiled slightly, as though her quiet conviction had pushed them back. "You're not alone in this," she said.

Her tone didn't waver.

It didn't beg.

It didn't demand.

It only spoke truth.

"Look to the light. It's always been there, waiting for you."

And then… The Redeemed entered the battlefield.

His presence was undeniable, unrelenting, muscling into the war like something beyond force, beyond destruction. He stood at the edge of the chaos, his glow burning against the storm, his voice cutting through the battlefield like judgment itself.

"The darkness is strong," he said, his words carried through the storm, undeniable.

"But it doesn't own me. It will not own you."

Marcus's forces recoiled, the shadows twisting violently, recognizing him, fearing him.

The Redeemed pressed forward, his gaze locked onto Marcus himself, challenging him, daring him.

And Marcus snarled.

"You think this light will save you?"

His voice was venomous, pressing into the storm, wrapping into the chaos like poison.

"You think faith alone will stop me? You're fools, every one of you!"

The storm collapsed inward, the mist lashing at the edges of the light, the shadows moving closer, suffocating the battlefield. The ground shuddered beneath the war's weight, cracks splintering outward, the swamp reacting to the battle, fracturing under the strain.

And at the center—Joshua stood, unmoving.

The scroll shook in his hands, his breath shallow, sharp, his gaze darting between the chaos and the golden light.

"I… I don't know what to do," he said, his voice breaking. "They're everywhere. The shadows… they're everywhere."

The war raged, crashing against the battlefield, demanding resolution…

And at the center of it all—Joshua remained caught between forces that refused to wait.

The choice was his.

The Eleventh Bell: God's Word

The eleventh bell hit—louder, sharper, heavier than anything before it. The force ripped through the swamp, shaking the surface, cracking through the unseen depths, pulling at the land like something desperate, like something starving.

The waters collapsed into themselves, then shot outward, scattering, unable to contain the movement. The mist dropped, smothering everything, leaving nothing untouched, nothing unclaimed. There was no space left to retreat.

The resonance pulsed outward, cutting through the storm, driving into the battlefield like a command that could not be ignored.

The golden light surged, expanding in furious waves, fighting for space, forcing back the dark. But the shadows did not retreat. They thrashed violently, clawing forward, writhing like something starving, desperate, frantic—their voices rising in guttural cries, a chorus of defiance and fear.

And then, they reached Joshua.

Darkness coiled, winding around his arms, his chest, his legs, tightening, pulling, refusing to let go. The scroll shook in his grip, its glow flickering, caught between warring forces, pressed into the fray with no escape. He staggered, breath shallow, hands trembling as the suffocating weight pressed into his chest.

"*You can't save me,*" he whispered, his voice raw, strained, barely audible over the roar of battle. His head hung low, the dim glow of the scroll casting fractured shadows across his face. "*I've done too much… lost too much.*"

"No!"

Gillie's voice slammed through the storm—sharp, unrelenting, refusing doubt, refusing surrender. She stepped forward, blade steady, stance solid, her resolve like iron.

"That's not how this ends!"

Her words cut through the battlefield, pushing against hesitation, pushing against the moment that threatened to pull Joshua under.

"My grandmother believed in a world worth fighting for—a world we could have again. She believed in peace. And so do I."

Her gaze locked onto Joshua—fierce, unyielding, refusing to let him fall.

"You're part of that, Joshua. You've always been part of that."

The words struck, pushing through the storm, pressing against the suffocating grip of the war. And for a fleeting instant—the mist thinned; the shadows hesitated.

But it didn't last.

The storm collapsed inward, the battlefield roaring with reckless fury. The ground cracked beneath the strain, splintering outward, forcing the swamp to recoil.

Joshua was at the center of it all.

The shadows coiled tighter, their tendrils digging into his skin, pulling, refusing to release him. The scroll trembled, its glow flickering wildly, caught between forces battling for control.

Ezekiel's voice cut through the chaos—deliberate, unyielding, an anchor against the abyss. His presence burned brighter; his words sharp as steel.

"The eleventh bell reveals the Word, but the God Forsaken Bell reveals the heart."

The battlefield lurched, forcing a beat of stillness, bearing down on Joshua, demanding recognition.

"You must be ready, for the final toll waits for no one."

The warning hung thick in the air, weight grinding against Joshua like judgment. The scroll shook in his hands, its glow surging outward, responding to the battle, to the war, to the choice before him.

The words etched onto its surface burned, alive with meaning, alive with power.

And then… Olivia stepped forward.

She moved through the battlefield without hesitation, her presence slicing through the chaos like a blade of light. Her voice was calm, but it carried force, surging into Joshua, pulling him back from the edge.

"It's not about worthiness," she said, breaking through the storm, pushing into the hesitation. "It's about grace. You don't have to carry this alone, Joshua. Let it in. Let Him in."

The words struck, pressing deep. For the first time—Joshua's head lifted.

His gaze found the golden glow, the battlefield, the choice waiting for him.

But the shadows weren't finished.

They pressed inward, frenzied, clawing, refusing to let him escape.

And then… Elana stepped forward.

Her form glowed softly, warm, inviting—wrong.

Her smile was gentle, her voice a quiet lure, each syllable winding through the battlefield like silk.

"I've always been here for you," she murmured, slipping closer, coiling into his hesitation like smoke. "You've carried so much pain, Joshua. Let me take it from you. Let me give you peace."

The battlefield tightened—the storm pressing inward, the war suffocating, demanding resolution. The light wavered under the pressure, bending but refusing to break. The darkness crept at the edges, waiting for the moment hesitation would let it in.

Joshua froze, his eyes darting between them all—Grace, Ezekiel, Olivia, The Silent Child, The Redeemed… and me.

And Elana.

Perfect. But wrong.

The scroll shook in his grip, its glow caught between forces, between choices, pulling him apart. The weight of it was unbearable, digging into his hands, seeping into his skin, as if the war itself was demanding his answer.

The eleventh bell's resonance lingered, refusing to fade, stretching through the battlefield like an unseen hand twisting everything tighter. It rolled over the storm, over the warriors clashing at the edges, surging into the cracks that had already formed. There was no more time for uncertainty.

And Joshua wavered—caught between the darkness and the light.

The God Forsaken Bell

The war erupted again, twisting violently, pressing into the clearing with reckless force, clawing at the battlefield, desperate to drown the light.

But then… everything stopped.

The storm hovered, waiting.

The battlefield held its breath, as though time itself had recoiled, stretching thin, fragile, charged with the weight of what was coming next.

The air trembled, thick with anticipation, with dread, as though the war knew—everything was teetering on the edge. The oak's golden light pulsed faintly, no longer expanding, no longer fighting, but watching. Holding. Waiting.

The fragments shimmered, delicate and beautiful, glowing with the remnants of everything lost. They floated just beyond reach, trembling in the charged air, caught between destruction and reclamation.

And at the center—Joshua stood.

The scroll gleamed faintly in his trembling hands, its glow uncertain, flickering like something afraid.

The swamp held its breath, but the shadows did not.

They crept closer, suffocating.

The mist grew thicker, heavier, curling into shapes that whispered in low, insidious voices. Their words were sharp, precise, slipping into the silence like blades pressed against skin.

And then... Marcus stepped forward.

His presence was towering, his voice cutting through the stillness like something weighted with finality.

"You've fought so hard to hold onto this light," he said, smooth, venomous. "But has it truly brought you peace, Joshua? Has it freed you from the pain that clings to your soul?"

Joshua didn't answer.

He hesitated, his grip on the scroll tightening, as though he might find an answer within it, something he had missed, something he had overlooked.

But the whispers grew louder, insistent, dragging at his mind.

"It's too much."

"You're not enough."

"Let it go."

Gillie stepped forward, her knife gleaming in the oak's dim light, her presence cutting through the voices like steel. "Joshua," she said sharply, her voice a blade through the fog. "Don't do this. Don't let him take this from you. We've come too far, fought too hard to lose it all now."

Joshua's hands shook, his breath uneven, his doubt etching itself into his face. "*I don't know what to believe anymore,*" he whispered. "*I don't know if I can keep fighting.*"

"You can," I said, stepping beside Gillie.

My voice shook, but I forced the words out.

"You already have. You've carried so much, but you've done it. You're here, Joshua. You've seen the light, felt it. Don't give up now. Don't let them take this from you."

Marcus let out a soft, mocking laugh, his shadows swirling around him like smoke, slipping closer, wrapping into Joshua's hesitation.

"This light you speak of," he said, disdain heavy in his voice.

"It's a fragile thing, Joshua. It's a fleeting flicker that burns brightly before dying out. You've clung to it for too long. Let it go. Step into my shadow. Find peace in the darkness."

Gillie's grip on her knife tightened, her jaw set, her stance unshakable.

She moved closer to the fragments, her breath steady, her resolve unbreakable.

The glowing piece before her pulsed, its light trembling in recognition.

"I won't let this be taken from me," she said fiercely.

"Not again."

I'm taking it back.

"I don't care what the swamp throws at me—I won't give up."

The shadows surged, clawing at the edges of Gillie's fragment, but the oak's beam flared brighter, fighting back the suffocating mist.

Gillie reached forward, her fingers brushing against the light, and the darkness shrieked, recoiling in fury.

I felt my own fragment pulsing before me, its glow flickering like a dying ember.

It hurt to look at it—hurt to acknowledge what had been stripped away, what was lost.

Marcus's voice curled around my thoughts like chains, dragging at my hesitation.

But I knew what I had to do.

With shaking hands, I reached forward, feeling the fragment's warmth press into my skin.

The shadows clawed at the edges of my resolve, the mist shrieking louder, the storm moving closer…

But the fragment's glow burned brighter, grounding me, filling the emptiness that had threatened to consume me.

Marcus snarled as Gillie and I reclaimed our fragments, his shadows twisting in fury, but his gaze never left Joshua.

"You can't reclaim what was never truly yours," he spat.

His voice was poison, enveloping Joshua and deepening his hesitation, feeding it.

Joshua looked at us, his hands trembling, his breath uneven. He glanced at the scroll, then at the glowing fragment hovering just beyond his reach.

And then… he looked at Gillie. His great-granddaughter stood beside the fragments, her stance rigid, her eyes sharp—not angry, not pleading, but desperate in a way she wouldn't allow herself to show. She had fought so hard to reach this moment. She had never doubted the light. Not once.

His gaze drifted to Grace—his wife—watching him not with sorrow, not with expectation, but with a calm that made the world feel still. She did not speak. She did not plead. She only looked back at him, steady and certain, her presence unwavering even as he trembled beneath the weight of his choice. Grace had always believed. She had always known.

And Joshua—Joshua had tried. But the doubt had consumed him, creeping in slowly, relentlessly, carving into his ribs, clawing into his thoughts, suffocating his faith.

He searched their faces—Gillie, fierce and unyielding. Grace, calm and certain. The light itself, waiting for him to choose.

He looked at me—not his family, not the one he had failed or loved, but I carried the weight as if I was. And in that moment, he saw it too.

And yet—he still couldn't find the answer.

His fingers tightened around the parchment, his breath uneven and raw.

A sound stirred—low and resonant, like the lingering hum of bells long since silenced. It coiled through the clearing like a memory half-remembered, settling into the space between breaths.

And from the edge of the battlefield, the Bellmaker returned.

The mist parted around him—not from force, but reverence. His figure was just as before: cloaked in tattered light, bones of time and sound stitched into silence. Joshua's breath hitched. Even the shadows seemed to hesitate.

"*You came,*" Gillie whispered.

The Bellmaker did not speak at first. His head bowed, and a chime rang—not from his lips, but from the very air around him. Then, in that layered voice that sounded older than sound itself:

"You have followed the tolls. Now you must choose whether to stand . . . or to be counted."

He raised one arm, finger pointing—not to the bell—but to Joshua's trembling hands.

"The last toll does not seek the fallen. It waits for the ones who remain standing."

Around his words, the air hummed—not as a warning, but as a memory. A soft harmonic resonance bloomed across the field, like the low, layered melodies once heard among the humming trees. It didn't simply fill the space—it moved through it, curled into the bones of the earth and the breath of the oak. As if the trees and the Bellmaker were of the same breath, the same song.

And the Bellmaker was no longer there.

A strange calm settled over Joshua amidst the chaos. His gaze fell to the scroll in his trembling hands. It wasn't about holding on anymore. A profound, unexpected certainty bloomed in his heart. It needs to fall, a quiet voice whispered within him, to take root in the earth, to become what it was always meant to be.

Joshua's hands lingered for a moment longer, trembling, his grip faltering, his gaze locked on the scroll as though it might still give him an answer, as though it might still save him. But the whispers pressed deeper, sharper, louder.

And Joshua…

Dropped the scroll.

The scroll did not fall by accident, nor was it a mistake that could be undone. It slipped from his fingers in a way that felt almost deliberate, as if his body had moved without hesitation, as if the moment had been written long before it arrived.

The parchment spiraled downward, its descent slow, deliberate—as if the very air held its breath. It caught briefly in the glow, suspended for only an instant before it fell—collapsed—gave way to gravity.

When it struck the ground, it wasn't the sound of paper meeting earth. It was something heavier—deeper—final.

It rang through the battlefield like the shattering of stone, like the splintering of something sacred—something that could never be remade.

A shockwave pulsed outward, carrying the toll of its fall, coiling into the air, into the marrow, into the silence left behind.

The swamp felt it. The mist recoiled, the ground tightened, and for a moment—everything knew.

But the light held.

It did not falter. It remained, burning, unwavering, holding steady in its radiance. It did not fade, did not flicker, did not shift. It simply waited.

Joshua no longer held it, but the presence of the scroll did not lessen. If anything, it seemed stronger now, more pronounced, as though the act of surrendering it had only secured what was to come.

The beam that connected it to the oak trembled, its glow flaring for just a moment before stabilizing. But beneath its roots, the earth reacted—cracking, splitting deeper, reaching outward as if the land itself was grieving.

Gillie staggered back, her breath shaking in uneven gasps, her body unable to process what she had just witnessed. She was trembling, though whether it was from shock or despair, even she did not seem to know. Her hands were clenched, fingers twisting into fists that could do nothing to change what had happened. When she spoke, her voice barely carried, weak and fractured, as if saying it aloud might make it real, might make it irreversible.

"Joshua, no!"

The Silent Child stepped forward. Their voice, soft and small, rang louder than thunder.

"It is done."

Across the battlefield, Ezekiel stood unmoving. His glow remained steady, untouched by the war unraveling around him, unshaken by the weight of the choice that had just been made. But his eyes—his eyes told the truth. He did not look surprised. He did not look lost. Only knowing. From the moment Joshua stepped forward. From the moment the shadows reached for him. From the moment his grip on the scroll loosened.

Still, Ezekiel did not move. Not to reach for Joshua. Not to stop what had already happened. Not to break the silence enveloping the battlefield. Because watching was not absence. Watching was knowing. And knowledge, when held too long, became power. Joshua's fall felt like prophecy fulfilled, a moment sinking into the battlefield, silent, suspended, holding onto the air like something sacred. The light did not mourn. It did not rage. It did not hesitate. It simply remained. Not a loss. Not a defeat. Something else. Something waiting.

Marcus let out a low, satisfied laugh, his shadows swelling, rising, feeding on the clearing, stretching across the battlefield like a claim he had always believed to be inevitable. *"You've made the right choice,"* he said, smooth, assured, drowning the battlefield in his certainty. *"Step into my shadow, Joshua."*

The clearing was still.

Too still.

The storm did not press forward. It thickened, folding inward, watching, waiting—recognizing that something had collapsed into finality. The swamp did not resist. It did not recoil. It only *shifted*, settling beneath the weight of the choice, absorbing it into the space where all decisions linger before they take shape.

Joshua stood at the center, the scroll at his feet, its light unmoved, unchanged, waiting. But he did not lift it. Time stretched, slowing into something unbearable, fragile, something too delicate to hold.

And then… Joshua smiled.

The first time they had seen it.

Not broken.

Not hesitant.

Not afraid.

A smile of acceptance.

A smile of knowing.

A smile that told them it was already too late.

But something else accompanied it, something unseen by Marcus, Elana, or Raven – a faint, internal glow that seemed to emanate from Joshua himself, a quiet radiance Gillie and I had never seen before.

Gillie's breath hitched, her hands shaking, clenched into fists, as if gripping something might pull her back from the moment.

Ezekiel shifted slightly, his movements tight, measured, controlled, as though any wrong motion might cause the battlefield to collapse entirely.

Marcus watched, calculating, knowing, his victory twisted into reality itself.

Joshua lifted his gaze, looking at them, his expression unwavering, his smile remaining.

And then… his voice broke through the silence.

"Don't. . . ."

His breath was uneven, but his words were steady, carved from something absolute.

"Don't make the same mistakes I did. Don't fight the law of faith and love. Don't give up the light."

The words were not shouted.

They did not need to be.

They settled into the clearing, into the silence, into the space that stretched between hope and despair. They etched themselves into the battlefield. Through the storm. Through the war that had stopped just long enough to listen.

The shadows twisted, recoiling, sensing what was coming next.

Joshua's breath hitched, his chest heaving, his voice breaking.

For a single, fragile moment, there was nothing.

No movement.

No sound.

Just the tremor in his breath.

And then—he screamed:

"REDEMPTION!"

Whether he said it before the toll or because of it… no one could say.

But the God Forsaken Bell answered.

The world fractured.

The toll crashed into reality with a force so raw, so unrelenting, the very air seemed to weep.

The ground didn't tremble.

It shattered.

Time did not freeze. It collapsed, folding inward, suffocating beneath the magnitude of the sound. The warriors stood motionless. The shadows recoiled, not in fear, but in understanding.

The light did not advance. It did not retreat. It simply remained, steady, waiting, unshaken—but mourning.

The bell did not chime. It howled. A sound that did not fade, did not die—it engraved itself into the battlefield, into the hearts of those who stood beneath the weight of its cry, into the very bones of the land. And Joshua's scream was not a plea. It was a reckoning. A declaration. An ending.

For the first time, the storm hesitated. The swamp did not consume. It watched. And in that moment—nothing would ever be the same again.

The Final Four Bells

I looked around, my breath shallow, my pulse pounding against my ribs, as if my body knew—this was it.

The moment where everything changed.

The battlefield wasn't unified in grief or triumph—it was divided.

Two forces.

Two reactions.

Two realities.

On one side—the army of darkness erupted.

Their voices rose like thunder, triumphant, consuming, celebrating what had just fallen into their grasp.

Shadows swelled around them, moving upward like smoke reaching toward a sky that had finally surrendered. Their figures illuminated by the twisting storm, their faces cracked open with satisfaction, their cheers pressing into the clearing like a wave swallowing everything in its path.

Their joy was visceral, alive, sharp—the kind of victory that didn't feel earned but stolen, devoured, taken.

And yet, for them—it was everything.

For the army of light—it was devastation.

Silence first.

Then—a slow unraveling of breath, of movement, of hope splintering beneath the weight of what they had just witnessed.

Their bodies stiffened, their gazes sinking, their expressions carved from disbelief, sorrow, loss.

Lightning flashed, illuminating their faces for a brief, brutal second—eyes stretched wide, jaws clenched, postures folding inward, gripping their weapons like anchors to a world that had suddenly tilted off its axis.

Gillie hadn't moved.

She had staggered back before—but now, she was frozen, caught between instinct and grief, between wanting to rush forward and knowing there was nothing left to save.

Ezekiel stood still.

Unmoving, unwavering—not because he didn't feel the loss, but because he understood it.

Because he had known it was coming before anyone else.

And I stood between it all.

I felt the storm twist against the battlefield, pulsing between these two reactions—feeding their triumph, sinking into their sorrow, mirroring the split in reality that could never be undone.

When the bell and Joshua's scream collided, the sound wasn't separate from the battlefield but carved into it.

A force that didn't exist in the air alone but in the very bones of war itself.

It didn't echo.

It embedded itself into the clearing, settling deep into the moment, into the faces of those standing within the storm, refusing to be ignored.

The war raged, but time had stopped, marking itself around this instant, refusing to move forward until it had etched itself into eternity.

This was the fracture.

The irrevocable divide.

The second where everything splintered apart.

And there was no escaping what came next.

Grace cried out, her voice fracturing through the storm, shaking as the earth beneath Joshua split wide open, a chasm yawning at his feet, its depths swallowing what remained of the light.

She fell to her knees, her sobs breaking, pressing into the battlefield, shaking through the clearing as though her grief alone might stop the inevitable.

The swamp howled in fury, the mist twisting violently, the storm coiling tighter, reacting as though it understood what was happening, understood that something irreversible had just begun.

From the chasm's depths, they came.

Demons.

Their forms jagged, shifting, unnatural, their bodies stretching in ways that should not be possible, their claws scraping against the edges of the abyss as they dragged themselves upward, screeching into the storm.

Their eyes were hollow pits, their mouths jagged chasms of teeth, gnashing as they reached for him, for the body, for the flesh they had been waiting for.

Joshua writhed, his body buckling beneath the constriction of Marcus's shadows, the chains twisting around his limbs, tightening like serpents, their coils digging into his flesh, clawing into bone.

And then… the demons reached him.

Raven descended first.

He didn't lunge, didn't tear forward like the others—he moved with purpose, deliberate, his fingers contorting into jagged claws as he pressed them into Joshua's ribs.

He felt it.

The flesh.

The struggle.

The breaking.

His grin was slow, sickening, spreading as his claws sank deeper, digging into muscle, twisting—pulling.

Joshua screamed, his voice fracturing through the battlefield, ripping through the storm, his body convulsing beneath the grip of the shadows, beneath the jagged claws raking into him.

Elana followed, her form shifting, twisting, her mouth stretching unnaturally wide—not in hunger but in satisfaction, in certainty.

She gripped Joshua's shoulder, her nails digging into skin, her grin cracked, grotesque, unrelenting.

And then… she tore.

Her teeth sank into flesh, ripping it away in one brutal motion, blood spraying across her arms, dripping from her grin as she devoured him.

Joshua's screams were raw, collapsing, faltering, not diminishing but breaking.

The other demons descended, their claws raking into his back, his legs, his chest, their jagged fingers clamping into open wounds, digging into torn muscles.

They did not feed with desperation.

They fed with certainty.

With victory.

The chasm widened, its edges splintering, crumbling beneath the weight of the darkness pouring from its depths.

Grace's sobs cracked, her voice shattering as she screamed his name, her hands digging into the ground, clawing at the dirt as though she could pull him back.

Ezekiel watched, silent, his hands shaking as he gripped the hilt of his sword, his knuckles white, his shoulders collapsing.

The Silent Child stood frozen, their light dimmed, flickering, struggling, their small frame trembling beneath the weight of the moment.

And Marcus…

Marcus laughed.

His shadows tightened, their coils driving deeper, suffocating, claiming, sealing the moment with absolute finality.

His voice rose, rich with satisfaction, dripping with triumph.

"This is the end," he said, smiling. "This is what you chose, Joshua. This is what you deserve."

The demons did not stop. They ripped, tore, devoured, their forms twisting as they consumed him piece by piece, their screeches merging into chaos, into the anthem of conquest.

The swamp stood still. The chasm pulsed, swallowing what remained of Joshua's cries.

Victory deepened, stretched, hammering down into the battlefield, settling into the air—not as an ending, but as a coronation, an undeniable proclamation.

Marcus tilted his head, listening, grinning. His soldiers raised their weapons, their voices merging, folding into the moment, lifting their triumph like something absolute. Unquestioned. Sealed.

They celebrated.

They announced it.

They believed it.

Everyone believed it.

None of them realized—it was never just a victory.

It was something greater.

Something waiting.

Something coming.

But in that moment—there was no resistance. No defiance. No challenge to their claim.

Only darkness.

Only triumph.

Only the certainty that light had lost.

The New Dawn

The Three Days of Silence

The first day was the worst.

Not because of pain.

Not because of battle.

But because of absence.

Joshua was gone.

And we were still here.

That wasn't supposed to happen.

We had walked into his purgatory. Entered his judgment. We knew the risk. We'd made the deal. If he fell, so would we.

So why were we still breathing?

Why had we been left behind?

It felt wrong. Off. Like some ancient law had been broken, or worse—bent.

The New Dawn

The scroll lay where it had fallen.

Untouched.

Unmoving.

Still glowing.

But it didn't reach for us. Didn't whisper or burn in our hands. It only waited.

Like everything else.

Gillie crouched by the roots of the oak, her fingers curled into the dirt. Not searching. Not moving. Just holding on—like the ground might give her answers if she gripped it tight enough.

But the earth gave her nothing.

No sign of Joshua.

No imprint of where he had stood.

No blood. No ash. Not even a shadow.

It was like he had been erased.

Beside her, Grace sat perfectly still. Her hands folded in her lap, her eyes fixed forward. She looked like a woman who had already said every prayer she knew. And none of them had been enough.

Ezekiel stood near the scroll.

Unmoving.

His arms at his sides, fists clenched just enough to keep from shaking.

He didn't speak.

Didn't look away.

Didn't dare touch the parchment.

Because whatever judgment Joshua had triggered—it hadn't fallen on us.

Not yet.

And that was the worst part.

We weren't spared.

We were waiting.

The deal had been clear.

One fate.

Shared.

So why were we still here?

Were we next?

Or had something… interfered?

The scream.

The final word he shouted.

Redemption.

And then—the bell.

Had he said it before the toll, or because of it?

Had it saved him?

Had it saved us?

Or had it only delayed what was coming?

None of us could say.

And the silence didn't offer answers.

But the demons didn't care.

They celebrated.

From the edges of the swamp—what remained of it—their cries echoed like laughter clawed from bone. Twisted voices rang through the shadows, shrill and triumphant. Their shrieks weren't rage.

They were joy.

Because they believed they had won.

They believed the light had fallen.

That Joshua had failed.

That nothing stood between them and the world anymore.

Their songs were mockeries of worship—howls of conquest, distorted into praise of their own corruption.

They danced in the distance, feeding on the aftermath, claiming victory not just over Joshua, but over hope itself.

It didn't matter to them that the scroll still pulsed.

Or that the battlefield still trembled.

They had seen the light drop.

And that was enough for them to rejoice.

Gillie finally broke the silence.

"Why are we still here?"

Her voice was quiet, but it carried.

I looked over at her. She didn't move her gaze from the dirt.

Grace didn't respond. Neither did Ezekiel.

Because none of us knew.

Had we been spared?

Or had judgment simply not arrived yet?

And if it hadn't…

Was it still coming?

The scroll offered no answer.

It only waited.

Like everything else.

The second day was worse—not because of grief, but because the world didn't stop for us to mourn.

Marcus's forces didn't rest.

They didn't hesitate.

They didn't even slow.

They rejoiced.

Their voices rolled through the swamp—sharp, cutting laughter, shouts that hit the trembling ground like distant thunder.

They didn't just move through the battlefield.

They claimed it.

Owned it.

As if nothing we'd fought for had ever mattered.

And we—we scattered.

Not in fear.

Not in surrender.

Not because we had lost.

We retreated because there was nothing left to fight for.

I sat near the roots of the oak, back stiff, hands loose on my knees, watching the shadows surge unchecked.

Gillie was beside me—rigid, silent, unmoving. Her gaze locked on the horizon, not blinking, not shifting.

Her fingers tapped lightly against the fabric of her coat, like she was counting something.

Seconds.

Breaths.

Everything we had lost.

Grace knelt at my other side. Her hands were pressed together—not in prayer, just resting, still.

She didn't whisper to the sky like before. Didn't close her eyes.

She stared forward, her gaze distant—like she was looking beyond the battlefield, searching for something that wasn't here.

Ezekiel was the only one standing.

He'd moved from the scroll to the tree, hands shoved deep into his coat pockets.

His shoulders squared, spine stiff—holding himself still like it was the only thing keeping him together.

He was never still. Not before battle. Not between them.

He paced.

He planned.

He tested the ground.

But now—he didn't move.

Not because he didn't want to.

But because he didn't know what movement meant anymore.

Gillie turned her hands in her lap, staring at her palms for a long, quiet moment.

Then, she pressed them against her knees—gripping just enough to keep herself here.

Her voice broke the silence, low and hoarse.

"Why did we live when he didn't?"

No one answered.

Not right away.

Her voice wasn't weak—it was tired. Bone-deep. The kind of exhaustion that doesn't sleep away.

There should've been words.

Something to give back.

Some explanation.

But there wasn't.

Because we didn't know.

I breathed slowly, eyes fixed on the ruins of the battlefield, watching as the weight of someone else's victory settled like ash over the land.

When I finally spoke, it was barely more than a murmur.

"The deal was clear."

The words didn't feel like mine.

They felt like something I was remembering.

"Win or lose… we were supposed to share Joshua's fate. But we didn't."

Gillie's hands curled against her knees.

Not clenched.

Just enough to show the tension unraveling beneath her stillness.

She shook her head slightly, eyes flicking to the dirt and then back to the sky.

"Then what happened?"

I didn't answer.

Because I didn't know.

We hadn't won. Not truly.

The rules had been set. The price agreed upon.

And we had broken it.

The second day was worse.

Not because of grief.

Not even because of fear.

But because the world didn't stop.

The demons didn't leave.

They celebrated louder.

Their laughter curled through the mist like smoke from a fire that refused to die. Their shadows danced just beyond the edges of the clearing, not hiding, not attacking—just watching. Just reveling.

We were still here.

And they knew it.

They circled us, their shrieks rising like twisted hymns. It wasn't torment. It was amusement. We hadn't been spared. We'd been forgotten.

Or maybe… delayed.

I sat by the oak, the same spot I hadn't moved from since the toll. My hands rested on my knees, my fingers numb from clenching and unclenching, over and over again. There was nothing left to hold. No sword. No answer.

Just the waiting.

Gillie sat nearby, cross-legged in the dirt. Her coat was wrapped tight around her, though the air wasn't cold. Her fingers tapped silently against her leg. A rhythm. Maybe a countdown.

"Two days," she said quietly. "He's been gone two days."

Her voice was too calm. Too still.

Grace hadn't spoken. Not once since the toll. She sat like a statue—praying maybe, or remembering. Maybe both. Her eyes were open, but her mind was far away. With him.

Ezekiel had moved only once—to press a hand to the soil. And then he stood. Unmoving. Guarding nothing. Protecting nothing.

Not pacing.

Not commanding.

Just… waiting.

Everything around us should've collapsed by now.

But it hadn't.

And maybe that was the scariest part.

Because it meant the rules weren't being followed.

Or they were being rewritten.

I watched the shadows shift at the edges. I didn't know if they were real. Didn't care. My eyes were too tired to tell the difference anymore.

Gillie spoke again. Not to anyone. Just into the air.

"We shouldn't be here."

Her voice cracked just slightly.

The rhythm in her fingers stopped.

"We went into his purgatory. His judgment. That was the deal. We die if he dies. So why…?"

The words hung, half-spoken.

No one finished them.

Because the truth was too big.

And too close.

I didn't respond.

Not yet.

I wasn't ready to say it out loud.

But the thought was there. Buried behind my teeth.

He bought us time.

Maybe with his scream.

Maybe with his sacrifice.

Maybe with his soul.

Whatever he did—whatever that last word was—he did it at the precise moment the bell tolled.

And now, here we were.

Alive.

Unjudged.

Uncertain.

And still surrounded by demons who thought they had already won.

Gillie pulled her coat tighter, her shoulders tense.

"He's not coming back," she said. "Is he."

It wasn't a question. Not really.

And I didn't lie.

"No."

Silence followed. Heavy. But no one argued.

Because deep down, we knew.

Even if we didn't understand it.

Even if it wasn't fair.

The demons laughed again, louder now. Joyous. Wild.

They still believed they had won.

And we—
We sat in the silence.
Not defeated.
Not delivered.
Just waiting for whatever would come next.
The third day didn't bring peace.
Or clarity.
Or hope.
It brought silence.
The kind that wasn't passive.
The kind that pressed down.
That waited.
We were still in Purgatory.
Still in the place Joshua had died.
And every second we remained here… we knew.
Judgment hadn't come yet.
But it would.

I sat at the base of the oak, hands flat in the dirt. My palms itched from the stillness. I couldn't bring myself to move. Every twitch felt like it might draw attention—might tip the balance.

Gillie sat nearby, still cross-legged, her eyes closed, her shoulders rigid. She hadn't said a word since night fell.

Grace sat with her back to the tree, her hands folded in her lap, her head tilted back. She wasn't praying anymore. Not out loud. But something in her expression looked like surrender.

And Ezekiel…

Ezekiel hadn't moved since sunrise. Not even to breathe. He stood like a sentinel made of stone, watching the horizon as if waiting for the sky to split open.

The demons weren't laughing anymore.

They were still there—lurking. We felt them. But they weren't celebrating now. They were listening. Watching. Waiting.

Because they didn't understand either.

Because maybe they hadn't won.

Or maybe they had… and were just waiting for the final part of the sentence to fall.

Gillie opened her eyes slowly. Her gaze drifted to me.

"We shouldn't still be here," she whispered.

I nodded. "I know."

She ran a hand through her tangled hair, then let it fall. "If the deal still stands… we're overdue. Something should've happened by now."

I didn't answer.

Because she was right.

And wrong.

Something had happened.

The bell had tolled.

The word had been screamed.

The scroll had been dropped.

But none of it had been clear.

Not yet.

She lowered her gaze to the ground. Her voice barely carried.

"What if… what if he changed the terms?"

I looked at her then. Not because the question was new—but because it had been mine, too.

"What if redemption didn't come too late?" she whispered. "What if it came just in time?"

I didn't answer.

I didn't know how.

Because the bell rang at the exact same moment he screamed.

No one could say what came first.

Or what it meant.

And that was the point.

Because in Purgatory, uncertainty is the punishment.

And in that silence, we waited.

Not for rescue.

Not for rebirth.

But for judgment.

It could still come.

Even now.

We all felt it.

That tension in the air.

That pressure under the surface.

Like the whole world was holding its breath.

The scroll still sat in the dirt where Joshua dropped it.

Untouched.

Unclaimed.

It still glowed faintly.

Not with power.

Not with promise.

With purpose.

Still waiting for someone to pick it up.

But none of us dared.

Because what if touching it triggered the end?

What if we weren't spared—only delayed?

What if judgment had simply paused?

We didn't speak of it.

But we all felt it.

The stillness before a verdict.

The breath before the fall.

The moment before the hand of God moves.

Day three ended with no answers.

No signs.

Just breath.

Just silence.

Just the weight of everything still unresolved.

The third day did not bring peace.

It brought pressure.

The kind that coils behind your ribs. The kind that makes you afraid to breathe too deep in case the world notices you're still here.

The air hadn't shifted in hours. The sky was still gray. Still stuck. The oak tree didn't move. Neither did the scroll.

And neither did we.

We weren't sure if we were allowed to.

Gillie sat on the same patch of earth, her fingers tangled in the grass like she was trying to root herself into the ground before it gave way. She hadn't said anything in hours.

Neither had I.

Neither had anyone.

Because what could we say?

We weren't supposed to be here.

Not like this.

Not after that.

Joshua was gone.

The God Forsaken Bell had tolled.

The war had ended.

And still—we remained.

But in Purgatory… that meant nothing.

If we were still here, then judgment hadn't come yet.

Or worse—it was still coming.

Gillie spoke suddenly, her voice hollow and too loud in the stillness.

"What if it wasn't over?"

I turned to her slowly. She wasn't looking at me. She was staring at the scroll like it might explode if she blinked.

"What if it didn't choose us," she whispered. "What if it's just… waiting to finish the job?"

I didn't answer.

Because I'd already thought it.

What if the demons had celebrated too early?

What if Joshua's scream hadn't saved us?

What if it had only delayed what we had earned?

The silence thickened. My stomach turned.

We were still in the swamp—still in the place between. Waiting.

Gillie stood, slow and unsteady. Her fingers twitched like she wanted to reach for her blade. But there was nothing to fight.

Not yet.

I followed her gaze.

The scroll hadn't moved.

Hadn't changed.

Hadn't pulsed.

But the air around it… was tight.

Tight like breath before a scream.

Like silence before a verdict.

Like the split second before the noose is pulled.

And then…

The scroll lit.

The Reckoning of Light

It did not ignite gently.

It did not rise like a flickering ember, nor did it pulse like something hesitant, unsure of its own existence.

It detonated.

A blast of radiance surged upward, consuming the battlefield in a flood of brilliance so vast, so pure, that the air itself shuddered beneath its presence.

It came like a tidal wave.

Like a storm reversed.

Crashing not with chaos—but with absolute, unwavering order.

An existence that could no longer allow darkness to remain.

The golden glow collided with the chasm, driving itself deep into the abyss, forcing its presence into the depths that had dared to claim Joshua. The earth recoiled, convulsing, shaking with the impact as the radiance poured into every crevice, every crack, every hollow pit of shadow.

Marcus's forces had been cheering.

Their victory claimed.

Their triumph celebrated—shouted, laughed into the battlefield as though nothing could defy it.

And then… the light touched them.

Their cheers twisted. Changed.

Screams fractured the air—high, broken, shrill.

The sound of conquest devoured by agony.

Of warriors realizing too late they had won nothing.

Their bodies did not burn.

They shattered.

The New Dawn

Raven was the first to fall.

He convulsed, limbs twisting inward, shadows writhing and recoiling, trying to retreat—But there was nowhere to go.

The light sank into his skin, threading through his veins, filling his bones like fire crawling through dry wood.

His scream was raw. Guttural.

His body fractured apart, piece by piece—Golden brilliance splitting through his chest, arms, throat, skull—Until he collapsed inward.

Pulled into the light.

Gone before his final scream had the chance to finish.

Elana was no different.

Her screech split the battlefield, her body writhing as the brilliance coiled through her limbs, her chest, her breath—Pressing into every fragment of existence that had once belonged to her.

She clawed at the air. Reached.

Struggled.

But there was no escape.

The light pierced her ribs, her spine, her throat—Until nothing remained.

The demons collapsed next.

Their twisted forms unraveled, dissolving, breaking apart—Limbs shrinking into nothingness, voices fading before they could comprehend their loss.

Their screeches fractured.

Then vanished.

Silenced by a wave of radiance that spared no shadow.

Not remnants.

Not ashes.

Nothing.

The swamp did not simply brighten.

It transformed.

The mist, once thick and suffocating, didn't just lift—It was eradicated.

The very air seemed to shudder.

The atmosphere compressed.

Pressure shifted.

Not into emptiness.

But into something untouched.

Something pure.

The waters, once blackened and tainted, rippled as filth fell away—Revealing depths so clear they mirrored the sky.

Vines, once dead and tangled, straightened.

They bloomed.

Not like they had returned—Like they had never been broken in the first place.

The transformation wasn't just a change.

It was a rebirth.

The swamp—once a pit of despair—became a sanctuary of light and purity.

The air no longer reeked of decay.

It carried the scent of blooming flowers, of clear water, of untouched earth.

The ground was no longer mud.

It was a carpet of green, vibrant grass that glowed with life.

The trees stood tall, unbowed.

Their branches heavy with leaves, rustling gently in a breeze that no longer pulled—But carried.

It was hard to believe this place had once belonged to shadow.

As if the essence of the swamp had been rewritten.

Its history erased.

Its story reborn.

The light that had erupted from the scroll hadn't simply driven away the dark—It had filled the swamp with a new kind of energy.

A life force.

A pulse.

The swamp was no longer to be feared.

It was to be *cherished*.

A testament to transformation.

A monument to the power of light.

Proof that even the darkest places can bloom again.

Marcus watched.

He did not retreat.

He did not blink.

But he could feel it.

The world changing.

Bending beneath the presence of something far greater than himself—Greater than anything he had ever commanded.

And for the first time in his existence—He felt loss.

True loss.

Not the loss of battle.

Not the loss of power.

But the kind of loss that can never be rebuilt.

Never undone.

He tried to speak.

The words caught in his throat.

Strangled by the brilliance flooding the battlefield—Tearing apart everything that had once answered him.

He could not look away.

The mist was gone.

Not faded.

Erased.

The waters—once mirrors of his own corruption—now ran clear.

Still.

Undisturbed.

Marcus trembled.

His shadows writhed and coiled, clawing at the ground, the air, at the very fabric of existence—Grasping for something to hold onto.

Something to drag back into the abyss.

But the abyss was gone.

Erased.

As though it had never existed.

The darkness had unraveled, thread by thread.

And now—only light remained.

He gritted his teeth. His breath shook.

"No."

It wasn't just a word.

It was a snarl.

A command.

A plea.

But the world didn't listen.

It didn't flinch.

It didn't stop.

His soldiers began to *fade*.

Not fall.

Not die.

But disappear.

Their bodies convulsed, shattered—Their screams collapsed into silence, ripped away before they could be heard again.

They were not destroyed.

They were *unmade.*

Raven—his fiercest weapon—cracked open, flesh splintering before he could draw a final breath.

Elana shattered—dissolving before she could even reach for something to save her.

One by one.

Every loyal shadow.

Every twisted echo.

Every follower.

Gone.

And Marcus…

Was *alone.*

He breathed.

Ragged.

Shallow.

Uncertain.

He watched the last remnants of his world collapse.

Burn.

Twist away into *nothing.*

And it tore through him.

A wound deeper than any blade.

A loss that stretched beyond time—

Beyond power.

Beyond redemption.

He screamed.

A roar that cracked the battlefield, tried to tear through the light—
But the light didn't yield.

It struck him.

One beam.

Then two.

Then a thousand.

It tore into him—splitting through bone, flesh, shadow—Ripping through the foundation of his being.

He twisted.

He fought.

He raged.

But the shadows no longer obeyed.

They died.

And Marcus—

Finally understood.

This was not punishment.

It was judgment.

His essence fractured.

Splintered with golden light.

Tearing through his chest, limbs, face.

He tried to hold himself together.

Tried to anchor to the power he once commanded.

But it was gone.

And so was he.

His final breath never came.

His final scream never formed.

He was not slain.

He was *erased*.

Shattered.

Gone.

Forgotten by the darkness he once ruled.

And the battlefield…

Was still.

The swamp was cleansed.

The war was finished.

And in the aftermath—

There was silence.

A silence so heavy. So sacred. So final—That it settled over the clearing like the last breath of existence.

Ezekiel stepped forward.

Slowly.

Like a man moving through a memory.

He removed his cloak.

Let it fall to the ground.

Then the satchel.

The sound of it landing felt loud against the stillness.

And then—

He knelt.

No drama.

No declaration.

Just a life laid down.

A burden set aside.

He placed one hand against the soil where the scroll had once fallen.

And whispered—

"Let it take root."

The Task Ahead

I woke with a sharp inhale, my chest tightening as if I had surfaced from deep water—as if I had been drowning in something unseen and had just now broken through.

For a long moment, I did not move.

I did not speak.

I simply breathed.

The world around me was strange—different, weightless in a way I couldn't immediately comprehend.

Warmth pressed into my skin—not oppressive, not suffocating, but gentle and steady, filling the air like a presence rather than a sensation.

I turned my head slowly, the motion feeling both effortless and impossibly heavy, as though my body had spent too long in stillness—as though I had only just remembered how to move.

And then—the sound. A quiet murmur of life shifting, stirring. Something familiar, yet distant. Like a world that had always existed just beyond reach.

For a moment, I thought I was still dreaming.

The golden light that had guided us in the swamp had faded, replaced by the gentle glow of sunlight filtering through a canopy of trees.

The air smelled different—clean, fresh, alive.

And the oppressive weight that had suffocated the swamp was gone entirely.

I sat up slowly, the movement sending a strange sensation through my limbs—as if I had been asleep for far longer than I had the right to be.

The scroll still rested in my lap.

Its weight felt different now—not heavy, but living.

Like it had become more than parchment—like it now carried the record of the light that had returned.

It pressed into me not with judgment, but with purpose.

Gillie groaned beside me, stirring.

Her body tensed, her breathing sharp as she woke suddenly—her chest rising and falling like she had just been pulled from something deep.

"This isn't the swamp," she muttered, her voice laced with confusion. "This isn't… Purgatory."

My heart raced as the memories flooded back—the eleventh bell, Joshua's scream, the chasm's eruption, the twelfth bell's toll.

"We're outside," I said softly, my voice trembling as the realization settled over me. "We made it out."

The words felt strange—like they didn't belong to me.

As if they had been given to me, placed in my mouth like a truth I had no choice but to speak.

Gillie's posture stiffened.

She looked around again—slower this time, deeper, searching for something familiar.
Something to anchor herself to.

"But how?" she asked.

Her voice was tight—not skeptical, not fearful, but unsteady. Like she already knew the answer wouldn't be simple.

"Were we… asleep?" she muttered.

She shifted, rubbing at her arms, her fingers pressing against her skin like she was testing if she was real.

"Were we carried here?"

I swallowed, my thumb brushing against the parchment, tracing its surface.

It wasn't pulsing anymore.

It wasn't shifting.

But it was still something more than paper.

"I don't know," I admitted.

I looked down at it, feeling its weight—not heavy, but present.

Like something alive.

Like something watching.

"Maybe the light brought us here. Maybe it carried us forward," I whispered.

She frowned. "Forward to what?" she muttered. "This doesn't feel like an ending. It feels like the next step."

I turned the scroll over carefully, its weight settling into my hands like a steady presence.

"Maybe that's what it is," I said, my voice stronger now. "The next step. The light didn't destroy us like it did the army of the dark. It didn't consume us. It didn't erase us."

"It sent us forward—for something greater."

Gillie nodded slowly, her gaze lingering on the horizon where the sunlight stretched endlessly ahead of us.

"Then we don't waste it," she said firmly. "Whatever this is— wherever we are—it doesn't end here. We carry the scroll. We figure out where it's supposed to go."

And though the path ahead was unmarked, uncertain, I felt no hesitation.

The light had brought us here—not as a reward, but as a calling.

The swamp was gone.

The shadows had fallen silent.

But our journey was just beginning.

She shook her head slowly, her eyes clouded with thought.

"Joshua—he didn't make it. But we did. Why? Why us? Why not him?"

The question cut through me—sharp and heavy.

I swallowed hard, gripping the scroll a little tighter.

"I don't know," I admitted, my voice trembling. "But I think... I think he knew. In the end, I think he knew what this was about. What it was for."

Her jaw tightened, and she looked away, her hands clenching into fists.

"He warned us," she muttered, her voice raw. "He warned us not to make the same mistakes he did. To hold on to the light, no matter what. Do you think... do you think that's why we're here?"

I looked down at the scroll again, its faint glow reflecting in the sunlight.

It no longer felt like an object.

It felt like a message.

A story—one that had died, risen, and was now ours to carry forward.

A responsibility.

A calling.

"I think it is," I said slowly. "I think... this is why we were chosen. To carry it. To bring it where it needs to go."

"Where it needs to go?" she repeated, her tone edging toward frustration. "And where's that? What are we supposed to do with it? The swamp's gone. The shadows are gone—what's left?"

"The world," I said simply, the words feeling both foreign and inevitable.

"The world is still broken. It always was. But this… this is the story that can bring it back.

The story of the light. The story of the return."

"The light, the truth—it wasn't just for us. It's for everyone. Joshua gave his life for that. We can't let it be for nothing."

She let out a sharp breath, her shoulders sagging as the weight of my words settled over her.

"So that's it," she said finally. "That's what we're doing now. Carrying God's Word back to a world that doesn't even know it needs it."

I nodded, my hands tightening around the scroll.

"It's what we're meant to do," I said softly. "The light showed us that."

For a moment, she didn't respond. She just stared at the horizon, where the sunlight stretched farther than I'd ever seen it—Illuminating a world that felt impossibly vast.

Then, slowly, she stood, brushing the dirt from her hands.

"Fine," she said, her tone firm despite the grief still lingering in her eyes.

"If that's the task, then we do it. No more waiting. No more doubting."

I stood as well, the scroll tucked carefully under my arm.

The air felt warmer now.

Clearer.

Like the world itself was waking up after a long, dark slumber.

There was still so much I didn't know—so much I didn't understand.

But for the first time, I felt… ready.

The swamp was gone.

The shadows were gone.

But the journey was just beginning.

Tempered and Refined

The silence was unlike anything I had ever heard before.

For so long, the tolling of the bells had dominated everything—each chime crashing through the swamp, shaking the earth, commanding attention with its unbearable weight.

But now, the sound was gone.

The God-Forsaken Bell had tolled its last note, and for the first time, its absence did not feel ominous or uncertain.

It felt like a beginning.

Gillie stood beside me, hands in her pockets, staring at the horizon where the light stretched farther than I thought possible.

The oak's golden beam had faded, its glow lingering softly but no longer blazing upward.

The world around us felt different—not empty, but full.

Full of something new.

Something waiting.

Something alive.

For the first time, the silence didn't feel like loss.

It felt like a moment of transition—a breath between what was and what would be.

Gillie turned slightly, her stance straighter, stronger.

I saw it in her eyes—the grief still present, but softened. Tempered.

Shaped into something else.

Something close to hope.

"We're supposed to carry it, aren't we?" she asked.

Her voice was even, steady—like she had already accepted the answer.

I nodded, gripping the scroll carefully.

Its glow had dimmed slightly in the sunlight, but its presence remained unchanged.

Constant.

"Not just carry it," I said. "We have to share it. The light wasn't just for us. It never was."

Gillie frowned, glancing toward the distance, trying to picture the road ahead.

"And how exactly do we do that? Just stroll into the world and tell them we've got the answers to everything? That we walked through Purgatory, heard some bells, and now we know better?"

"It's not about knowing better," I said quietly, though the weight of the task pressed heavily against my chest.

"It's about showing them. About giving them the chance to see the light like we did."

She let out a short, breathy laugh, shaking her head.

"You make it sound simple."

"It's not," I admitted, turning the scroll over in my hands, tracing the edges of the parchment.

Its faint glow caught the sunlight, reflecting something steady. Something unshaken.

"It's never simple. But it's—right. This is what we're meant to do."

Gillie was quiet for a moment, unreadable.

Then, almost absently, she adjusted the strap of her satchel—her movements sharp and practiced.

"I don't know what we're walking into," she said finally, her tone thoughtful, distant.

"But for the first time, it doesn't feel hopeless. It feels—like maybe we've got a shot."

I caught the faintest trace of something softer in her expression.

A flicker of belief.

A trace of certainty.

A glimpse of hope.

"We do," I said more firmly now. "Because we're not walking into this alone."

She glanced at the scroll, then back at me, smirking faintly.

"So," she said, teasing, "we're just supposed to walk out there and fix the whole world, huh?"

I smiled, despite the grief still lodged deep in my chest.

"Something like that," I said, tucking the scroll securely under my arm.

"Though I wouldn't mind knowing exactly where to start."

Gillie let out another short laugh, shaking her head—though there was no bitterness in the sound.

No frustration.

Only something quieter.

Steadier.

"Right. A divine mission without a map. Sounds about right for us."

It should have felt uncertain—daunting, even—but it didn't.

There was something oddly fitting about it.

Something that made sense in a way the world hadn't for a long time.

We had walked through fire.

Through ruin.

Through loss that had nearly broken us.

And still, we remained.

Maybe that was the lesson.

Maybe the journey was never meant to be written down in careful directions.

Maybe it had always been about stepping forward, even when we didn't know exactly where the road would lead.

There was no marked path ahead.

No guiding stars to steer us.

Only faith.

The kind that had been tested, fractured, nearly lost—but never fully extinguished.

And maybe, after everything, that was what mattered most.

The war had ended.

The bells had tolled.

The reckoning had come and gone.

And yet, in the stillness, something remained.

For all the suffering—for all the loss—something had been left behind for us.

Not victory.

Not relief.

But something larger than grief.

Purpose.

A task.

A weight that did not crush—but called.

I reached into my pocket, my fingers brushing against the edges of the coin.

It was still there.

Solid.

Unchanged.

Carrying the weight of something greater than myself.

My thumb ran over its surface slowly, tracing its worn edges.

Feeling its presence—not as a burden, but as proof.

Of endurance.

Of what we had left to do.

For so long, it had felt heavy.

Unbearable.

Like something meant to break me.

But now…

I turned it in my palm, letting the sunlight catch the metal.

Now it was just a coin.

Gillie watched me, her expression softening, her breath a quiet exhale as she shifted her gaze toward the horizon.

"He's gone," she said, grief lingering but no longer raw.

No longer suffocating.

"But he gave us something, didn't he? Something bigger than all of this."

I tightened my grip on the coin, then the scroll—feeling their warmth settle in my hands.

Not as remnants.

But as responsibility.

As the path we had to forge ourselves.

I met Gillie's gaze and nodded.

"He did."

Her fingers lingered at her side for only a moment before she turned fully toward me, resolve settling deep in her stance.

"Then we don't waste it," she said.

"We set out. We carry the scroll. We do whatever it takes to make sure this light reaches the people who need it."

"They do need it," I said, certainty threading through my voice.

"They might not even know it yet, but they do. The world's been broken for too long."

The first steps forward carried no hesitation.

We left behind the clearing, the oak, the lingering echoes of a war that had finished—but would never be forgotten.

There was no road ahead.

No carved direction.

But there didn't need to be.

The light wasn't in the world yet.

It was in us.

And it would guide us forward.

For the first time, I felt the faintest flicker of something close to hope.

The weight of the past still clung to me—to both of us—but it didn't hold us down.

It was part of us, yes, but it didn't define where we were going.

What defined us now was the purpose we carried.

The task ahead.

The journey was just beginning.

But it wasn't one we had to face alone.

The horizon stretched wide.

Golden.

Waiting.

The world was quiet.

Watching.

Expectant.

We had no map.

No carved direction.

But we didn't hesitate.

The light had set us forward—not just as survivors, but as those chosen to bring it beyond the battlefield.

To a world still in need.

The New Dawn

I tightened my grip on the scroll, its glow steady in my hands, and the words rose unbidden in my mind—meant to be spoken, meant to be carried forward.

The light had won.

Not just in battle, but in the hearts of those who chose to believe.

It was a victory that transcended the physical.

A triumph of sacrifice.

Of renewal.

Of truth that could not be undone.

And in that silence—something remained.

Not just the echoes of battle,

but the truth we had carried forward.

The bells had tolled.

The last cry had been heard.

And whether or not it had been answered no longer mattered.

Because I understood now—through the fire, we were tempered. Through the trial, we were refined.

And now—through the light, we would carry it forward.

Epilogue: A New Beginning

The light was no longer distant—no longer something imagined, something wished for. It was here, stretching across the horizon with quiet certainty, threading through the air like a presence rather than a mere glow.

The world we had walked through—fractured, drowning, suffocated by despair—was beginning to breathe again.

At first, the change was imperceptible. A quiet shift beneath the earth, beneath the air, beneath the weight we carried. But as the days stretched forward, something more deliberate unfolded—not just recovery, but recreation.

The first day, the land stretched itself toward the sky, as if recognizing, for the first time, that it no longer needed to hide beneath shadow. Fields of green spread beyond the hills, broken only by clusters of wildflowers that hadn't bloomed in years. They rose slowly, cautiously, yet without resistance—an answer to the war rather than a scar from it.

The second day, the stagnant waters stirred. Streams that had been suffocated beneath decay now ran clear, twisting silver beneath the sunlight, alive with movement. The rivers, hesitant yet unstoppable, followed the pull of something unseen—something greater than the weight that had once held them still.

The third day, the trees answered. Once strangled by shadow, once bent beneath the pressure of darkness, they stood tall again, their leaves whispering softly in the breeze. The wind did not pull them down this time—it carried them forward. It belonged to them again.

It wasn't perfect.

But it was alive.

And that was enough.

We had carried the scroll through the swamp, through the trials, through Joshua's sacrifice. Its light had guided us through the abyss, its truth burning steady even when we faltered. Now, it rested in my pack, carefully wrapped in cloth.

Its glow had dimmed since we had left Purgatory, but it was still there—constant, like the faint, steady beat of a heart.

Waiting.

Not for us, but for the world.

Waiting for the moment its words would be spoken aloud—carried to those who needed them most.

Gillie walked ahead, her silhouette framed by the warmth of the afternoon sun. Her steps were firm, yet something had changed in her—the weight she carried had shifted, softened, though her sharpness remained. The path stretched before us, winding through hills bathed in gold, and as we moved forward, a quiet understanding settled between us.

We weren't alone.

At first, we thought we were—just two figures against the vastness of the road, the uncertainty of what lay ahead—but slowly, almost imperceptibly, others began to follow.

The fourth day, the sky stretched without obstruction. At night, the stars emerged in full force—brighter than they had been in years, unburdened by mist, uninterrupted by shadow. They scattered across the heavens like markers, reflecting the quiet rebirth beneath them.

The fifth day, sound returned. Birdsong filled the air—not loud, not overwhelming, but deliberate, as though the silence had held its breath for long enough. The call was light, careless, yet it carried something absolute.

Gillie exhaled softly, shaking her head with a faint smile. "Even they knew it was time."

On the sixth night, as the fire flickered between us, a young girl approached me. Her hair was tangled, her clothes patched and frayed, but her hands were steady as she held something out to me—a flower.

Its petals glowed faintly, catching the starlight with an ethereal shimmer.

She looked at me with certainty.

"For him," she said, and placed it in my hands.

I froze, the weight of her words settling over me like a wave, pressing against something deep and unspoken within me. My throat tightened as I took the fragile gift from her hands.

"*Thank you*," I whispered.

She nodded, her gaze unwavering, far older than her years. "He's still here," she said. Then she turned and ran back to the group gathered at the edge of the camp.

I sat by the fire that night, turning the flower over in my hands. It was beautiful and delicate, but resilient in a way that felt impossibly profound.

Its glow was faint, but unwavering—just like the light we carried.

Just like everything we had fought for, lost, and somehow still held on to.

Epilogue: A New Beginning

Gillie sat beside me, silent as always, but I caught the faintest trace of a smile tugging at the corner of her mouth. The firelight flickered between us, casting long shadows, stretching toward something unseen but unbroken.

"I keep thinking about him," she murmured, barely above the crackling flames.

I nodded. "Me too."

Her fingers tightened around her sleeves, her shoulders stiffening. "He didn't have to fall."

The words were sharp, edged with something tangled between frustration and grief.

I let the silence linger. Gillie did too.

Then—"What do you think he was trying to tell us?"

I swallowed, adjusting the scroll in my grip. "I think he already knew he wasn't coming with us."

Gillie exhaled sharply, shaking her head. "That's not fair."

"No," I admitted. "It isn't."

She stared into the fire, watching the way the embers flickered, twisting upward into the sky.

"Grace believed in redemption. She kept fighting for it. Joshua did too, but in the end…" She hesitated, voice frayed. "…he wasn't fighting for himself."

I tightened my grip on the parchment.

"He knew what had to happen for the light to break through."

Gillie clenched her jaw. "You think that's the truth? That Joshua wasn't supposed to make it out?"

I hesitated. Then— "I think he was never going to leave. Not because the swamp wouldn't let him, but because he wouldn't let himself."

Gillie closed her eyes briefly, exhaling slowly.

"So what do we do with that?"

The wind shifted around us, gentle but deliberate.

I traced the edges of the scroll, feeling the warmth still pulsing beneath the fabric.

"We make sure it wasn't for nothing."

Gillie didn't respond right away—just nodded once, firm, steady, accepting. The kind of acceptance that wasn't surrender but resolution.

I thought of Ezekiel—his silence, his final act of surrender in the light. He had laid down his burdens without fanfare, as if his part in the story had been completed long before the last bell tolled. I hadn't seen him since. But maybe that was the point. Maybe some lights are meant to pass quietly, their work already done.

In the corner of my eye, I thought I saw the Silent Child—still watching. A small silhouette bathed not in firelight, but in something purer, more radiant. But when I turned, the shape was gone. And in its place— only light. Not the soft flicker of the campfire. Not moonlight. Something deeper. Something that didn't belong to the night. Something that watched back.

My thoughts turned, unexpectedly, to the family that had cast me aside. The ones whose betrayal had driven me into the swamp in the first place. I didn't know where they were now—or if they'd ever understand what had been given for them. But the light wasn't just for those who had followed it. It was for those who hadn't yet seen it. Even them.

And as dawn broke the next morning, the sunlight spilled across the hills like a promise, warming the earth, warming the people who walked with us. It did not rush. It did not claim dominion. It arrived simply because it was meant to.

Epilogue: A New Beginning

We packed up camp quietly, moving through the remnants of night, stepping forward as if we had always known the way, even before we could see it.

The fire's embers had faded, their warmth lingering only in memory, and the ground beneath us felt steadier than it had in days—no longer heavy with exhaustion, no longer pressed beneath uncertainty.

The scroll rested in my pack, wrapped carefully in cloth, and as I lifted it, I felt the slightest weight shift.

As though it had settled into this moment.

As though it knew.

I adjusted the straps on my shoulders, pressing my hand briefly against the fabric, feeling the familiar hum beneath my fingertips. Its glow had dimmed since we had left Purgatory, but it had not disappeared—not truly. Not entirely.

This journey was no longer just about the scroll.

It was about all of us.

About the light that bound us together, the faith we carried forward, and the hope we shared with a world that had been waiting.

Gillie walked ahead, her strides steady, her posture straight, but I could see the faint trace of something unreadable in her movements— something cautious, something considering.

Joshua's final cry echoed in my mind as we crested the next hill.

Redemption.

It hadn't been spoken in vain.

It hadn't been lost to the abyss.

It had been carried forward, in the earth beneath us, in the water that now ran clear, in the sky that no longer hid behind mist.

The scars of the past remained, but they were no longer wounds.

They were reminders of everything that had been overcome.

Gillie slowed slightly at the top of the hill, her breath hitching, her gaze flickering toward the horizon.

I frowned. "Gillie?"

She didn't look at me.

She was staring at something—far ahead, too distant, almost blending into the glow.

For a second, her fingers twitched, like she wanted to reach forward—like she saw something I didn't.

Then—she shook her head, exhaling sharply.

"*Forget it*," Gillie murmured.

Her voice was quiet, but edged with something heavy—something unfinished.

I adjusted my grip on the scroll, pressing my hand against the fabric.

Its glow had dimmed.

Not gone.

Not fading.

Just waiting.

For a fleeting second—I thought it pulsed.

Not in warning.

Not in struggle.

But in recognition.

Gillie noticed. She stopped, staring at the scroll wrapped tightly within the folds of my pack. Her breath was steady, yet something had shifted in her gaze—something uncertain, questioning, as if she felt it too.

She lifted her head slightly, eyes flickering toward the sky, then beyond it, as if searching for something neither of us could name.

"You realize it's been seven days, right?" Gillie said.

Epilogue: A New Beginning

Her voice was quieter than usual—less of a statement, more of a thought spoken aloud.

I blinked. Seven?

I gripped the strap of my pack a little tighter, rolling the number over in my head.

Seven days.

Since the war ended.

Since the darkness broke.

Since everything changed.

I exhaled slowly, adjusting my hold on the parchment, shifting its weight between my fingers.

Its glow may have faded, but the steady pulse beneath my grip had not.

It was still there.

Still waiting.

Not for me.

Not for Gillie.

For the world.

Gillie hesitated, her fingers brushing against the fabric of her coat, her posture straight but tense, as if she was caught between speaking and staying silent.

"You think He's doing it again?" Gillie asked.

This time, her voice wavered—not with doubt, but with something deeper.

Something bordering on reverence, hesitation, awe.

I swallowed, but I didn't answer.

I didn't have to.

The answer was already here.

It was in the steps we took forward, pressing into the earth as if carving out something new, something untouched.

It was in the breath between hesitation and belief—the moment between knowing and understanding.

It was in the light, not merely enduring, but beginning again.

I tightened my grip on the parchment, the weight of it grounding me, settling me in the truth of what had come before and what had yet to unfold.

Then, slowly, I lifted my pack over my shoulder, feeling the presence of every step ahead before I even took the first one.

And so began A New Beginning.

And in this new beginning, there was light.

Next in the Scrollbearer Saga

<u>Lighting the Shadows of Joshua Clay</u>

Book Two of The Scrollbearer Saga

The war is over—but the mission has only begun.

With the scroll in hand, Gillie and I journey beyond the battlefield, carrying the light to those who still walk in darkness. But when we encounter others who once followed Joshua Clay—now lost, turned, or worse—we realize our greatest challenge is still ahead.

Joshua is still alive.

But he's no longer the man we followed.

Bound to the dark, surrounded by familiar enemies, and haunted by the scream of redemption, he stands between salvation and ruin. And if there's any hope of bringing him back—we'll have to face what he's become… and what we're willing to sacrifice to bring him home.

Light must go where shadows dwell.

Coming soon.